Stardancer

A novel

by

Jean Cummings

Copyright © 2000
Jean Cummings

Rx Ranch Enterprises
2609 E. Fruitport Road
Spring Lake, Michigan 49456

Library of Congress Control Number 00-190937
ISBN: 0-9679959-1-4

Other titles by Jean Cummings:
Why They Call Him the Buffalo Doctor
Alias The Buffalo Doctor
Buffalo in Our Backyard
Shinglebolt

Printed in the USA by
Morris Publishing
3212 East Highway 30
Kearney, NE 68847 • 800-650-7888

Contents

Contents

Introduction

Though *Stardancer* is a work of fiction, the saving of the American buffalo from extinction happened in a way akin to Gitty's protecting buffalo calves.

In South Dakota, James "Scotty" Philip, a cattleman, was married to a woman of Indian blood. She saw that the buffalo, long respected by the Indian people, was being systematically eradicated from the plains. She suggested to her husband that they capture buffalo if they could. Philip purchased the Dupree buffalo herd and moved the animals to his ranch near Ft. Pierre.

By 1918 this herd had multiplied to 500 animals, and some of these buffalo were used to seed the herd at Custer State Park in the Black Hills. Today many of the buffalo found in private herds throughout the United States are descendents of these Philip buffalo.

Chapter 1
Green Gold

Saturday, June 1, 1844

His rawboned body moved alongside the oxen, guiding them and the cart they pulled through the shallow water. The hard-packed wet sand was easier to walk on than the fine dry sand farther from the shoreline. Hours ago the water had soaked through his boots. His feet were a dull ache at the end of his throbbing legs. The late spring air was balmy, but the water of Lake Michigan still carried the chill of melting ice.

At the age of twenty-five, Conway Carleton was reaching out into the world to begin a new enterprise. He was going to become a lumberman.

Conway absently flicked his switch over the backs of the oxen. His blue eyes narrowed as he thought of the promise that lay ahead of him here in Michigan. *Green gold,* he whispered to himself—that was what all those tall, straight cork pines were! Now that the lands to the west were being settled, he was certain that the demand for lumber would become enormous. The territories of Iowa and Minnesota soon would be admitted to the Union as states. Then settlers would rush in. Though the prairies of the West were rich with fertile soil, they lacked trees, necessary to provide lumber for houses, barns and outbuildings.

I'll have lumber ready for them, Conway vowed.

His thoughts were interrupted by whimpering. Conway turned and saw that his oldest child was stumbling along the beach in the powdery white sand, her chubby short legs struggling to keep up.

"Come here, darlin'," he said, holding out his arms to Cathy. "Let me carry you a ways so you can rest."

The little round face burst into a happy smile. Blond curls bounced as she ran to him. Conway hoisted Cathy onto his back. Her soft arms circled his neck, and she buried her face against his shoulder.

He trudged onward. In just moments the whistling breathing of the child on his back told him she'd fallen asleep. Poor thing. Only five years old. No wonder she's tuckered out from all this walking! But the little cart just didn't have room for all of them. He looked back at Ruth. On his wife's lap nestled the dark head of three-year-old Rebecca, and cradled in Ruth's left arm was their infant son, John. She gave Conway a tired look. As their eyes met, the baby fussed, and Ruth pulled her bodice aside to feed him.

Conway thought of Ruth's breasts, those white globes that had been his to tease, to pet, to enjoy. But now they were the baby's. As he felt himself grow aroused, he flushed. A quick swat to the oxen hurried them along. While she nursed a baby Ruth wouldn't let him near her breasts. Conway wondered if his touch really would curdle the milk as Ruth claimed. Or was she keeping him away, fearing another pregnancy?

He rubbed his auburn beard and squinted out across the endless water, where the sun was sliding lower and lower in the sky. The big lake seemed more like an ocean. Eighty miles from shore to shore! All that way across to Wisconsin Territory!

The water scarcely rippled. One more night of sleeping without shelter. Just thinking of it made Conway's neck itch. Blasted mosquitoes! With no wind the swarms would be out tonight. Thank the Lord he'd brought mosquito netting for Ruth and the children! Too bad he didn't have enough for himself. His freckled face and neck were blotched with swollen bites from last night. He was grateful for his thick beard, which gave protection to his lower face.

"I think we'll stop here, Ruth," he said. "Best get settled in before dark."

She nodded, her hazel eyes cool and tired as she patted Rebecca's back to wake the child.

Last night they'd climbed a tall sand dune and slept in shelter under trees.

"Another bad night for mosquitoes," Conway sighed. "Not a breath of wind. I think we're better off right here on the beach tonight."

He turned to unhitch the oxen. "I'll build a fire—put wet sticks and grass on it. Smoke away the mosquitoes. Cathy, Becky!" he ordered. "You girls pick dune grass for Joe and Josie."

2

Rebecca leaned against her mother, small fists rubbing her sleepy eyes.

"Now!" Conway barked. "Becky, help your sister right now, or I'll switch you!"

Becky's lower lip quivered, pushed over her upper lip, but she followed Cathy up the steep side of the dune to pull bunches of grass for the oxen.

Ruth Carleton laid baby John, wrapped in her shawl, on the soft sand. She walked along the shoreline, gathering dry pieces of driftwood for the fire.

Conway watched his wife's supple body moving and bending along the white sand. How slim and beautiful she was—her waistline as trim as the day he married her six years ago. She looked just the same, except that her breasts were bigger now because of the milk. Again, he felt that warm feeling begin, and he quickly looked away, fussing with the oxen.

He swallowed, thinking of being settled in their log house with a real bed for him and Ruth, a cradle for the baby, and a loft for the girls. Then he and Ruth would have their privacy again,...He cleared his throat and howled, "Cathy! Becky! Hurry up with that grass! These animals are hungry!"

By the time the huge red sun disappeared into the lake, the odor of frying sidepork filled the summer air. Ruth lifted out the browned pork and poured batter into the skillet. Flapjacks smothered in molasses had been their fare for two days. Conway groaned silently. There was nothing else, he sighed, and flapjacks *were* filling and nutritious.

"That's the end of the sidepork," Ruth sighed, "and a good thing. By tomorrow t'would be tainted."

As darkness dimmed the sky they ate in the flickering light of the cookfire. When mosquitoes began to bite, Conway threw wet leaves and pine needles onto the fire. Soon smoke cloaked them.

With a briar-scratched fist Cathy rubbed her eyes and sniffled.

"I know, darlin'," Conway sympathized. "Smoke smarts the eyes. But it's better than being eaten alive by these monsters!" To Ruth, he muttered, "Damn, but I don't remember them being this big in Indiana!"

"Everything's big here, I think," she answered, her voice a whisper. "The lake's so large you can't see across it. These sand dunes are higher than our Indiana hills. Trees are taller. Why shouldn't the bugs be bigger?" She shrugged listlessly as she opened her blouse and offered her brown nipple to baby John.

His son's pink lips grasped the nipple, and Conway watched lazily as the drowsy baby suckled noisily and steadily, all without opening his eyes.

A feeling of well-being spread over Conway as he watched his family resting on the sandy beach. He *knew* he was doing the right thing—leaving the worn-out farm in Indiana and coming to Michigan to take the timber. This beautiful timber here was a crop already planted and cultivated by The Lord. The trees awaited harvest. Conway was going to harvest them.

Ruth's voice broke into his thoughts. "The girls are awfully tired, Conway. Would you fix the canvas and quilts so they can sleep?"

Conway jumped up to get the bedding out of the cart. He spread quilts on the canvas, and the two girls, Ruth and the baby snuggled together. Gently, Conway covered them with the protective mosquito netting.

Though exhausted and aching, for a long time Conway remained sitting up, smoking his pipe, keeping close to the smoldering fire for protection from the buzzing insects.

It's going to be a good life! Ruth will like it, too. I'm sure she will! Conway told himself. But then he thought of the tearful parting last week when she said good-bye to her parents and two married sisters. He shook his head. Ruth would miss the closeness of relatives, the get-togethers for quilting and barn raising, holidays and baptisms. Ruth was made of softer stuff than were the women Conway grew up with—the Carleton women and their Indiana neighbors. Ruth's father was a schoolmaster. She'd been reared in a brick house in Salem, a house filled with books and echoing with discussions of politics and philosophy. At the time Conway met Ruth she was studying under her father such topics as Xenophon in Greek and Cicero in Latin. Conway sighed.

Even after six years he was still bewildered that Ruth Denny had returned his love. Her father was an educated gentleman, while he, Conway Carleton, was a gaunt farm boy with little education. Why, Ruth had never even lived in a house made of logs until she married him! She'd never lived on a farm. Her life had been spent in towns.

Conway smiled as he remembered how fate had thrown them together. He'd just happened to be in Salem that day, getting a wagon axle repaired. As he left the blacksmith's shop the sound of pounding

4

hooves came from his right, and with horror, he saw a runaway team barreling down the street, the wagon behind them rocking crazily. Rooted with fear, a young woman stood in the middle of the dusty street. Conway had rushed to her, pulling her out of danger.

Even now he could remember the dazzling smile she'd given him. How he'd love to see that smile these days! Ruth seldom smiled anymore. He tried to make her life as pleasant as he could, but it was hard for her to get used to rugged farm life. And now he was pushing her into an even harsher frontier experience. For a moment Conway frowned, swept by doubt. Then he remembered his dreams, his belief that he could succeed. Conway intended to become wealthy, or at least better off than Ruth's schoolmaster-father. When he succeeded, he'd give her all the things he couldn't provide now.

He thought of their destination, the village of Mattigan and how small it was. But it'll grow. All this part of the country will grow. And my family and I, we'll grow with it and prosper!

※   ※   ※   ※

Their cabin had been built in a stand of white pines, quaking aspens, and oak trees. The previous occupants had begun to clear a small area for a garden, though the planting had to be done around two huge pine stumps. The trembling aspen leaves quivered, twinkling their pale undersides in the sunshine.

Conway cut away all the aspen trees that leaned toward the cabin. Aspen trees were unlucky trees. You didn't want them pointing at your home. Years ago Granny Carleton had told him this. She claimed that the cross of Calvary had been made of aspen wood, and ever since that time aspen trees were avoided by good Christian people. Aspen leaves fluttered constantly, grieving over what had happened long ago in the Holy Land. Conway pursed his lips. He didn't know if all that was true. But just the same, he planned to get rid of the quaking trees near his home.

It was late to be planting a garden. Conway worried whether there was enough growing season left. But he had to try. Using a borrowed cultivator and his oxen team, he worked the sandy garden bed until it was ready for their precious seeds. While Ruth planted carrots and peas, he hoed the far edge of the garden into hills for corn. The hills would help the roots take hold, the Indians said. Chubby Cathy walked along with him as they moved from hill to hill, dropping four kernels into each

5

mound. Smiling happily, Cathy recited along with him over and over again:

> *One for the beetle,*
> *One for the crow,*
> *One for the cutworm,*
> *And one to grow.*

Just beyond where Conway was planting corn, a path entered the big woods. It led into the perpetual green dusk to their nearest neighbors, the Andersons, and then on to Mattigan. The Anderson cabin wasn't far, but the forest was so dense that their cabin was out of sight.

One evening at dusk Cathy and Rebecca scrambled around the front dooryard chasing fireflies whose greenish-yellow blinking lights beckoned. Childish giggles floated on the still summer air. Conway squinted, peering around the clearing into the darkening woods. He couldn't see Joe and Josie. He sighed. He'd have to go into the woods to drive them nearer to the cabin for the night. Bears still lived in these woods, though the townspeople said they were getting scarcer each year as more and more people arrived.

When Conway started down the path into the deep woods, pine needles above him hummed. Fallen needles crunched under each step. "Joe! Josie!" he called as he moved farther into the woods. Finally, on the far side of the Anderson's cabin he spotted the two big oxen.

With a stout switch he drove them onto the path. Slowly the oxen plodded toward home. A small shadow moved in the thicket to his left. Conway's heart jumped. His scalp prickled. A bear cub? If it was a cub, the she-bear wouldn't be far. The sour taste of fear oozed into his mouth. He crackled his switch against Josie's lumbering flank. "Git! Go!" he roared, glancing anxiously at the dark cub.

A high-pitched bleat came from the animal. All the pent-up air in Conway's lungs exploded in a laughing sob. Not a bear cub at all! It was the Anderson's pet black lamb! Conway's tense muscles relaxed and he coughed.

The next morning Conway lifted Rebecca up onto the pine bench beside him as Cathy slid onto the bench beside her mother. Conway looked across the hewn pine table. His eyes met Ruth's.

"Shall we pray?" he asked. As they lowered their heads Conway recited their ritual blessing, which ended with "Bless this food for its intended use." After a short pause, he added, "And God bless the trees! Amen!"

6

Cathy's blond head jerked up the moment he said "amen."

"Why did you ask God to bless the trees, Papa?"

Conway's pale eyes twinkled. "Because trees are going to make us rich. All these tall trees are going to be turned into lumber. People are going to buy that lumber from me. In a few years you girls and your Mama won't be wearing calico. It'll be silk for my beautiful darlin's."

He took a swallow of coffee, sputtered and choked before managing to swallow it.

"I'm sorry, Conway," Ruth apologized. "We're out of coffee."

Conway pointed to the yellow Johnny Cake in the center of the table. "See we're out of flour, too."

"I don't mind the Johnny Cake so much," she said, "though I wouldn't want it every day. But I do hate starting a day without coffee. My, how I do enjoy my coffee!"

Conway sipped the substitute brew from his mug and agreed that the homemade "coffee" wasn't very good. Ruth made it by toasting old dry bread and then crumbling it into granules, which served as the "coffee" grounds.

Day before yesterday Conway had tried to get both flour and coffee, but there wasn't any to be had in Mattigan. A tradesman the villagers called "Elnathan" was supposedly due any day now from the south. He was bringing a wagonload of supplies, they said.

＊   ＊   ＊   ＊

Pale eyes half-shut with contentment, Conway leaned back in his chair and sucked on his pipe. He glanced at Ruth, seated on the other side of the big brick fireplace. Her knitting needles clicked at the brown yarn which she was turning into a pair of stockings for him. Every so often her foot tapped the wooden cradle on the floor beside her rocking chair, and the cradle swayed gently, soothing the dozing baby John.

Conway smiled. When he'd come up here last spring to buy the cabin and its furnishings, the folks he'd bought out wanted to keep the cradle. "We have a new baby," he'd insisted. They gave in, agreeing that the cradle went with the other furnishings. Ruth seemed to enjoy having the cradle. It freed her hands for doing other things. The cradle was a luxury they didn't have when Cathy and Rebecca were babes.

The glow from the fireplace caught Ruth's hair, forming a halo of gold around her brown hair, which she wore swept in a chignon at her

7

neck. Her beauty overwhelmed Conway. How fortunate he was to have courted and won her! Sometimes he wondered why Ruth had been attracted to him, with his rough ways. During their six years of marriage she'd always corrected his poor grammar. Sometimes it'd been tiresome and even humiliating; but now that he spoke like a gentleman, Conway was proud. Using proper language would serve him well one day when he began dealing with bankers and financiers. He wouldn't act like a country bumpkin, nor would he be treated like one.

The children, too, had benefited by Ruth's grammar. Young as they were, the girls spoke proper English. They'd become fine ladies. He'd see that his ladies were dressed in the most elegant frocks.

They'd been living in their Mattigan cabin for a month. A lot had been accomplished. Conway had registered his timber claim at the county seat. He and Ruth had planted a small vegetable garden, though he didn't know how much they'd harvest from it.

He'd even formed a partnership with George Gordon, a single fellow not much older than he. George seemed to be just as enthusiastic about the future of lumbering in west Michigan as Conway was, and George had cash to invest. Conway had decided that additional capital would move their lumbering enterprise along faster, and he happily formed the partnership.

Ruth's listlessness bothered him. She went about her duties silently, her face expressionless. He'd hoped she'd be pleased with the cabin. It was larger than their home in Indiana. Conway glanced at the log walls chinked with mud. The fireplace was bigger and better-constructed than theirs in Indiana. He'd built several shelves for Ruth and added pegs in the corners to hold jackets and other clothing.

But Ruth complained about the floor. "Sand gets into everything!" she sputtered.

Their cabin in Indiana also had a dirt floor, but there the dirt was hard clay. Here, it was fine sand.

"Soon we'll have a plank floor, Ruth," Conway promised. With all his timber, once he and George got the mill into operation, he could give her all the board floors she wanted. He'd tried to gather Ruth into his arms, but stiffly, she evaded his reaching arms and bent over the cradle to check on baby John.

Conway had looked forward so much to their soft feather bed built into one corner of the single-room cabin. Since a roomy loft provided beds for the children, Conway had anticipated having privacy for their lovemaking.

Ruth refused to let the girls sleep in the loft.

"Rebecca is much too young to climb that ladder!" she insisted. "I wouldn't think of letting her go up there for another year or two. She could break her neck!"

Conway built another bed in an opposite corner of the cabin. Sadly, he resigned himself to more years of silent groping and hurried lovemaking, spiced with Ruth's whispers of "Be quiet. Don't let the children hear!"

✳   ✳   ✳   ✳

Rustling sounds of squirrels running over the outside log wall beside Conway woke him. Squinting, he peered at the greased paper window and saw with surprise that it was daylight. He was even more amazed when he rolled sideways and saw Ruth still sleeping beside him, her long hair cascading over her pillow, even spilling onto his. His fingers gently stroked those soft strands.

How many months had it been since he'd awakened before Ruth? Since baby John was born last February, she'd been up feeding the baby at least once during the night and then again early in the morning. Conway swung his bare legs off the bottom of the bed, moving slowly, not wanting to waken Ruth. Poor dear. Let her sleep while she can before the baby starts crying for his milk.

The flannel of his gray nightshirt stuck against his damp back. Today's going to be a scorcher! Already, it was hot.

As Conway walked quietly across the sandy floor he glanced down into the cradle. His breath caught in his throat. Gasping, he bent closer. The baby—baby John!

Baby John's eyes stared sightless, straight up. His mouth was open and contorted, as if gasping for breath. His always pink face was dark, mottled purple and blue.

Conway's hand flew to his mouth. He bit on his index finger to keep from crying aloud. My son! My son! He reached down and touched the tiny head covered with auburn fuzz, the color of his own hair. Baby John was cold. Conway turned away. He squeezed his eyes shut as a wave of nausea clutched him. Bitter acid rose in his throat. He swallowed. My son is dead! He wanted to throw open the door, rush outside and shake his fist at the heavens roaring, "My son is dead! God! You let my son die!"

A rustling on the bed brought him out of his confusion. Ruth was sitting up. She mustn't see the baby! Conway dropped to the bed beside her, gripped her shoulders firmly.

"Not now, Conway," she snapped. "I have to feed the baby. My breasts are so full I'm sore!"

"Ruth, uh, you can't see the baby. You mustn't!"

A flicker of fear passed across her eyes. "What's the matter?"

"Baby John." He choked and swallowed. "Baby John is dead."

Her hands flew to her throat momentarily, then with a swift jerk, she moved to look into the cradle next to her side of the bed.

Conway pushed her back. "No! Don't look, Ruth! Please!"

Her brown eyes looked deep into his. Her mouth opened, a shrill keening came from deep within her chest. Over and over a high-pitched wail.

Wakened by their mother's screaming, Cathy and Rebecca began to cry. They pattered to their parents' bed. The whimpering of the girls clashed against their mother's crazed wailing.

Conway needed help. This was too much for him.

"Cathy, darlin', you've got to be my big girl."

As his attention turned momentarily to Cathy, Ruth snatched her baby from the cradle.

The hair on Conway's neck crawled as he watched his wife hug the cold baby to her breast. Her keening quieted to a sing-song moan. She rocked, clutching the baby.

Conway got off the bed. He patted Cathy's blond curls gently. "I want you to be my big girl now, Cathy. Get dressed. Run over to Anderson's cabin. Tell Mrs. Anderson that Mama is sick and would she come over right away?"

Cathy's blue eyes streamed tears, her lips quivered. "Get dressed now." Conway gripped her shoulders and turned her toward her bed, giving her a pat on the bottom. "Hurry!"

Rebecca howled with fear. Conway picked her up and cuddled her, stroking her back and crooning, "It's all right, darlin'. It's all right." With relief he saw Cathy's chubby shape, clad in a shapeless calico dress, run to the door and tug it open. Her bare feet flashed as she tore out the doorway.

Suddenly, Conway realized that he must get out of his nightshirt before Amelia Anderson got here. Setting the now quietly sobbing Rebecca on her feet, he reached for his trousers. As he stepped into them and buttoned the fly, he threw an uneasy glance toward Ruth, still rocking and crooning to dead baby John. Her eyes didn't move but stared into the empty cradle.

As soon as he was dressed, Conway turned his attention to Rebecca, who looked like a young version of her mother. Often when Conway looked at his younger daughter he thought, *so that's how Ruth looked as a child!*

"Papa! Papa!" Cathy cried as she burst into the cabin followed by a red-faced Amelia Anderson, her stout body puffing. She frowned with concern as she entered the cabin. Her eyes darted, taking in the sobbing Rebecca, glassy-eyed Ruth sitting crosslegged on the rumpled bed, hugging her baby. Amelia Anderson's eyes met Conway's, her eyebrows rose questioningly.

"The baby," he whispered, shaking his head. "He's gone." His voice cracked. A sob broke from his chest.

Mrs. Anderson walked to the bed and reached down toward Ruth. "Give me the baby, Mrs. Carleton," she said gently. "He's dirtied hisself. Needs to be washed. While I'm acleaning him, I wants you to get dressed. You be having visitors today. You don't want to meet visitors in your nightgown, now, do you?"

"Come on, now," she persisted. "Give me the baby. He needs cleaning. You get dressed," she ordered, her voice stern.

Like a sleepwalker, Ruth handed the baby to her neighbor. Mrs. Anderson pulled a flannel blanket out of the cradle as she moved across the room carrying the baby's body.

"Help your wife get herself dressed," she said to Conway as she passed him. "Her best dress, for the buryin'."

She moved toward the open door. "I'll take him to my place to clean him. Mr. Carleton," she added, "move that cradle to a dark corner somewheres. Cover it so's she don't have to look at it. Cathy, child, you come with me. I need you to run an errand for me."

Conway was forever grateful to Amelia Anderson for taking charge and arranging the burial of baby John. His hands were full just controlling his own sorrow and handling Ruth. As soon as Mrs. Anderson took the baby from her arms Ruth stopped her eerie keening. Rebecca settled into wide-eyed silence. Hardly moving, she sat on the edge of her bed and stared at her mother.

By the middle of the afternoon villagers began arriving. Amelia's husband, Hobart Anderson, had made a rough pine coffin. He carried it

11

to the Carleton cabin where it was placed on a chair beside the fireplace. Conway looked into the small box and saw that Mrs. Anderson had lined the coffin with a bleached white flour sack. A wet cloth lay over baby John's face, concealing it.

When Conway looked inquiringly at Mrs. Anderson, she answered, "The face is going fast. It's the awful heat. I'm trying to keep cool water on his face, poor babe." Her chin bobbled sadly.

George Gordon, Conway's new partner, arrived. He embraced Conway, then held him off at arm's length. "Are you all right, friend?" he asked.

Conway nodded silently. "Thanks for coming, George."

Quietly, George spoke to Conway, glancing doubtfully toward Ruth who was hunched over, sitting on the bed. "I dug the grave, and I found a Bible," he said. "It's a small graveyard, only about ten graves, but they've set aside enough land so's a church can be built there someday."

"It's time to go to the graveyard, Mrs. Carleton," Amelia Anderson spoke. "Come kiss your babe good-bye before we close the coffin lid."

Ruth shook her head "no."

Gently, Mrs. Anderson slid her ample arm around Ruth and coaxed, "My dear, tell your baby good-bye."

Eyes blazing, Ruth glared at her neighbor. "I will not say 'good-bye' to him. Never!"

Dutifully, Cathy and Rebecca let themselves be led by Mrs. Anderson to the small pine box where they kissed the cold blue skin of their baby brother's cheek.

At the graveyard, George Gordon read comforting passages from the Bible. Conway glanced uneasily at Ruth, who stood dry-eyed and expressionless beside the deep hole which would hold their tiny son for all eternity. The lump in Conway's throat felt enormous enough to choke him. He'd dreamed of a lumbering empire, working with his son and then with grandsons to build wealth and security for the Carleton family.

The coffin was lowered into the grave. Everyone walked past the hole and dropped in a fistful of dirt.

"Everybody come to my place," Mrs. Anderson spoke firmly. "We eat. That will help the heartache."

For two days Conway didn't leave the cabin. He would've preferred to be out in the woods with George, or planning their sawmill on the banks of Lake Mattigan. Keeping busy would've helped him deal with his grief. But Ruth needed him and his companionship, though she still was in a stupor.

Sitting unmoving for hours, she seldom spoke. Cathy and Rebecca sat silently, their eyes large and frightened. Conway tried to coax them to go outside to play, but they were afraid.

Ruth prepared meals, but aside from that, she sat in her rocking chair, white knuckles gripping its arms tightly.

"I need to go into the woods today, darlin'," Conway said. "George and I have to get some timber surveyed. Besides, this is bread-making day. Aren't you going to make us bread?" he reminded her gently.

Silently, Ruth rose and moved to the fireplace where she got down her bowls and Dutch oven.

It was nearly suppertime when Conway returned to his cabin. As he walked along the worn path through the woods he smelled smoke. Ruth must be cooking supper. As he neared the cabin he saw thick, dark smoke billowing from the chimney.

Why such a big fire? It was a hot August day. He ran.

When Conway opened the cabin door a rush of heat blasted him. Ruth, her face red and perspiring, stood in front of the fireplace swinging a hatchet and throwing boards into the roaring flames. Animal-like grunting sounds came from her clenched lips as she hacked with the hatchet.

With relief Conway saw that the girls were out of the way. Huddled on their bed, they were tearfully hugging each other.

As Conway approached Ruth, she glared at him defiantly.

He saw the object of destruction—the cradle, which Ruth was hacking apart and burning.

"Oh, Ruth," he said softly, his heart aching for her in her anguish. "You shouldn't burn the cradle." He stretched his hand out toward her. "We'll have other children."

With a frenzied lunge, Ruth threw the remains of the cradle into the fireplace.

"No," she said. Her voice was so cold it made Conway shiver. "No. There will be no more children."

Chapter 2
Not All the King's Horses

Sunday, April 20, 1851

Cathy sat up straight in the church pew, her blue eyes dutifully fastened on the Reverend Campbell and his waving arms. She wasn't listening to him. Sunday morning in church was her time to daydream, to let her imagination fly off to strange lands. Now that she was twelve years old, Cathy saw Mattigan as a pretty dull place. Such a tiny town and so isolated! She sighed. Everything here was boring. But then some days she enjoyed playing games with old friends. Cathy felt mixed up. She was too old to be a child, yet she didn't feel like a young lady.

Reverend Campbell's voice roared, jerking Cathy from her thoughts. As he pounded the lectern, making a point, his dark, curly hair fell over his forehead. Rev. Campbell *was* a handsome man. Cathy knew that many church women agreed with her. The silly women fawned over him following church services. Cathy's eyes turned to the prim Mrs. Campbell, who sat in the choir loft. Her lusterless brown hair was parted in the middle and drawn backwards into a severe bun. Cathy wondered if Mrs. Campbell had been pretty when she was young. Whatever would've drawn such a nice-looking person as Reverend Campbell to such a plain mouse as Mrs. Campbell?

Cathy's thoughts drifted from the Campbells to her own family, Pa and Mama sitting on her right and Becky on her left. For almost as long as she could remember Cathy had sensed that her family was not like other families in Mattigan. Of course, now they had a nicer house and more clothes than most others. But even when they still lived in their little log cabin, Cathy knew that they were different. The below-the-surface tension in the Carleton household didn't exist in her friends' families.

Sometimes Cathy walked to the edge of town and sauntered past their old cabin, which had been in deep woods when they lived in it. Now a dirt track passed in front of the cabin door. A one-story frame house had been built across the road from the cabin. Cathy counted back. It was seven years ago that they had come to Michigan. She didn't remember that long trek. Pa sometimes talked about it, telling how Cathy had walked much of the way because the ox cart was small and she was the oldest. "You were a brave little darlin'," he'd say.

Cathy did remember when her baby brother died. She never would forget Mama's terrible screaming. And Mama was never the same after baby John died. She seldom smiled, and she went about her duties silently. Joy had gone out of her life.

Even when they moved to their elegant frame house near the center of town—the house Pa had ordered built especially for them— Mama hadn't perked up.

"See, Ruth?" Pa had proudly pointed to the gleaming oak flooring. "Real oak floors! No more sand in the porridge, hey?"

Without a word, Mama passed through the entrance hallway and headed for the kitchen. A glance at Pa's crestfallen face told Cathy how disappointed he was that Mama didn't appreciate the nice house he'd worked so hard for.

For almost three years now they'd been living in the new house. Mama saw that the floors were waxed to a glowing shine. Every Monday she baked bread, every Sunday she attended church. That was her life.

An undercurrent of discord filtered through the Carleton household. Cathy noticed one glaring difference in her family. Mama and Pa slept in separate bedrooms. In the households of her girlfriends, Ellen Stearns and Judith Peters, Cathy learned that their parents slept together, and not just in the same bedroom, but in the same bed.

Her parents not sleeping together preyed on Cathy's thoughts. She suspected that this was a key to why her family was different from other families, and unhappier. When Pa was home he was jovial and friendly to her and Becky. As his lumbering interests grew, he traveled more and more, and was away from home often. He grew short-tempered if around home for very long.

Cathy was startled out of her reverie when the congregation rose for the final hymn and benediction. She jumped up. Becky snickered and poked her in the side. Cathy nearly made a face at her sister, then thought better of it. After all, they *were* in church. At the conclusion of the service parishioners filed out of the sanctuary. Reverend Campbell shook hands with each person. When he grasped Rebecca's hand he patted her bonnet and said, "Such a lovely child you are, my dear. So like your mother."

Cathy put her small hand into Reverend Campbell's, and he smiled gently, "Nice to see you, Catherine."

Next he clutched Mama's hand. "You're looking lovely this morning, Mrs. Carleton."

Cathy gasped as she looked at her mother's face. Mama was smiling; her eyes actually shone. Mama looked absolutely lovely. Never had Cathy seen her mother glow. Of course, she seldom saw her mother even smile.

As Cathy walked down the church steps it occurred to her that Reverend Campbell had praised Rebecca's looks as well as her mother's. He'd said nothing about Cathy's appearance. Just then Pa squeezed her shoulders.

"Am I ugly, Pa?" Cathy's face crinkled unhappily as she looked up into her father's freckled face.

"You're beautiful, darlin'." He tweaked a golden curl that peeked from beneath her bonnet.The curl snapped back. "Your hair is like spun sunshine."

"I'm too fat!" Cathy protested as they walked down the board path toward home.

Pa pinched her round cheek. "It's just baby fat," he reassured her. "You'll lose it in the next couple years. You're becoming a young lady, you know." He reached into his pocket. "Oh, by the way, I have a present for you." He handed her a small object wrapped in crumpled brown paper.

As he unwrapped it, he added, "Of course, you're to share this with your sister, you understand."

The present was maple sugar candy.

"Thanks Pa!" she breathed as she popped a piece into her mouth. "Here, have some," she offered. He broke off a chunk.

A strange sensation tickled Cathy's tongue as she chewed. It was like having a mouthful of hair. She stopped chewing and looked at Pa, who had also stopped chewing.

Pa spat the stuff into the street; Cathy did likewise.

"Bah!" Pa grunted, "Indian maple sugar! I got this from Jake Newton. He said his sister made it!" He spat again.

"Why are there hairs in it?" Cathy asked.

"When the Indians boil maple sap while they're making sugar, they cook rabbits, squirrels, any animals in the boiling sap. Almost always there's animal hair in Indians' maple sugar." Pa squeezed her hand. "Sorry about the disappointment. I'll keep my eye out for some clean maple sugar, darlin'."

When they arrived at the Carleton home Cathy took off her bonnet. She stroked it lovingly. Made of white figured muslin and delicately trimmed with ribbons and roses, it was shaped like the cup of a morning glory. She hung it on an arm of the huge ornately-carved hall tree. A glance in the mirror told her that her hair was mussed.

She frowned as she patted her blond curls into place. She could see that she wasn't as pretty as Rebecca and Mama. She wasn't ugly, but they were prettier. Remembering how beautiful Mama had become when she smiled at Reverend Campbell, Cathy grinned at her reflection. Yes, even she looked prettier when she smiled. She'd have to remember to smile a lot.

Suddenly, Rebecca's face appeared next to hers in the hall mirror. "See anybody I know in there?" Rebecca teased.

Mama came into the hallway. "All right, girls, you can help me finish getting dinner ready." Cathy noticed that her mother's expression was once again somber. Maybe Cathy had only imagined the glowing smile Mama had given Reverend Campbell.

✳   ✳   ✳   ✳

Pa had been gone so often that Cathy felt strange having him eating with them at the table once again. He'd just returned from a long stay in St. Louis where he'd negotiated the sale of thousands of board feet of his lumber. From this fabled Mississippi River port he'd brought each of his "three ladies" a long cashmere scarf. The scarves were identical, feather-soft, dyed the blue of a summer sky.

"And guess who I saw in St. Louis?" Pa asked. "Jenny Lind, the famous Swedish opera singer. She's lovely, and she sings like a bird!" He reached for another piece of fried chicken.

"Becky, pass me the gravy boat, will you darlin'? I think I'll have a tad more gravy."

18

He turned to Mama. "Even the finest hotels can't duplicate your delicious chicken gravy, Ruth. Home cooking is always best."

Cathy watched her parents' eyes lock momentarily, then Mama looked down and toyed with her applesauce. Puzzled, Cathy wondered what had passed unsaid between them.

"All right, girls, remove the plates, please." Mama rose. "Bring the dessert plates from the kitchen."

Cathy set the four gold-banded porcelain plates at her mother's left while Mama placed a still-steaming cherry pie on the table. As Mama cut through the pastry and lifted out the wedges, Cathy could almost taste the flaky, golden crust covering the scarlet cherries.

Cathy had just popped the first bite of pie into her mouth when Pa suddenly howled, "Ugh!" He jumped up from his chair, tipping it backwards, and spat a mouthful of half-chewed cherry pie onto the shiny, waxed floor boards.

Cathy looked from her father to her mother. Mama's pretty face turned the color of a ripe plum.

"A cherry pit!" Pa yelled. "I bit into a damned cherry pit, woman! Do you want me to lose my teeth? Can't you learn to cook properly and get the damn pits out of the cherries?"

Silently, Mama rose and went to the kitchen. Returning with a rag, she wiped up the mess.

Hot tears stinging her eyes, Cathy stared at her piece of pie. She loved Pa, but his temper was getting worse. Usually after one of his out-of-town trips he seemed better-natured. But here he was, losing his temper, and he'd been back only one day! If confined in Mattigan very long, he growled around the house, acting like those stereoptican pictures of caged lions snarling out at the world.

The following Saturday Cathy spent all afternoon with Ellen Stearns at Ellen's house. First they'd played outside with their sticks and hoops, racing each other down Hickory Street hill, then climbing back to the top for another race.

When the sultry heat had them perspiring, they found something to do inside, away from the hot sun. They spent the rest of the afternoon admiring the lovely new fashions of Godey's Lady's Book.

As dinner hour grew near, Cathy headed home so she could help Mama. Papa was in town, and he'd be eating with them tonight.

When she stepped into the cool, dark hallway, Cathy hung her bonnet on the hall tree and headed for the kitchen. Her nose told her that dinner was cooking.

She kissed her mother on the cheek. "What're you making?" Cathy looked at the counter where two unbaked pie shells awaited filling.

"Pie? What kind today?"

There was an unusual gleam in Mama's hazel eyes as she brought a majolica bowl out of the ice chest and removed the dampened tea towel that covered it. The bowl was filled with freshly-washed cherries.

Cathy's eyebrows rose. Cherry pie again? So soon after Pa's temper fit over biting into a pit?

Deliberately, Mama poured half the cherries into one crust and the other half into the remaining crust.

"But Mama!" Cathy cried. "The pits! The pits! You haven't removed any of the pits from the cherries!"

Silently Mama added the flour and sugar and dotted the cherries with dollops of fresh butter. As she carefully placed the pastry tops over the unpitted cherries, a look of pleased satisfaction crossed her face. "Yes, I know. Perhaps your father will learn to appreciate an *occasional* pit."

Friday, June 27, 1856

Cathy smiled indulgently as her friend, Elizabeth Benton, opened her birthday gifts, squealing over each one. Elizabeth was celebrating her sixteenth birthday.

Cathy preferred the companionship of her old friend, Ellen Stearns. Ellen was more fun than Elizabeth. She was livelier and more imaginative. But Elizabeth had one fascinating advantage over Ellen: Elizabeth was being courted by John McAffery.

Cathy found it hard to remember when she first fell in love with John McAffery. She supposed it was that day two years ago when Pa brought him home for Sunday dinner. During the entire meal her heart had fluttered whenever she looked at their guest. John was the superintendent at the sawmill. Pa seemed to think a lot of him. Cathy loved his thick brown hair, his eyes the color of brandy. His full moustache made him look older than he was. Pa said he was only about twenty.

She took a secretive peek at John McAffery sitting casually on the needlework-covered footstool near Elizabeth. How could he be so smitten with the insipid Elizabeth? Cathy acknowledged that Elizabeth was tall and slender, with lovely long blond hair, but she was so bland! No pep or gumption! It had to be her money that John was after. He was an ambitious fellow, and it just had to be the money. Years ago, Elizabeth's wealthy parents had been killed in a train crash, and Elizabeth was left a well-to-do young girl. Elizabeth's Aunt Carolyn, a sister to her mother, was raising her.

No matter how hard she tried, Cathy couldn't manipulate John into being alone with her. For almost a year now she'd been trying. He hardly knew she existed. She'd promoted the friendship with Elizabeth in hopes that more opportunities for time with John would arise. Instead, it caused Cathy untold pain because of having to watch John's open adoration of Elizabeth.

After the birthday gifts were opened, Elizabeth's Aunt Carolyn announced that cake and punch were ready on the dining room buffet. When Cathy jumped up to see if she could help, she caught her heel in the fringe of the rug and gave her ankle a wrench.

Elizabeth and her Aunt Carolyn fussed.

"John," Elizabeth said, "You'll help Cath get home, won't you? Or should we hitch up the carriage?"

"No, no," Cathy protested. "It's not far. If I can lean on John's arm, I can make it with no trouble."

As John helped her down the front steps, Cathy found it hard to keep from grinning. At last she had her chance to be alone with John McAffery!

After they rounded the corner and were out of sight of Elizabeth's house, Cathy drew John into the yard of a vacant house. "Oh, let me sit on this porch a minute," she sighed. "Just a minute to rest my ankle."

"Is it paining you much?" he asked.

"Some," she lied. It wasn't hurting any more.

"John," she held her hand out to him, "sit beside me."

Obediently, he seated himself beside her on the wooden steps.

She turned, and her round breasts brushed against his arm. A whistling sound told her that he had sucked in his breath.

"Kiss me, John," she breathed. "Please." Again, she leaned her bosom against his arm and touched her lips to his. John's moustache pressed gently against her upper lip, then his lips crushed against hers. Cathy threw her bare arms around his neck, and with a quick movement she slid onto his lap. Her fingers played with the longer hairs lying on his neck. John's lips pressed against hers insistently. His hand moved over her bodice, stroking her breast. Slowly the warm hand slid across the skin of her neckline and downward inside her bodice. The sweetness of his lips pressing on hers made Cathy's head feel light.

21

With a hoarse cry, John pushed her off his lap. He jumped up. "I'll walk you home now, Cath."

She tried to throw her arms around his neck, but he caught them in a firm grip. "No," he said. His voice rasped harshly. He cleared his throat. "I'm going to marry Elizabeth, and this isn't right."

Tears filled Cathy's eyes. "You're going to marry her?" she whispered.

"Yes. Elizabeth has loaned me money, and I'm going west to buy us suitable cropland. Now that Iowa has become a state, I want to farm that rich soil. Around here, there's nothing but sand."

Cathy's thoughts whirled in chaos. "When are you leaving?"

"Next week. I've already given notice to your Pa. I'm training a new mill superintendent to take my place."

That night Cathy lay in bed crying silently; she didn't want Rebecca in the next room to hear. How could she explain that she was in love with someone who was going to marry another person? Oh, John, she moaned softly. *Don't marry Elizabeth! Marry me!*

✳   ✳   ✳   ✳

Independence Day dawned with not a cloud in the sky. The village of Mattigan was celebrating the 80th birthday of the United States. Pa and George Gordon contributed lumber, and a speakers' stand was erected in the square near the school. Early in the morning, Cathy and Rebecca, along with Elizabeth, Ellen, Judith and a handful of young matrons, decorated the stand with aromatic cedar boughs, forming a shaded bower for the speakers.

Elizabeth strung red, white and blue bunting across the front of the stage, and Judith and Ellen pinned a large American flag across the backdrop. Later that morning the flag's 31 stars would remind the audience of how far the union had come in 80 years.

Across the square Cathy could see men working the spit, turning the roasting pig over the coals. At noon everyone would eat barbecued pork, immediately after the orations and before the street-dancing.

After breakfast Cathy and Rebecca got ready for the celebration. Cathy chose a frock of blue barege and a bonnet of fancy straw trimmed with white ribbon. Now that John had left Mattigan, she wasn't nearly so interested in her appearance. Who was there to pretty herself up for?

22

The orators gave their speeches, waxing long on the glories of America, of Michigan, and especially of Mattigan. A ladies choir sang two hymns, some children performed a skit, and then it was announced that the barbecue was ready and serving would begin at once.

A long line waited for the barbecue, so Cathy and her friends moved to the table serving lemonade. As they sipped lemonade they examined the crowd for interesting strangers.

"Look! There's Daniel and Willie!" Ellen cried, pointing. Her motioning hand bumped Cathy's glass, and lemonade poured down the front of Cathy's frock.

Everyone gasped. Ellen apologized, her blue eyes bright with tears.

Cathy laughed. "It's nothing, Ellen. It'll wash out. I'll run home and change." As she moved off toward her house, she called, "Save me a place in line!"

As she neared her house, Cathy heard a rumble like dynamite exploding in the distance. A few seconds passed. A second rumble. Strange. In the spring it was common to hear dynamite explosions. Sometimes loggers broke log jams by blasting. But the log drives were over for the season. Cathy couldn't imagine who'd be blasting.

She scurried up the steps and entered the front hallway. The house seemed strangely silent.

"Mama?" Cathy called.

There was no answer. Cathy walked to the kitchen. Mama was always either in the kitchen or in the small sitting room, doing handwork.

A search of the kitchen and sitting room was fruitless. Perhaps she'd gone to the celebration. No, Mama wouldn't go. Mama never went anywhere but to church and to market.

Cathy climbed to the second floor. "Mama?" she called softly.

Mama's bedroom door was open. Cathy stepped into the bedroom. She gasped. She was face-to-face with a madwoman, gray disheveled hair hanging around her face, eyes wide and glassy. The creature was holding a double-barreled shotgun.

Mouth open, Cathy stared, unable to move, as the woman cracked open the shotgun. The wild woman replaced the expended shells with two fresh shells, one in each chamber. Fleetingly, the thought occurred to Cathy that the woman was Mrs. Campbell, Reverend Campbell's wife—but she looked crazy, hardly recognizable. What was she doing here?

23

Cathy's eyes focused behind Mrs. Campbell to Mama's bed. Two people lay on the bed. Cathy tried to call "Mama!" but no sound came from her throat. She forced her legs to carry her toward the bed, the red bed. Oh, the bed was so red!

Neither of the people lying on the bed had a face. One of them wore Mama's clothes, but where Mama's face should have been there was only blood and hair—no face. The other person wore a man's dark suit and a pastor's clerical collar, but his head was gone, spattered onto the wall behind the bed.

Cathy felt her head come loose from her shoulders and float upward. Slowly, she turned to the madwoman. The woman raised the gun and swung it toward Cathy. Cathy turned her back and covered her face with her hands.

Don't blow away my face!

A cannon-like boom. Cathy's legs buckled.

The next thing she remembered was being on the settee in the parlor. Next door neighbors, Mr. and Mrs. Glenn, hovered over her.

"You're all right, dearie," Mrs. Glenn fussed.

"She didn't shoot me?" Cathy whispered. "She pointed the gun at me. I heard it go off! I thought..."

"She turned the gun on herself. You must've fainted, poor thing. Don't blame you."

"Mama?" Cathy's voice cracked.

"We sent for the doctor. He'll be here soon."

Cathy shook her head in a rhythmic motion. No doctor could help Mama. No doctor could put Mama's head back together.

Cathy grasped her legs and pulled them to her chest, hugging them tight. She rocked forward and backward. A repetitive whimper, monotonous and dreary, came from her lips. Over and over she droned, "Not all the king's horses, nor all the king's men can put Mama's head back together again."

Chapter 3
If a Stone Falls on an Egg...

Pa hired Miss Grace Oliver to supervise the Carleton household and act as chaperone. Her presence in the kitchen was a constant reminder of Mama's absence.

On the surface the Mattigan people had been kind. For two weeks a procession of townspeople, mostly women, came to the Carleton house "to see if there was anything they could do to help."

Cath wanted to scream, "Yes, you can help! Get the accusing look out of your eyes! I don't want your pity, and I don't like what you're thinking about Mama!"

Most callers praised Cath, saying how brave and strong she was to bear up under the burden of what she'd seen. Then they'd look at Cath expectantly, waiting for her to entertain them with the gruesome details of what she'd seen in her mother's bedroom that day. When Cath met their scrutiny with silence punctuated with a defiant look, they soon left.

The men who came calling seemed more sympathetic. They spun their hats in their hands and shuffled their feet. Most didn't even bring up the scandal. Usually, they said they were calling to see if the two Miss Carletons were getting along all right since they knew Mr. Carleton had to spend so much time out of town. Cath didn't see them as gentlemen conniving to take advantage of two young ladies at a time of distress. These men were community leaders, concerned in a paternal way for the girls' well-being. There was one exception. Jason McDaniel was not making his calls out of a feeling of paternal duty.

Every day Jason McDaniel presented himself. Cath knew that for nearly a year Becky had been seeing him. In the past Cath had brushed it off as Becky's first romantic involvement. After all, Becky was only fifteen.

But the devotion and consideration that Jason McDaniel showed to Becky, and even to Cath, was impressive. It showed a maturity beyond a heart pulsing with love and passion. Awkwardly but sincerely, Jason conversed with Pa, those times when Pa was around, which weren't many.

Cath couldn't blame Pa for finding more business reasons to keep him out of town. How humiliating this must be for him! Then she remembered that Pa hadn't slept with Mama for years, and her heart hardened toward him. If he'd been more loving to Mama...

Shaking herself, Cath stopped herself from thinking that way. Pa was alive. He was living, and he had to make the most of his life, just as she and Becky did. No wonder Pa fled to his out-of-town concerns—the silly women in Mattigan already were pursuing him.

Cath noticed that they got more female callers on evenings when Pa was in town. Some of the ladies weren't even subtle. They brought cakes and pastries and praised their own cooking. Remarks like, "I always say, a woman should appreciate her man. She's his servant, obedient to his wishes," floated about the parlor.

Cath sighed. Pa seemed pretty old to have all this attention from females. He was nearly thirty-seven. But she supposed this fine house and all the money was attractive to many ladies.

On the other hand, if Pa seemed too old to be flirted with, Cath worried that Becky was too young. Of course, Jason McDaniel did seem mature for his eighteen years. And hadn't Mama said that she and Pa were only nineteen when they married?

Soon after Mama's funeral Cath began thinking about leaving Mattigan. She longed to get away from the busybody tongues and leering faces. The only thing keeping her here was Becky. And if Becky were to marry Jason McDaniel?—this would free Cath to leave. Cath promised herself that she would do nothing to promote the relationship. If it was meant to happen, it would. Cath wouldn't push her sister into Jason McDaniel's arms just so she could leave Mattigan.

She suddenly became aware of a silence, a void in the conversation between Rebecca and Jason McDaniel.

"Oh, Mr. McDaniel," Cath gushed, "has Rebecca shown you any of her fine handwork? She's just completed some beautiful tea towels to be used in her own home someday. Becky, do show him your lovely tea towels."

When Becky left the room Jason McDaniel's pale eyes fastened on Cath's. "I know she's just a wee lassie," he spoke in a harsh whisper, "but I love her!"

Soberly, Cath regarded him. "I'll not stand in your way, Jason McDaniel. I think you'd make a fine husband for my sister."

His eyes opened wide. "You approve of me?"

"Of course," Cath replied. "But I'm not the one to court. You must convince Rebecca. And then, of course, you must ask my father's permission."

Jason's face contorted into a surprised smile. He looked like someone who was about to steal an apple pie, and then found it handed to him.

"I have no doubts about your sister's desires, Miss Cath. She wants to marry me—after the period of mourning is over, of course."

When Becky returned with her embroidered tea towels, Cath saw the raw look of love on Jason McDaniel's face. She sighed. She'd been so entwined in their family tragedy that she'd forgotten that in spite of death, life goes on. Pa has his business, selling timber, making money. Becky continues her love for Jason McDaniel.

And I? I have mourned Mama with single-mindedness. But then Cath remembered that only days after Mama's death she'd begun thinking about her own future—a future away from Mattigan. And, being honest with herself, Cath realized that whenever she thought of leaving Mattigan she also was thinking about John McAffery out there in the West.

If she left—no, *when* she left Mattigan, she'd find him. He was out there somewhere, using Elizabeth's money to buy a farm. If only I can find him! I know I'll be able to make him forget Elizabeth. He'll fall in love with me. I just know he'll love me. He has to! A soft sob broke from Cath's chest.

Both Becky and Jason stared at her.

Becky jumped up and ran to Cath. Dropping to the floor in front of Cath, Becky hugged her sister's legs and cried, "That's all right, Cath! Go ahead and cry. It's time you cried!"

Cath swallowed and patted Becky's dark head. She couldn't admit that her heartache was for John McAffery and not for Mama.

Gently, she pushed Becky away and stood up. "I have no need to cry."

✳   ✳   ✳   ✳

Their boots made squeaking sounds on the hard-packed snow as Cath and Rebecca walked down the street toward Elizabeth Benton's house. Grudgingly, Cath had to admit that Elizabeth had been a true friend during the six months since Mama's awful murder and the shame that went with it. Elizabeth always was inviting Cath to do something with her, keeping her busy, trying to prevent her from brooding over the shooting and the whispered gossip of the village people.

It was really very thoughtful of Elizabeth since she herself was suffering with worry over John McAffery. Cath worried about him, too. John hadn't returned from the West. Handsome John, who had borrowed money from Elizabeth last July and gone west to buy an Iowa farm, hadn't been heard from since.

Cath held her mittens over her mouth and breathed the warmer air. My but it was cold! Perhaps it was too cold for the ice skating party Elizabeth had planned. But Elizabeth said that Pete, the sleigh driver, would build a campfire so they could warm themselves.

A big sleigh was parked in front of Elizabeth's house. Two huge draft horses stamped their dish-sized hooves, and the silver sleigh bells on their harness jingled merrily. Cath brightened. Perhaps it would be fun after all. Already Ellen and Judith were climbing into the straw-filled sleigh. As Cath walked nearer she could hear the girls giggling as they flirted with Darrel and Charles Rayburn. Jason McDaniel, his flaming hair blowing in the wind, waved eagerly at Rebecca. Cath peeked at her sister and saw two rosy spots appear on Rebecca's cheeks as she returned Jason's wave. Jason McDaniel and Rebecca Carleton were "a couple." Cath expected Rebecca to announce her engagement any time. Even so, Rebecca's adoration of Jason was a puzzle to Cath. He seemed far too much like Pa. Why, he even looked something like Pa, with his red hair.

Ever since her mother's horrible death Cath had found it hard to be loving and respectful to Pa. If only Pa had given Mama the love she craved! Then Mama wouldn't have turned to Reverend Campbell! Cath grew angry with Pa whenever she thought of how he'd slept in a separate bedroom away from Mama.

Jason McDaniel hurried to meet them. "Hi, Becky, Cath." He took Rebecca's mittened hand. "Climb into the sleigh and warm up." As Jason helped Rebecca into the sleigh, Elizabeth came down the steps of her house. She and Cath embraced.

"No word?" Cath asked.

Elizabeth shook her head, and her eyes grew shiny with tears. Cath almost felt angry with John McAffery for letting Elizabeth worry so. He should get word to her somehow.

"The *Marie* is scheduled to arrive tomorrow from Chicago," Elizabeth said, speaking of the weekly arrival of the lumber schooner, which also brought mail. "Oh, Cath," she cried. "Will you go with me tomorrow morning to meet it? I don't think I can bear waiting there on the dock alone!"

Cath squeezed Elizabeth's hand. "Of course, I'll go with you. Now, let's enjoy your sleigh ride and ice skating. It's so nice of you to arrange this. Winter gets long and boring!"

Cath and Elizabeth sat deep in the box at the front end of the sleigh directly behind Pete, the driver. Judith and Ellen flirted openly with the Rayburn brothers, and beyond them, Rebecca and Jason whispered intimately.

"I think you're going to have Jason McDaniel for a brother-in-law," Elizabeth commented quietly.

"Ugh," Cath grunted.

"Don't you like him?"

Cath cocked her head. "I guess I don't. He reminds me too much of my father."

Elizabeth patted Cath's coat sleeve. "You really shouldn't be so hard on your father."

"My Mama would be alive today if he'd been more loving, more considerate."

"Cath, you don't know what went on with them. Maybe you're jumping to the wrong conclusion." Softly, Elizabeth suggested, "Why don't you have a talk with your father about it?"

"Talk with Pa about his not sleeping with Mama?" The very thought made Cath gasp. Her cheeks burned with embarrassment. "I couldn't!"

"It would be hard," Elizabeth agreed as she studied her mittens. "I feel shame talking about it with you. Still, it might be worth it. You could find out that you're being too hard on your father."

Suddenly, one side of the sleigh reared up as its runners climbed a deep snowdrift. Young people tumbled through the straw into the laps of others on the down side. Everybody laughed. Someone started singing, and others joined in.

When the sleigh arrived at the frozen beach of Lake Mattigan not far from the channel into Lake Michigan everyone piled out. In a matter of minutes Pete had a huge fire crackling. Men and boys dragged sturdy logs near the fire for seats. Cath and Elizabeth began fastening ice skates onto their boots.

"The ice looks smooth as glass," Cath said. "A perfect day for ice skating. I thought we'd have to shovel snow first."

Elizabeth grunted as she struggled with a skate. "Pete says in this area the wind usually keeps the ice free of snow. That's why he picked it."

Arm-in-arm, Cath and Elizabeth skated in circles on the smooth ice. Once, their skates locked and they tumbled to the ice, sliding to a giggling stop.

Later, they warmed themselves at the fire, sipping mugs of hot spiced cider and munching Aunt Carolyn's freshly baked crullers.

On the return sleigh ride to Elizabeth's house, everyone was in high spirits, singing and throwing straw at one another.

Judith Peters sat on Elizabeth's left, holding hands with Darrel Rayburn. She turned to Elizabeth, "Thanks for having this party, Elizabeth. It's been fun. Too bad John isn't here. You know, I never thought he was that kind of fellow—to beg money from a body and then take off!"

Darrel laughed. "He really took you, didn't he, Elizabeth? You'll have to admit he pulled a fast one!"

"Hush!" Cath snapped. "Don't speak such nonsense!" When she reached for Elizabeth's hand, the girl's whole body was quivering.

As soon as the sleigh stopped in front of Elizabeth's house, Cath stood, brushing straw from her coat. She patted Elizabeth's cheek. "I'll be here bright and early tomorrow morning. We'll go to the docks and wait for the *Marie*. I know you'll get a letter from John tomorrow!"

Elizabeth nodded listlessly as she turned, walking toward her house. Cath pitied her. Privately, Cath agreed with Judith and Darrel. She was almost certain that John McAffery had taken Elizabeth's money and run. Cath's face flushed as she acknowledged that she hoped this was so. If John *had* fled, that would mean that he was out there somewhere, free, and that someday she and he...

The next morning Cath strode vigorously toward Elizabeth's house. Though it wasn't windy, the air was bitterly cold. It was going to be nasty waiting down on the docks. Whatever had prompted her to promise Elizabeth that she'd accompany her? Guilt. Always, she felt guilty around Elizabeth—guilty for coveting her fiance.

Cath rang the doorbell. Elizabeth's Aunt Carolyn opened the door.

"Good morning, Cath, come in, come in. You're up and about mighty early."

"Yes, Mrs. Jones," Cath answered. "I promised Elizabeth I'd go with her to the docks to wait for the *Marie.*"

"Ah, yes," the stout woman sighed. "Poor Elizabeth. She's so worried. She seemed especially sad last night, which surprised me. I'd hoped the skating party would cheer her."

"Some friends teased her, saying that John took her money and ran off," Cath explained. "That's why she felt so miserable."

"Oh, no!" Mrs. Jones gasped. "How terrible!"

"Where's Elizabeth?"

"She's not up yet, which is strange," the woman replied, looking thoughtfully at Cath. "Especially if she planned to wait for the boat with you. I'll wake her," she said, turning to climb the steep stairway.

Cath absently ran her fingers across the marble top of an ornately carved console table in the front hall. If they were late meeting the schooner, at least they wouldn't have to freeze, waiting on that cold dock.

A high-pitched scream echoed down the stairwell. A second scream tore through the quiet, followed by a heavy thud and the sound of breaking glass.

Cath raced up the stairway, heart pounding in her chest. She turned right toward Elizabeth's bedroom. In the silence she could hear a strange squeak. It sounded like the noise a ship makes as it strains against its moorings at the wharf.

Upon bursting into Elizabeth's room, Cath nearly fell over Carolyn Jones, crumpled on the floor. The dark velvet draperies were drawn over the windows, and light in the room was dim. As her eyes adjusted, Cath squinted toward the creaking sound and saw a long white shape suspended from the chandelier.

Cath's hands flew to her mouth. Elizabeth? Elizabeth trying to hang herself? Cath rushed to the center of the room and hugged Elizabeth's hips, trying to lift her so the cruel rope couldn't strangle her. Through the white Indian muslin nightgown Elizabeth's legs felt cold and stiff. Cath looked up into her friend's face. Elizabeth's eyes were half open; her tongue filled her mouth in an ugly grimace.

With a sob Cath let go, jumped over the unmoving form of Elizabeth's aunt, and tore down the stairs. She ran outside, looking up and down the street for someone who could help Elizabeth. An approaching wagon rumbled around the corner. Cath ran toward it.

"Oh, please help!" she cried to the bewildered drayman. "Come with me!"

The man tied his team to a tree and raced behind Cath to the Benton home. Cath's white face and wide eyes told him it was urgent.

As great sobs shook Cath's body, the man sawed with his pocket knife at the rope holding Elizabeth to the chandelier. When the rope was cut nearly through, the last strands tore, and Elizabeth's body thumped noisily to the floor. Her lifeless form lay twisted like an abandoned rag doll.

Cath touched Elizabeth's cold cheek. "Oh, Elizabeth," she moaned, tears streaming down her cheeks. Why did you do this? Why? No man—not even John McAffery is worth dying for!

Mrs. Jones stirred, and Cath turned to give the older woman attention. Elizabeth was beyond feeling anything.

The funeral was a sad affair, taking place in the basement of the small, unfinished Episcopal church to which the Benton family belonged. The room was crowded, just as the Methodist church had been crowded for Mama's funeral. Why did people flock to tragedy?

There was one especially noticeable difference between Mama's funeral and Elizabeth's. Because it was wintertime, there was not a single flower in the room. That brought tears to Cath's eyes. So young, Elizabeth was, and not even a bunch of wildflowers on her coffin.

There was another difference between this funeral and Mama's. The congregation would not go to the cemetery after the services. Elizabeth wasn't to be buried yet. Her coffin would be stored in the warehouse of Anderson's Furniture and Mortuary. Because the ground was frozen, graves weren't dug during the coldest winter months. Cath shivered, hating the thought of Elizabeth being stacked up with other dead people waiting for spring to thaw the earth.

Following the services, Cath walked down the church steps with Rebecca and Jason.

Judith Peters sidled up to them. "I always knew Elizabeth was peculiar, and this certainly proves it. She was out of her mind!"

"No, Judith," Cath hissed with cool fury. "She knew her own mind. Her heart was broken. Your embarrassing her in front of everyone about John taking her money was cruel!"

"Well, Miss Uppity," Judith snorted, "since when did *you* become a moralizer? We know what *your* mother was! That gives you no right to preach to decent people!"

"That's enough, Judith!" Jason McDaniel's strong voice intervened. "Come, Becky, Cath." He smoothly stepped between Rebecca and Cath and, taking their elbows, guided them down the street.

Once inside their front hallway, as they removed their coats, both Rebecca and Cath burst into tears. They fell into each others arms, sobbing and sniffling.

"How could that horrid Judith say such a thing!" Cath cried. "And in front of all those people!"

Miss Grace bustled into the hallway from the kitchen.

"Was it an awfully sad service?" she asked, her tiny bird eyes blinking.

"I think Rebecca and Cath could use some camomile tea, Miss Grace," Jason suggested. "It's been a difficult time."

The housekeeper nodded and disappeared.

Cath studied Jason through lashes flecked with tears. She was grateful to him for extricating them from the contemptible scene in front of the church. She appreciated his take-charge attitude.

Jason's strength and obvious fondness for Rebecca made it easier for Cath to consider the plans she'd fostered these past two days. The only thing keeping her here in Mattigan was Rebecca. As soon as Becky was safely married to Jason, Cath vowed she'd slip away.

Rebecca stopped her quiet sobbing and rested her forehead against Jason's shoulder. Absently, he patted Rebecca's back.

"Oh, Jason," Cath sighed. "Why? Why did it happen to Elizabeth? She was so sweet and so innocent, so trusting."

Running his lean fingers through coarse, unruly hair, Jason said, "Something my grandmother used to say comes to mind in thinking of Elizabeth. Grandmother said, 'If a stone falls on an egg, too bad for the egg. If an egg falls on a stone, too bad for the egg.'" He looked at Cath to see if she understood.

She nodded. Elizabeth was fragile, like an egg. Cath took a deep breath. I'll not be a delicate egg! I'm a stone, and the people of Mattigan won't shatter me!

In February Jason asked Pa's permission to marry Rebecca. The wedding date was set for May 23. For the remainder of the winter and throughout early spring Cath helped Rebecca make her wedding dress, hem tea towels, embroider aprons and pillowcases—all the items a young bride needs.

Most of the time Cath hummed happily because Rebecca's marriage was giving her the freedom to leave Mattigan. She could head west to look for John McAffery. At any rate, Cath wouldn't have left until warm weather arrived. She wasn't foolish enough to face the rigors of winter in her journey west. May would be the best time to leave. It would allow her months of warm weather for her search.

The wedding ceremony was lovely. White and lavender lilac blooms decorated the church, and Rebecca looked gloriously beautiful, her dark hair set off by the white satin bridal gown with its trimmings of blond lace. Her short gloves with embroidered tops were worn fastened over the band of the long lace sleeves. The lacy veil formed a crown where it was caught up over Rebecca's curls before it trailed to the floor.

Following the ceremony and the dinner held in the church basement, the newlyweds retired to the one-story bungalow Jason had constructed during the spring months. Cath breathed a sigh of relief. Now she could leave. The sooner, the better!

The weather was warm. As soon as Miss Grace was asleep tonight Cath planned to slip away. She figured she'd walk along the beach until she got to Gordontown, where she'd catch the stage. She knew she could do that. Hadn't she walked all the way from Indiana when she was only five years old?

Cath's major concern was safety while traveling. She knew it wasn't proper for a young lady to travel alone. Decent women didn't travel unaccompanied. Cath feared if she did, male travelers might assume she wasn't a lady.

Chin on hands, she stared vacantly out the front window, worrying. Her eyes fell on Tommy Glenn. The neighbor boy was playing marbles in the street. His clothes drew Cath's attention. What a splendid idea! She jumped up and hurried outside.

"Hi, Tommy," she called.

He stood up. His eye level came to about Cath's cheekbones. Just about her size.

"Tommy," she began, "I need an outfit of boy's clothes, and what you're wearing would be just right."

34

His brown eyes looked puzzled, and he frowned.

"I'll give you a twenty dollar gold piece for the clothes you're wearing—your boots, too."

There was a long pause.

"Please, Tommy."

"Gee, Cath, I can't do that," he said. "Ma would find out that the clothes were missing and she'd lick me good! I wouldn't dare! What could I tell her, about what happened to them?"

Cath thought for a moment. "Tommy, I'll tell you exactly what I'm going to do with them. I'm going to be leaving Mattigan tomorrow. I'll be gone. And then you can tell your mother the truth about your clothes, and why I had to have them. I'm going out West, and I've got to dress like a boy in order to travel safely. So just tell your mother the truth—that I had to have your clothes in order to be safe. I'm sure she'll understand. The twenty dollars will buy you brand new clothes with money left over. I know your mother would approve of your helping me travel safely. She wouldn't want anything bad to happen to me."

Tommy looked at Cath for a long time. He kicked the toe of his boot into the sand. "You're really going out West all by yourself?"

"Yes. And you can make it safe for me," she pressured him.

Reluctantly, he consented.

"Go change your clothes and bring them to my house. Then I'll give you the gold piece," Cath said. "Don't forget the boots!"

The exchange was made. Cath waited until after the evening meal to try on the clothes. Throughout dinner it was hard to keep from squirming. Only she and Miss Grace were eating, as Pa had gone to Grand Rapids in the early morning hours.

At last Miss Grace brought two bowls of applesauce from the kitchen. After finishing dessert Cath excused herself. "I guess I'm exhausted from all the activity of Rebecca's wedding."

Once in her room she undressed quickly and slipped on the pale blue linen shirt. Stepping into the trousers, she stuffed the shirt-tails inside and struggled with the small buttons on the fly. A glance in the gilt-framed mirror told her that both shirt and trousers were a loose fit. Her reflection also pointed out her breasts. She frowned, pulling off the shirt. Something had to be done about that. A bosom would be a sure giveaway. Cath solved the problem by wrapping her breasts tightly in a tea towel retrieved from her hope chest, sewing the towel's ends together.

Now when she put on Tommy's shirt, her bound breasts gave her the appearance of having a broad chest. With a sigh, she picked up the worn gray wool jacket and thrust her arms into it. There. That was even better. Her breasts were hidden.

The ankle-high boots weren't a bad fit, for which she was grateful. She expected to be doing a lot of walking in her search for John McAffery.

And now she had to conceal her long blonde curls in the cap. Cath bent from the waist, lowering her head until the tips of her curls nearly swept the floor. Slowly, she filled the crown of Tommy's cap with her hair as she moved the cap toward her head and settled it there. Holding it with both hands, she rose. Watching in the mirror, she stuffed wisps of escaping hair into the cap. When all of her hair was concealed, she tipped the cap to a jaunty angle. Cath examined her reflection. A wide smile spread across her face. Grinning back from the mirror was a young boy of about thirteen—exactly the image she was trying to create.

Suddenly a scratching sound came from behind the highboy. Cath whirled. A gray mouse scurried across the floor and out of the room.

Cath looked back toward her reflection. With dismay she saw that because of her quick movement, most of her hair had tumbled out of the cap. Cath gritted her teeth. That would never do.

She grabbed the cap from her head and threw it at the mirror. For a long time Cath studied her reflection, stroking her long curls. She swallowed. Tears sprang to her eyes as she moved toward her sewing basket. Angrily, she brushed the tears from her eyes. Cath picked up the long shears. Back in front of the mirror she grabbed a handful of golden curls directly over her left ear. Holding the shears close to her head, she snapped closed the scissor blades. Cath stared at the amputated curls clutched in her left hand. With a defiant toss of her head she threw the curls onto the floor. The silver shears flashed again. Soon the floor was covered with blond curls.

The reflection looking back at Cath was no longer Cath, but the image of a blond-haired boy. Cath moved closer to the mirror and worked at smoothing out the choppy haircut. The image before her kept blurring; she squeezed her eyes so her vision would clear.

She retrieved the cap from the floor and once again placed it on her head. Now she could pass for a young boy, for sure.

Cath checked her carpetbag to make certain her gold coins were packed safely, along with her blue silk dress and the dainty print calico. She had put in her favorite morning glory bonnet to go with the silk frock and a linen bonnet to match the calico. Once she found John, she'd want to look pretty for him.

Unconsciously, her hand flew to her shorn head. Would John think she was ugly? In public her bonnets would cover her hair. She would hate being stared at on the street, or made fun of. Cath sat at her oak secretary and began her farewell note. "Dear Pa, Becky, and Miss Grace," she wrote. "Please don't worry about me. I shall be fine. I've gone to the West, where I believe my future lies. I can't bear to stay in Mattigan any longer. Please understand. I have taken money, so I shall be fine. I'll write when I get located. Yours affectionately, Cath."

She left the letter unfolded on the top of her secretary where Miss Grace was sure to find it tomorrow morning.

Not a sound came from the rest of the house. Miss Grace must be asleep by now. Cath picked up her brocade carpetbag, glanced around her bedroom. There was nothing here for her. Her future lay in the West. Her future, her love. Silently she tiptoed down the stairway.

Chapter 4
Wade Stanton, Riverboat Gambler

Thursday, June 25, 1857

As Cath waited for the stagecoach she thought about her two weeks' journey from the deep woods of Mattigan to this rolling, treeless prairie of Illinois. She was incredibly tired of traveling! The only thing that kept her heading west was the image of John's handsome face which she'd concentrate on every time she thought of returning home. Or she'd remind herself of how Mama had disgraced them all. Cath's cheeks burned when she thought of having to face the knowing looks of people like Judith Peters. Already she missed Pa and Becky. Someday, when John and she were married and living in a fine mansion she'd invite Pa and Becky to come visit.

Cath watched as her carpetbag was stowed securely on the rear boot of the Concord coach, along with the baggage of other passengers and a mail sack.

The stage driver constantly scratched himself. His filthy hands dug at every part of his body, and he smelled worse than an old Billy goat.

Cath climbed aboard. Already three men filled the forward-facing seat. Cath sat facing them. A young man with an older woman whom he called "Mother," seated themselves next to Cath. The woman waved a lacy handkerchief in front of her nose.

"That driver!" she gasped. "Filthy creature! Ugh!"

The man in the middle stroked his bushy, black beard. His dark eyes sparkled devilishly as he spoke. "These overland drivers and the stock-tenders all have lice. For years they never wash the blankets they sleep on. They rarely bathe. Know how they get rid of lice?"

Cath felt an awful urge to scratch, but she forced her hands to remain in her lap.

The black-bearded passenger chuckled. "When warm weather comes, on a spring morning the drivers spread their underclothes and blankets on an ant hill. By evening the ants have eaten all the lice. This gives the drivers relief from scratching—only for a while though, until the lice eggs hatch. Then they're back to scratching." His eyes danced as he saw the discomfiture his tale was causing Cath and the lady passenger.

I do believe he told us that just to see if we'd squirm, Cath thought. She raised her eyes in time to see an amused glitter in the man's dark eyes as he studied her. Cath's cheeks grew warm as his gaze swept her body. He was certainly enjoying her uneasiness!

The coach swayed as the driver climbed up on the front boot and placed his feet against the footboard. Behind his feet was a water bucket and a buffalo robe. He gave a rasping cry to the horses, and the carriage jerked ahead.

As it moved along the rutted road the coach swayed both from side to side and fore and aft. Though Cath had never been a passenger on a large boat, she wondered if riding the swells of Lake Michigan might be like this rocking ride.

The ticket agent had said they'd stop at way stations twice that day for meals. He'd assured her that meals would be reasonably priced. For several days Cath had worried about her shrinking supply of cash. She hadn't been realistic about the amount of money she'd brought. In her innocence she hadn't known how much everything would cost. Her gold coins were nearly gone, yet her stomach growled its hunger. It seemed forever before the coach slowed and they pulled into a station.

Inside the way station, the six passengers were told to sit at a long plank table with pine benches. As Cath slid onto the bench, she saw that the table was filthy. Old dried food formed lumps on its surface, and fresh sticky chunks attracted buzzing flies.

"If that awful driver sits with us, I shan't be able to eat a thing!" the older woman announced to the table.

The food was expensive. Cath hesitated, but she had to eat. Maybe if she ate a lot this time she could get by on one meal today.

There was plenty of hearty food but it was bland. Bowls of beans and hominy, a platter of bacon, bread but no butter, only sorghum molasses. Cath stuffed herself with more than she wanted. She was determined that at the next meal stop she wouldn't eat. Dessert was dried apple pie. Cath lifted her fork and poked at a small black speck lodged in the upper crust. There was another — and yet another. Her lips curled. Mouse droppings! Cath clamped her lips together firmly. Mustn't be sick!—mustn't lose the meal. She closed her eyes and began counting backwards from one hundred to focus her mind on something else.

A clatter of dishes let her know that the manager was removing plates. She opened her eyes as he reached for her pie plate.

"What's the matter, kid?" he asked. "Don't you like apple pie? Never heard of a kid who don't like apple pie!"

Cath's eyes flashed. "Your apple pie is filthy, sir. And I object to paying for filth."

"Well, now, boy," he drawled, "my mama taught me that we all will eat a peck of dirt in our lifetime."

Cath stood up to get away from the food-encrusted table. "Yes, sir. My mama taught me that, too, but I don't like getting my whole peck of dirt at once!"

The manager's face flushed darkly while the other passengers roared with laughter.

"Well, said, sonny!" the black-bearded man bellowed, as he clapped Cath on the back with a whack that jarred her teeth. The man's dark eyes twinkled as they swept her body. When his eyes locked with hers for a moment, he raised an eyebrow rakishly.

Could it be that he suspects I'm a girl? Cath wondered. Cath spotted the outhouses in back of the station and turned in that direction. The man joined her.

When they arrived at the outhouse which said "Men" on it, the man opened the door and entered. He held the door for Cath. You can come on in, son. It's a two-holer."

Cath's face reddened.

"It's okay, son." The man seemed to be suppressing laughter. "There's room for two."

Cath swallowed. "I'm sorry, sir, but I've got what my Pa calls 'bashful kidneys.' I can't pee in front of anyone."

"Do tell!" The man flashed her a broad grin. His teeth gleamed white against his dark beard. Chuckling, he shook his head and closed the outhouse door.

At this moment Cath wished she had dressed as a female.

41

Surely it would be safe with another woman in the stagecoach. But there was yet tonight where they all had to sleep at a station.

Later, as the coach with fresh horses rocked through a drier countryside, dust poured into the passenger section, covering them with a fine layer of grit.

An hour after sundown they pulled into the station where they would spend the night. The woman was given the one private room. Males were handed blankets and pillows and told to make themselves comfortable on the floor. Again, Cath wished she was not masquerading. If she'd been traveling as herself perhaps she could have shared the private room with the older woman.

Cath decided not to eat. She said she was too tired. And from the smell of the cooking—it smelled like bacon and beans again—she could skip supper without regrets.

Picking a corner, Cath rolled up in her blanket and dozed off. Dimly, she heard the men come into the room after they'd finished eating. Cath shifted her position and fell asleep again.

A loud click near her ear awakened her. Eyes wide, she stared into the dimly-lit room. A flash of silver gleamed near her face. Someone was pointing a revolver at her! At her head! Cath sat upright.

The muzzle of the gun didn't follow her, but stayed pointing where it was.

"Just scootch back across the room where you were, fellow," a voice whispered. "I'd hate to pull this trigger."

There was a scuffling noise. Cath saw the dark shape of a man slide away.

In spite of the dim light Cath recognized that the man with the gun was the black-bearded passenger. He lay against the wall with his head near hers and his feet stretched in the opposite direction.

It had happened so fast Cath hardly had time to be frightened. But now that it was over her heart thumped against her ribs. Her breath came in short gasps.

"You okay?" the black-bearded man whispered.

"Yes. Thank you."

The rest of the night Cath didn't close her eyes. She was quite sure the black-bearded one didn't either.

As dawn lightened the room, Cath saw that the person who'd tried to accost her during the night was the man traveling with his mother.

He must suspect she was a girl. And what about the black-bearded one? Did he suspect, too? Did he feel he must protect her?

Stiffly, Cath boarded the Concord coach for another day's travel. Throughout the long day dust seeped into the swaying carriage, coating her face with powdery grime. As twilight approached, Cath's body ached. Last night's fitful sleep hadn't been restful. She was bone tired. At dusk the stagecoach creaked to a stop. With surprise Cath looked out the window and saw that they were on a wharf. Toward the west lay a brown expanse of dark water which had to be the Mississippi River. Far across the wide river twinkled the lights of a town.

Cath climbed out and stood waiting as the driver unloaded baggage. She was now the only female passenger, since the woman and son had gotten off earlier. The stage driver hung a lantern on a tall post.

"That's a signal for the ferry boat to come over to pick up passengers," the black-bearded man explained. "You'll be getting on a different stage with fresh horses over there at Keokuk. Across the river, that's Iowa."

Ah, Cath sighed. Iowa—where her true love had gone. The state of Iowa was actually in sight. Stooping, she rummaged through her carpetbag to check on her gold coins, what remained of them. Frantically, she dug through the bag. The coins were gone! Her money was gone! Cath plunged her hand into her trouser pocket. Three quarters! That was all the money she had left!

She burst into tears. Great spasms heaved from her chest. The other passengers stared, but she couldn't stop sobbing.

A flatboat driven by a steam engine bumped against the wharf. The coach passengers stepped on board.

"Come now," the black-bearded man said softly. "Big boys don't cry," he chided. "Get on board before the ferry leaves without you."

Cath's sobs grew even louder. Her shoulders shook.

"What's the matter? Why are you crying?" the man asked.

"My money!" she gasped. "It's gone! It's not in my carpetbag!"

The man took Cath's arm and pulled her aboard the ferry, paying her fare along with his.

"Thank you," Cath sniffled.

"Don't you have a handkerchief?" he asked.

She shook her head.

From his coat pocket he pulled a white linen handkerchief. He handed it to her. "Blow. And stop crying. Big boys like you don't cry!"

43

Cath looked up at him. Though his face was blurred through her tears, it seemed that his lips quivered. Was he suppressing a smile?

Side-by-side they stood at the wooden railing of the small ferry watching the lights of Keokuk grow closer. "So you don't have any money?" the man asked.

Cath bit her lower lip to keep from bursting into new tears. "No," she whispered, voice quavering, "just this." She brought the quarters out of her pocket.

"Well, you'll have to stay with me tonight then," he said. "That is, if you don't mind sleeping on a couch."

"Do you live here?" Cath asked.

He laughed. "No, thank God! But I do live on that steamboat moored over there," he pointed to the left where six side-wheelers were docked. "I live on the *Sally Anne*. She's the longest one there."

Cath's thoughts raced. She was stranded with no money. Here was an offer of shelter for the night. Yet could she keep from him the fact that she was not a boy? Her eyes darted upward to search his face, but he had turned away. He stared across the dark water toward the western shore. She didn't have much choice unless she wanted to sleep on the wharf with the rats. At least he'd said there was a couch. She wouldn't have to share his bed!

As they walked off the ferry onto the Keokuk wharf the man turned to Cath. "Well? Are you going to accept my hospitality? Or are you waiting for a better offer?" In the dark Cath could see his dark eyes glinting.

"No, sir!" she cried. "I mean, yes sir. I want to accept your offer. It's very kind of you, sir." The words tumbled out in a rush.

"Very well, come along." He began walking briskly along the dock. His boots tapped sharply on the thick planks. Cath scurried to keep up. The odor of fish drifted up from the water beneath the wharf.

Cheerful orchestra music came from one docked side-wheeler called *The North Star*. Cath couldn't get over how huge these steamboats were. She was accustomed to the lumber schooners which sailed into Mattigan, and she'd always thought they were large, but these steamboats were much bigger.

At the gangplank of the *Sally Anne* the man turned to Cath. "I'm forgetting my manners," he said. "Forgive me. I'm Wade Stanton." He held out his hand.

Cath slid her hand into his large one. "I'm, .. uh, I'm Tommy Carleton," she stammered.

A strange look flashed across his eyes, then was gone. "Nice meeting you, ...uh, Tommy," he grinned. In the near-darkness his teeth gleamed white against his dark beard.

For a moment Cath thought he was laughing at her. He moved up the gangplank. "This," he said, "is the main deck, where the engines are, where the machinery is located." He led her to a stairway. "The staterooms are on the saloon deck. I'll show you around the boat tomorrow." They walked down a covered hallway, flanked by stateroom doors on one side and open air and dark river on the other.

"Here it is," Wade Stanton said, stopping before one of the doors and opening it. In the darkness Cath heard him strike a match. Shortly, warm light flickered through the room from a lamp on a dresser.

The room was elegantly furnished: Aubusson rug, ivory brocade-covered couch, mahogany clothes press, bed covered with a bright crewel work counterpane in shades of blue.

"As you can see," Stanton said, "the couch isn't large," he pursed his lips. "But you're a small fellow. Perhaps it'll suit you." He gave Cath a wide smile.

He set his leather luggage beside the clothes press. "I have business which will take me an hour or so. While I'm gone I'm going to have a chambermaid bring you a tub and hot water." With his thumb he traced a slippery path across her dusty cheek. "Feel good to get clean?" he asked, teeth flashing.

"Oh, yes," Cath breathed. How thoughtful!

When the colored chambermaid began bringing pails of hot water, Cath tried not to stare. She'd never seen a person with such dark skin. Cath wanted to touch the girl's bare arm to see if dark skin felt like white skin. The girl appeared to be near her own age. When the metal tub was half full of steaming water, the chambermaid asked, "Ain't you gettin' in, mastah?"

"Not until you're done bringing water," Cath answered, raising her chin defiantly.

The girl laughed, her white teeth gleaming against wide pink lips. "Bashful, huh, boy? Why, you be down underwater, at least alls the parts of you that you want tuh hide from me!"

Adamantly Cath shook her head. "I'll wait."

At last the dusky chambermaid said she was done bringing bath water. She handed Cath a cake of soap, a wash cloth, and a fluffy towel. "Have a good bath, mastah," she called over her shoulder as she closed the door.

Quickly, Cath pulled off Tommy Glenn's grimy clothes and stepped into the tub. The warm water was murky—apparently Mississippi River water, but warm, oh so warm! She lathered herself with foamy suds, rubbing the washcloth briskly over her skin. Working soap suds into her short hair, she splashed water on her head. How good it felt to be clean after two weeks of dust! Cath relaxed, dozing. When the water began to feel cool, she reluctantly stood up.

Just at that moment the door to the stateroom opened, and a strange man carrying a silver pitcher entered. With a shriek, Cath dropped back down into the round tub, splashing water onto the rug.

"It's me!" the man announced, grinning broadly. "Wade Stanton! I got a shave and haircut."

Wide-eyed, Cath stared. It *was* the black-bearded man, now without the beard. Only a dark mustache remained. Clean-shaven, he was a handsome man; charming dimples creased his cheeks when he grinned.

Dropping to his hands and knees, he began mopping at the spilled water. "I brought a pitcher of warm water to rinse you off," he said. "A pretty gal like you doesn't want to leave soap on tender skin."

Cath looked at him sharply. "You know I'm a girl?"

He leaned over the rim of the tub and grinned at her wickedly. Their eyes were not ten inches apart. "You didn't think I'd ask a *boy* to share my cabin?"

Cath's mind raced. What was she to do? What did he have in mind?

"Stand up, Sunny, while this water is still warm. I'll pour it over you to rinse off the soap."

"I will not! And don't call me 'sonny!' I'm a girl!"

"Yes." The dimples pressed deep into his cheeks. "I see!"

Stanton picked up the pitcher. "Sweetheart, I was calling you 'Sunny' S-U-N-N-Y," he spelled, "because your hair is the color of bright sunbeams. Now stand up! I've seen worse sights than naked girls before!"

Slowly Cath rose from the soapy water, her eyes squeezed tightly shut, arms folded across her breasts. She felt warm water pour over her head and wash down her skin, taking the soapsuds with it. When the water trickled to a stop, she felt a soft towel wrapped around her nakedness.

As she stepped out of the tub Wade Stanton picked up her carpetbag. "Did you bring any female clothing?" he asked, poking in the bag.

He pulled out the blue silk and whistled. "Nice dress! Sunny, you surprise me. You're running from money, aren't you?"

Haughtily, Cath replied, "There're more important things in life than money!"

"Oh, little Sunny," he grinned. "You're so young. It's a lot more fun to be rich than to be poor. I've been both. Money isn't important unless you don't have enough of it." He appraised the silk garment.

"I'll get the chamber maid to press this dress for you, then I'm taking you to dinner. It's time we had some good food after that slop they fed us at the stage stops."

By the time he returned with her freshly-pressed frock Cath had gotten into her underclothing. She stood waiting in the middle of the stateroom, morning glory bonnet covering her shorn head. Her white petticoat with the heavy horsehair stiffening waited to give her dress the look of a hoop skirt.

Wade Stanton handed the rejuvenated frock to Cath. As she wiggled into the dress, Wade's eyes flashed.

"If you were any sort of gentleman, sir, you'd turn your back!" she sputtered.

"It appears to me," he drawled, "that a gentleman would assist a lady in distress. I think you're going to tear this lovely frock before you get it on. Here, you have it twisted," he said, reaching out and pulling the skirt down. As the dress dropped over her body, his hands brushed lightly across her breasts.

Cath caught her breath, shocked at the sensation his light touch caused in the pit of her stomach.

His brown eyes sparkled. "You look ravishing," he said, as she smoothed the foulard silk. She knew it was a lovely dress with its rows and rows of blue velvet ribbon trimming the edges of the flounces.

Taking Cath's elbow, he steered her out of the stateroom. "We've missed the dinner hour," he said, "but the steward promised he'd put some food out on a sideboard for us."

Cath gasped at the elegance of the long saloon flanked on either side by the staterooms. Painted a dazzling white with gilded ornaments and scrollwork, its ceiling was the same brilliant white, but was contoured with scrolls and patterns.

At one side of the saloon on a mahogany sideboard covered with a white linen cloth was arranged an assortment of food—a platter of sliced roast beef, a porcelain tureen filled with delicious-smelling stew. Sprigs of fresh mint and lemon slices garnished the serving dishes. At the far end of the sideboard was an array of rich pastries, cakes, ices, fruits and nuts.

The steward hovered near, seeing that they were properly served. They seated themselves at a table for two at one side of the saloon. They ate hungrily.

When her immediate hunger was appeased, Cath looked up from her plate. Wade Stanton was watching her, his eyes alert and twinkling. On his right hand he wore a gold ring in which a huge diamond was imbedded.

"What do you do, Mr. Stanton?" she asked.

He dabbed at his mustache with a linen napkin. "None of this 'Mr. Stanton!' I'm older than you, but that makes me feel ancient. Call me 'Wade.'" He returned the napkin to his lap. "I'm a gambler, a riverboat gambler."

He seemed to be watching for her reaction.

"Is it a legal profession, or must you do it secretly?"

"Oh, I'm not secretive about it," he laughed. "In fact, the better known I get, the more people want to play with me. As to if it's legal, I can't say. I just work on boats where the captain approves of me and my brand of poker. Some captains won't allow any kind of gambling. Captain Tilby of the *Sally Anne* permits all kinds—honest and dishonest."

"Which kind of gambling do you do? Honest or dishonest?"

"I play an honest game of poker with honest cards. If a player gets in his cups and plays poorly or bets imprudently, I don't tell him to go to bed and come back when he's sober." Wade's dimples deepened. "And I'm not above buying him a drink or two, either!"

Cath played with her food. She was so full she feared her seams would give.

"Now it's my turn for questions," Wade said. "You said you were Tommy Carleton. How about your real name?"

"Cath. Cath Carleton."

"I think I prefer 'Sunny.'" He reached across the table and pulled a short curl from beneath her bonnet. "And how did your golden curls get shorn?" he asked.

Cath was annoyed at his familiarity. How dare he touch her hair! Yet something held her back from saying anything. It was by his generosity that she'd been fed. He'd seen that she had a warm bath, a roof over her head tonight. I must be nice to Wade Stanton, she reminded herself. I'm lucky to have found him. Whatever am I going to do? I've got to find John McAffery! Then everything will be all right.

Unaware that her facial expression had changed when she thought of John, Cath opened her mouth to answer his question.

"What thought just crossed your pretty little mind?" Wade asked, studying her closely.

She'd been thinking about her irritation with him, reminding herself to be grateful to him. She couldn't tell him that! Then she remembered.

"Oh, I thought about finding my brother, John. That's what I'm doing out here—looking for him. A year ago he came out to Iowa to buy a farm. He never returned."

She didn't notice the narrowing of Wade's eyes or the tightening of his lips as she talked of John.

"And the hair?" he prompted.

"When I decided to dress like a boy, for safety reasons you understand, I couldn't get my hair to stay inside the cap. It was long, kept falling out, so I cut it off!" She lifted her chin defiantly as tears filled her eyes.

"Poor Sunny," he sympathized. "You're a brave girl. Maybe not too sensible, but you've got nerve."

On their way back to the stateroom, Wade pointed out the washrooms. "Now you can use the one marked 'Ladies,'" he laughed. "You don't have to share one with me anymore."

Cath flushed, remembering the outhouse at the stage stop where he'd tried to coax her to share it with him. "Did you know I was a girl then?" she demanded, her blue eyes snapping.

"What do you think?" he drawled as he disappeared inside the men's washroom.

Back in the stateroom as they prepared to sleep, Cath moaned, "I don't have anything to sleep in! I don't want to wear those filthy boy's clothes, but I'll wrinkle my dress if I sleep in that, and my petticoat..."

Wade reached into his luggage and brought out a white nightshirt. "Here," he said, tossing it to her. "You can wear that."

"But what will you wear?" she stammered.

"Does it matter?" he asked, raising one eyebrow.

Cath's face grew pink.

"If it makes you feel better," he said, "I have two nightshirts."

"Will you leave the room while I undress?" Cath asked.

For a moment their eyes locked, and Cath feared he was going to refuse.

At last he muttered, "As you like," and stepped out the door.

Cath rapped sharply on the door as soon as she was ready for bed. Quickly, she curled up on the couch.

Wade strode into the room. Wordlessly, he went to the lamp on the bedside table and turned the wick down. The room became pitch dark. There wasn't even a window to let in moonbeams.

The rustling of clothing told Cath that he was undressing. When the bed creaked, she figured he was in bed.

Tired as she was from the long day and her nearly sleepless night last night, for a long time Cath couldn't fall asleep. Heavy, regular sounds of Wade's breathing came from his bed; she could tell he was asleep. Rolling from side to side, she tried to get comfortable. The couch was quite adequate—certainly far softer than the floor last night! Maybe her awareness of Wade sleeping near kept her senses tingling and body taut.

Cath shook herself crossly. Don't think about Wade Stanton! Think about why you're enduring this! You're here because you want to find John McAffery. The thought of John and his handsome amber eyes soothed her. Soon she slept.

Chapter 5
Sweet Gandy Dancer's Garters

The clang of a loud gong brought Cath up off the couch, her eyes wide. What was it? A fire bell?

A groan came from the bed. Wade rolled over.

"What is it?" Cath cried. "What's the matter?"

"It's six-thirty. That's the wake-up bell. Breakfast is served at seven."

Cath became aware of a throbbing noise. It sounded like engines. "Are we moving?" she asked.

"Yes. Don't you feel it?" Wade answered.

Glancing down at her bare ankles, Cath said, "I'd better get dressed."

Wade sighed. "Last night I left my room to allow you to dress in private. This morning I'll not go out there in my nightshirt. Turning my back is the best I can do." With that he rolled over, facing the wall.

Cath dressed quickly, putting on her calico print dress. It was wrinkled, but the freshly-pressed blue silk was much too formal for morning wear. "I'll go to the wash room to give you privacy," she sniffed as she left the stateroom.

The breakfast gong sounded at seven. A long table nearly filled the length of the saloon. It was covered with steaming platters of ham, eggs, flapjacks, and biscuits. As soon as Cath and Wade finished eating, their dishes were removed, and waiting passengers took their places at the table.

Wade offered to show Cath around the boat. "This saloon area is known as the 'gentlemen's cabin,'" he said, "but as you can see, it's also the dining area. Aft and farthest from the engines is the ladies' cabin. Only men acquainted with lady passengers may enter the ladies' cabin." He opened the door, and Cath peeked in. The ladies' cabin was even more elegantly furnished than the main saloon.

They strolled outside. Below, the dark river boiled, churned by the huge paddle wheels. Bluffs covered with green forests bordered the banks of the wide river. "Where is the boat going?" Cath asked.

"St. Louis. The *Sally Anne* goes back and forth between St. Louis and Keokuk, hauling cargo and, of course, passengers."

He told her that St. Louis was two hundred miles downstream from Keokuk. "We'll probably put up in Hannibal tonight to take on cargo."

Pointing to the deck above them, Wade explained that it was called the 'hurricane deck.' "The cabin up there is called 'the texas,' and that's where the officers of the boat live."

On the hurricane deck overflow cargo was stored—steam engines, boilers, plows, furniture, hogsheads, and barrels. Perched above the hurricane deck was the pilot-house, enclosed in glass all the way around. Cath could make out the pilot's distant figure up there in the pilot-house.

Below on the main deck was more cargo and a huge supply of wood to feed the fireboxes of the two engines. On either side of the steamboat huge paddle wheels creaked as they churned through the water, pushing the boat forward.

Side-by-side Cath and Wade stood, leaning on the railing. Wade half-turned to look at Cath. His eyes twinkled dangerously. "Last night I explained to the steward that I was recently married, and that you're my bride."

Cath gasped. "I beg your pardon!" she cried. "How dare you!"

Wade's dimples deepened. "Well, for your sake I dared. Because you were sharing my cabin, I thought your reputation would be protected if you were supposedly married to me. An unmarried woman occupying my cabin would have an unpleasant title."

She stared at him, her eyes snapping.

"Of course," he went on, "if you prefer that the passengers and crew think you're my concubine, that's your choice. Your reputation would suffer more than mine. Gentlemen are forgiven many peccadilloes."

He turned back toward the brown river. "But I see that you're angered by my lie. I'll explain to the steward that you're merely 'a friend.'

I should warn you, though, that you'll find yourself feeling uncomfortable in the ladies' cabin once your unmarried situation becomes known. Ladies are very insistent about keeping non-ladies at arm's length. Guess the pure ladies think the tarnish of the soiled doves will rub off."

Cath felt cornered. What could she do? No money, no friends, no relatives. She sighed. Her life right now seemed to be at the mercy of Wade Stanton.

"Well, never mind," Cath retorted. "The damage has been done. Best to leave things as they are."

Wade pulled a long cigar from his vest pocket and lit it. "You needn't worry about marriage, Sunny," he smiled, though Cath detected a grimness to his smile. "I'm already married. Have a wife and daughter in Philadelphia. In fact, I'm just returning from there where I visited my daughter."

Unaccountably, Cath felt her disposition darken, as if a cloud had passed in front of the sun. "I wouldn't think your wife would like your working out here so far away from her," she commented, her voice prim.

Wade took a long pull on his cigar. "Doesn't matter what my wife likes. Been separated for years." A flash of pain crossed his forehead for a moment, and then was gone.

He told Cath that he was thinking of someday working on a steamboat which would go up the Missouri River. He said that steamboating on the Missouri River was less luxurious and more dangerous than on the Mississippi, but it was said to be more exciting and much more lucrative. "The West is opening up," he said. "There's money going up the Missouri. All sorts of manufactured goods are shipped all the way to Ft. Benton. Then the boats bring back furs and buffalo robes."

That evening in the saloon just before dinner Wade introduced Cath to Captain Tilby.

"My dear Mrs. Stanton," the captain boomed, "what a lovely bride! You must sit on my right at dinner. Stanton, you old rascal," he turned to face Wade and strenuously pumped the gambler's hand. "How did you ever persuade such a lovely little bird to nest with you?"

At the head of the table the captain stood, carving a dripping beef roast with the assistance of a colored steward. Twenty waiters, all colored, hurried back and forth along the table carrying platters of food. One waiter held a huge silver tureen while another ladled creamy leek

53

potato soup into the passengers' bowls. Cath admired the dainty flowered Spode bone china dishes, so delicate.

It was easy to chat with the captain since he did most of the talking. He seemed happy to have a fresh ear for his old stories of steamboat races and near catastrophes.

There were several choices for dessert. Cath chose shortcake covered with scarlet, juicy strawberries nearly smothered in thick whipped cream.

After dinner Wade took Cath's elbow. "Shall I escort you to our stateroom, or would you rather spend some time in the ladies' cabin?" he asked.

"Where are you going?" Cath asked.

"I'm going to work, my dear," he said. "Someone has to pay for our room and board, you know." There was a hint of sarcasm in his voice.

Cath flushed as she was reminded that she was destitute and living on his charity. "I'll pay you back, Wade!" she said stiffly. "It will take awhile, but I'll get money and I'll pay you back! I don't take charity!"

Wade's brown eyes flashed humorously, as they swept across her body, lingering on her breasts before they met Cath's blue eyes. "You can repay me, little Sunny. But it's not your money I want."

Gasping, Cath's gloved hand flashed across his face. A red streak appeared almost immediately on his cheek. Cath felt her own face flush. Her mind worked quickly. Wade had no right to make such a suggestion, one part of her thoughts said. But the other part of her mind reminded her that she had agreed to accompany him, to share his room, and that she was dependent upon him for food and lodging. She could understand how he might think that she was not a proper lady.

"May I remind you that I am a lady, sir!" she snapped. She hoped that the quaver in her voice didn't let Wade know how fearful she was.

Thoughtfully, he studied her for a moment. "My dear, even ladies have passions. Unless, of course, they're foolish enough to stifle them or to misdirect them."

She frowned. *What did he mean by that?*

"I really must be going, my dear. There's money in the saloon waiting to be transferred from the pockets of certain gentlemen into mine." He held his arm out for her to take. "Which will it be—the ladies' cabin or the stateroom?"

Cath decided to spend some time in the ladies' cabin. The elegance there was breathtaking. In Mattigan her family had been one of the wealthiest in town, but the furnishings of her home were positively plain compared to this opulence.

From the white ceiling bounded by delicate scrollwork hung a large chandelier. Soft light glowed from eight opaque round globes, and suspended from these were long fingers of cut glass, sparkling like diamonds. Two ladies sat on a rosewood settee. Cath made her way to the far side of the room where she saw a lacquered Regency writing table. She sat down at the table and opened a drawer. Inside was a bottle of ink, several quill pens, and sheets of thick, ivory-colored stationery.

It was time to write to Rebecca. For nearly three weeks Cath had been gone from Mattigan. Pa and Becky would be frantic with worry. Dipping the pen into the dark ink, she began:

> June 27, 1857
> Mrs. Jason McDaniel
> Mattigan, Michigan
> Dear Rebecca,
>
> As you can see by this letter, I am well. I am writing this from a steamboat docked at Hannibal, Missouri. Tomorrow we shall continue on toward our destination—St.Louis. I shall try to mail this letter in St. Louis. I am presently in the employ of a wealthy widow, Mrs. Christopher Stanton, in the position of companion. It is a very elegant life, and it suits me much better than life in Mattigan.
>
> I do hope you are happy, and that all is well with you. I shall write you again when I am settled into a more permanent position. Please give my best to Papa and to Jason.
>
> > Affectionately,
> > Your loving sister,
> > Cath

In the ladies' wash room Cath scrubbed herself and then retired to the stateroom. On the wall beside the door hung a framed piece of pink satin upon which were printed the rules of the boat. Gentlemen were forbidden to go to the table without their coats. No one was to pencil or otherwise injure the furniture. Gentlemen must not enter the ladies' saloon without permission from them. Cath smiled at the last rule which said, "No gentleman was to lie down in a bed with his boots on."

She undressed quickly for fear that Wade would come in at any moment. She needn't have worried. Over the ensuing hours as she tossed restlessly, trying to get to sleep on the couch, Cath realized Wade was staying out very late. Though she didn't have a timepiece, she believed it must be the middle of the night.

When she finally did sleep, she slept so soundly that she only vaguely heard Wade enter the stateroom and get into bed.

The nightmare oozed into her sleeping mind exactly as it had the other times when she'd suffered the horrible dream, a nightmare which reenacted Cath's finding her mother's mutilated body last year. Once again she was slowly climbing the stairs toward her mother's bedroom, her legs feeling as if grindstones were tied to them. Cath was whimpering, "Mama? Mama?" Her heart raced faster, as in the dream, she reached the top of the stairs and turned toward her mother's room.

Then she was walking slowly, so slowly, toward the bed, where lay the two doll-like figures. When she looked down at her mother's shredded face a terrible scream rose from her throat. Again, the scream filled the stateroom, waking her.

"What is it?" Wade leaped from his bed. Cath buried her face in her hands and bit her lip to keep from screaming once more. Terrible sobs began deep in her chest. She began crying uncontrollably. Wade gathered her into his arms like a child, rocking her and stroking her hair.

"Everything's all right, Sunny dear," he soothed. "I'm here. Everything's all right."

When her sobbing quieted, Wade rose and lit the lamp on the dresser. The soft glow warmed Cath's heart. The horror slid farther back in her mind. She almost smiled as she realized that she and Wade were dressed in identical nightshirts.

"Maybe you should tell me about your nightmare," Wade said softly, as he sat down again beside her on the couch. Lifting one of her hands, he stroked it gently. "Sometimes talking about fearsome things helps, and troubles don't seem as awful."

Cath never had talked about Mama's adultery and murder. She had acknowledged it with Elizabeth, but they hadn't dwelled on it. Cath was just too embarrassed.

Sniffling, Cath began telling Wade Stanton about Mama's horrible involvement with Reverend Campbell. By the time she got to the part where she was in Mama's bedroom, she was moaning. Wade put his arm around her shoulders and held her tightly to him. "Oh, it was so awful!" she cried.

56

"Poor Sunny," he whispered, kissing the top of her head. "That was rough! No wonder you have bad dreams about it!"

He stood up and padded barefoot to his suitcase, where he felt around inside it. "Brandy will quiet your nerves," he said as he extracted a silver bottle. The lid of the flask served as a tiny cup. He filled it with brandy.

"Sip this," he instructed, handing her the silver cup. The brandy burned her throat. She could feel its searing trail all the way down to her stomach, where it warmed her.

Wade studied her thoughtfully. "I imagine you're quite angry with your mother," he said.

Cath gasped. "Angry?" she cried. "She's dead! No one should be angry at someone who's dead—especially your mother!"

"I think you should be very angry at her," he said softly. "She disgraced your family. She got herself killed where she couldn't be around anymore. She humiliated you in front of your friends and townspeople. Why shouldn't you be angry?"

Cath stared at him. Her face burned with heat. She pressed her lips together.

"Sunny," Wade said, "you don't have to hate your mother. Just hate what she did. She hurt a lot of people. What she did wasn't right, but that doesn't make her a bad person. She did a bad thing. Who doesn't?" He poured more brandy into the cup. "You don't know why your mother got involved with her parson. But something like that doesn't just come about. She had needs that weren't being met, and she used the parson to help fill those needs."

He sighed. "You're very young, Sunny. But try to be a little understanding of your mother." Wade gave Sunny a broad smile. Cath found herself grinning back. His dimples were *so* handsome.

He was stroking the soft skin between her fingers when Cath glanced down at their intertwined hands. How clean and soft his hands were! The large moons on his fingernails were very white, and his nails were spotlessly clean—so different from the hands of the men in her past. Pa, John McAffery, her brother-in-law, Jason. They all worked with their hands, and their fingers were calloused, the nails not always clean. Cath glanced up and caught Wade scrutinizing her, an affectionate look on his face.

Afterwards, she never knew if the brandy had warmed her emotions and released her inhibitions, or whatever had made her so bold.

Abandoning all reserve, she threw her arms around Wade's neck. "Oh, thank you for being so nice to me, Wade," she cried as she nuzzled her nose into his warm neck.

She felt the muscles in his arms tense as he drew her body against his. His lips bent to cover hers, and a thrill raced through Cath's body at the touch of his mustache on her skin. With one hand he held her body tightly against his, and his other hand cupped her cheek, the thumb caressing her chin. Only their flannel nightshirts separated their bodies, and Cath could feel the quickening of Wade's breathing. His soft mustache was sliding down her chin and onto her neck, where he nibbled gently. His lips traced her jawline, stroking her skin softly, seductively.

Strange feelings coursed through Cath's body. How sweet this was to be cuddled close against Wade's warm chest! His hand slid down from her neck to her breast and rested there. When he began stroking her enlarging nipple Cath took a deep, shuddering breath. She felt herself sliding into a world of promising pleasure, where everything was warm, moist and sweet.

Wade stood, scooping Cath into his arms. Huskily, he murmured into her neck, "I think you've slept on the couch long enough."

As he laid her on his bed he began tugging on the oversized nightshirt she was wearing. "Let's get rid of this ridiculous thing," he said. His dimples creased deeply into his cheeks as he grinned at her, his dark eyes sparkling with fire.

For a moment Cath protectively clutched the nightshirt to her body, but as his soft hand slid under the nightshirt and began caressing the fullness of her naked breast, she relaxed and closed her eyes. Wade began squeezing her nipple gently between his thumb and forefinger. Fuzzily, as if in a dream, she felt him slip the nightshirt over her head. Again, his mustache was upon her lips, teasing her, challenging her. His lips slid down across her neck and onto her breast. Cath's breath caught in her throat when his lips fastened onto her hard nipple. His tongue began a long, slow caressing of the pink nipple. Waves of warmth washed through her body.

"I'll try not to hurt you, Sunny," Wade whispered hoarsely as he lay atop her. His naked body felt hard, his muscles firm under Cath's touch. But then came the pain, the awful pain. Cath cried out. Wade smothered her cry with his mouth, pressing hard against her lips. He was moving his body faster and faster, but the terrible pain gripped Cath's body. She lay perfectly still, praying the hurt would stop. At last Wade uttered a harsh cry and stopped his hurtful thrusting. He lay still, burying his lips in her neck under her ear.

Cath squeezed her eyes shut, and a tear slid down her temple. What had happened? She'd felt so wonderful. Everything had been so pleasurable—but then such pain!—and all the good feelings had stopped. Well, not all. Tenderly, she stroked the hard muscles on Wade's back. Warmth still spread throughout her body. She just no longer had that rising, insistent passion.

Wade rolled off her. "Turn over, Sunny," he said. "Turn your back to me so I can cuddle you."

As she did so, he snuggled his naked body close to hers, holding one of her breasts gently in his big hand. Into her ear he whispered, "I'm sorry it had to hurt, Sunny. It always does the first time, but it'll get better and better. You'll see." His hand stroked her breast and brushed across her nipple. In only a few moments Cath could tell from Wade's deep breathing that he was asleep.

For a long time Cath lay awake. She savored the closeness and warmth of his naked skin, but she was confused by the strange feelings flowing through her body. Eventually she slept.

She awoke feeling confused. She couldn't figure out where she was. Then in a rush of embarrassment she realized she was in Wade Stanton's bed, naked as a newborn babe. The lamp on the dresser was still burning. Cath was lying on her back, and Wade's left arm lay across her breasts. Hardly daring to move, she turned her eyes sideways. Wade was awake and watching her.

He gave her a roguish grin. "Don't look so crestfallen, Sunny. Now you're a woman, and a *real* woman, I might add." He pulled her toward him, enveloping her body in his arms. Softly at first his lips stroked Cath's, but then the pressure grew stronger and more demanding. He pressed and kneaded her breasts, gently pinching her nipples. His hands were all over her body, teasing her and arousing her passion.

Without meaning to, Cath grunted when Wade entered her. She was sore, and it hurt, but not so much as last night. Even so, it hurt enough that her pleasurable feelings were drowned by pain.

Afterwards, Wade stroked her stomach gently. "Still hurts?" he asked. "I'm sorry, Sunny, I really am. Before long it won't hurt, I promise you. It'll be pure pleasure."

Cath swallowed, blinking back tears. Here she was, doing "that thing" that she and Ellen Stearns had whispered about, giggled about, with a man she hardly knew. John McAffery was her true love. What was she doing in Wade Stanton's bed?

Wade nuzzled her neck. His moustache tickled, sending shivers through her body. I'm here, Cath reminded herself, because I have no money, no way to pay for my room and board. She flushed when she realized that she might be paying for her keep by sleeping with Wade Stanton. Her cheeks burned. She closed her eyes. I'm no better than a tart!

With his thumb Wade brushed the wetness from her eyes. Ever so gently, his lips touched hers. "Please don't cry, Sunny. Don't be unhappy. Next time it may not hurt at all, and pretty soon you'll like it. I'll make sure you like it!"

Cath's lips quivered. Next time! How often did he intend to do this? The way she felt now, maybe it'd be better to just starve to death.

The breakfast gong rang, interrupting her gloomy thoughts.

Wade jumped out of bed. "Sweet gandy dancer's garters! Am I hungry! You've given me a real appetite, Sunny!"

He turned his back to reach for his shirt, and Cath found herself admiring his muscular body. She'd never seen a naked man before. His buttocks were so round and smooth...Cath caught herself, and shut off those thoughts. Slowly she climbed out of her side of the bed. How sore she was! Glancing back toward the bed, she saw that there was blood on the sheets. Painfully, she moved toward her clothes. This wasn't an easy way to pay for her keep. But what else could she do?

Chapter 6
On the Mighty Mississippi

Two years had passed since Cath cut her hair and fled from Mattigan to end up in Wade Stanton's bed aboard the *Sally Anne*. Once again her hair fell down her back. It was long enough to draw back into the fashionable "waterfall" coiffure. Cath patted her curls contentedly. No more did she look like a boy or a freak.

For only two months she and Wade had remained aboard the *Sally Anne*. From there they'd transferred their possessions to *The Redeemer,* and then in November Wade moved them to the lower Mississippi River where they wintered in warmer climes. Wade was a restless man, changing steamboats two or three times each year. He changed boats when his gambling wasn't going well. He said moving to a different boat changed his luck.

Sometimes Cath wondered how she could have stayed with Wade Stanton for so long. The purpose of her life was to find John McAffery. How could she reconcile her love for John with being Wade's kept woman? She knew the answer—money. Without money, Cath couldn't travel around Iowa looking for John. Remaining with Wade seemed the best she could do in continuing her search.

At every port during the past two years Cath had inquired concerning the whereabouts of her "brother," John McAffery. At first she'd tried to convince Wade that John was her brother, but he only grew furious. "Don't lie to me, Sunny!" he'd stormed. "Don't ever lie to me! I'll take a lot, but no lies! We play it straight with each other! From the very beginning I told you I was married. I didn't let you think I could marry you someday. Don't *you* lie to me!"

When Cath discovered that her inquiries about John upset Wade, she did her questioning more discreetly, away from Wade's hearing. It seemed strange that Wade actually might be jealous of John, someone he'd never met. Wade never had professed love for her. He'd pat her bottom affectionately and tell her that he guessed he'd keep her for awhile. Though Wade gave no declarations of love, Cath suspected that he cared for her more than he was willing to let on. Or perhaps, because he was a gentleman, he felt it wrong to declare affection for her when he wasn't free to marry.

Cath was leaning against the railing of *The Blue Lady*, their newest floating home, which was moored to the levee at Keokuk along with eleven other sidewheelers. The wharf was covered with freight of all descriptions—wheat, corn, oats, potatoes, boilers, plows, threshing machines, furniture, bar iron, hardware, hogsheads and barrels of sugar and molasses. Scores of drays and wagons were moving the stuff. In front of the business houses great numbers of wagons were unloading pork and produce and loading groceries, salt, and iron for merchants in the central and northern parts of Iowa and Illinois.

Cath had found her chance this morning, the opportunity to slip ashore without Wade so she could ask merchants if they knew of a farmer named John McAffery. She had told Wade that she needed some new blue ribbon for a bonnet.

Wade was good to her. He delighted in buying her frocks in the latest fashions, although he did ridicule the hooped skirts which were the style now. "I want you to be fashionable, Sunny," Wade grumbled when she modeled a prospective purchase for him. "I guess you'll have to wear the silly hoops, but I hope this absurd fashion goes out of style in a hurry."

No one in Keokuk had heard of a John McAffery. In her zeal to question many merchants she forgot to buy the ribbon. When she returned to the steamboat empty-handed Wade threw her a dark look and sullenly walked away. Amanda sighed. Sometimes it seemed as if Wade Stanton could read her mind. Almost always he could guess when she was thinking about John.

Cath had learned to enjoy Wade's lovemaking. He was tender and caring about her feelings. At times they made love languidly and sensuously. Other times they tickled each other and giggled and caroused. Only once had Wade taken her brutally.

On that unpleasant occasion she and Wade had been lying on the bed one afternoon, resting. With a finger Wade was lazily tracing the outline of a flower on her print dress. Cath's face was partially averted from Wade, and her thoughts were roaming to John McAffery's whereabouts.

Suddenly, in a rage, Wade had grabbed her by one shoulder and pulled her off the bed. She staggered and would have fallen if his hand hadn't been grasping her shoulder. The fragile chambray tore. Cath looked up into Wade's eyes. They were glinting dangerously. Without taking his eyes from hers he pulled off his white shirt and began unbuckling his belt.

"Get out of that dress!" he growled as he stepped out of his trousers and tossed them onto the rug.

Bewildered, Cath stood still. Wade's fist gathered a handful of material and yanked. The whole bodice came loose from the sleeve. He continued ripping the dress apart while Cath trembled, too frightened to do anything. She had never seen Wade like this before. After tearing off her hoop and pantaloons, he swung her roughly onto the bed and pinned her there, holding her wrists against the counterpane above her head.

His kiss on her mouth was bruising. As he took her forcefully, he gasped between gritted teeth, "I'll make you forget him! You'll forget him!"

Whenever she thought of that frightening time a shiver of apprehension ran up Cath's back. They'd never spoken of it. She thought Wade was ashamed that he'd shown he was jealous of her thoughts about John McAffery. His rage had momentarily given him away. Wade had revealed a vulnerable spot, a hint that he could be hurt. Sometimes Cath thought about her feelings toward Wade. She didn't dwell on it long, though. The confusing emotions made her uncomfortable.

Cath felt warmth and gratitude toward Wade. He provided shelter, food, clothes, and yes, .. affection. She loved how his brown eyes twinkled, caressing her, his gaze lingering and brushing gently across her body.

Sometimes Cath thought that if she weren't in love with John McAffery, she might fall in love with Wade Stanton. But then Cath would remember her mother and what could happen when you married someone who wasn't your own kind.

Wade was a Southerner, a riverboat gambler. He spoke with a slow, slurring drawl. Wade believed gambling was a profession, while farming and lumbering were simple, hard labor.

Now John McAffery, Cath thought, was her own kind. They had the same values...

Far down the wharf she saw Wade's tall figure striding toward *The Blue Lady,* wending his way around the crates and barrels. The snugly-fitting pale trousers showed off his well-muscled legs, and Cath felt a surge of pride that he was "her man."

When he looked up and saw her waiting for him, he grinned and returned her wave. From the stairwell behind her she could hear the clatter of his Wellington boots as he took the steps two at a time.

He burst out on the deck, caught her around the waist, and planted a happy kiss on her lips. Wade seemed to be amused about something. His dark eyes danced merrily.

"Something is funny?" Cath asked archly. "Do I have a smudge on my nose?"

"No," he laughed. "I just saw the damnedest thing over on Main Street. A lady was walking a black French sort of dog. I saw this man run up to her and tap her arm. I thought maybe he meant her harm, so I walked toward them. The man, it turns out, was the dogcatcher, and for some reason he was after her dog. This lady looked at the dogcatcher and kind of sniffed. Then she lifted one side of her hooped skirt. The little dog scurried under, and she let her skirt fall back down, concealing the dog. Sweet gandy dancer's garters! You should've seen the look on that dogcatcher's face! He was furious! People had gathered, and they clapped and whistled, encouraging the lady. She stood her ground, and eventually the dogcatcher stomped off." Wade chuckled. "I've hated these silly hooped skirts ever since they came into fashion. But at last one has performed a useful purpose."

Shortly after noon *The Blue Lady* pulled away from the levee and headed upriver, bound for St. Paul. They passed the *Floating Palace,* a powerless theatrical barge upon which a stock company presented plays varying from *Hamlet* to *Ten Nights in a Bar Room.* Wade had taken Cath to several of these productions, even though it meant he had to give up an evening's work. They'd sat in the section containing eleven hundred arm chairs. Behind them were five hundred cushioned settees, and nine hundred gallery seats. The whole theater was exquisite with much gilt and cut glass.

Cath never had been on the Mississippi River above Keokuk. On this warm August afternoon, she strolled on deck. On the river banks slender willows, elms, white maples and cottonwoods grew right to the river's edge.

The upper Mississippi was different from the river between Keokuk and St. Louis. Though still a wide river, it was narrowing. Burlington was a charming town. Buildings seemed southern in style, and Cath wondered if the citizens were chiefly from the South. Most of the houses were painted white. They had a plaza and portico, and many had a gallery above with large windows looking toward the river. Because of the dazzling whiteness of the houses, the city made a striking appearance as seen from the river. Bluffs formed a staircase upon which the houses perched, rising one above the other.

At dusk one evening as they were approaching Davenport Cath leaned against the railing, watching the sky change from salmon pink to rose. Wade stood beside her, puffing on a cigar. *The Blue Lady* rounded a bend, and suddenly ahead of them were the cities of Davenport on their port side and Rock Island on the starboard. Cath was amazed to see a long bridge spanning the river, linking the two cities.

"I didn't know there was a bridge crossing the Mississippi!" she said to Wade. "Why, even at St. Louis there's no bridge!"

"Along its entire length," Wade drawled, "this is the only bridge crossing the mighty Miss. Five spans and a drawbridge. It is a fine bridge." A far off look crossed his face. "Three years ago last spring I took an unexpected swim under that bridge."

"You did?" Cath exclaimed.

The bell of *The Blue Lady* rang, announcing its approach to Davenport.

"What happened?" she wanted to know.

"Well, steamboat pilots hate the railroads, you see," Wade began. "They're afraid the railroads will take away their business—hauling goods and transporting people. It was early in May, and I was on the *Effie Afton* bound from St. Louis for St. Paul. The Effie was almost a brand new steamer. This bridge was only a year old at the time. As we slid under the draw, the *Effie Afton* rammed the bridge, right over there," he pointed and paused, taking a long pull on his cigar.

"I'm sure it was intentional. There wasn't that much wind or current. The pilot had to have meant to destroy the bridge. Anyway, as the bridge fell, all the steamboats docked at the wharf at Davenport and across the river at Rock Island turned loose their whistles and bells, rejoicing over the damaged bridge.

"Right away the *Effie Afton* began taking on water. Soon it listed badly. Thank God I was wearing my money belt, so all I lost was my luggage and clothes in my stateroom. And my Wellingtons. I pulled them off as soon as I saw that we were going to sink. I jumped in and struck out for the wharf over there. But I'm telling you that river was cold! Snow run-off had ended only a few weeks earlier, and that water was miserable. The old Mississippi seemed mighty wide to this one, I'll tell you! But I made it, as you can see." He grinned and gave Cath a bow.

"Wade, how terrible!" she sympathized. Then a frightening thought occurred to Cath . Her gloved fingers flew to her mouth. "Wade," she turned to face him, and her eyes were large with fright. "I don't know how to swim!"

Wade choked as he exhaled a blue cloud of smoke. He sputtered. "Well, we'll have to fix that! We'll just have to find a secluded, sandy bayou, and I'll teach you to swim. Or at least you can learn to float on your back. Then if our boat sinks, I can swim and just tow you to shore."

Cath looked up into his dark eyes twinkling with devilment. "Are you serious?" she asked.

"Of course."

But then another thought struck Cath. "But I don't have a swimming costume!"

Wade let his eyes slide lazily over her body. "Mmn, yes, I know," he replied lazily. "That's why I said we'd find a 'secluded' bayou."

Cath laughed and with her fingers tapped him on the arm. "You scoundrel!" Her cheeks grew rosy.

Wade threw back his head and roared.

"What's so funny?" she snapped.

When he finally quit laughing, he looked down at Cath . "That's one of your more charming traits, little Sunny. Though you've spent over two years as a kept woman, you still have the ability to blush."

She sniffed, raising her chin. "I'm *not* a tart!"

Once again, Wade dissolved into howls of laughter.

There was a slight jolt as *The Blue Lady* bumped against the levee. The crew bustled, hurrying to secure her to her moorings.

"Wade," Cath began. She looked up into Wade's eyes, then lowered her own eyes shyly.

"Oh, boy," he sighed, "here it comes. I know that look. You're about to wheedle something from me." She knew by the deep dimples in his cheeks that he wasn't annoyed.

She swallowed, then looked up at him defiantly. "Wade, I want you to teach me to play poker!"

66

Wade's eyebrows flew up. He removed the cigar from his mouth. "Ladies don't play poker."

Cath tossed her head. "Since when did I qualify as a 'lady'? Ladies don't travel with gentlemen who aren't their husbands."

"But everyone thinks I'm your husband. The passengers and crew all respect you. They treat you like a lady," he protested. Then, taking Cath's arm, he gave her a shake. "Sunny, you wouldn't like the way they'd treat you if they thought you weren't a lady. You wouldn't like it at all! And if you played poker, they wouldn't consider you a lady!"

"Oh, Wade," Cath sputtered, "I have no intention of playing poker in public. I just want you to teach me in the privacy of our stateroom. I could practice at it, and it would give me something to do. I get so tired of just doing needlework and making bonnets! Besides, who knows? Perhaps someday it'll be permissible for a lady to play poker. Or," and she looked at him archly, "perhaps someday I won't care to be considered a lady any longer."

When he looked at her Wade's eyes bore a new look. Along with the affectionate twinkle was an admission of respect.

✳   ✳   ✳   ✳

The secret poker lessons had been going on for a year and a half, and Wade admitted to Cath that she had become an excellent player. During the long evenings when Wade was off gambling with gentlemen passengers she'd practiced and played with imaginary opponents. Cath didn't know what she would do with this new talent, but she had a feeling that somewhere, someday, it might come in handy.

Sometimes she and Wade played for fun. During these games Cath often was tempted to suggest they play for money. She had a terrible need to accumulate money. If only she had money of her own, she could strike out and search for John McAffery on her own.

But she never made the suggestion that they play for money. Intuition told her that Wade Stanton was really a better and far more experienced poker player than she, at least in the long run. Cath feared that if they played for money, she might end up being in debt to him. She could end up like an indentured servant! Wade could own her for years!

In November when they headed for Natchez, as Wade did every winter, Cath sighed with unhappy resignation. She despised going south.

By spending the winters on the Natchez-to-New Orleans stretch, she missed five months out of the year searching for John.

Since they'd left for the lower river right after the election of Abraham Lincoln as President of the United States, Wade had said that this probably would be their last winter in the South. "My home state of South Carolina and other cotton states have repeatedly said they'd secede from the Union if a Republican's elected," he said.

"You mean they'd form a new nation?" Cath was shocked.

"That's what they say."

"What would happen then?"

"War," Wade said softly.

"War?" Cath cried. "You mean some of our states fighting other states?"

"Yes. If even only one state secedes, Lincoln will have no choice but to force it back into the Union."

That conversation had occurred almost three months ago. During those three months seven southern states had seceded from the Union. South Carolina, Wade's birthplace, had been the first. Cath glanced dreamily out the window of their stateroom. How nice it was to have a window! They were traveling near the western bank of the river, and she could see the huge cypress trees draped with the eerie Spanish moss. Their large stateroom was by far the most elegant they'd ever had. Sitting in a brocaded stuffed chair, his boots propped on the foot of the bed, Wade was smoking a cigar and reading a newspaper.

"Sweet gandy dancer's garters!" he blustered. His boots hit the floor with a crash. "Fools!" he roared. His brows drew close together in a scowl.

"What is it, Wade?" Cath asked.

"This is an Atlanta paper," he said, tapping the newspaper sharply with his forefinger. "They're saying that since the enemy was elected, there must be war. Listen to the idiots. They say, 'Let the consequences be what they may, whether the Potomac is crimsoned in human gore, and Pennsylvania Avenue is paved ten fathoms deep with mangled bodies or whether the last vestige of liberty is swept from the face of the American Continent, the South will never submit to such humiliation and degradation as the inauguration of Abraham Lincoln.'" He threw the paper to the floor.

"When is the Inauguration?" Cath asked.

"Early March," he answered, "I think the fourth or fifth." Wade stared out the window absently. "I believe we'd better plan to return north sooner than usual. I don't want to get caught in the South when war starts. I might get drafted into the Confederate Army, and you..." His dimples deepened as he looked at Cath , "with your Yankee accent, the Confederates are apt to stand you up before a firing squad."

Wade stood up and paced about the room. "Yes, definitely, we'll go north soon as I can get us passage." He scratched his moustache. "Only trouble is I don't know if going to St. Louis is far enough north. When it comes to choosing sides, I'm not sure which way Missouri will go."

The second week in March Wade got them out of the Deep South. Once they arrived in St. Louis he booked passage for them aboard *The Dragon Lady*, a sternwheeler bound for the upper reaches of the Missouri River. Cath was thrilled about this opportunity to travel a new route because it would give her a chance to look for John McAffery along the western border of Iowa. Adventure twinkled in Wade's dark eyes whenever he talked about "The Big Muddy," the Missouri River. Once he'd drawled, "They say the Missouri is nothing but mud—too thick to drink and too thin to cultivate."

The Dragon Lady was moored at the St. Louis levee. Roustabouts were loading her with cargo, but she wasn't scheduled to embark for another three weeks.

Cath sat at a gleaming, highly-waxed Chippendale desk in the ladies' saloon writing a letter to Rebecca. For almost four years Cath had kept up the fiction that she was traveling as a companion to the wealthy "Mrs. Christopher Stanton." She was able to receive mail from Rebecca by giving her the address of Edgar and Rose Henright in St. Louis. They were old friends of Wade's, now also friends of Cath's. Whenever their current steamboat docked at St. Louis, Cath and Wade always visited the Henright's home. Often there was a letter from Rebecca.

The very first letter she'd received from Rebecca had given her the news that John McAffery had returned to Mattigan a month after Elizabeth's suicide. According to Rebecca, John was devastated, but eventually he pulled himself together and returned to the Iowa farm he'd purchased with Elizabeth's money. Cath was disappointed that Rebecca had not borne a child. Early in her marriage Rebecca had become pregnant, but in the beginning stages she had miscarried. Whenever Cath thought of her hopes of Rebecca's having a child, she felt so grateful that there wasn't any chance of herself getting pregnant. Wade said he'd contracted mumps soon after the birth of his daughter. He didn't think his seed was good anymore. Cath had no interest in having a child. She supposed that if she found John, he would want children. She guessed she'd face that when the time came.

But Cath did hope Rebecca would have a child. It would give Pa a grandchild—something that would help ease the emptiness in him that, according to Becky, was left by Cath's leaving. Cath hoped someday, after she was settled down with John, that Pa could come visit them and see how happy she was. Of course, to have Pa visit her now was impossible. And never, never would she return to Mattigan!

Quill pen poised above the stationery, Cath's thoughts were far off when Wade burst into the ladies' saloon waving a folded newspaper.

Since they were the only passengers at present, Cath had the room for her own use. Wade was returning from doing some business in the city. He was excited about something in the paper.

He pulled up a delicate rose velvet footstool and sat down. "A week ago today, Lincoln was inaugurated President," he said. "In his inaugural speech he reminded us that the Union is older than the states. He said secession is illegal and a revolutionary act. He promised to show forbearance for a time, but he warned that he'd try to enforce federal laws in all the states, and that he'd keep possession of federal property. By that he meant, Ft. Sumter in Charlestown harbor.

"Let me read you the last part of his speech," Wade said, his dark eyes gleaming. "Here, Lincoln is speaking to the South. He says, 'In your hands, my dissatisfied fellow countrymen, and not in mine, is the momentous issue of civil war. The government will not assail you. You can have no conflict without being yourselves the aggressors. You have no oath registered in Heaven to destroy the government, while I shall have the most solemn one to preserve, protect and defend it. I am loath to close. We are not enemies, but friends. We must not be enemies. Though passion may have strained, it must not break our bonds of affection. The mystic chords of memory, stretching from every battlefield and patriot grave, to every living heart and hearthstone, all over this broad land, will yet swell the chorus of the Union, when again touched, as surely they will be, by the better angels of our nature.'"

By the time Wade finished reading, Cath had pulled a lace handkerchief from her sleeve and was dabbing at her eyes. "He'll make a great President, won't he?"

"I think so," Wade agreed. "He's showing the South the right combination of velvet glove and iron fist."

That evening Cath and Wade went to a dinner party at the Henrights. Two other couples were guests—a local judge and his wife, and an elderly ship owner and his daughter, a lovely auburn-haired girl who seemed to be about Cath's age.

Rose Henright was French, so wine always was served with her dinners. Cath stroked the graceful stem of her wine goblet and admired the formalized rosebuds and bluejay engraved upon it. Dinner talk centered around the problem of the rebellion. Wade didn't say much about President Lincoln, Cath noticed, since the others seemed to favor the right of states to secede. The judge hoped Missouri could stay neutral in any conflict.

"But, Judge," Wade protested, "there can't be neutrality! Missouri is a part of the Union. If the Union is attacked, Missouri can't say 'I'll not fight.' What if St. Louis were attacked by the Rebels?"

"The seceded states won't attack anyone. They don't want war."

Wade shook his head. "I wish I could believe that."

After dinner the men retired to the library for their cigars and brandies, while the ladies moved to the parlor. Rose Henright seated herself on a velvet settee beside the fireplace where she began pouring demitasse coffee. Cath sat beside her friend, helping pass the delicate cups and saucers to Rose's guests. Just as Rose handed Cath her own cup, a burning log rolled onto the hearth. In an instant the hem of Rose's skirt was aflame. She gasped, staring at her burning skirt.

Cath jumped up and ran around the table to get at the flames. Her wide hooped skirt touched Rose's flaming one, and Cath's own skirt burst into flames. Quickly, Cath snatched the silver pot and poured coffee on her flaming skirt. With loud sizzling the flames dwindled to smoke. Cath poured the rest of the coffee on Rose's skirt, but the flames had gained too much headway. Rose screamed.

"Call the men!" Cath shrieked. "Get help!"

She wanted to tear the flaming dress from Rose's body, but because of her own voluminous skirt, Cath couldn't get close enough. There was only one thing to do. Cath ripped off her own dress. Not bothering with buttons or fasteners, she tore away the soft material and jumped out of the hoop cage. Now, clad only in camisole and pantaloons, she scooped up an oriental throw rug and covered Rose's flaming skirt with it, smothering the flames.

71

When the men burst into the smoky room Cath was pounding out the last of the smoldering material.

Edgar Henright rushed to his wife.

"She's all right," Cath panted. "But you'd better send for some water in case the flames start up again."

Rose quietly sobbed, "How can I ever thank you, Cath ? You saved my life!"

Everyone stared at her. Cath shivered.

"Let me see your hands, Sunny," Wade said quietly.

Cath held out her right hand, as if she were presenting her hand to be kissed.

Wade turned her hand over to examine the palm. "She's burnt her hands," he said to the room in general.

Two maids hurried into the parlor carrying pitchers. Their eyes grew wide when they saw Cath.

"Would you please bring a robe for Mrs. Stanton?" Wade asked. "Her dress is burned." He took off his jacket and covered Cath's bare shoulders. Cath blushed scarlet. She was wearing only undergarments.

"Oh, no, Wade," she protested, "my dress isn't burned, not badly. I had to tear it off so I could get near Rose to put out the fire. When her skirt first caught fire I tried to put out the flames, but my skirt touched Rose's and mine flamed up, too." She smiled ruefully at him. "You've always hated hooped skirts, but I didn't know they could be dangerous."

The maids brought a blue velvet robe for Cath. A huge, heavy-set colored woman bustled into the room carrying a pot with a strange-looking plant in it. "You burnt, chile?" she knelt in front of Rose.

"No, Mammy," Rose answered, "well, perhaps a little on my limbs. You can care for them upstairs. Mrs. Stanton has burned her hands, though, while saving me. Please treat her hands, Mammy."

The stout woman rubbed the white sticky juice from the plant onto her palms. Whatever it was, it was soothing. The smarting lessened.

In the carriage on their way home, Wade kept a protective arm around Cath all the way to *The Dragon Lady*. "You're a brave lady, my little Sunny. You're one of a kind," he whispered softly as he picked up her hand and kissed the pink tender skin of her stinging palm. "Not many ladies would drop their modesty as you did." He swallowed. "Sunny, I..." He stopped abruptly.

Though he said no more, Cath had the strange feeling that he had nearly said, "I love you."

72

Chapter 7
Jumping Ship

When *The Dragon Lady* left St. Louis and heading north on the Mississippi River, Cath stood near the bow, enjoying the springtime green of the distant river bank. Never would she forget the sight of the murky, yellowish Missouri River flowing in on their port side to join the dark Mississippi. As the pilot steered into the brown water and pointed the bow west, a shiver travelled through Cath's body. Surely the Missouri might prove to be the river of her dreams, the stream that would carry her to John McAffery.

For four days they steamed in a northwesterly direction across the state of Missouri past tobacco farms and apple orchards, stopping frequently to take on passengers and goods and to get wood at the woodlots.

The Dragon Lady was a long, low ship with a lofty superstructure. The American flag flew from the jackstaff forward. Two shiny black smokestacks were spanned by the wrought iron figure of a Chinese dragon, its nostrils spouting red-painted wrought iron flames.

The main deck was filled to the guard rails with bales, crates, bedrolls, trunks, and cordwood for the engines. Three hulking Conestoga wagons with bright red wheels and blue beds were parked end-to-end near the stern. At one side was a whole barnyard of mules, horses, hogs, and sheep. Clucking and crowing sounds came from dozens of chicken coops, and Cath was surprised to see a large cage filled with cats. Wade said that in the West, cats were scarce and very prized, worth more than ten dollars apiece. They were valued as mousers, to keep mice and rats from destroying foodstuffs.

Cath saw several Indians wrapped in colorful blankets, their bronze faces devoid of expression. There were mountain men in greasy deerskins. They reminded her of the louse-covered stagecoach driver in Illinois four years ago, on that fateful trip when she'd met Wade. At times Cath thought that she might have found John long before this if her time and attention hadn't been so diverted by Wade. But then, thinking realistically, she had to admit that she more likely would be dead from starvation, exposure, or sickness.

On a balmy spring afternoon they moored at St. Joseph, the second largest city in Missouri. According to Wade, the initial trip of a ship each spring always precipitated celebrations at all the river towns on the journey upriver. A ball usually was called for when two steamboats met or docked for the night at the same town. In fulfilling this custom, *The Dragon Lady* had been lashed to another sternwheeler, *The Aurora Borealis*, which was also making its maiden trip of the year up the Missouri River. With the two sternwheelers tied together, the passengers mingled back and forth. The saloon of *The Dragon Lady* was being prepared for dancing in the evening. The saloon of the Aurora would be used by those who wished quiet conversation or gambling.

Wade had gone ashore to see an old friend, a banker. Wade trusted very few banks. Lately, his gambling had been bringing in a great deal of money, and he had begun depositing it in certain banks that he believed to be stable. He said he had no intention of leaving any money in southern banks, or even in Missouri banks. Wade still didn't trust Missouri. He said the state's southern sympathies and the fact that it was a slave state made Missouri's long range loyalty to the Union questionable. Cath knew he wasn't leaving money in a St. Joseph bank. She understood that he trusted his banker-friend to get his money safely transferred to a Pennsylvania bank which he believed to be sound.

When Wade believed that he'd saved enough money, he planned to quit the nomadic existence on the steamboats, he said. He wanted to open an elegant, honest gaming house, where there was a wide variety of ways to gamble. He said there would be music, jugglers, all sorts of performers to entertain his customers. Entertainment, he said, would entice them inside his doors, and once inside, the lure of the wager would tempt them to gamble.

Cath smiled to herself as she strolled along the hurricane deck, absently watching the bustling activity on the wharf. Already she had decided upon the dress she would wear for the ball this evening, having chosen the pink satin gown overlaid with pink crepe and draped with flounces of satin looped up with pink tuberoses. It was a favorite of

Wade's. He said it made her look like a Dresden china doll. Cath was excited about tonight's ball because it meant an opportunity to meet a whole shipload of traveling people. There was always the hope that one of them might be acquainted with the whereabouts of John McAffery.

"Sunny!" Wade's voice came from down the wharf. Cath threw him a wave. He was accompanied by a gentleman.

When Wade stepped out onto the hurricane deck he turned to his companion, then smiled broadly at Cath. "Sunny, I'd like to present Will Babcock, an old and trusted friend. Will, this is Sunny, or 'Cath,' I guess I should say."

Will Babcock bowed. "A pleasure to meet you, Miss Cath," he said.

How strange. Wade always introduced Cath as "Mrs. Stanton." But to this Mr. Babcock, he just said "Cath." She studied the gray-haired, slender man. His blue eyes seemed kind and honest. Had Wade told him the truth about their relationship? No disapproval appeared in the man's eyes.

Wade stepped between Will Babcock and Cath, taking each of them by an elbow. "Let's go to our stateroom, where we can have a cigar and tell Sunny the news," he said.

Babcock stopped and stared at Wade in amazement.

Chuckling, Wade gave his friend's arm a tug. "Sunny isn't like most ladies. She appreciates the aroma of a good cigar. She allows me to have a smoke whenever I want to." He turned to Cath and flashed her an appreciative grin.

Once in their stateroom and after the men's cigars were lit, Wade propped his boots on the footboard and drawled, "Guess what news came over the telegraph this afternoon?"

Cath leaned forward.

"My glorious home state began firing today on Ft. Sumter in Charleston harbor! The insurrection has begun. South Carolina has fired upon the American flag."

"Then it's war?" Cath asked.

"Has to be. Open rebellion such as South Carolina is showing will have to be checked," Will Babcock said. "Lincoln has no choice but to use force, and if the southern states resist, then it's that saddest kind of war— civil war—fighting where cousin may be against cousin."

A dark shadow crossed Wade's face as he added, "Or even brother against brother."

Will Babcock seemed to be a fine gentleman. Cath could see how Wade would trust him. Babcock seemed at ease chatting with them, though he must guess that Cath was not Wade's wife. It was obvious that this was "their" joint stateroom. Wade hadn't made even a pretense that this was either his or her room.

At dinnertime the usual sit-down dinner was dispensed with. Instead, a long sideboard buffet was set up at one side of the saloon, which had been cleared of most of its furniture to make room for dancing. When Cath entered the saloon on Wade's arm she could sense gentlemen turning toward her. She was sure that Wade noticed it, too, taking male pride in showing off his well-dressed, blond Dresden doll.

The Brussels carpets had been rolled up and stored out of sight. The gleaming waxed oak floor was sprinkled with sawdust for dancing. The orchestra, which was set up in the aft section of the saloon, struck up a lively waltz, and Wade took Cath in his arms. Cath's hooped skirt slithered and swished, as the satin material swayed with her movements. She looked up into Wade's dark eyes and laughed merrily. What fun to be dancing!

At the end of the waltz Will Babcock approached them. "Wade, old man," he asked, "may I have the honor of a dance with Miss Cath?"

Wade dipped his head in a partial bow and placed Cath's hand in Babcock's.

Cath had been dancing for only a minute with Babcock when a tall, blond fellow tapped him on the shoulder and asked if he might have the pleasure of the lady's company.

Over and over, strange gentlemen from the *Aurora Borealis* took their turn dancing with Cath. She was having a wonderful time. Wade had disappeared. She supposed he was playing poker with the *Aurora* gentlemen.

After some time, when a waltz finished, Cath was gasping for breath. "I'm terribly thirsty, sir," she said to her current partner, a stocky, dark-haired fellow. "Could we have some punch? I'm parched!"

They strolled toward the table bearing a large crystal punch bowl. Cath's dancing partner handed her a Bristol champagne glass filled with a scarlet liquid containing a single cherry. "May I present myself, ma'am?" he said with a slight bow. "My name is Geoffrey Addison of Sioux City, Iowa."

Iowa! Then, remembering herself, she responded, "I'm Mrs. Wade Stanton." She rushed on. "How interesting that you're from Iowa,

Mr. Addison. Perchance, would you happen to know a Mr. John McAffery, originally from Michigan?"

Geoffrey Addison nodded his head. "Yes, I know him. Not well, but he bought a farm wagon from me last year."

Cath was only vaguely aware of the shattering sound of breaking glass as her goblet crashed onto the oak floor. The room darkened. For a moment Cath feared she was going to faint.

Alarmed, the gentleman took her elbow. "You're very pale, Mrs. Stanton. Let me help you to a seat."

In a daze Cath allowed herself to be led to one side of the saloon. Gratefully, she sat. This man said he knew John McAffery! She inhaled great gulps of air trying to calm herself.

"You really know John McAffery?" she gasped. "He'd be about twenty-five years old. He has brown hair and very light brown eyes, ...oh, and a moustache. At least he had a moustache five years ago. I haven't seen him in nearly that long."

"That sounds like him. That's what he looks like," Geoffrey Addison answered.

Breathlessly, Cath asked, "Where does he live?"

"His farm is about twenty miles from Sioux City."

"Is that on the river?"

"Yes."

"When I get to Sioux City," she asked, "how could I find him—find his farm?"

Addison frowned, thinking. "The best thing to do would be to check with Henry at Henry's Emporium. Everybody in western Iowa buys dry goods and supplies from Henry. He could give you the best directions."

At that moment Wade sauntered up. "Ah, Mrs. Stanton," he addressed her formally. "I see you are resting. Are you too tired to dance with your husband?" He partially bowed and held his arm out for her.

Quickly, Cath introduced the two men, and then Wade whisked her off to the dance floor.

"There's a suspiciously excited twinkle in your eyes, Sunny, and a rosiness to the cheeks," Wade commented, watching her closely. "Do I have a rival in Mr. Geoffrey Addison?"

"Fiddlesticks, Wade," she retorted, "you know me better than that! But having so many gentlemen wanting to dance with me has certainly been flattering. And fun," she added.

Wade studied her thoughtfully as he whirled her around the floor.

Cath tried to erase the elation from her face, but she knew it was impossible. At last she had learned the whereabouts of her beloved John. This very steamboat, *The Dragon Lady*, was carrying her up the Missouri River to Sioux City and John McAffery.

At midnight Cath retired. Lying alone between the crisp sheets, she began to plan her escape. Her excitement was so great that she still was awake when, hours later, Wade climbed into bed. Cath feigned sleep, and in moments, Wade's heavy breathing told her that he was sound asleep.

Ever so slowly she slid out of bed. Groping in the darkness, she felt for Wade's clothes. She touched the smooth silk of his tie, the rough linen of his breeches. At last Cath's fingers found his calfskin money belt. Carefully, so as not to let the gold coins clink together, she pressed on the money belt. It had been a good night for Wade. She had planned to take only two coins. Surely there were enough in the belt that she could extract four without their being missed. One at a time, she slid twenty dollar double eagles from the belt.

Cath hid the four gold coins under the rug. Tomorrow when she had the opportunity she'd sew them into her pantaloons. Quietly she slipped back into bed. Once before when she'd had the chance to strike out on her own, back when she left Mattigan, Cath had miscalculated badly the amount of money she needed. She didn't want to make that mistake again. This time, she'd take as many gold coins as she could. Tomorrow night she'd remain awake and get more coins.

As she pulled the cool sheet to her chin, she told herself she wasn't stealing the money. If I were Wade's wife, he'd give me money. He introduces me as his wife, therefore I can act like a wife. Besides, it's money won by gambling. Just a few hours ago those coins belonged to someone else.

In the dark she smiled to herself. Now the coins belonged to her.

When *The Dragon Lady* was unloaded, the captain rang the departure bell. Slowly, the great stern wheel churned against the muddy water, and the steamboat moved against the current of the swiftly rushing Missouri River. Cath and Wade stood on the hurricane deck. To keep warm Cath wore her blue woolen coat with the fox collar. Puffs of frosty breath burst from their mouths when they spoke.

As they steamed farther north, the spring weather kept growing chillier. The trees bordering this more northern and western part of the river showed no trace of greening. The river's current was swift, and the muddy water carried tree branches, sometimes even whole trees that had been torn from their banks. The pilot had to be watchful to avoid these dangerous snags.

A fellow passenger joined them at the guard rails. He seemed knowledgeable about the river towns they were passing. He talked about Ft. Calhoun on the Nebraska side, and DeSoto, situated handsomely in a cove, half-surrounded by a pretty crescent bluff.

Later, off to the starboard they saw Sergeant's Bluff City. The bluff from which the town derived its name was three miles farther upriver, the site where Sergeant Floyd had been buried over fifty years ago by his companions, Lewis and Clarke, while on their expedition to Oregon.

Six miles farther on, *The Dragon Lady's* bell announced their arrival at Sioux City. Cath's eyes sparkled. She tried not to let Wade see her face. She knew her excitement was bubbling to the surface. Ever since the ball in St. Joseph when she'd found out that John McAffery farmed near Sioux City, she often caught Wade regarding her with a thoughtful look. He suspected something. Cath felt some guilt over stealing from Wade's money belt. She wondered if he suspected. Altogether now, she'd taken thirteen double eagles. Each coin she'd sewn securely into her spare pantaloons, using a patch over each coin.

Since it was not yet time for their evening dinner, Wade suggested they stroll ashore. Cath found Sioux City to be a pleasant town, though obviously it was an outpost of civilization. The town fronted on a land inhabited by savage Indians. Altogether there were seven dry goods shops that they passed. Cath was relieved to see Henry's Emporium, the largest of the lot. This was where she was to learn the exact whereabouts of John McAffery.

Cath's mind worked furiously. She had no idea how long *The Dragon Lady* would remain docked at Sioux City. It probably would leave in the morning.

That evening when Wade was off gambling, she located the steward to find out exactly when *The Dragon Lady* was scheduled to depart. He said departure was at six in the morning.

Early in the evening Cath dozed, but she was too excited to sleep soundly. From the time that Wade quietly climbed into bed beside her she lay awake, staring into the darkness, listening to Wade's harsh breathing. She waited for what she guessed would be about an hour, then slid stealthily out of bed. Slowly she felt her way across the dark room.

Wade continued the heavy breathing of deep sleep. Cath found her clothes, lying where she had laid them out last evening. Silently, she slipped into them, being extra careful as she slipped on her pantaloons not to let any coins clink against each other. Just before easing out the door, she put her farewell note on top of Wade's clothes.

Cath had agonized over the note. Nothing sounded right. No matter how much she apologized, her leaving seemed unforgivable. Finally, she had just scrawled, "I'm sorry, Wade, but this is the way it has to be. Take care of yourself, Cath."

Out on the hurricane deck the frosty air was crisp. In the dim light of the wharf she could see her breath. From under a tarpaulin she extracted her carpetbag, having hidden it there last evening. A glance around revealed no one on deck. In the semi-darkness Cath crept quietly down the gangplank onto the dock. Quickly, she slipped into the deserted office of the shipping company. Cath knew she dared not walk on the streets of Sioux City at this hour. No decent woman walked alone in darkness.

The small, empty office was chilly because the fire in the woodstove had gone out. Cath wondered when the shipping clerk would come on duty. Minutes crept by in slow agony for Cath. At last activity began on *The Dragon Lady*. The crew bustled about on deck and wharf, loading crates, lashing down barrels. Cath tried to sit quietly, but her body seemed to react to every gold coin sewn into her underwear. When the gangplank was pulled up, her breath caught in her throat. One long blast from the steam whistle, and *The Dragon Lady* moved away from the wharf, her bow pointing upriver, heading for the Far West.

Cath closed her eyes. She imagined Wade sleeping peacefully in their bed, being transported without his knowing it, away from her. She brushed her cheek with her hand, surprised that she was weeping. She rummaged in her reticule for her handkerchief. By the time she found it, she was sobbing, wretching with hiccoughing cries of grief.

For a long time Cath wept loudly in the deserted, chilly room. No clerk reported for duty, and she had the spartan waiting room to herself. Soon after dawn Cath managed to stop weeping. It was time she left the shipping office. Carrying her heavy carpetbag, she made her way toward The White Horse Inn, a respectable-appearing hotel she had seen yesterday when she and Wade strolled the streets of Sioux City. Few people were about at this early hour. Her heels clicked noisily on the wooden walk, and Cath glanced around uneasily. She grew even more apprehensive when a bearded man on horseback stared at her rudely, and a one-eyed wagon driver offered her a ride.

Cath breathed a sigh of relief when she climbed the steps of The White Horse Inn and entered the small lobby. No one was in sight, but a small hand bell sat on the counter. She shook it.

From a door behind the counter a bald man wearing thick spectacles entered. A look of surprise crossed his face, and the startled expression remained as he spoke. "Yes? May I help you, ma'am?"

Cath said she'd like a room.

"Will you be staying with us long?" he asked, a wary look on his round face.

"Perhaps," she replied. "It's uncertain. I'd like one of your larger, brighter rooms."

Almost with reluctance the bald clerk allowed Cath to register for one of his rooms. He handed her a large key. "Go back outside and turn right," he instructed. "You'll see the stairway going up the side of the building to the guest rooms. Yours will be the fourth room on your right."

Cath took the key. "Where can I have breakfast?" she asked.

The clerk pulled a gold watch from his vest pocket. With a start Cath realized that the watch and the very motion of the man looking at it reminded her of Wade. Her eyes welled with tears. The desk clerk didn't notice. He jerked his head to his right. "The White Horse Inn dining room will open in half an hour."

Cath climbed the outside wooden stairway leading to the rooms of the hotel. Her room was large, with a good-sized window opening out onto the street which ran in front of the hotel. She was anxious to get her dresses out of the carpetbag before they became hopelessly wrinkled. There was no clothes press, only wooden pegs in one corner. She hung her frocks on the pegs. This was the frontier, the far shore of civilization. What could she expect?

After breakfast of black coffee and a soft-boiled egg—Cath was too excited to eat more—she set out for Henry's Emporium.

Mr. Henry was helpful but maddeningly curious about why Cath wanted to locate John McAffery. Cath explained that she was his cousin, bringing family news. Mr. Henry didn't act as if he believed her. He said there was a twice-weekly stagecoach which went right past John's farm, but the next coach east would be two days hence. He suggested that she rent a buggy at Pierson's Stable and ask them directions of how to get to the Dubuque Stage road. "You'll spot McAffery's farm easily," he said. "The only two-story frame house on the road. High-toned, big barn. You'll know it when you see it."

Cath set out to find the stable. By now there was much activity in the streets, which were jammed with farm wagons. Cath didn't know how she could get to John's farm. Having been raised in town, she'd never learned to ride a horse or drive a team. She'd have to hire someone to drive her there.

After talking with the stableman, Cath understood the distance of John's farm. "It's a full day's drive for a horse, ma'am," he said. "You'll have to rent the rig for two days."

"All right," she agreed. Then she added, "And I need to hire a driver."

"Where will he sleep?" The stableman squinted his eyes.

"I have no idea," Cath snapped. "In the barn, I suppose."

When arrangements were completed, Cath climbed into the buggy. Her driver was a young fellow named Fred. His brown hair fell across his eyes, and he was so thin she wondered when he had last eaten. Cath doubted if he'd seen his sixteenth birthday. Fred slapped the reins, guiding the chestnut gelding through the crowded streets and out onto the stage road to Dubuque, which lay clear across the state on the east border, on the Mississippi River.

The minute the buggy left the shelter of the buildings and houses of Sioux City and the bluffs of the Missouri River and drove out onto the treeless prairies, the chill wind blasted Cath. She pulled the buffalo robe around her, grateful that the stableman had provided it. The tawny dry buffalo grass remaining from last summer swayed in the wind. The rolling expanse of land reminded Cath of Lake Michigan and the wider portions of the Mississippi River. The buggy was a ship sailing on a sea of ruffling brown grass.

The sun was halfway between its zenith and the horizon when Cath caught sight of a two-story frame house. Her breath caught in her throat. "Is that it?" she whispered.

"Yup," Fred said. "That's McAffery's."

Cath's heart thumped. As Fred guided the horse into the lane, a tall figure emerged from the red barn. The person stopped and stared at the approaching buggy.

82

Squinting, Cath tried to make out if the man was John or not. The clippity-clop of the horse's hooves kept time with her racing heart. She was nearly close enough to make out his features.

Yes! There was the moustache, the thick brown hair blowing in the wind. His face was weathered, and he'd become muscular.

In the buggy Cath stood, letting the buffalo robe fall to her ankles. "John!" she called, waving frantically. "Oh, John!"

Chapter 8
Finding True Love

The buggy wheels had scarcely stopped rolling when Cath leaped to the ground, clutching her skirt tightly against her legs. "It's me, John!" she cried. "Cath! Cath Carleton from Mattigan!"

For a moment a confused John McAffery scratched his cheek, then with eager strides he hurried toward the buggy. The chill spring breeze tossed his silvery-brown hair, which was almost the color of dry prairie grass.

Cath watched, breathless, as he neared. And then he was standing before her, staring down at her, topaz eyes glittering in the fading sunlight. With a loud whoop he grasped her around the waist and actually lifted her into the air. "What are you doing out here in this godforsaken wilderness, you lovely little doll?" he blurted. He set her down on the ground and shook his head in wonderment. He seemed unable to believe that she was actually here.

The glow in his eyes showed he was pleased to see her. "I was stopping in Sioux City for some business," Cath improvised, "and I heard that you lived out this way. I thought I'd pay an old Mattigan friend a visit." Coyly, she glanced up into his gentle eyes. She added, "It's been a long time, John."

Though John McAffery looked happily stunned, Cath tried to figure out if her arrival was a marvelous event for him, or if she presented a problem.

As if in answer to her unspoken question, from beyond John's shoulder Cath saw the farmhouse door open, and a small woman and a little boy stepped out on the porch.

"Pa!" the child called. "Pa! Who came in the buggy?" The boy jumped off the porch, and ran toward them.

"My son, Abner," John explained, as he scooped the boy up into his arms.

Pain stabbed Cath's chest. His child! John had married! Slowly she turned toward the farmhouse porch to face the woman who must be his wife. How could John have married someone else? John, why didn't you wait for me?

John was saying something. "What?" she stammered.

"Come meet my wife," he repeated, taking Cath by the elbow and leading her toward the house. Even through the heavy wool of her coat sleeve Cath felt the heat of his fingers gripping her arm. Her legs trembled. She didn't want to meet Mrs. John McAffery, the woman who had borne him a son, who shared his bed. She stumbled, but John's grip steadied her.

"Martha," John's voice sounded husky, "Meet Miss Cath Carleton from Michigan. Her father was my boss back in Mattigan. Cath, this is my wife, Martha."

Cath faced the figure standing on the wide front porch, dreading what she would see—some ravishing, gorgeous lady who had swept John off his feet, someone who had made him forget his love for Elizabeth. A woman who had made him forget Cath .

Cath's eyes met the small bird-like eyes of a tiny, plain woman. Her straight, pale brown hair was parted in the middle of her head and drawn back severely into a bun at her neck. She wore a faded blue-checkered gingham dress, and a gray woolen shawl covered her thin shoulders. Her dark eyes regarded Cath uneasily. No expression of welcome came from those eyes. The woman's brow was furrowed. She looked frightened. Martha McAffery resembled a small brown sparrow watching a cat slink toward her nest.

The two women nodded to each other. "Please come inside, Miss Carleton, out of the chill. We'll have some tea." Martha hesitated. "Uh, what about your man,—your, uh?"

John chortled. "That's no man, Martha. That's Fred." Out of the corner of his mouth he explained to his wife, "A young tad who hangs around Pierson's stable."

He turned and called to Fred, "Make yourself at home in the barn loft, Fred. We'll fetch you for supper when it's time."

Instead of going to the parlor, John led them to the spacious dining room just off the kitchen. He took Cath's coat and held a chair for her at the table, which was covered with faded blue oilcloth. "Out here," he explained, "we don't entertain in the parlor hardly ever. That's only for the parson's visits and christenings. Here in the West, people sit around the kitchen or the dining room table." He took off his gray and black checkered jacket and seated himself in a chair opposite Cath. The top button of his shirt was unbuttoned. Cath had to concentrate hard to keep from staring at the silvery, curling hairs showing at his throat.

"Well, what have you been doing these past years?" he asked. "How long has it been?"

It's been five long years! she wanted to scream. *How could you forget?* Instead, she answered, "I left Mattigan four years ago, and you had left, I think, somewhere about the year before that." She lowered her voice. "I heard that you learned about Elizabeth."

John spoke very softly, too. "Yes, I went back for her in the fall of '57 but it was too late." John's folded hands gripped each other until the knuckles whitened, and he frowned. Other than that, he showed no grief. I was right, Cath thought. It *was* Elizabeth's money he wanted. It seems he'd kept the money she loaned him and used it to buy this place for himself, and a topnotch farm it seemed to be.

"Have you been married long?" Cath asked.

"I met Martha on my way back here from Michigan. She was a farm girl of fifteen." He leaned back in his chair and clasped his hands behind his head. "How is your father?"

"I haven't been home to see him, but my sister writes that he's well. Do you remember my sister? She married Jason McDaniel."

Martha McAffery hurried into the dining room carrying a tray bearing a blue china teapot and three teacups with unmatched and chipped saucers. She returned to the kitchen and shortly reappeared carrying a hot pie tin. She protected her hands by holding the pie with hands wrapped in her bleached flour-sack apron.

"What kind of pie, my dear?" John asked.

Martha's sunken eyes lowered. "Mock apple pie," she answered as she began cutting the first piece. "That's about all I can fix this time of year, unless you bring me some dried peaches from town."

Martha McAffery's voice was shrill and high-pitched, like the voice of a child.

Martha placed a wedge of pie on a small plate and then hesitated. She nearly handed it to John, paused, and after a tortured decision, she passed the first piece to Cath.

"What have you been doing since you left Michigan?" John asked.

Cath gave her usual tale about being the companion to Mrs. Christopher Stanton. She found herself regaling the envious couple about her travels up and down the picturesque Mississippi River, describing how they wintered in the sunny, temperate south,—before the rebellion, of course—then moved northward with the blooming of the apple blossoms.

An expression of awe covering her small brown face, Martha McAffery stared at Cath open-mouthed. "How exciting that must be!" she murmured.

Taking pity on the mousy creature, Cath said, "This pie is delicious! You called it 'mock apple pie?' However did you make it?"

"Oh, it's just a can of soda crackers and water with essence of lemon, nutmeg and sugar added. It do taste a lot like apple pie, don't it?" the small woman answered, her cheeks blushing red at the unexpected compliment.

The little boy, Abner, whined, and Martha McAffery pulled him onto her lap. His nose was running, and she dabbed at it with her apron. The boy looked nothing like John. His dark eyes set close together were a duplicate of his mother's. Though now his hair was towhead-white, Cath suspected it would turn to a nondescript dirty blond like Martha McAffery's. It was too bad that more of John's handsome traits hadn't been passed on to the boy.

"Do you plan to stay in Iowa long?" John leaned forward slightly, clearing his throat.

Cath's answer surprised herself. As if she were in a trance she replied, "I'm starting a small business in Sioux City. I plan to design and make millinery items and perhaps even expand into creating fashionable ladies' garments."

As if at a great distance she heard John reply that this should be a good venture. "Right now, I think the ladies have only the choice of buying ready-mades brought by the steamboats, or sewing their own. You might do very well," he added.

That night, sunk deep in a featherbed in the McAffery guest bedroom, Cath couldn't fall asleep. Her mind was in turmoil, trying to deal with the terrible disappointment of John's being married. One moment she silently moaned into the darkness, "how could he!" and the next moment she dissolved into tears, struggling to keep silent. She wouldn't want her anguish heard. It seemed impossible to her that John had married such a gray little shadow. Was he looking for a chore girl, someone to handle the duties of a farm wife? Surely, he couldn't have been interested in her as a lover? But then she thought of the two sleeping in the same bed in the adjoining bedroom, and tears flowed again.

The next day when Cath was leaving to return to Sioux City she thanked Martha McAffery for her hospitality. "When you get into Sioux City, be sure and look me up," Cath said, not meaning it a bit. "Right now I'm at the White Horse Inn, but if I carry through with my plans for business, I'll have to find a suitable establishment."

John walked with her toward the buggy. Fred had the chestnut gelding harnessed. Sitting in the driver's seat, Fred looked impatient to leave.

The huge sky hung over them like a giant overturned blue washbasin. The vastness of the treeless landscape was overwhelming. Having grown up in the forests of Michigan, and after years traveling the tree-lined Mississippi River, Cath found this prairie expanse awesome.

When they'd walked out of earshot of Martha and before they moved too close to Fred, John whispered into Cath's ear, "I'll come see you in Sioux City. You're at the White Horse Inn? What room?"

At his question Cath's heart gave a great thump. Waves of heat radiated through her body. Almost without expression, she told him how to find her room.

"I'll be there tomorrow," he murmured. When they reached the buggy he helped her climb aboard. Gently, John spread the furry buffalo robe across her lap. As soon as John stepped away from the buggy, Fred clucked, urging the horse forward. The buggy rolled down the lane toward the stage road.

Cath didn't look back. She wore a smug smile. Tomorrow she'd be seeing her true love. Hadn't he said so? And he wasn't coming as a gentleman paying a formal call. The yearning in his amber eyes told her why he was coming to town. Cath closed her eyes. She could almost feel his strong arms around her body, holding her close. How long she had waited for the chance to be held in John McAffery's arms! After all those years of dreaming about it, her wishes were about to come true. Tomorrow John was coming to her! With a start, Cath opened her eyes. Fred was studying her with interest, and she didn't like the knowing look on his young face. She'd have to be more careful. Like Mattigan, Sioux City was a small town. Gossip would be a favorite pastime. Cath wouldn't want Martha McAffery to grow suspicious. She didn't want to be murdered like her own Mama. She must conceal her emotions. She must be very, very careful. If she really was going to open a millinery-design shop, she must keep her reputation respectable. Otherwise, the town matrons wouldn't patronize her.

✳   ✳   ✳   ✳

Much to the bald room clerk's displeasure Cath ordered a tub and hot water brought to her room. Though they charged her far too much for the service, Cath believed it worth the price to soak in the cleansing warm water. She wanted to be fresh and clean for John. She had no idea what time of the day he'd arrive. He'd said only that he'd "be there tomorrow." She supposed that he would leave his farm in the morning and arrive in Sioux City mid-afternoon.

After the bath tub had been hauled away, Cath debated about what she should wear to greet John. Her wardrobe was severely limited. All she had was what she'd been able to stuff into her carpetbag before sneaking away from Wade and *The Dragon Lady*. There didn't seem to be any need of pretense for getting all dressed up for John. He wasn't coming all the way into Sioux City to see her dressed in a gown of the latest fashion. No gentleman would come calling for a lady at her hotel room door unless he had intimacy in mind. Cath shrugged. Why bother with the petticoats, hoop, pantaloons and dress? Her delicate cambric dressing gown was the practical garment for the occasion. It was comfortable. It revealed her feminine curves. Cath glanced at her reflection in the mirror. The ivory-colored gown showed off the high color of her complexion. The flush of her cheeks showed her anticipation of John's visit.

Cath was still fluffing her damp curls when there was a knock at her door. She assumed it was the chore boy come back to retrieve something he'd forgotten. Instead, when she opened the door to her hotel room, there stood John McAffery, holding his dusty hat.

"Let me in!" he hissed, furtively glancing down the hall.

Quickly, she opened the door, and he slipped inside.

90

"I wouldn't want anyone to see me," he said. "Too many people in town know me. And," he added, "of course, I wouldn't want to damage your reputation either."

A wave of irritation drowned Cath's elation. This reunion, though private, didn't seem any more romantic than the one day before yesterday at John's farm, with his wife and child looking on.

John tossed his felt hat onto a chair. Putting his arms on Cath's shoulders, he said, "Let me look at you, lovely lady. What a beautiful woman you've grown to be!" His eyes examined her appreciatively. Cath felt better.

Those brandywine eyes, always so attractive, now glowed with eagerness, with passion. His thumbs stroked her skin, playing with the soft lace circling the neckline of her dressing gown. Abruptly, he pulled Cath toward him, crushing her against his chest with one arm, and with his right hand he cupped her jaw and tipped her lips to his. His mouth came down on hers hard and moist.

With the sound of harsh breathing in her ears, Cath thought how often she'd longed for this—to be smothered in John's powerful arms. Just as years ago it hadn't mattered to her that he was betrothed to Elizabeth, neither did it now matter to her that he was wed. John was her true love, and true love has no rules.

"I want you, Cath," he rasped. "And I think you want me. I remember that before I left Mattigan you tried to seduce me. You're even lovelier and more desirable now." His hand moved from her jaw to her bodice, and he began kneading her breast through the thin cambric. Cath's nipple grew large at his touch. His fingers continued to caress her breast. His breath whistled as he murmured into her ear, "You're so lovely, so lovely!" His fingers drew aside the top of her gown. Slowly, he dipped his head toward her breast. When his mouth fastened upon her erect nipple, she threw back her head, feeling the waves of passion enliven her body. Fumbling, he pulled off her dressing gown and picked her up.

In bed he took her quickly, with no further caresses or endearments. Afterwards, while John dozed, they lay side-by-side in the hotel bed. Cath gazed fondly at her loved one. She forgave him for his self-centered lovemaking. He was so excited about seeing her after all these years! And after being stuck with that dowdy wife for so long, who could blame him for being inconsiderate in his loving?

Perhaps his uneasiness about making illicit love in a small town hotel room might have contributed to John's haste in bed. She decided to find a small cottage away from the center of the business district, yet situated not too far from customers. That way she could run her millinery business and have a tryst for meeting John, all in one rent payment! Smiling softly, she studied his handsome profile, so vulnerable now in sleep. It seemed like a dream come true. For so long she had looked forward to this moment. John actually lay beside her in bed. He'd just made love to her. Over the past years while she'd searched for him, sometimes her faith had faltered. At those times she doubted if she'd ever see John McAffery again. Facing reality, she'd acknowledged the vastness of the frontier. When she'd grown discouraged in her search, she'd told herself she was wasting her life in a fruitless hunt. Now, reality was this—John's warm body sleeping next to her. Cath was amazed at her good fortune.

Thursday, July 4, 1861

Cath had leased a neat cabin nestled in a grove of hickory and basswood trees on the edge of town. The trees gave the cabin privacy, and their shade cooled down the scorching heat of the summer sun. Though Cath had planned the cottage as mainly a love nest for herself and John, to her surprise her millinery business flourished. Cath had a talent for combining straw, ribbons and swatches of material with unusual colors. The ladies of Sioux City flocked to her shop to get a custom-designed "Catherine Creation." In fact, so successful had the bonnet-creating business become that she hadn't even considered expanding into other clothing items. Designing and making one-of-a-kind hats kept her busy.

Her business was large enough that she should hire a seamstress to do the tedious sewing. This would free Cath to spend more time on designing. However, she was reluctant to have anyone else in her shop. As long as Cath was alone, John could come and go freely through her rear entrance. The way it was now, when he stayed overnight, he didn't have to hurry to leave; if she hired a seamstress, he'd have to slip away before the employee arrived.

About once a week John came to town and spent the night.

"Did you come to town this often before I arrived?" Cath asked him one day.

"Of course not!" he laughed. "What was there to come to town for?"

"How often did you come to town?" she persisted.

"Oh, about once every two, three months."

Cath studied him. "Wouldn't that make your wife suspicious, now?"

John shrugged. "Suspicious? So? What can she do about it? She's not the kind to leave. She has no one but me."

The hairs on Cath's neck prickled as she thought of five years ago today. Mrs. Campbell probably hadn't been the kind to leave, either. She was a colorless creature. In fact, Martha McAffery resembled Mrs. Campbell. Cath shuddered.

"What if Martha should get it in her head to do away with me?" Cath asked, her voice trembling.

"Martha? Do what?" John asked, incredulous. Then his face smoothed out. "Oh, you're remembering what happened to your mother."

Cath stared at him. Of course she remembered. How could she forget?

John squeezed her arm. "Don't fret, Cath. Martha doesn't know one end of a gun from the other. She's terrified of guns. She makes me keep them hidden, because of Abner, you know."

Cath bit her lip. She wasn't convinced. She doubted that Mrs. Campbell had known anything about guns, either. Even so, the Rev. Campbell's mousy wife had changed the lives of the Carleton family with terrible destruction. Though Cath felt no affection for Martha McAffery, she felt sympathy for the helpless woman. A finger of guilt prodded her. Then she remembered that John didn't feel worried about his wife's guessing the reason for his frequent trips to town. If John could be callous enough to disregard his wife's misery when he had to look into her eyes daily, certainly Cath could ignore guilty feelings toward a woman she scarcely knew. She didn't feel guilty, but she feared Martha McAffery. If ever Martha felt backed into a corner, well...Cath shook off these thoughts. She was being maudlin because this was an anniversary of Mama's terrible death. Strange, though, that she had gotten herself into a triangle, just like Mama. Cath looked up at the endless western sky. Like mother, like daughter, they said.

The closest stores and warehouses were nearly a half mile from her log cottage with the storefront windows. Earlier in the day she heard the band playing at the Independence Day celebration. When the fireworks began Cath clapped her hands over her ears. Explosions on the Fourth of July brought back too much horror. Sometimes Cath wondered when that awful memory would fade away.

It was after sundown. Arm in arm, Cath and John sauntered out of the front door into the shelter of darkness where they breathed the cooler outdoor air. Cath suddenly became aware that the whole western half of the sky was rosy red.

"Look, John!" she cried. "What is it?"

"Prairie fire."

Cath clutched at him. "What should we do?"

He squeezed her protectively. "Nothing. It's across the river in Nebraska. Can't cross the river. Don't be afraid. Why, at night a prairie fire can be seen as far as 25 miles. When a fire catches in redtop bunch grass or in big bluestem, it goes!"

She shivered. One of her patrons had once been nearly killed in a prairie fire, and her description of the roaring, smoking fire was frightening.

"Think it's time we go to bed, love?" John asked softly, giving her hand a tug toward the cabin.

Cath wanted to resist. She didn't want to go back into that sticky, smothering cottage. She wanted to be outside where the air was cooler. She wished they could stroll into town and mingle with the celebrating crowds. But she knew that was out of the question. John was a married man. No one must ever see them together.

With an unconscious sigh, she let herself be led into the sweltering cabin. As Cath stepped out of her dress and then the lace camisole, carefully hanging them up, a strange thought occurred to her. Though for four years she'd lived in only a steamboat stateroom with Wade, never once had she felt confined or cooped up as she did so often here in Sioux City. But Wade's lovemaking had been exciting, coaxing. Wade could make her whole body light up, like turning up the wick in a lamp.

Astonished, Cath stood perfectly still. What a strange thought. Her mind must be playing tricks on her—perhaps the heat. Why on earth would she be thinking fondly about Wade Stanton? After all, John McAffery was her real love. Hadn't she searched the whole West looking for him?

Even so, as she crawled into bed between the sticky sheets and slid into John's arms, part of her mind was thinking of Wade Stanton and the cool, rippling waters beneath their many steamboat-homes.

Cath almost had quit thinking of what John did to her as "lovemaking." The word wasn't right—he didn't make love to her. He entered her, shuddered, left his seed, which she certainly didn't want, and then rolled over to doze.

Once again he completed his act and fell asleep. Perspiring, Cath lay on her back weeping tears of frustration. All those years she'd spent searching for John McAffery mocked her. Had she been mistaken? Surely John was her true love. She must be patient. He needed time to get used to her and to know her and her needs. He was still too infatuated with the newness of her body.

She reminded herself to be patient. She'd have to use her wits to teach John how to be a good lover. If John ever suspected that she was sexually more sophisticated than he it would drive him away. She'd lose him, for sure.

Chapter 9
He Calls it "Sinning"

During the four months that Cath had been living in her storefront-cottage on the edge of Sioux City's growing business district she had grown fond of it. Behind her cabin a creek which her patrons called "Grasshopper Creek" gurgled cheerfully as it rushed over rocks. Its clear water made life possible for the hickory and basswood trees growing along its banks. In the spring months Cath had listened to the peeping of the frogs in the slough on the other side of the creek. Toward the end of June she'd relished picking wild strawberries in the swales. In less than half an hour she'd filled a tin bucket with tart, juicy berries. As summer progressed she discovered dewberries, gooseberries, currants and wild grapes.

Cath thrilled to the singing of the yellow-breasted meadowlarks who had nested in the prairie grass across the road from her cottage. When she walked through the tall grasses, prairie hens thrummed away from her footsteps.

Now, with summer drawing to an end, katydids rubbed their green gossamer wings together to sing their warning of the frost which in a few weeks would cloak the countryside.

Her cottage reminded Cath of her childhood, when she and Becky had frolicked in the woods surrounding their log cabin on the edge of Mattigan. After their move into town Cath had lost touch with the pleasures of nature. Of her four years with Wade on their succession of different steamboats, Cath had been almost a captive of each steamboat. Nature was something she'd observed from the deck of the boat. She'd looked at the scenery on the passing riverbanks as one would observe a painting. Here, in the cozy surroundings of her cottage, she lived with trees, birds, and a huge raccoon who washed his dinner every evening in Grasshopper Creek.

At last she'd found herself enjoying a new feeling, a sense of independence. On the front door Cath posted the hours that her shop would be open, from ten in the morning until two in the afternoon. Though her customers begged her to remain open longer, Cath held to her limited hours. It was necessary for her to work many hours each day outside of these shop hours to design and sew the bonnets. She kept aside time so she could walk the countryside, enjoy the fragrance of nature.

The short hours that her millinery shop was open also made it possible for her to be free for John's unannounced visits. Cath never knew when he might arrive. Sometimes a week would pass without his coming to town. Other times he'd return in only two days. Cath knew that his wife had to suspect the reason for his frequent trips to Sioux City, since before Cath's arrival he'd seldom come to town. Only a dull-witted woman would believe the excuses he said he gave to Martha — frequent broken ax handles and endless cracked horseshoes. Cath continued to worry about Martha McAffery and what jealousy might do to her. John insisted that Martha was no problem; no provocation would tempt her to confront Cath. Nevertheless, apprehension hung over Cath like a dark cloud, preventing sunlight from reaching her.

Cath broke the black thread with which she was sewing. She studied the bonnet. Mrs. Caudle would be pleased with this new creation, a bonnet of black velvet and corded silk. The bunch of artificial currants and red feather tacked to one side contrasted with the black material. The hat had a jaunty appeal.

Through the open doorway came the sound of horse's hooves trotting on the hard-packed dirt road which passed by her cottage. Cath tipped her head, listening. Perhaps it was someone passing on their way north. But, no. The hoofbeats were slowing. It must be John.

Fiddlesticks! Why does he have to show up now — just when I'm getting ready to take a walk along the river bank to look for bittersweet! Cath's hand flew to her throat. She had surprised herself with her lack of enthusiasm for John's showing up. She held her breath, waiting for the feeling to go away, but the irritation at John's arrival stayed, lying heavy over her heart. What had happened to her raging love for John? For years all she'd thought of was John McAffery. Just the thought of him and his soft topaz eyes had been enough to kindle a warm feeling in her stomach. Now that she was John's paramour, the raging flame had gone out. Cath couldn't remember when the fire of her love had begun to flicker. But dim it had. Now what love she had left for John remained as a withered thing, dried up and limp. Her flames of love had burned to ashes.

As Cath stared unseeing at the velvet bonnet in her hands, she heard John's boots hit the ground in her front dooryard, and his tall figure filled the doorway.

"Cath!" he cried, gasping.

Cath jumped up from her chair and ran to him. "What's the matter, John?" she asked, gripping his dusty sleeve. "What's happened?" He appeared exhausted. Dark circles underlined his eyes; his voice was hoarse.

He took deep breaths while Cath led him to the chair beside her workbench.

"Can you come home with me?" he blurted. "I need you to help me take care of little Abner and Martha. Abner has scarlet fever, and Martha's been nursing him, but this morning Martha couldn't get out of bed. She thinks she's got the cholera!" John leaned his elbows on his knees and let his head sag limp between his knees.

Cath tucked two calico dresses into her carpetbag, along with underthings and stockings. Glancing around her shop, she had the wistful feeling that she might be leaving it for good. She shuddered. Would she get cholera and die? Nonsense. What else could she do? A child and a frightened woman needed care. She'd do it for the child and Martha. Not for John McAffery. She didn't owe John anything.

"All right," Cath said. "Ride to Pierson's stable. Rent a horse and a buggy. While you're doing that I'll go to the apothecary shop to get medicines and herbs I'll need. Pick me up at...no, I'll meet you at the stable."

"It'd be faster if I rented you a riding horse," John protested.

"That may be," Cath answered tersely, "but I never learned to ride a horse."

During the long trip to John's farm they scarcely spoke. John seemed paralyzed with fear. Cath went over and over in her mind the various potions and methods of treatment Mr. Morgan had told her about when he dispensed the medicines to her. When darkness closed around them John slowed the horse's speed, but once the nearly full moon rose above the horizon, there was enough light to resume almost full speed.

At last John turned up the lane toward his darkened home. Not a lamp burned. Cath shivered. The tall house shown a ghostly white, reflecting the pale moonbeams. She hated the thought of entering this house of sickness, this home of John and his wife and child. What was she doing here, anyway?

John carried Cath's carpetbag while Cath clutched the flour sack full of medications from Mr. Morgan. The minute they opened the kitchen door Cath heard the far-off whimpering of the child. John moved ahead into the dark kitchen. She heard him fumbling, trying to find a lamp. At last, she heard the scratch of a sulphur match. A small flame glowed, and Cath made out John's silhouette leaning over a lamp. When the wick caught, a soft glow spread through the kitchen.

"Light another, John," she suggested, "so we can each have one."

As she reached out for the second lamp she instructed, "Show me where Abner is."

John led her up the stairway to a tiny room under the eaves. The boy lay on his rumpled bed, fussing weakly. His eyes were closed. He seemed unaware of their arrival. Cath placed her palm on his forehead. His skin was hot and dry.

"He's feverish," she said. "I'm going to mix up a medicine that Mr. Morgan said was good for scarlet fever. You're to give him a spoonful every hour. It's important to cool him; you must sit beside him and bathe him constantly with cool water until his fever breaks. Understand?"

"Won't you be helping me take care of him?" John asked plaintively.

"No. I'll be caring for Martha. If she does have cholera, we certainly don't want to expose Abner to it. We'll stay apart. I'll take care of Martha; you take care of Abner. They don't know what causes cholera, but in his weakened state, Abner might be especially susceptible to any miasmas around."

Downstairs in the kitchen Cath opened the flour sack and removed the medications she'd brought. Into a small cream pitcher she dropped one grain of sulphate of zinc, one grain of foxglove, and a half teaspoon of sugar. To this she added two tablespoons of water and mixed it. Finally, she added half a cup of water to the concoction and stirred it thoroughly, leaving the spoon in the pitcher.

When she delivered this medication upstairs to Abner's bedroom she saw that John had gotten a white china basin of water and was sponging the child's hot skin. "That's right," she nodded approvingly, as she set the cream pitcher down on the nightstand beside the bed. "Be sure and give him a spoonful of this every hour." She turned to go, sighing, "I'll tend to Martha now."

She didn't have to be shown the way to Martha McAffery's bedroom. Last April, when she'd first arrived in Sioux City and had stayed overnight with the McAfferys, Cath had said goodnight to John and Martha as she stood outside the guest room door. She remembered how envious she'd felt as she'd watched them go together into their bedroom.

The minute she stepped over the threshold into Martha McAffery's bedroom, the sour stench engulfed her. Cath held the lamp high to see her way into the room. She gasped when she saw the sick woman. Martha's closed eyes were sunk deep into the darkened sockets. Dried vomit stuck to her thin cheeks and ran over the wrinkled sheets, down the side of the bed.

Taking the lamp with her, Cath hurried out into the dark hallway. "John? Where do you keep your fresh bed linens?"

Cath heard him stand up; his footsteps sounded on the floorboards of the bedroom.

"No! Don't come out here!" she cried. "Just tell me where they are. I'll find them."

Later, when she'd managed to wash Martha McAffery and get clean sheets on the bed, she began administering the variety of medications Mr. Morgan had recommended. Most important, he said was calomel and opium. Cath began with that mixture, using ten grains of calomel to one of opium. She placed a mustard poultice across the woman's emaciated abdomen.

By dawn Abner was better, his fever having broken. John moved him downstairs where he could look after him and also prepare food, draw water from the well, and briefly feed the horses and livestock. Cath asked John to pick a dozen ears of field corn. As Mr. Morgan had instructed, she had John boil them with the husks on. These she placed alongside Martha's frail body. She instructed John to keep bricks warming in the oven at all times, and she kept exchanging warm bricks around Martha's body, to keep her warm. The boiled ears of corn were to draw poison out of the body.

Twice that day Cath fell asleep sitting upright in a hard, straight-backed chair. Through the window in the bedroom she could see that daylight was fading. How could she stay awake another night? A squeaking noise drew Cath's attention to the head of the bed. Martha was conscious, her thin hand fluttering helplessly. The small dark eyes were like raisins stuck in her yellow face. From the shriveled face the raisin eyes watched Cath fearfully.

"John asked me to take care of you, Martha," Cath explained gently, patting the thin arm. "He's taking care of Abner, and keeping bricks warm for your bed. He can't possibly take care of both of you and the livestock, too, you know." Cath tried to smile cheerfully, but she knew it was a false smile.

"Thank you," the woman whispered. "I'm so worried about the baby."

Cath leaned closer to Martha. "I beg your pardon. I don't think I heard you. You're worried about what?"

The thin voice wavered. "The baby. I'm in the family way." Martha pinched her lips together tightly, and a flush of embarrassment mixed with the yellow tint of her complexion.

Cath's heart thumped harder. How could this woman be pregnant? Her stomach is flat. She'd seen it herself when she covered Martha's abdomen with the mustard plaster.

"How far along?"

Eyes closed, the woman sighed, "I just missed my third monthly."

Cath gulped. A hot blush of anger ran through her body. So John was making love to his wife this summer, even when he came into town to her! Cath felt betrayed.

"Do you think you can swallow?" Cath asked. "You should be taking more fluids. I'd like to give you some warm mint tea."

Spoonful by spoonful Cath got nearly a cup of herb tea down her patient's throat, along with another dose of calomel and opium. Martha fell back into a sound sleep. Cath leaned forward and rested her forehead on the counterpane.

With a start, Cath awoke. Rubbing her eyes and blinking sleepily, she studied the gold chatelaine watch Wade had given her. It was after five in the morning. Guiltily, she squinted toward Martha McAffery. The woman was awake, looking alert. Dark sunken eyes watched her. Martha's skin had lost its deep yellow cast. Her eyes were brighter; they seemed able to focus.

"You look better," Cath spoke softly. "How do you feel?"

"Some better. I do so want to live—for Abner, you know, and the baby." A fierce look crossed the sick woman's face. "Why don't John come see me?"

"I told him to stay away from both you and me," Cath replied. "Since he's taking care of Abner, we don't want the miasma to spread from this room to Abner, do we?"

Martha threw Cath a hard look. "What do it matter?" she sighed bitterly. "I've lost John to you, anyway. I can see that plain and clear."

"No, you haven't," Cath retorted. "You're wrong. In fact, as soon as you're well enough for me to leave you, I'm moving away from Sioux City."

The raisin eyes studied Cath's face suspiciously. Finally, Martha asked in her thin, high-pitched voice, "Why do that? John says you have an important business, that you're making lots of money."

"That's true." Cath stared thoughtfully at the glowing lamp, turned low, which sat across the room on the highboy. She loved her cottage surrounded by green trees and the little creek which bubbled behind her cabin. She delighted in creating elegant bonnets. It was hard to believe how much ladies were willing to pay for her inventions of fancy. Why had she told Martha McAffery that she was going to leave Sioux City? Frowning, Cath concentrated. For one thing, she was going to leave to get away from John. It was time she got out of his life. Just looking into this sick woman's sunken eyes made Cath sick over the heartache she'd caused this woman. And then there was the fear she'd been living with— the worry that Martha McAffery's misery might cause her mind to snap, and that Cath might suffer the same fate as her mother. No reason to tempt fate to cause history to repeat itself. But there was something else, something that kept nagging at her.

Cath's hands rested in her lap, nervously pleating and unpleating folds of her skirt. Finally, the truth wriggled into her mind. She wasn't giving up her beloved cottage and her profitable millinery business out of an act of kindness for this sick woman.

She missed Wade. She wanted to find him, to be engulfed in his loving arms again. Oh, how she wished she were cuddled against his chest right this minute! Whatever had possessed her to leave Wade?

Martha McAffery was saying something.

"I'm sorry," Cath said, "I didn't hear."

"I asked where you would go."

"I'm going to try to find a very special man," Cath said softly, smiling at the unfortunate woman lying on the bed. "I left him to come here, which was a terrible mistake for all of us. Now I'm going to look for him. I pray to God that I can find him, and if I do, I'm going to beg him to take me back." Cath studied her hands sadly. "I wonder if he'll forgive me," she murmured. "I couldn't blame him if he didn't. For a long time I treated him shabbily. I used him shamelessly. I had a very precious thing, and I didn't value it until after I'd thrown it away."

Martha slept most of the morning. At noon when the sick woman awakened, Cath fed her chicken broth. Cath smiled gently at Martha as she bathed her with a cloth. In a spontaneous surge of sympathy for the miserable woman, Cath pulled her delicate cambric nightgown out of her carpetbag.

"Here!" she said, holding up the gown. "Let's get you into a soft, clean nightgown. Gently, she rolled the gray flannel gown off Martha, and like dressing a child, Cath guided Martha's arms into the sleeves and tugged her gown into position.

Martha's eyes filled with tears as she fingered the flimsy, white material.

"Never seen such elegant material," she said. "But I'm afeared I'll soil it for you."

"It's your gown, now, Martha," Cath said. "My present to you."

Martha clutched Cath's hand. "You're so good to me," she said. "I'm so grateful to you for coming. John did right to ask you."

Embarrassed, Cath looked away.

It was late in the afternoon when the bleeding began. Martha writhed with painful cramps. Between the pains, Martha wept quietly. "It's the baby. I'm losing the baby."

Her pains grew closer together. Cath was terrified that the woman would bleed to death. There was so much dark blood trickling from the tiny woman. How much blood could a body lose and survive? Finally, a mass of clots and tissue the size of a hen's egg was expelled, and the bleeding slowed.

"Was that the baby?" Martha wanted to know.

"I think so," Cath answered.

Martha turned her face to the wall and bit her lip.

"Perhaps it's for the best," Cath said softly. "The cholera may have poisoned the baby or marked it in some hideous manner." She patted the woman's hand. "Try to accept it. Tell yourself that it was meant to be this way. When you're stronger you'll have more children."

Martha turned toward Cath , her face showing hope for the first time. "Do you reckon so?" she breathed.

"I'm sure of it!" Cath replied firmly. Her assurance was sincere.

After a week of care both Martha and Abner were on their way to recovery. Abner couldn't be kept still. He raced about the house, knocking over chairs and rattling doorknobs. When Cath and John decided he was well enough to play outside, he chased the cackling chickens around the barnyard and threw stones at the pregnant calico cat.

Her sleeves rolled up above the elbows, Cath's hands were plunged in steaming water as she washed the breakfast and lunch dishes. John entered the back hallway, stamping his boots to loosen hay and straw before coming into the kitchen. He glanced at Cath uneasily, quickly turning his eyes away.

Something was troubling him. "Do you have something to say to me, John?" she asked.

At her words John started, and he looked at her wide-eyed. "How'd you know?"

"You look like a man with something on his mind."

John shuffled his feet. "Cath, I just want to say how grateful I am to you for taking care of Martha. I don't know what I would've done without you. I can never repay you for what you've done. I think you've saved both Abner's and Martha's lives."

He cleared his throat and went on. "That's what makes saying this so awful difficult. Cath, I'm not going to come in to Sioux City to see you anymore. I know this sounds ungrateful, but it has to be this way. I can't live with my conscience anymore. It's almost like my sinning with you brought on the sickness in my wife and child. Understand?"

Mouth agape, Cath stood in front of the dry sink, her hands resting in hot suds in the dishpan. *Sinning with her! Indeed! So that's what he called his grunting contortions!* She felt her cheeks grow hot.

"I know it's going to be hard for you, Cath," he continued. "But it's something we never should've started in the first place. And remember, *you* were the one who looked me up. I didn't come hounding after you. I think if you keep busy with your little bonnet business, your heartache will lessen with time. By and by, you'll meet someone you can love, and you'll marry. Just be patient, and don't turn your heart against others. And don't be too particular. You aren't getting any younger, you know."

Cath removed her hands from the dishpan and slowly dried them on the flour sack tied around her waist. Her blue eyes snapped.

"What will you do, Cath?" John asked. "Will you be all right?"

"What will I do?" she repeated his words slowly. Her chin lifted. "I shall return to my former life on the river."

"You mean as a companion to that rich old lady?"

"Not exactly. You see, *Mrs.* Stanton is really *Mr.* Stanton."

John's jaw fell open. "You were with a man? Before you came to me?" he sputtered.

"Yes! And he's twice the man you are! I was out of my mind to leave him for you! And The Lord forgive me for causing him pain."

"You dare to call upon The Lord, you..., you whore!" He was shouting now.

"Shush," Cath warned. "Do you want Martha and Abner to hear? It's time I left. If you work very hard, you can get by. Don't work Martha too hard for awhile. She's been very sick, you know. Do you have a neighbor who can take me back to town? *You* can't take me, because you mustn't leave Martha alone yet."

The next morning John's neighbor to the east rode up the lane. He harnessed the rented horse to the buggy and tied his own horse behind it. It was a bumpy trip back to Sioux City, but Cath hardly minded. She bubbled with excitement and plans. She'd lain awake much of last night, figuring the best way to find Wade. At last her mind had seized upon what seemed to be the most reliable plan.

This very day, the moment she arrived in Sioux City, she'd go to the steamship office and buy a ticket for the next downriver steamboat to St. Joseph. There she'd locate Will Babcock, Wade's trusted banker friend. Cath felt sure that Wade always kept Babcock informed of his current steamboat-home so that correspondence and legal papers could be sent to him. She'd find out what boat Wade was on, and she'd intercept him somewhere on the river.

It took Cath four days to settle everything to close out her business. She finished three bonnets which had been in the final stages of completion, but returned money to twenty customers who had placed orders for bonnets they'd never receive. Once again, Cath sewed her gold coins carefully into her undergarments, and added a cloth money belt, musing that she was leaving Sioux City with a great many more coins than what she'd arrived with—coins stolen from Wade. Cath smiled to herself. *And now I can pay him back. Won't he be surprised! He thinks he'll never see me or his coins again.* She threw her head back and laughed. She could picture the quizzical look on Wade's face when she found him. The dimples would crease his cheeks, and he'd hold his arms out for her. But then she sobered.

What if Wade won't forgive me? Maybe he's found another woman! At this thought, tears rushed to her eyes.

For a time she wept. Finally her chin snapped up. *Perish the thought. Don't borrow trouble!* Even so, the nagging worry stayed with her.

Chapter 10
Lac Qui Parle, Lake Which Speaks

Wednesday, September 18, 1861

Cath's trip down the Missouri River to St. Joseph was aboard *The Lone Star,* a small, modestly decorated sternwheeler. The depth of the yellow-brown river was low, the current sluggish. The daytime weather was gloriously warm, but after sundown the autumn air grew chilly. Cath became acquainted with a young couple from St. Louis, and her chats with them caught her up on facts about the insurrection that she hadn't known. All summer she'd been so caught up in her involvement with John that she hadn't paid attention to war news. Sometimes patrons of her shop mentioned the rebellion, but usually they talked about what young man had gone off to fight the rebels or the latest word about who'd been wounded. Cath grew alarmed when she learned that in July the Union suffered a terrible defeat at Bull Run. She'd been sure that the North would crush the insolent rebels quickly.

By the time *The Lone Star* docked at St. Joseph, Cath's legs trembled from nervousness. She was anxious to find Will Babcock. Yet what if he refused to tell her Wade's whereabouts? She didn't know what Babcock's attitude toward her would be.

In the steamship ticket office she explained that she was looking for Mr. Will Babcock, a banker, but that she didn't know with which bank he was connected. The shipping clerk frowned, scratched his head. "I don't know," he said, "but Yancy probably does. Yancy knows everybody in St. Joe."

The clerk stepped out from behind the ticket counter and walked out the door. He squinted, looking down the pier, spotted his target. "There," he pointed toward an old man in ragged clothes sitting cross-legged on a huge coil of hawser.

Cath approached the old man. She saw an unkempt white beard, feet bound in rags. When she stood before him, she cleared her throat and began, "Excuse me."

"What can I do for you, ma'am?" he asked, jumping quickly to his feet.

"I'm looking for a Mr. Will Babcock, a banker, and I was told that you might direct me to the proper bank."

"That I can," he answered, bobbing his head. "St. Joseph State Bank. Will's President."

"Where might I find that bank?"

The old man pointed. "Walk two blocks up that street to Whalen's General Store. Turn left, and the bank will be on your left."

"Thank you so very much," Cath said. She made herself give the strange fellow a smile, turned to leave.

"Ma'am, just a moment."

Cath wondered what he wanted.

He was holding out his hand, palm up. "I expect a fee when I give information. How else is an old man to support himself without turning to begging?"

"How much of a fee?" Cath reached inside her reticule.

"Four bits would be adequate."

After paying, Cath hurried off, anxious to put distance between herself and the peculiar fellow.

When she turned left at the general store she saw the sign of the St. Joseph State Bank. The man's directions had been correct. She hoped he was right about this being Will Babcock's bank.

Inside, Cath approached an iron-barred teller's cage and told a clerk she wished to speak with Mr. Babcock. As she spoke she saw Will Babcock moving through the aisle behind the tellers' cages. He was in shirt-sleeves, black elastic bands around his forearms. Cath would've known him anywhere because of his distinctive silver hair.

"Mr. Babcock!" she called.

He stopped and turned. At first, his face was blank, but when recognition registered in his eyes, his forehead wrinkled. Quickly, he strode to the far end of the row of barred cages and opened a solid oak door. He motioned for her to follow.

Will Babcock ushered her past the tellers' cages into a large office. Apparently it was his, because he swept his suit coat off the chair and put it on. Taking Cath's arm, he led her to a chair.

"I'm delighted to see you, my dear," he said. "What can I do for you?" He leaned back in the oak swivel chair with a polite smile. Cath decided the banker wasn't as old as she'd thought. His skin was tanned and smooth. His hair must have whitened prematurely.

Swallowing, Cath mumbled, "I'd like to find Wade."

"Why?"

Cath studied his face. He didn't look hostile, but he wasn't making this easy.

"I made a terrible mistake, Mr. Babcock. I left Wade."

"Yes, I know."

"You knew about it? Wade told you?"

Babcock nodded, watching her closely.

"It was an awful thing for me to do. I don't know what got into me! I had this silly idea that I was in love with a ...well, it was a childhood sweetheart thing. I heard he was farming near Sioux City so I slipped away from Wade."

"You found the childhood sweetheart?"

"Yes," Cath replied softly.

"And?"

Cath's cheeks grew hot. Her eyes stung. *Oh, dear God, please don't let me cry!* She took a deep breath. "The man was married. My past love for him was delusion on my part. I realized it was Wade I cared about."

Babcock looked at her sharply. "You still care for Stanton? Are you sure it's not the security of his money you care about?"

Cath jumped up. Her impulse was to walk out. But she remembered why she was here and the information she needed from Will Babcock. To find Wade she had to coax his whereabouts from Babcock. Cath forced herself to be seated.

"Sir, I've been supporting myself for four months and doing very well at it!"

"How did you support yourself?"

"I opened a millinery-design shop. I designed and sewed one-of-a-kind bonnets. Apparently I have a flair for it because the ladies were willing to pay me a great deal of money for each bonnet I designed for them."

"I can check that, you know," Will Babcock said slowly, watching her. "I have connections in Sioux City."

"Check it," Cath replied, looking Babcock straight in the eyes.

111

After a long silence where the banker and she stared at each other, Cath spoke. "You sound antagonistic, Mr. Babcock. Does that mean that you won't help me locate Wade?"

"You want to find him." Babcock's blue eyes pierced into hers. "Why?"

"I want to beg his forgiveness. I want to tell him how much I've missed him. I want to tell him I love him, only him."

Babcock continued studying her. At last he spoke. "All right. I believe you, and I'll do what I can. I think you should know, though, that you did a cruel thing, leaving Stanton as you did. I've never seen him so devastated. You really tore him up." He paused and added softly, "You see, he really loved you."

Cath pulled her linen handkerchief from her sleeve and dabbed at her nose. "Mr. Babcock," she asked, voice trembling, "do you think Wade will take me back?"

"My dear, I have no idea. But I can say this. If I were in Wade Stanton's boots, I think *I'd* give you a second chance." He hesitated, gave Cath a wistful smile, and added, "But, then, I always did have a soft spot for pretty ladies. And, of course, you haven't wounded me as you have Stanton."

Thursday, September 26, 1861

The roustabouts scurried around the pier, busy securing *The Blue Belle* to her moorings on the dock at Lac qui Parle, the tiny settlement where, according to Will Babcock, she would find Wade. Cath was astonished to learn that Wade had given up his nomadic river existence and gone to a frontier settlement. She'd always thought that when he quit the boats, he'd settle in St. Louis. Wade was sophisticated, cosmopolitan. She thought of him as a city-dweller, not a pioneer.

Cath grew breathless from anxiety. She trembled. What if Wade wouldn't even see her?

What if he was so angry that he wouldn't give her a chance?

When the gangplank was set, Cath was among the first passengers to disembark. Everyone seemed to be going in the same direction, so she joined the crowd moving up the street. Then she saw the sign, "The Last Chance Gaming Parlor." All the men were headed toward that building. It must be Wade's place. Cath hung back until the passengers of *The Blue Belle* had crowded inside. Then she pulled open the door and stepped in. The light was dim. Cath stood unmoving, waiting for her eyes to adjust

112

to the semi-darkness. She began to make out shapes of billiard tables and other gaming tables. From a distance came the music of fiddles.

A figure wearing a loose blue tunic was at her side. "Madam?" the person said. "Can I help?"

Cath squinted, turning in the direction of the voice. A Chinaman! Where on earth had Wade collected *him*?

"Yes," she answered. "I'd like to have a few words with Mr. Stanton — privately, that is."

"Did he send for you?" the fellow asked in a sing-song voice.

"No, I'm an old friend. A surprise for him."

The heavy eyelids narrowed. The Chinaman studied her. At last he spoke. "I put you in private dining room. Not used this time of day. Follow please."

In the dining room he spoke again. "I tell Mr. Stanton who calls?"

"No. I want to surprise him." Cath was so unsure of herself that she feared if Wade knew who it was, he might refuse to see her. He might tell the Chinaman to show her out.

The small man hesitated, then left, his blue tunic fluttering about his thin body.

Though the man had motioned for her to be seated, Cath stood. She was too nervous to hold still. To pass the time, she paced, circling the gleaming mahogany table, concentrating on placing her footsteps within the oval designs in the carpet.

The door handle rattled. Cath stopped pacing and stared as the door opened. Wade was halfway through the doorway when he recognized her. His astonished look showed that he hadn't expected her. Still gripping the door handle, he stopped in the doorway.

"Wade," Cath began. Her voice cracked. She swallowed and tried again. "Wade, can you forgive me? I beg you, forgive me!"

She ran to him and clutched his hand. He bent his head and gave her a stiff peck on the cheek. With the heel of his boot he kicked the door shut. "Where the hell did you go?"

Cath held back nothing. As she related her life and whereabouts during the past four months she began weeping, and the last part of her explanation was told through sobs. "And then I realized it was you I loved and nobody else," she finished, looking away from those unfriendly eyes.

"So you're penniless, have no place to go, and you thought you'd freeload with me for awhile again, eh?"

Cath took a step backwards and thrust her chin forward. "I'm not penniless! I have a lot of money! I told you my bonnet business was very successful. And I intend to repay you for the money I borrowed from you, too!"

His face softened a little. "Sunny," he said, his voice tight, "when you left me you broke my heart. I'm just starting to heal up. I don't feel like getting wounded again."

Cath realized she was still holding Wade's hand, stroking it, playing with his huge diamond ring. She clutched his hand harder and looked into his eyes. "I love you, Wade. I really love you. I was a child not to realize it before. But now I've grown up. I know how much I care for you. Wade, please take me back! I don't want to live without you!" She dropped his hand and threw herself against him, weeping silently.

For a long time Wade stood motionless, arms dangling limp at his sides. Finally, his hands gripped her shoulders. He thrust her away from him, looked into her eyes as if he wanted to read her mind. He took a deep breath, let it rush out. "Oh, Sunny gal! Are you really back?"

"To stay. Forever. With you."

"You know I can't marry you," he said.

"I want only to be with you."

Again, he searched her eyes, weighing her sincerity.

At last Wade grinned, and the dear dimples creased his cheeks. How long it had been since she'd seen them!

"Welcome home, Sunny," he said. His strong arms went around her, and she felt herself being crushed into his chest. Ah, this was as she'd dreamed, how she'd hoped it would be! Wade *was* forgiving her! She tipped her head back to look into his face. In the moment before Wade's lips pressed hard against hers, she saw tears in his eyes.

When Wade finally took his lips from hers, he spoke softly, his mustache tickling the skin of her cheek. "I'm glad you came back, Sunny. *Damn* glad!"

Suddenly, Cath remembered the coins sewn into her pantaloons. "Oh, Wade!" she cried, "I do want to repay you, and I'm sorry I stole your money."

Wade grinned his old roguish smile. "Steal? And how much did you steal?"

"Thirteen double eagles," she admitted. Then she began pulling at her crinolines, lifting up her voluminous skirt.

"Hey!" Wade laughed. "What are you doing? Put your skirt down, you little tease. One-Two might come in."

"But I have to get into my pantaloons to get the coins to repay you. That's where I keep them!"

Wade gave her a rakish grin. Taking her elbow, he said, "We'll worry about getting into your pantaloons upstairs in my quarters."

Friday, November 15, 1861

Cath relaxed in the comfortable sitting room in Wade's apartment above the gambling casino. The cheerful room let the afternoon sun sweep through the west window. Cath put the finishing stitches on a new bonnet for herself. Wade said that next week they'd go to St. Louis to spend the winter. Cath wanted sophisticated hats suitable for the city.

Their new life was idyllic. Her relationship with Wade had changed from what it had been before she "jumped ship," as Wade referred to her leaving him. Before, each had kept an emotional distance from the other. Neither had ever spoken the word "love" regarding their feelings toward the other. They'd lived tentatively, without any sense of permanence. Now, they each openly vowed their love to the other. They agreed that their relationship was permanent. If Wade had been free to marry, they would have married.

As Wade grew more secure, trusting Cath's love, they were able to joke about her foolish adventure of hunting down John McAffery.

"Well, sweet gandy dancer's garters!" Wade said the first time they discussed it. "I wasn't pure when I met you, and I haven't been a monk since you left. But, Sunny," he paused, then went on softly, "was he worth it?"

"Actually, Wade, he wasn't worth spit," Cath said, her eyes snapping at the unwelcome memory. "He was interested only in his own pleasure, with no thought to mine. It made me feel terrible to think of how I'd taken you and your ways so for granted." She looked down at her hands and then met his steady gaze. "The only good thing that came out of my running off is that now I appreciate you so much!" Cath threw herself into Wade's arms and smothered his face with kisses.

Laughing, Wade responded, and before long they moved into the bedroom.

After Cath confided to Wade that she hadn't enjoyed John McAffery's lovemaking, Wade grew more trusting. One day he laughingly confessed to Cath that he hadn't missed the coins she'd taken from his money belt. "If you hadn't confessed, my little Sunny, I never would've known."

Slowly, the story of Wade's last five months came out. At first he seemed hesitant to let her know how devastated he'd been over her desertion, but as he gained confidence in her love he talked about how horrible it had been for him. He had remained on *The Dragon Lady* and journeyed with it all the way up the Missouri River to Ft. Benton.

"Sioux City," he said, "was the last stop where there was a woodpile at the landing. From there on we had to live off the country. We shot antelope for meat; the second class passengers helped the crew cut wood. At the Yankton Agency while we were loading wood, the Sioux chiefs came aboard for a dole of whisky. Twice, once on the way up, and again on the way down, we were stopped for nearly half a day by a giant herd of buffalo crossing the river. Each time we filled the food locker with plenty of meat. Coming down, the crew caught nine buffalo calves. They penned them up on the boiler deck. At Ft. Berthold they caught a young grizzly bear and two coyotes. Along with all the bales of hides, we took interesting live cargo back to St. Louis."

Wade said he hadn't gambled at all on *The Dragon Lady* after Cath left. "I couldn't," he explained. "I think if I had, I would've lost everything. My heart wasn't in anything. I just sat in the saloon, drinking. The steward helped me to my stateroom when he saw that I couldn't get out of the chair by myself."

Wade picked up his Chinese houseboy, Won-tu, on that trip far up the Missouri River. Won-tu, or "One-Two," as everyone now called him, had run away from the heavy labor of laying steel rails of the spreading western railroads. His frail body hadn't been up to the long hours of hard labor. He was near starvation when Wade spotted him. Finding him to be a Chinese who spoke understandable English, Wade took him under his wing. The ever-grateful One-Two apparently had mothered Wade and helped bring him out of his despondency.

Cath was relieved that she and Wade trusted each other enough to be honest. And she *had* been totally honest with him, answering whatever questions he'd asked about her five-month absence. She'd been dishonest with Wade only once, and she didn't consider it being dishonest. Rather, she'd withheld information from him.

Soon after she arrived at Lac qui Parle and moved in with Wade, Cath feared she might be pregnant. She told herself that she was late because of her traveling and the nervousness she'd gone through trying to find Wade and worrying whether he'd take her back. When she began to feel nauseous in the morning she grew alarmed. She wouldn't have John McAffery's baby. She would not! She'd hate the poor thing — just looking into its eyes she'd be reminded constantly of how she'd hurt Wade, how she'd risked Wade's love for foolishness. Cath wasn't sure that Wade would accept a baby into their household. She didn't want one, either. A gambling casino in a frontier town was no place to rear a child. She would *not* have this baby.

Cath developed a plan. She persuaded Wade to give her riding lessons. "I've never ridden a horse, Wade. Certainly if we're to live here in the West I must learn to ride. How else can I get around in these huge distances?"

Wade was going to buy her a horse. At Cath's insistence, he postponed the purchase.

"I don't know if I'm going to like riding, Wade," she protested. "Can't you rent me a horse to practice on?"

Wade agreed, selecting a horse for her at the livery. Cath hated every minute of the riding lessons. She was afraid of horses. During the first lesson when Cath's rented white mare turned her head and gazed at her with huge eyes, Cath was sure the look was threatening.

"She wants to bite me!" she cried.

"Nonsense!" Wade laughed. "That mare is the gentlest horse in the stable."

By the third day, Wade decided it was time for Cath to learn to sit a trot. Though she hated the bouncing trot, Cath stuck with it because it was precisely this jostling that she hoped would loosen the baby from her womb.

After a week of daily lessons, Wade still didn't believe Cath's balance and confidence were where she was ready for cantering. This was fine with Cath. Terrified at the thought of streaking across the prairie on the back of a galloping horse, she was content to bounce on the wide back of the trotting white mare.

On the eighth day of Cath's riding lessons Wade had been instructing her for nearly an hour when a tumbleweed blew across the brown prairie in front of Cath's mare. Cath remembered the horse shying, and her fear when she realized the mare was rearing. After that she remembered nothing — not hitting the ground, nor how Wade got her to their apartment and into bed. When she opened her eyes, she looked around in confusion. Wade sat beside her, holding her hand. She'd been unconscious for six hours, he said.

Aside from a pounding headache, she'd suffered no ill effects. "I hate horses!" she'd grumbled.

"In that case, no more riding," Wade said. "If you want, I'll teach you to drive a horse from a buggy."

"Let's wait and see," she replied.

The day after she was thrown from her horse Cath saw the desired result of the riding lessons. She was no longer pregnant, if she had been — whether from the bouncing on the horse, or from the jarring fall, she didn't know. She was grateful there'd be no baby. This probably had been her one opportunity at motherhood since Wade seemed sure that his seed wasn't fertile. Even so, the thought didn't make her sad. She guessed she didn't have a strong urge to be a mother. Besides, her life style wasn't suitable.

With her silver sewing scissors she snipped the thread on the bonnet she was making. Holding it at arm's length, she admired her newest creation. It should be just perfect for winter in St. Louis.

Saturday, April 19, 1862

Since it was only a few blocks to the Henright's home, Cath decided to walk. It was a warm spring day, and she strolled happily, admiring the trees, nearly leafed out in tiny newborn leaves. Rose Henright had sent a messenger, letting Cath know that two letters had arrived yesterday, one for Cath, the other for Wade. As she thought of the awaiting letter, Cath walked faster. Surely the letter would announce the safe arrival of Rebecca's baby.

When she and Wade had arrived in St. Louis last November, Cath was delighted to find five letters from Rebecca awaiting her. Rose had kept them for her all that time. Rebecca's letter written in October had announced that she was "with child." Ever since, Cath's excitement had grown with the passing months.

At the Henright's three-story mansion, Cath tapped the door knocker. Austin, the Henright's British butler, opened the door.

"Good afternoon, Mrs. Stanton," he stepped aside for Cath to enter.

"Good afternoon, Austin. I've come to pick up letters that have arrived for me. Mrs. Henright sent word that they were here," Cath said.

"Yes, ma'am, I shall get them at once. Mrs. Henright is in the north parlor doing needlework. May I announce your presence?"

"Is she alone?"

"Yes, Mrs. Stanton."

"Very well, Austin. Please announce my arrival."

As Cath stepped into the parlor behind the butler, she admired the room. Its dark mahogany furniture contrasted nicely to the all-white walls and ceiling. A large crystal chandelier dominated the room, its facets sparkling from the reflections of the flames from the fireplace. Rose sat on a brocaded chair the color of a robin's egg. Head bent in concentration over her handiwork, her dark curls fell alongside her long, slender face. The moment the butler announced Cath's presence, Rose jumped up. After embracing Cath, Rose turned to the butler. "We'll have coffee, Austin, if you please."

Breathlessly, Cath spoke, "Oh, Rose, if you don't mind, could Austin get my letter first? I hope it's word from my sister that I'm an aunt!"

Rose smiled and nodded her assent to the butler. She motioned toward the Hepplewhite companion chair next to hers, and Cath seated herself, though she sat on the edge of the seat.

When Austin returned with the letters, Cath could scarcely contain herself. "Would you mind terribly, Rose?" Cath held up the letter.

"Read it, my dear," Rose laughed. "I'm dying to know, too."

Cath tore open the envelope. "A girl! Oh, Rose, it's a girl!" Cath cried, smiling broadly. "Listen to this. Dear Cath, On the second of this month Jason and I were blessed with an adorable baby girl. She has soft fuzzy auburn curls exactly the color of Jason's hair — and Papa's, too, of course. We've named her Gitty Anne. Jason says "Gitty" is a term of endearment for infants in Scotland. He says that since she is the dearest babe in the world, her name must be Gitty. Anne was my choice, so we have combined the two names. I keep calling her Gitty Anne, but Jason says only Gitty. I suspect our daughter will be known as Gitty.

"Oh, Cath, how I wish you could see your beautiful niece! I do hope you will try to come visit us soon. Your loving sister, Rebecca McDaniel."

Cath laid the letter in her lap. Her eyes were moist.

"We must send gifts," Rose announced. "What do you think we should get?"

119

At that moment Austin brought the coffee. While she prepared to pour, Rose said, "We must go shopping tomorrow, Cath. Shopping for infant gifts." It was said as a statement rather than as a suggestion. Cath smiled. Money gave power to a person. Rose's wealth gave her the confidence to make decisions according to her whims. Cath hoped to someday have so much money that she'd be like Rose.

Later, when Cath was leaving, Rose said, "I'll pick you up tomorrow at two and we'll shop."

Cath had walked perhaps two blocks from the Henright Manor when she passed a brightly-dressed young girl who walked so slowly that she scarcely moved. Cath realized the girl was crying. Turning back, Cath asked, "What's the matter, dear? Why are you crying?"

Between sobs, the young woman blurted out that she had no place to sleep and no money. Dark smudges smeared her cheeks. Cath saw that the girl was wearing an extraordinary amount of cosmetics. Could she be a tart? Cath studied her closer. She was a pretty young thing. Brown curls framed her face, and though her nose was sharp, her features were fine. Blue eyes, reddened from crying, were fringed with long lashes. Cath doubted that the girl was more than sixteen.

"Why are you homeless?" Cath asked.

At first, the girl was reluctant to talk, but when Cath made it clear that she was aware of her occupation, she seemed eager to cry her woes.

"Mizz Veronica toss me out!" she raged. "Just because I keep a bottle of French perfume a customer give me! A stinkin' bottle of perfume, and she boot me! No other house in St. Louis will hire me now!" she wailed. "Mizz Veronica will see to that!"

The girl's name was Jennie Tucker.

"I'll tell you what, Jennie Tucker," Cath said. "You can come home with me tonight. My husband is a gambler, and we have a casino up north on the Missouri River. I've been wanting to expand and have hurdy-gurdy dance girls to entertain and to dance — for a price — with the customers. This might be something you could do. It's only from May through November. Then we return to St. Louis for the winter. I guess you could make enough in six months to live quite well in St. Louis the other six."

When Wade returned to their apartment late that afternoon he was astonished to see a young stranger sitting in their parlor. Cath introduced them, then walked to the fireplace and picked up a letter lying on the mantle. "I picked up our letters at the Henrights today. This one's for you. And Wade, guess what! Becky had a little girl! I'm an aunt!"

"That's wonderful, Sunny," Wade murmured and kissed her absentmindedly. Cath could see that his thoughts were on the envelope in his hand.

"Read your letter," she said. "Who's it from?"

Frowning, Wade tore open the envelope. "It's from my Aunt Ophelia in Philadelphia. He scanned the letter. "Just a short note letting me know that my brother, Beauregard, is a cavalry officer fighting with Brigadier General T. J. Jackson. She says he was wounded in The Battle of Fair Oaks, but that she got word that he was mending."

"I didn't know you had a brother, Wade," Cath commented.

Uneasily, Wade cast a look at their visitor.

Cath caught his look. "Jennie, would you excuse us for a minute? We'll be right back." Cath strode toward their bedroom, Wade following.

Once inside the bedroom with the door closed, Wade burst out, "Sunny! Sweet gandy dancer's garters! What's that tart doing in our parlor?"

"She has no place to stay tonight. I've invited her to use our guest room."

"Have you lost your mind?" Wade exploded.

"No," she smiled sweetly. "I'm thinking of opening a hurdy-gurdy dancehall in connection with your casino. One dollar a dance, and the girls keep half. I think we could make money."

Wade regarded her thoughtfully. "Just how much money do you want, Sunny?"

Cath cocked her head, thinking. "I want so much money that I never have to ask how much something costs."

"That's a lot of money," he answered. Then, as if brushing off an unwelcome thought, he asked, "What are we going to do with Miss Tart out there?"

"We'll have dinner with her and get to know her to see if she's a good candidate for The Last Chance Gaming Parlor. Not everyone could take the isolation there."

"I'll not have dinner with a whore!" Wade hissed.

"Oh, fiddle! Men!" Cath clucked her tongue. "You'll sleep with them, but you won't eat with them. Silly! Of course, you'll join us for dinner!"

121

"No thank you!" Wade turned on his heel and reached for the doorknob. Before opening the door, he turned to Cath and said, "Have a pleasant dinner with your new friend! Good night!"

Chapter 11
The Lucky Pearl

Sunday, June 15, 1862

Cath managed to gather eighteen girls willing to leave St. Louis and try their luck as hurdy-gurdy dancers at the Last Chance Gaming Parlor at Stimsonville on the muddy Missouri River. Wade's original hostility to Cath's idea had given way first to patronizing amusement and eventually to a reluctant acknowledgement that the girls were popular with his patrons. Cath knew that the girls were more than just "popular," though she didn't press it with Wade. She was positive that the presence of attractive girls available for dancing drew many steamboat passengers who might not be enthusiastic about gambling, or have the wherewithal to chance losing it at the faro or poker tables.

While still in St. Louis, during the weeks before they boarded the northbound boat, Wade kept busy courting steamboat captains and steamship line owners, persuading them to schedule overnight stops at Stimsonville so passengers could spend an evening gambling at his casino. Wade used the persuasive arguments that the passengers would enjoy the diversion, and that his Last Chance Gaming Parlor was indeed their last chance on the way upriver.

In May they boarded *The Golden Eagle,* a graceful white steamboat bound for Ft. Benton. Huge paintings of handsome golden eagles decorated the massive wheel covers protecting the paddlewheels on either side of the boat. None of Cath's collected girls had ever been aboard a steamboat before. They squealed with excitement over the opulent furnishings. Though Cath had lived aboard many steamboats, she was impressed with the beauty of *The Golden Eagle's* decorations. The ceiling of the main saloon projected above the hurricane deck, forming a clerestory to provide skylights. Supporting the ceiling was a double row of white columns on each side with elaborate capitals from which sprung carved arches embellished with pendants and finials. A large mirror at the stern reflected the whole saloon, making it seem twice its actual length. During daylight hours the saloon was a kaleidoscope of color from the light flickering through the bright skylights. At night it became a glittering fairy palace, each facet of the glass prisms dangling from the chandeliers beaming prickles of light which were reflected in all the mirrors.

Once aboard *The Golden Eagle* Wade seemed astonished at the numbers and colorfulness of Cath's retinue of eighteen St. Louis "ladies of the night," as he had begun to call them after he saw how angry Cath got when he called them "whores."

Firmly, Cath insisted that the girls tone down their flamboyant cosmetics. "Study the other female passengers," she told them. "Wear only just a hint more color than they're wearing. You are dance girls — artists. You can wear theatrical makeup when you're working, but none of this heavy-handed tart coloring in public! You're starting a new life — a more respectable life!"

Once they arrived at Stimsonville Wade hired carpenters to build a barracks-like addition to The Last Chance. The front of the new addition, which butted up against the rear of the original building, served as a dance floor, and the rear of the new structure was housing for the hurdy-gurdy girls. Wade was going to build one large room like an enlisted man's barracks, but Cath insisted upon individual rooms for each of the eighteen girls. "They can be small rooms," she said, "but each girl must have her own room!"

Squinting, Wade looked down at her, his dark eyes twinkling, dimples creasing his cheeks. "I thought your girls were going to be hurdy-gurdies," he grinned.

Cath tossed her bright curls. "Well, yes," she said, "for now. But we'll see what develops. These girls are ambitious and adventurous. I'm guessing most of them will want to make more money than dancing brings. I won't push them into anything, but I want to make sure they can expand their talents if they choose. I want a separate room for each of the girls!"

Wade shook his head, smiling. He instructed the workmen to build partitions, making individual bedrooms in the new building.

While the new construction was going on, the inside of The Last Chance Saloon was brightened. Huge oil paintings of flamboyantly buxom nude women were hung on the walls. Replacing the mirror over the bar was a colorful painting of a naked woman reclining on a burgundy satin drapery. The bright coppery-brown hair which cascaded across the subject's bare shoulders was unusual. Wade said the painting was over two hundred years old and that he considered it an investment. He'd paid dearly for it, but paintings by this artist were appreciating in value. This artist's name was "Titian," and he'd always painted women with that color of hair, Wade said. Cath didn't think it was particularly special. Pa and Jason's hair was that color, and she'd never thought it attractive. She preferred men with dark hair like Wade's. Then Cath remembered that little Gitty's hair was auburn. Cath cocked her head and studied the portrait of the nude lady. She decided that copper-colored hair was attractive on a woman.

On the far end of the long mahogany bar were arranged exquisite decanters of silver and cranberry glass, surrounded by sparkling bottles of fine brandies.

Wade installed new lighting fixtures which corrected the former dimness of the casino. Now, with Cath's hurdy-gurdies here, it was important for the lighting to be brighter to show off their loveliness.

Since faro was becoming a prestige game, Wade set up two more faro tables. Faro was at least as popular as poker. Interested onlookers crowded around the big faro tables, watching players place bets on the colorful waxed cloth which had every card from ace to king painted on it. On a high stool perched the "lookout" who watched for trouble or for a player shifting his bet while the cards were being drawn from the faro box.

Along the inside wall of the casino were long tables where patrons played keno. The dealer turned the bird-shaped wire cage called the "keno goose," and then drew a number from it. A happy cry of "Keno!" meant the number was the one a patron had been waiting for.

The poker tables were just as popular as faro, but because faro was such a colorful game to watch, the faro tables were always more crowded. Wade played nothing but poker, and then only for high stakes with special patrons.

On a small raised stage far back in the casino four fiddlers tuned up, getting ready for their evening's entertaining.

Carried by the warm south wind, the clang of a steamboat bell announced its imminent arrival. In the few weeks they'd been here, seldom had a steamboat passed without stopping. Whether this was due to Wade's

125

persuasive powers with the captains and steamship line owners in St. Louis, or whether it was from word-of-mouth praise from satisfied patrons, they didn't know. But Cath knew Wade was pleasantly surprised at the increase in business and in the number of boats mooring for the night so their passengers could enjoy the pleasures of The Last Chance Saloon.

As Cath's gaze swept the casino she saw Wade strolling toward her, weaving his way through the faro tables. When he reached her side, his hands stroked the bare skin of her arms, and she shivered with pleasure at his touch.

He pulled his gold watch from his vest pocket. "Four o'clock. I'm betting this boat puts up for the night. Sunny, my dear, it seems we have a thriving business!" As he grinned down at her, his teeth gleamed white against his dark moustache.

Wade sent One-Two to meet the boat. With him One-Two carried a handwritten invitation to the captain to be the dinner guest of Wade Stanton this evening.

Less than an hour later boat passengers filled the casino. As Cath maneuvered her wide hooped skirt among the dancers the silvery head of a customer caught her attention. Looking more closely, she realized that the man, who was examining the casino with interest, was Will Babcock. Quickly, she hurried toward him.

"Will! Will Babcock!" she called.

He turned, smiling broadly when he recognized her.

"What on earth are you doing here?" Cath asked.

"Well, news of your and Wade's success has reached even St. Joseph, my dear," Babcock said. "I'm here on business, with an investment proposition."

"Wade will be so glad to see you." Cath took the banker's arm. "Let's go find him." Into Babcock's ear she whispered, "He *did* take me back you see, and we're very, very happy."

He squeezed her arm. "I'm rewarded to hear that."

They found Wade in the dining room checking preparations for dinner. He was delighted to see Babcock. "One-Two!" he bellowed in the direction of the kitchen. "Set one more place at this table!" Immediately, the small Chinese man floated silently into the dining room, carrying another place setting of delicate Spode. Cath watched One-Two as he fastidiously arranged the silverware and folded the white linen napkin into a tulip blossom shape. One-Two was fast becoming more than a houseboy. He ordered groceries, planned menus and bossed the cook unmercifully. He tried to assert his opinions and rules on the dance girls, but so far they'd ignored his scoldings.

Soon they were joined by Captain Logue, whose sidewheeler, *The Lucibelle*, had moored at the wharf. While Wade questioned the captain and Babcock about late news of the war, One-Two poured into their wine glasses a fine Beaujolais-Villages, which was chilled, unlike most red wines. Wade insisted that Beaujolais tasted its best when it was served exactly as it comes out of the casks in the cellars among the rolling French hills where it is produced.

The captain brought welcome news that the Union had retaken New Orleans, Baton Rouge and Natchez. "We'll free the Mississippi of those rebels," he said, his sharp, pointed nose twitching with distaste. "They hold Vicksburg and Port Hudson, but we'll rout them out of there."

The main course was buffalo hump steak, roasted brown and crisp on the outside, pink and juicy within. Cooked in the meat juice and served with the meat was a hearty Yorkshire pudding. Captain Logue dabbed at his blond moustache. "This is absolutely delicious, madame. My compliments to the cook."

Cath nodded graciously.

"No wonder your place is so popular, Stanton, with food like this!" he continued.

"We don't feed our customers," Wade explained. "We have a bar for liquors, but that's it. You see, they have your excellent food on your boat, and they don't need to dine here."

Will Babcock cleared his throat. "And that brings me to my business and why I'm here. Word travels fast up and down the river. Your set-up here has become the talk of the river. Everyone wants to come here. It's like taking the waters at a new, well-touted spa. I'm here to propose that we build a hotel nearby so that patrons can spend a few days if they wish. I've some money to invest, and I can't think of a better place to put money right now."

"I don't have either the time or the inclination to run a hotel," Wade protested.

"No, I don't imagine you do," Babcock agreed. "But I can find and send up an experienced hotel manager, chef, and there will have to be chambermaids and housing for hotel workers."

Her head almost whirling, Cath dreamed of boarding houses being built and people moving to Stimsonville until it was a bustling frontier town like Sioux City.

By the time the men finished their plans for the new hotel, Captain Logue had become a partner with Will Babcock and Wade. Following dinner the three men toasted their future with glasses of cognac.

Sometime in the middle of the night, the casino began to empty. Cath noticed that many dance girls had disappeared, and she guessed they were in their rooms with their dance partners. She bit her lip. Somehow she had to figure a system where she made sure she got fifty percent of everything, and not just the dance tickets. Already she was getting fifty cents out of the dollar dance tickets, but she wanted a percent of the bedroom favors. Someone trustworthy would have to be put in charge of recording appointments and collecting the money.

Wade stepped out of the shadows. "Tired?" he asked.

"A little," she admitted. "Let's slip out and walk by the lake." They went through a side door and walked to the shore of the small lake which was less than fifty yards from The Last Chance. A quarter moon dimly lit the rippling surface of the water. Though there was scarcely any breeze, tiny wavelets lapped against the shore, making whispering sounds. Hand-in-hand, she and Wade strolled along the soft, sandy shore shaded by willows, hickories, and cottonwoods. Cath could see why the French had named the lake, "The Lake Which Speaks."

"Sunny, my love," Wade spoke softly, "I think we're going to be a hell of a success."

"It does look that way, doesn't it? If a banker and a boat captain believe enough to invest their own money, we must have a good chance." She swatted a mosquito off her bare arm.

Wade stopped walking and turned Cath to face him. Cupping her cheeks with both of his hands, he kissed her lips gently. Cath gripped his dark head from behind and pulled him toward her lips. With that, he drew her body to his and enfolded her in a hard embrace.

When Wade released her, he took her elbow in his hand, guiding her toward the dark shape of The Last Chance. "I think it's time we retired for the night," he grinned.

Cath squeezed his arm and giggled girlishly. Wade could make her forget about managing the business and making money. When she was in Wade's arms she felt like a young girl.

It was nearly noon when she awakened. Wade already had left. When Cath went to the kitchen for coffee One-Two was muttering to himself. She seated herself at the small kitchen table and sipped the strong brew.

"All right, One-Two," she said, "what's the matter? Tell me!"

After much garbled gibberish Cath discovered that One-Two was disgusted with Wade. One-Two said that last evening Wade had won fifteen hundred dollars from two Wisconsin youths who were on their way west to make their fortune. "They loss they fahtune!" One-Two sputtered. Apparently, this morning Wade arose early to get to *The Lucibelle* before she left. He returned the fifteen hundred dollars to the two surprised young men with the warning that they should never gamble again.

One-Two thought Wade foolish to return the money. Cath smiled softly as she sipped the steaming coffee. Wade was a gentleman — a warm and thoughtful person. How good of him to return his winnings to those boys! Perhaps he'd taught them a lesson they'd never forget.

Absently, Cath watched One-Two fuss around the kitchen, his long black queue wound tightly around his head. One-Two said the fashion of Chinese men wearing a queue dated back to the Manchu conquest of China two hundred and fifty years ago. The men were required to shave the front part of their heads and braid the rest of their hair in a long braid tied with a heavy black silk tassel. Though One-Two twisted his queue around his head when he wanted it out of his way, Cath noticed that as a sign of courtesy, he always loosened it before serving meals or answering the door.

Friday, August 15, 1862

Two months later a three-story frame hotel, The Golden Swan, was not only erected, but in business, its forty rooms always being three-quarters occupied. Though nothing great in appearance — Wade called it "The Yellow Goose" — the hotel was comfortable, and with One-Two planning menus and keeping a close rein on the chef, the cuisine was declared "excellent" by the guests of The Golden Swan.

During those warm summer months Cath persuaded Wade to let her plan a secluded garden and ladies' beach area on the shores of Lac qui Parle. Using solid boards, at Cath's direction workmen erected a six-foot high stockade enclosing a sizable area between the girls' living quarters and the edge of the lake. Once completed, Cath explained to the girls that this was their private area for their use during their off-hours to enjoy the cooling breezes from the lake.

When Wade saw how much Cath's girls enjoyed relaxing in the fresh air, he ordered trellises erected for shade so the girls were protected from the harsh sun. He bought a canoe, the kind of boat the Indians and mountain men used, so the girls could paddle about the lake.

Late in July Cath had another idea. She had been puzzling how she could make female steamboat passengers feel welcome. She knew that no lady would enter a gambling casino, but Cath suspected that there were some wives who resented having to remain alone aboard ship. And that meant that there were husbands who either didn't go ashore to visit The Last Chance, or if they did, they probably dared not remain for long. Finally, Cath thought of a solution. Her girls seldom used their outdoor garden and beach in the late afternoon or evening because they went to work in the casino at mid-afternoon and sometimes, earlier, if a steamboat docked.

Cath talked to her girls, explaining her plan. "After three in the afternoon, the garden is not to be used by any of you. I'm going to install a gateway from the outside into the garden, and after three o'clock the garden will be for the use of lady ship passengers, if I can persuade them to use it."

Each time a steamboat docked, One-Two was dispatched to the wharf to deliver a dinner invitation to the captain, and to invite ladies of the boat to use a special ladies' garden on the shores of Lac qui Parle. At first, no ladies came. Then late one afternoon four wives let themselves in through the outside gate and looked about uneasily. Quickly, Cath asked One-Two to make his special brand of Chinese tea, and to serve it to the four ladies in the garden along with some of his special Chinese cookies.

One-Two put on an outstanding performance as he went through his imaginative and elaborate motions of serving tea, Chinese style. Thoroughly enchanted with their Oriental host, the ladies lingered for nearly two hours, enjoying the whispers of the water and the cooling breeze. Word spread, and female passengers began to frequent the shoreline garden. Cath had scored another victory. The Last Chance moved a step closer toward gentility. The unspoken code of ethics now decreed that it was proper for wives to partake of The Last Chance's hospitality as long as they remained outdoors. One-Two enjoyed performing his tea service for visiting ladies. Cath believed it was a small price to furnish tea and cookies and a bit of One-Two's time to woo the ladies. Dealers reported that male passengers were staying longer and gambling higher stakes now that their wives weren't displeased or feeling abandoned. Patrons commented favorably about the entertainment for their wives and expressed appreciation for it.

Slowly during those summer months a change began to take place. More and more, passengers entering the casino referred to it as "The Lucky Pearl." Puzzled at first, Wade finally figured out that this was the frontier pronunciation of the French name "Lac qui Parle."

Down on the wharf a passenger would ask another, "Are you going to The Lucky Pearl?"

"If that name sticks," Wade laughed, "I think we'll have to change the old Last Chance's name."

"I think 'The Lucky Pearl' has a nice ring to it — especially for a gambling house," Cath offered. "The word 'Lucky' has got to be a great asset and 'Pearl" makes you think of riches. I think we should change the name."

Then came the day when one of the patrons spoke to Cath, calling her "Pearl." Startled, Cath looked up at the customer, wondering who he meant, but then she understood. He believed that she was "the Pearl" of "The Lucky Pearl."

When she reported this to Wade, he burst out in gales of laughter. "You asked for it, Sunny!" he howled. "Pearl sounds like a madam's name! If the shoe fits..."

Cath reached down, pulled off her kid slipper, and hurled it at Wade, who ducked, laughing.

Actually, Cath didn't mind being called "Pearl" by their patrons. "Mrs. Stanton" seemed too formal for casino language, as well as dishonest, though everyone but Will Babcock thought she and Wade were married.

Cath didn't feel like a madam, perhaps in part because of her appointment of Vera to supervise the scheduling of clients and the collection of advance fees. From the beginning, as soon as they'd arrived from St. Louis, Cath was aware that Vera disliked dancing with customers. She even seemed to have a quiet distaste for bedding them. A shy girl, Vera was the plainest and the least desired of the eighteen girls. When Cath approached Vera to suggest she consider devoting her time to collecting fees and keeping records instead of entertaining customers, the girl's face lit up in a delighted broad smile. Cath never had seen Vera so animated. Congratulating herself on her choice, Cath smiled to think how well Vera filled the roll. In a large ledger Vera kept all the financial records, recording each transaction with meticulous penmanship. Vera's eyes took on a new sparkle as she relished her work as "bookkeeper," and "appointment secretary."

One-Two made Wade and Cath's life easier. Daily, Cath's respect and admiration for him grew. She suspected that much of their nearly instantaneous success was due to the talents of this remarkable Chinaman. Gliding silently about the casino, he supervised everything.

However, one thing disturbed Cath — the attitude of her hurdy-gurdies toward One-Two. They attempted to order him around, and they paid no attention to his requests or commands. Tittering and laughing, their attitude toward him was that he was a strange and silly buffoon.

One day Cath was in the girls' parlor, a spacious room which served as a lounging area for the girls when they weren't working. She was helping Vera apply hot milk to freckles which had appeared on her hands after Vera neglected to wear gloves outside. One-Two entered the parlor and announced that water was heated for baths for two ladies.

"It's your turn for the first one, Elsa," Vera called to a dark Latin beauty across the room. At that moment Nancy, a pretty blonde, entered the room wearing only cambric pantaloons. Her naked round breasts bobbed as she strutted across the room. "It's my turn for the second bath," she told One-Two.

Cath's hands flew to her throat. Nancy wasn't the least bothered at showing her nakedness to One-Two! No one else seemed to think anything of it, either. Apparently, the girls didn't think of One-Two as a man. Cath walked toward One-Two. A trickle of perspiration slid down his temple.

"Nancy, go cover yourself," she muttered to the girl. Nancy threw Cath a puzzled look. Cath jerked her head toward the door. With a shrug of her shoulders, which set her breasts to bobbing again, Nancy flounced from the room.

That evening Cath couldn't get One-Two out of her thoughts. He was a special person. She felt sorry for him in his isolation, far from his country and countrymen. That night as they got ready for bed, Cath spoke to Wade about it. "Wade, I've been worrying about One-Two. He needs a wife, but where on earth could we find a Chinese girl?"

Wade straightened up from the bootjack, and with a grunt he pulled his foot out of his boots. "One-Two already has a wife back in China. That's what he's working and saving for — to get enough money for her passage to California. When that day comes, he'll go to San Francisco to meet her boat, he says."

132

Raising her brows at this new information, Cath thought about it. "And when One-Two goes to California to meet his wife, we'll lose him," she said.

"It'll be years before he gets enough money."

"I wouldn't be so sure," Cath warned. "Last week I saw him give money to a patron, and later that same patron gave One-Two a goodly amount of money. One-Two just might get a big win."

"Damn that Chinaman's yellow hide!" Wade stormed. "I told him he wasn't allowed to gamble — not in my casino!"

Cath laid a restraining hand on Wade's arm. "Wade, let me make a suggestion. One-Two needs a woman. He's a young man, he's exposed to all these pretty young things here. Let's loan him the money to send for his wife. That way he'll have a woman, and I think he'd be so grateful that you could count on his services for the rest of his life. He's a valuable asset, and you know it. Besides, it would be a kind and Christian thing to do."

"When did you begin to think about the Christian way to do things?" Wade raised his eyebrows. "As a matter of fact, One-Two's no Christian."

"Doesn't matter. Oh, Wade," she cried, "It would please me so much if we could do this for One-Two."

Looking at her sharply, Wade said, "It'll be a lot of money to loan him. When he goes to California to meet her, he'll be gone a long time. It's a dangerous trip. We might never see One-Two or our money again."

"One-Two's worth a lot of money," Cath said softly.

At breakfast the next day when Wade and Cath were sipping their first cup of coffee, One-Two glided silently into the room with a tray of steaming biscuits.

"One-Two," Wade drawled, leaning back in his chair, "Miss Cath has suggested that we loan you money for ship passage to America for your wife. Would you accept the loan?"

One-Two's always unreadable expression crumpled. He set the platter of biscuits down on the table so hard that several biscuits fell off, rolling across the white tablecloth, leaving a wake of golden flakes. Quickly, he pulled a large white handkerchief from the sleeve of his blue tunic and buried his face in it. He uttered not a sound, but from the heaving of his thin shoulders, Cath could tell that One-Two was crying.

At last he stopped shaking. The handkerchief was returned to his sleeve. "Thankee, missee," he said bowing and bobbing to Cath. "Thankee, misser," he bowed to Wade.

"Get the letter to your wife written, One-Two," Wade said. "Then on our way down river in November we'll stop in St. Joseph. Will Babcock should know how to go about sending money to China."

One-Two became a new man. The inscrutable expression disappeared. Now he moved through the casino with a broad smile on his face, chattering happily to himself in his native tongue. He even began to put on a little weight, losing the wraith-like look. It was good to see him happy. Cath hoped it wouldn't take too long to bring his wife to California.

Chapter 12
One-Two and Ten-Fu

Saturday, August 23, 1862

Cath and Wade were sleeping when the caravan of three Conestoga wagons led by four men on horseback rumbled into Stimsonville. Dimly, Cath heard the excited barking of dogs. It was the shouts of "Indian uprising!" which brought her wide awake. In his nightshirt Wade ran to the window.

"Where's the uprising?" he called down to the riders. "And where are you going?"

Her heart pounding, Cath slipped on a velvet robe and joined Wade at the window. The wagons had stopped next door in front of The Golden Swan. Each wagon was driven by a woman wearing a calico dress. Cath couldn't make out the women's faces because of the huge brims of their sunbonnets.

The rider on the lead horse removed his straw hat and called up to Wade, "First the red devils attacked the Lower Agency and Fort Ridgely. Was about eight hundred of 'em, they say. Then the Injuns turned on New Ulm and burnt it. Most people escaped. Now them Injuns is spreading out all over these parts, burnin', stealin', killin'!"

Wade called, "Where are you headed?"

"Why, we come to Stimsonville," the rider answered. "Safety in numbers, ain't they?"

"Well, sir," Wade answered grimly, "I guess there's numbers here all right, but I doubt if there's a dozen guns in town. The population of Stimsonville is mostly dancehall girls, card dealers and chambermaids — hardly what I'd call a protective body."

The rider was silent while he thought this over. Finally, he made up his mind. "Be that as it may, we be a sight safer here than out on our farms miles from nowheres. Our womenfolk is scared witless out there." He motioned back toward the sweeping prairie to the east.

And so the farmers settled in to camp in the street in front of The Lucky Pearl and The Golden Swan. When the farm women discovered that their sanctuary was a gambling casino they were horrified. They chose to remain in their wagons rather than accept Wade's offer of putting them up in the casino. Wade provided meals for the eight adults and twenty-one children who'd taken refuge outside his establishment. Several of the dancehall girls helped One-Two carry meals out to the wagons. The children stared wide-eyed and frightened at the Oriental, while their mothers glared at the brightly-dressed hurdy gurdies.

Word of the Sioux uprising spread quickly throughout the western waters. The river boats steamed past, no longer stopping at Stimsonville. Though passengers might wish to gamble their money, they had no urge to gamble their lives.

Wade owned four pistols. The day the refugees arrived he took Cath and One-Two out to the edge of the settlement to teach them how to shoot. Quickly, One-Two showed himself to be an accurate marksman.

"Are you sure you've never fired a pistol before?" Wade gave his Chinese houseboy a suspicious look.

One-Two smiled his mysterious grin. "Why would poor Chinaboy shoot gun?" he asked with a shrug of his thin shoulders.

Cath was not good with the pistol. She hated the loud reports. She kept closing her eyes just before she squeezed the trigger.

Finally, Wade gave up on her, deciding it was a waste of ammunition to continue. "The main thing, Sunny," he said, "is that you know how to load it and how to pull the trigger." He looked at her soberly, his dark eyes burning into hers. "If the Indians come and if it appears they're going to overwhelm us, I want you to put this pistol to your head, right here," he tapped her temple, "and pull the trigger."

Cath gasped. Her knees buckled, and she would have fallen if Wade hadn't grabbed her elbows.

With his index finger he touched her cheek, tracing the curve of her cheekbone down to her chin. "Better dead, Sunny, than to be taken captive by the Sioux. Believe me. They torture their prisoners. The squaws are even more vicious than the braves. Kill yourself, Sunny, or they'll kill you a piece at a time in hours, days, or weeks of unspeakable suffering."

Wednesday, October 15, 1862

Late in September General Henry Sibley defeated the Sioux near Wood Lake and seized fifteen hundred prisoners, successfully putting down the fearful uprising. The farm families camping in front of The Lucky Pearl hitched up their teams and returned to their homes. Late one morning when Cath arose she glanced out the window and saw they were gone. According to One-Two, they left before dawn without saying so much as "good-bye" or "thank you." Cath was relieved to have them gone. The disapproving glares from the farm wives had irritated her. Though she felt no guilt over her present position, Cath felt a certain loneliness for female companionship. It would've been nice to chat with the women a bit, to hear about their children and what their lives were like. Except for Vera, her hurdy gurdies were too immature and frivolous to be companions. The frontier was a rough and lonely place for women. There were so few women. Cath thought they should stick together and be supportive.

Steamboats still docked at the wharf to unload supplies, but the passengers stayed aboard. Even the captains declined Wade's invitations for dinner. No one wanted to come ashore and risk getting scalped.

One-Two said that when he went to the wharf to deliver dinner invitations and to encourage passengers to disembark and spend time in The Lucky Pearl, the passengers leaned against the guardrails and called down to him, "Hey, Chinaman! You're goin' to lose your pigtail!"

"Inyuns all gone!" One-Two tried to reassure them.

Finally, Wade himself went to meet a steamboat, but no amount of coaxing could convince the captain and passengers that the area was safe again. This made Wade decide that they might as well close The Lucky Pearl and The Golden Swan early for the winter.

The hurdy gurdy girls were delighted at the prospect of returning to St. Louis. Though all of them had a better life at The Lucky Pearl than they'd had in St. Louis, they were isolated and a little bored in Stimsonville. St. Louis offered them the variety and excitement of a city.

One-Two went ahead to the wharf with the girls and all their baggage to get it loaded on the steamboat. Wade turned the key in the front entrance door to The Lucky Pearl, and patted the white post supporting the canopy. "Goodbye, old girl," he said to the casino. "Take care of yourself. We'll see you in spring."

Tuesday, December 31, 1869

Cath smoothed her blond curls lovingly with long strokes of her boar-bristle brush. She was looking forward to the New Year's ball at the Henright mansion this evening. Having completed her bath, she had only to arrange her hair and she'd be ready. Earlier, Wade had left their quarters, saying he'd have a surprise for her when he returned. Cath suspected it had something to do with the ball this evening. His eyes had been twinkling when he left.

Cath gazed in the mirror, examining the skin at the corners of her eyes for signs of aging. Now that she had turned thirty, she knew she'd lost her girlish freshness. She'd put on weight, though Wade insisted she'd put it on in the right places. Wade had changed hardly at all. His body was still muscular, lean and firm. The dark hair at his temples had turned a becoming gray, only adding to his handsomeness. One concession to age Wade had been forced to make now that he was forty-three years old was to wear spectacles for reading. For a long time Wade had avoided using eyeglasses. Every year he had been forced to hold newspapers farther and farther from his eyes. When he began squinting Cath had interfered.

"Wade, for heaven's sake, how can you be so vain?" she'd burst out. "Get some reading spectacles! You'd look a lot less silly wearing them than you do trying to stretch your arms to twice their length!"

As she continued brushing her hair Cath thought about the past years and how good they'd been to her and to Wade. Of course, the ending of the war had been good for everyone. Wade's Aunt Ophelia had written that his brother Beauregard had survived the war, but that the family plantation house had been burned by the Yankees. Without their slaves the Stantons could no longer harvest cotton, and the aunt didn't know how the family could survive. In a very broad hint, she suggested that Wade send money. Cath wondered if he had.

Of her original eighteen hurdy gurdies, eight were still with Cath. Three had been lost to marriage. They'd boarded an upriver steamboat and disappeared with their new husbands into the treeless expanse of the West. Each winter one or two girls were lost in St. Louis, having succumbed to overdosing themselves with the popular but deadly laudanum.

138

In May the whole nation celebrated when the Union Pacific and the Central Pacific Railroads met in Utah. It seemed almost a miracle to think that now one could cross the country by rail in relative ease from New York to California. It seemed even more of a miracle when Cath thought of the difficulties One-Two had undergone in getting to California six years ago, when he journeyed there to meet his wife. The moment that Vicksburg was recaptured by the Union in 1863, the Mississippi River was once again available to the Union as a road to the sea. As soon as normal riverboat traffic resumed, Wade and Cath had put One-Two on a steamboat for New Orleans, where he transferred to an ocean-going vessel bound for Panama.

Two years later, in April of 1865 the rebels had surrendered to General Grant at Appomattox, but One-Two had not returned from California. Gruffly, Wade said he'd probably used the money to buy his own passage back to China, or perhaps he'd been drowned at sea. Cath was sure that One-Two hadn't returned to China. From little things he'd said she had the impression that One-Two couldn't go back. Perhaps there was a price on his head back there in The Celestial Empire. Cath missed the efficient and droll little Oriental. She worried a lot about him. Perhaps because it had been her idea to loan him the money to go to California, she felt responsible for his well-being. If tragedy had befallen One-Two, Cath believed she was to blame. Those times when she was feeling especially blue, she chastised herself for sending him off. At best it was a perilous trip, but for a small foreigner whose knowledge of American customs and ways was even less than his ability with the language, the way was barred by all sorts of pitfalls. Time after time, Cath pictured the little Chinese robbed and dead, lying in some forgotten alley of New Orleans or San Francisco.

On a steamy, hot July afternoon in 1865 Cath had been relaxing outside The Lucky Pearl in the secluded garden when the outside door had opened and two dark shapes moved into the garden. With a gasp Cath jumped up and ran toward the taller figure. It was One-Two! He *had* returned! She hugged him and hugged him. Sobs of relief wrenched at her chest. Tears of happiness ran down her cheeks as she clasped the thin Chinaman to her. When at last she was able to control herself, One-Two stepped back a pace. He introduced a lovely little woman, his wife.

"Miz Cath, please meet my wife, Ten-Fu," he said in almost perfect English.

When Cath moved to embrace the timid woman she realized that Ten-Fu was carrying an infant swaddled in a dark gray cloak.

"A baby!" Cath cried. "One-Two, you've got a baby!"

"Yes, missy," he bobbed and rocked with pleasure. "I have fine son."

"What's his name?"

Beaming, One-Two replied, "Henry W. Longfellow Hung."

Cath smiled. One-Two would not be returning to China. Not with a son named Henry W. Longfellow Hung.

Ringing a silver bell for service, Cath asked her current maid, Elsie, to make tea.

"Ah, no," One-Two protested. "May I? Ten-Fu has brought special tea leaves from China. I should like to prepare them properly."

"Of course," Cath agreed. "One-Two, your English! Your English is almost perfect! How did you do it?"

"I am to teach Ten-Fu English, so we made pact not to speak Mandarin for six days out of every week. She has learned English fast, and it has improved mine," he explained.

As they sipped the aromatic tea prepared by One-Two, he gave a sketch of his life during the past two years. Once his ship anchored at the isthmus of Panama, One-Two had walked across Panama following a mule train. Men with machetes led the way ahead of the train, hacking away the overgrowth of vines which continually tried to reclaim the path through the jungle. In the tropical heat, he walked through ankle-deep muck. Mosquitoes had been terrible. Right then One-Two had vowed that on his return trip, when he had his wife along, he would rent horses, which are faster, though more expensive, than mules. On the Pacific side of the isthmus he boarded a small two-masted brig called the *Victorine*. Twenty-five days out of Panama it ran out of rations. Passengers had nothing to eat but tea and, twice a day, a spoonful of molasses. As if that weren't trouble enough, the ship sprang a leak. All able-bodied passengers had to man the pumps. At last they had anchored at Old San Diego, a coaling station. One-Two went ashore, leaving the *Victorine* behind.

Once in San Francisco he waited months for Ten-Fu's ship to arrive. When it arrived, Ten-Fu was in ill health. One-Two decided they should remain in San Francisco until she regained her strength. After three months, when he thought her well enough to withstand another ocean voyage, he booked passage on *The Golden Gate,* a beautiful Vanderbilt Company ocean liner which plied the ocean between California and New York, rounding treacherous Cape Horn on each voyage. Passengers bound for the western United States disembarked at Panama. One-Two had been assured that this ship would offer a safer voyage than his perilous one on the leaky, scantily-provisioned *Victorine*.

Their voyage to Panama had gone smoothly. One-Two hired horses to cross the isthmus. This helped them avoid some of the hardships of that grueling twenty-five-mile tramp through jungle.

On their trip northward through the Gulf of Mexico they encountered violent storms. As their ship tossed in giant waves, both One-Two and Ten-Fu suffered terrible seasickness.

"By the time we arrive in New Orleans Ten-Fu was a shadow," One-Two said, his gaze turning toward his wife. "I fear for our not-yet-born child. We stay in New Orleans, wait for Ten-Fu to get stronger. I feed her rice and fish, good for strength. She gave me Henry," he grinned, waving at the baby.

＊　　　　＊　　　　＊　　　　＊

As she continued brushing her hair, Cath smiled happily at her reflection. How wonderful it was to have One-Two back at The Lucky Pearl, running the kitchen, keeping the girls in line! Though Wade hadn't said much, she knew that he was delighted, and surprised, at One-Two's return.

Little Henry W. Longfellow Hung was now four and one-half years old, a happy, screeching child, though a bit spoiled by the attentions from the hurdy gurdies. One of the girls who knew how to swim had taught Henry to float and to swim on both his back and on his stomach. Almost daily, the residents of the Lucky Pearl lined the shore of Lac qui Parle to watch Henry demonstrate his swimming prowess. Since few onlookers knew how to swim, the admiring "ahs," and "ohs," were sincere.

Cath smiled as she remembered those serene days last summer at The Lucky Pearl. So much had happened in the past years! She began arranging her hair on top of her head. First, the terrible killing of President Lincoln, then President Johnson had been spared impeachment, and now General Grant was President of the United States.

The door burst open, and Wade entered their bedroom, carrying several large boxes. "Surprise, Sunny, my love," he said, grinning. "For you."

Cath jumped up and ran toward the bed, where Wade had dropped the boxes.

"Now that those silly hooped skirts are going out of fashion, I want you to get rid of yours, Wade said. "I thought you'd need some frocks to try the new style." He held up a ball dress of white Chambery gauze trimmed with white satin folds and blond lace. "I thought you might like to wear this to the ball this evening."

He opened another box and held up a green silk dress accompanied by a mantilla trimmed with black lace. A bonnet decorated with red roses also nestled in the box.

"Oh, Wade, you spoil me!" Cath cried as she threw herself into his arms. "Whatever would I do without you?"

She pulled the lacy ball dress from its box and held it to her shoulders while she danced around the spacious bedroom. As Cath frolicked, Wade removed a cigar from his vest pocket and, never taking his eyes from Cath, inserted it between his lips. If Cath had noticed the loving adoration in Wade's eyes, she would have been stunned at the depth of his feelings.

Sunday, June 10, 1877

Not a breath of air moved. The steady breeze of the prairie was strangely silent. The wavelets which nearly always made talking, lapping noises on the sandy shore uttered not a sound. Sitting alone in the enclosed garden on the shores of Lac qui Parle, Cath fanned herself with a month-old newspaper. Faintly, from far off she heard the ringing of a steamboat bell announcing its approach to The Lucky Pearl Landing. With a smile, Cath thought of how the name "Stimsonville" had been replaced by the name, "The Lucky Pearl," which now designated this steamboat landing.

Cath wondered if Wade might be aboard this steamboat. Though he'd been gone only eight days, her world turned colorless and dull without him. Wade had gone to St. Louis to hire more dealers. Last month, shortly after they'd arrived at The Lucky Pearl, One-Two had discovered that two faro dealers and two blackjack dealers were skimming profits from the casino. Wade had dismissed the four men. Left short, Wade had to go to St. Louis to select replacements.

A faroff murmuring came to Cath's ears. Passengers from the steamboat were beginning to fill the casino. Apparently, Wade wasn't aboard this arrival, or he would've been here in the garden by now. Cath closed her eyes. She hardly realized that she had dozed. The startled jump which her body gave in response to a touch on her arm made Cath realize she'd been asleep.

Quickly she sat up, blinking, looking for Wade. As drowsiness fell away, her eyes fastened on silver hair.

Cath shook her head. What was Will Babcock doing here? She was expecting Wade. She squinted at her visitor. Yes, it definitely was Will.

"Will?" Her voice was scratchy from sleep. "How nice to see you! But what are you doing here?" She stood. "Where's Wade?"

The banker was holding his hat in an almost ceremonial attitude. His face wore no smile. The silver hair framed a forehead wrinkled with sadness. Finally, Cath forced herself to look into Will Babcock's eyes.

"Will?" she cried, "what's the matter? What's happened to Wade?" She grabbed the banker by his jacket lapels. "Tell me!" The last was a scream.

Will firmly closed his hands around Cath's wrists and removed them from his jacket. "Sit down, dear," he said. "I want you to listen."

Like an obedient child, Cath allowed herself to be returned to her chair. For a moment she studied her hands. Then with a fierceness which surprised even herself, she grabbed Will's hand. "Tell me why you're here, Will," she said. Her voice was low. "Tell me now!"

"It's about Wade," he answered.

"Yes," she whispered, "I know." Her eyes stared into his.

"Wade hired the new dealers," Will said. "They were all aboard *The Turtle Dove* coming upriver between St. Louis and St. Joseph. Their boat encountered *Intrepid*, a sternwheeler manned by a captain with special rivalry with the captain of *The Turtle Dove*. They engaged in a race. Apparently, the two boats were bow to bow when the captain of *The Turtle Dove* hung a keg of nails on the safety valve of the boiler. The boiler exploded. There were few survivors."

Unseeing, Cath stared into Will Babcock's grieving eyes. She didn't believe this. This was a terrible nightmare. Soon she'd awaken and shiver to think what a terrible dream she'd had.

Since it was only a dream, Cath thought she'd go along with it. "How do you know Wade didn't survive?" she demanded.

The banker answered softly, "I identified his body, arranged for his burial."

"I don't believe you!" Cath retorted stiffly. "You were mistaken. It wasn't Wade!"

Slowly, Will Babcock reached out and grasped Cath's hand in his. As in a nightmare, Cath watched his other hand reach into his pocket and bring out a shiny object. Cath looked into the banker's sad eyes, glanced at the object, which he placed in her hand. Cath stared at the sparkling thing with repugnance. Why should a glittering piece of metal and stone turn her body cold?

She took a deep breath. Another breath. In her right hand she held Wade's diamond ring. If the diamond was here, where was Wade? Where was his finger? It seemed like a nightmare. But it was no dream. The ring was here. Wade was not. "Wade?" she whispered. Once more she glanced at the shining, sparkling diamond in her palm. She didn't want Wade's ring. She wanted Wade.

When she looked into Will Babcock's eyes, she couldn't avoid the truth. His eyes told her that neither he nor she would ever see Wade again.

Cath couldn't stand it. She looked down at the cold piece of jewelry in her hand. It wavered and blurred. Mercifully, she fainted.

Chapter 13
Up the Muddy Missouri

Tuesday, July 10, 1877

It was exactly one month ago this day that Will Babcock had brought Cath the devastating news: Wade was dead.

She swallowed and took a deep breath. The first days had been a scarlet blur of disbelief. Now, soothing numbness enveloped her. Cath was able to go about the tasks of administering The Lucky Pearl. Her mind was kept busy trying to learn all the details of what Wade had done to make the casino function.

As yet Cath couldn't bring herself to sleep in the big bed she'd shared with Wade. Instead, she curled up on the lumpy divan across the room. There, she could sleep a little, though it was a restless sleep. A glance in the hand mirror told her that dark smudges marred the skin beneath her eyes. The drooping, downward curl of her lips showed the tension and despair she lived. Cath sighed and stood. It was time to walk through the casino. She must at least give the appearance of being concerned.

The moment Cath stepped out of the stairway and entered the casino she found herself looking for Wade. She reminded herself that she must stop expecting to see Wade around every corner. Cath sniffed the air and realized what had made her expect to see him. Cigar smoke, apparently from the same brand of cigars Wade had smoked. That was what had triggered her anticipation of seeing Wade. So many things made her think of him: her clothes, all of which he had chosen, everything in The Lucky Pearl was his doing. The last day or two, Cath had even begun to consider the possibility of moving The Lucky Pearl to a new location, changing the furniture and appearance so she wouldn't be so painfully reminded of Wade at every turn. The next time Will Babcock visited she'd discuss this possibility with him. She supposed he wouldn't be happy about her leaving because of his one-third interest in The Golden Swan hotel, but still, he could find someone else to run this operation.

Her thoughts were interrupted by the shriek of a dance girl. Cath hurried toward the sound. The crowd at the third faro table dispersed, patrons backing away, some pushing frantically. Chairs tipped over, clattering to the floor. When Cath neared the table she saw a wild-eyed man and the shiny revolver he pointed at Earl, the dealer. A battered brown felt hat covered the man's head. His faded denim shirt was open at the throat, a red bandanna kershief knotted there. He looked like a local farmer, except for his wild eyes. The whites of his eyes framed dark centers.

"Hand it over now, fella!" the man screamed at Earl. "Every bit, or I blow your head off!"

Cath's heart pounded. She couldn't breathe. But she had to do something. Earl appeared to be paralyzed with fright. His face was as white as the linen handkerchief in his vest pocket. He seemed incapable of moving.

"Just a minute," Cath heard herself say in a high-pitched tone. She moved toward the gunman.

Swiftly, the long silver barrel of the revolver turned toward her. Cath stared in horror down the muzzle of the gun.

It happened so quickly. She heard a crack which sounded like a pistol shot. Simultaneously, another crack. The revolver was knocked from the man's hand and clattered to the floor. The gunman and Cath glared at each other.

"Do not move, please!" One-Two's singsong voice rose over the patrons' cries. Cath turned. The little Oriental stood on top of a poker table, pointing Wade's revolver at the robber. "One move, I kill you," One-Two warned the surprised man.

The man gazed at his hand in wonder. He shook the hand as if he was surprised to find it still a part of him.

Patrons leaped on the thief. They bound his hands behind his back and led him out of The Lucky Pearl. It wouldn't take them long to find the sheriff.

Cath sank onto a chair beside the faro table. Now that danger was over, she began trembling violently. One-Two was at her side. "Come, missy," he said. "You need rice wine." He pulled her to her feet. As he pushed her toward the dining room door, he called back over his shoulder, "Drinks on house!"

In the dining room, Cath dropped heavily into a chair. One-Two poured clear rice wine into a cloisonne goblet and ordered, "Drink. All."

One-Two was refilling her goblet when Ten-Fu and Henry burst noisily into the room. Soberly, One-Two assured his wife and son that he was safe. Ten-Fu trembled and wept.

"For heaven's sake, One-Two," Cath gasped, "have them sit down and give them some of this!" She held up the dainty goblet. "I've stopped shaking already because of it."

Ultimately, Cath persuaded One-Two to join them in sipping his wine. "I can't visit with you in a civilized fashion when you're hovering around like a frightened servant. You're not a servant, One-Two, and you know it! With Wade gone, The Lucky Pearl wouldn't have lasted a week without you. We both know it! Now I need to know more about you, if we're going to be partners."

Cath picked an imaginary crumb off the white linen tablecloth, looked at the calm face of the Chinese man. His hooded eyes told her nothing. "All right," she sighed. "First: Where did you learn to shoot like a marksman? You didn't get that good from those lessons Wade gave us during the New Ulm uprising!"

One-Two's eyes turned to Ten-Fu. Cath thought she saw an almost imperceptible nod from Ten-Fu.

The slender Oriental began the tale of his background, of how he happened to leave China. One-Two explained that Chong Kuo, which Cath called "China" was also known as "The Celestial Empire" because its ruler bore the title, "Son of Heaven." The Chinese, he said, called themselves "the black-haired race," and for centuries they had felt superior to the rest of mankind, whom they called "the red-haired devils," who were to the Chinese merely barbarian wanderers.

"The English," his eyes snapped with anger, "brought opium into China. They promoted its use. The evil drug destroyed thousands of Chinese, threatened to destroy whole Celestial Empire. The British start war about 25 years ago. During this time firearms were distributed to people to defend China. Before that, few Chinese allowed to have firearms. I was given gun, learned how to use."

He told how at the end of the war, the victorious English demanded 21 million pounds in reparations, which nearly destroyed the Chinese economy. Both the Yellow and Yangtze Rivers overflowed their banks and inundated fertile cropland. At the same time, the secret society known as the Triad, who were dangerous banditti, made life and property insecure.

A religious leader, Hung Hsiu-Ch'uan, rose and rebelled, forming T'ai P'ing T'ien Kuo, the Heavenly Kingdom of Great Peace. Hung had been exposed to some Protestant Christian teachings and he embraced them wholeheartedly. His followers considered foreigners as "foreign brothers" rather than "foreign devils." One-Two had joined the T'ai P'ing rebellion. He had learned something of Christianity, even a smattering of English words.

"For awhile," One-Two said, "I thought we had chance of overthrowing the Manchu dynasty, but then the English," — he nearly spat the word — "decided they could sell more opium if the dynasty remained. They helped put down our cause. One day I decided to quit fighting, get out of China." He glanced at Ten-Fu. The woman wept silently. Henry stared in fascination at his father. Apparently, One-Two had never told his son about his past.

"The day I parted from Ten-Fu with promise that I would go to America, earn money to send for her, was execution day for one of her brothers and two of mine," he said, his dark eyes burning with painful memories. "Fifty-three T'ai P'ing followers were executed that day. I was disguised as woman. Ten-Fu, her mother and my mother watch with me and other relatives." He told how into their town of Kwangsi, in the Canton outlands, rode Mandarins with red, white, blue or yellow buttons. Some were carried in palanquins. Each victim was carried into the town square in a bamboo cage, hands tied behind his back, legs in chains. From the neck of each hung a board on which his sentence was written. Following the caged victims came musicians, armed servants and standard-bearers. When the men were taken out of their cages it was obvious that they were emaciated and weak. Some crumpled to earth, unable to stand. Each man wore long hair, the pigtail attached to the crown worn much shorter in the fashion of the Mings, the Chinese dynasty defeated by the present Manchu."

One-Two stood, paced the dining room as he recalled that day. "Executioner was dressed in red blouse. He wore copper crown with two pheasant feathers above ears. He held heavy cutlass two feet long — back of blade two inches thick with crude wooden handle." A Mandarin wearing a white button held a board showing the order of execution. Ten-Fu's brother was first. He was made to kneel before the executioner, who held the cutlass with both hands. One swing severed the head. The assistant floored the victim with a kick."

148

Cath swallowed, trying not to be sick. She glanced uneasily at Ten-Fu and was surprised to see that the little woman had stopped crying and was watching One-Two with fascination.

"After three or four decapitations," One-Two continued, "executioner change weapons to get sharp one. When last head falls, Mandarins leave. Executioner picked up all fifty-three heads, threw them into large chest. They took chains off bodies and left." He said that the moment they were out of sight, all the women, shrieking loudly, dashed toward the headless bodies, trying to identify their own men. The search went on all day amid mournful cries and sobs. One-Two stopped his pacing and stood motionless. "On that day, I watch the suffering of my mother, Ten-Fu, and her mother. I decide I not shed my blood for The Celestial Empire."

Ten-Fu's voice, surprisingly strong and firm, came from across the table. "On that day I agree: My husband and unborn children not become headless carcass."

"Did that all really happen?" Henry asked, his dark eyes wide and shining.

"Yes," One-Two said softly. "I not much older than you — just few years."

"I'm grateful," Cath said, "that you had practice with guns. You saved the day today, One-Two." Suddenly she remembered. "I must see to poor Earl. He looked terrified. I'd better make sure someone is helping settle his nerves." She stood.

"What can I say? 'Thank you' isn't enough. All I can say is, I hope I have the chance to return the favor some day."

"No," One-Two said. "I owe you favors for rest of my days for your help of Ten-Fu join me. I never repay that, missy."

When Cath returned to the casino she was satisfied, though surprised, to find activities going on as usual. The bar was more crowded than ever.

She recalled One-Two's shouted order that drinks were on the house — a shrewd decision on One-Two's part. The patrons deserved something to calm their nerves, and furnishing free drinks served as an apology on the part of the casino for the fright they'd suffered. One-Two had made one of those instant decisions that a good manager makes. Wade would've done the same. One-Two was certainly much more than a servant.

149

Cath would have to discuss with Will Babcock what sort of legal status she should arrange for the strange partnership which had developed between her and One-Two since Wade's death.

Tuesday, July 31, 1877

Three weeks after the attempted robbery and One-Two's dramatic rescue, Cath was moving past the keno tables when she saw Will Babcock walking toward her.

"Will!" she exclaimed. "How delighted I am to see you! I've been wanting to talk over some business problems with you."

Will's usually serene and smiling face remained sober, his forehead wrinkled. He seemed disturbed.

"There's someone who wishes to talk with you, Cath," he said. He turned to a man following him, a large man wearing a white suit. "May I present Beauregard Stanton, Wade's younger brother?"

Cath's hands flew to her throat as she faced Wade's brother. It was as if she were looking at Wade again, but in a flawed mirror, its reflection twisting features. The brother's face was narrower, his lips thinner than Wade's. This man's hair was brown instead of black. Feature by feature she supposed he didn't really look like Wade. But his eyes! His eyes were Wade's! Twinkling, mocking, teasing dark eyes. It was as if she were looking at a distorted tintype of Wade.

"There are matters of business to discuss with Mr. Stanton, Cath," Will Babcock prodded Cath.

"Oh, yes, yes," she said, recovering. "We'll go to my quarters. Please follow me."

Gripping her skirt, lifting it as she climbed the stairway to her living quarters, Cath wondered what business Beauregard Stanton had with her.

"Please be seated, gentlemen," Cath motioned toward the comfortable chairs facing the divan where she'd been sleeping at night. Thank goodness, Elsie had removed the pillow and quilt!

As they seated themselves, there was a knock at the door. One-Two stepped in, hooded eyes alert. "What refreshments for gentlemen?" he asked.

Good old One-Two! His eyes were everywhere. He didn't miss a thing going on at The Lucky Pearl.

"Brandy for the gentlemen," she answered, raising her eyebrows at Will Babcock for assent. He nodded, and One-Two disappeared.

150

"I won't even take time to lie and say I'm sorry about Wade's demise," Beauregard Stanton said, his voice a low growl.

Cath sucked in her breath. His voice was identical to Wade's! If she were to close her eyes, she knew she'd think Wade was speaking to her in his soft Carolina drawl.

"There was no love lost between my brother and me—ever!" Beauregard went on. "After he deserted our family and the South and sided with Yankees, I considered him my enemy. I don't normally do business with concubines, but Mr. Babcock here has persuaded me..."

"Sir!" Will Babcock's voice thundered; he rose quickly. "You will not speak to Miss Carleton in such terms!"

"Well," Stanton drawled, "I was always taught to call a spade a spade, but I'll withdraw the term."

One-Two entered, bearing a tray holding a Waterford glass decanter and brandy snifters. The Oriental poured brandy. As soon as the door closed behind One-Two, Beauregard Stanton continued. "I've come to claim the casino and all of Wade's estate for his daughter, Estelle."

Cath gasped. She threw Will Babcock a frightened look. "But," she swallowed, "all *my* money is in The Lucky Pearl! I've put all my money into the furnishings, the building." She glared at Beauregard Stanton. "You can't just take it! It's partly mine! Wade wouldn't take it from me and give it to his daughter! What would *she* do with it?"

Stanton swirled the brandy about in his snifter. "I intend to run it for her for the time being to see if it'll continue to be a profitable venture. You see, that's the one thing Wade and I had in common. We both loved to gamble. In fact, he taught me how to play poker when I was just a tad."

"Will," Cath's eyes begged the banker to support her. "He can't take The Lucky Pearl, can he?"

Will Babcock cleared his throat. "I'm afraid he can, Cath." He paused. "Though," and he threw a hard look at Stanton, "no gentleman would do so. Apparently years ago when Wade left Philadelphia he made a will leaving everything to his daughter. His wife kept that will, and I imagine Wade forgot it existed. I'm sure if he'd remembered, he would've made a new will leaving The Lucky Pearl to you. That's usual procedure for partners in a business: each leaves the other the business in case of his own death."

Cath studied her hands which lay limp in her lap.

151

"So I'm to lose my home *and* my place of business — everything. How soon are you taking over?" she asked Stanton.

"Right now," he answered. "This very day. But you may stay on as madam, or whatever position you hold. We can see if it works out."

"No thank you!" Cath retorted, her eyes sparkling with angry tears. She jumped up and hurried down the stairway to the dining room, Will following. After Will entered, she closed the door.

"Will, I want to set up a casino and dance hall in The Black Hills. Last year 75,000 men searched for gold there, and now that the Indians have been driven from the area, there must be thousands more men with gold fever swarming there. I don't want to stay here. Everything reminds me of Wade. Would you consider backing me?"

Will Babcock rose, stepped toward Cath, and grasped both her hands. "My dear, of course I shall! I know you'll be a success anywhere. But are you sure it's safe from Indian attack?"

Cath smiled at the silver-haired banker. "I think it's probably safer than this area was when we set up here years ago."

Cath assembled the employees, from Elsie the maid to the dealers and hurdy gurdies in the casino. Briefly, she told them that Wade's brother was taking over The Lucky Pearl, and that she was going to move to The Black Hills in Dakota Territory where she would set up another Lucky Pearl. "One-Two has already said he chooses to go with me," she announced. "If any of you care to move with me, I'll be most happy to have you."

"Now wait a minute there!" Beauregard Stanton shouted from across the casino. "You can't do that! I own The Lucky Pearl!"

"You don't own the employees, Mr. Stanton," Cath retorted. "They're not slaves."

"They belong here with the gambling establishment!" he insisted, his voice a harsh growl.

Angrily, Cath turned her back on him. "Does anyone want to join up with me in this new venture farther west?" she asked the workers. "I'm sure it'll be primitive, and I won't fool you— it's at the very edge of the earth. But anyone who wants to, please feel welcome to join me."

In the end all but two of the hurdy gurdies followed Cath. Five faro and poker dealers decided to risk the unknown farther west.

Stanton blustered and roared, but he couldn't stop the employees from leaving. Cath told them to pack their belongings quickly, that they were going to St. Joseph first to pick up furnishings for their new business.

Her mind reeled with thoughts of everything they'd need — supplies ranging from dozens of decks of playing cards to faro cloths, beds, chairs — so many things.

Tuesday, August 7, 1877

Cath could hardly believe how much she'd managed to accomplish in the one week since she left Stimsonville and came to St. Joseph. She'd sent One-Two to St. Louis to pick up supplies they couldn't get in St. Joseph. He'd returned to St. Joseph yesterday and in a short while their steamboat was scheduled to leave for the upper reaches of the Missouri River. Cath and her retinue would disembark at Ft. Pierre, Dakota Territory. There, they'd join a wagon train bound for The Black Hills. All their furnishings would be loaded aboard Conestoga wagons and carted across the prairie.

Smiling to herself, Cath thought of the many details she'd thought of, such as bringing a gold scale. Figuring that many of the miners would want to use gold for currency, she would be ready to take their gold dust.

Before the boat departed, Cath had to take care of one last detail. She wanted to write to Rebecca about her change of residence. Cath was sitting in the women's saloon of *The Merry Widow*, an elderly but regal sternwheeler, when she began her letter.

August 7, 1877

Dear Becky,

Mrs. Stanton died recently, and I am now moving to The Black Hills in Dakota Territory where I will establish a millinery business. As soon as I have a proper address I shall let you know. I didn't want you to worry if you didn't hear from me for awhile. I don't know how remote The Black Hills will be as far as mail service goes.

It's hard for me to imagine Gitty being fifteen years old! I try to picture what she must look like with Jason's auburn hair and green eyes. She must be a beauty! I do hope I can see her someday. Right now, however, I must concentrate on making my future secure. Since gold has been discovered in The Black Hills, boom towns have started, and there are fortunes to be made there. When I make my fortune I want to see you and my darling niece!

Hoping this finds you all well, your loving sister,

Cath

Cath gave Will Babcock the letter to mail. Will leaned casually against the guard rail and studied Cath. A smile played at the corners of his mouth.

"Something amuses you?" Cath asked, raising her eyebrows.

He smiled. "Yes. In the past I always thought that Wade was the organizer, the person behind the huge success of The Lucky Pearl. This past week I've learned otherwise. I think you're a whirlwind of an organizer, and with One-Two as your partner, The Black Hills is about to be hit by a cyclone of success. Those people out there don't know what's coming their way. There's gold dust out there about to be moved from miners' bags into your bank account!

The whistle blew twice, and a steward moved about the decks crying, "All ashore who's going ashore!"

Her arm through his, Cath walked with Will toward the gangplank. At the gangplank he stopped. Cath held out her gloved hand. "There aren't enough words for me to thank you for believing in me, Will. I hope our new Lucky Pearl will make you good money on your investment."

The banker took Cath's hand and smiled warmly. "I have no doubt that I've made a good investment." Quickly, he brushed her cheek with his lips, turned, walked briskly down the gangplank. When he reached the pier he walked in the direction of the bank. Just before the corner, Will Babcock turned, looked back.

Cath waved exuberantly, white handkerchief fluttering in her hand. Will gave a saluting gesture and disappeared.

Cath shrugged. She guessed he didn't like saying good-by. There was no way she could know the turmoil going on with the banker's emotions. Will Babcock, happily married man, father, successful banker, was wishing that he had the courage to throw away his success and respectability and join Cath in her casino operation in The Black Hills. He knew that he never could do it, but just wishing that he could was enough to throw his usually serene disposition into chaos.

The roustabouts loosened hawsers holding the boat to the pier. With a shrill whistle *The Merry Widow* headed up The Missouri River carrying Cath and her retinue of card dealers, hurdy gurdies, and Orientals into the raw and almost unknown Dakota Territory.

PART 2

GITTY

Chapter 14
The Fate of the *Henry Leigh*

Monday, April 2, 1878, Mattigan, Michigan

With his napkin Conway Carleton dabbed at his gray moustache. Years ago his auburn beard had turned gray. Thinking it made him look old, Conway shaved the beard. For awhile he'd felt nearly naked. He'd kept the moustache to help him adjust to his shaven chin. Though the hair on his head was flecked with gray, it still was auburn. His moustache, though, was decidedly gray.

Conway's pale eyes softened as he glanced across the table at his only grandchild. These past few years her slender, childish body had rounded, and now Gitty McDaniel was a young woman. She looked up and caught him watching her. Her brilliant green eyes regarded him soberly for a moment, then her face broke into a broad smile. "Well, Grandfather," she teased, "are you trying to decide what you're going to get your favorite granddaughter for her sixteenth birthday?" She tossed her head. Auburn curls swung across her shoulders, shining copper bright in the rays of the early morning sun streaming through the east window.

Conway returned her smile. "Now, darlin'," he said, "you know I wouldn't leave an important decision like that until the last day."

As she jumped up from her chair, Gitty popped the last of a honey-drenched biscuit into her mouth. "I've got to rush, Grandfather. Late for school." She hurried around the table, pressed a wet, noisy kiss on his cheek and hurried out of the dining room. Her green silk skirt swished softly against the door.

"Happy birthday!" Conway called, his gaze lingering on the empty doorway.

He lifted a crystal bell and shook it. His housekeeper scurried in from the kitchen. She carried a silver coffee pot.

"Ah, yes, Mrs. Tarkington," Conway breathed. "I'll have more coffee, please."

As she filled his moustache mug with steaming coffee, she asked if she could get him anything else.

"No, thank you," he murmured. "Might as well leave the pot here. I'll want more with my pipe."

As he sucked on his pipe Conway's thoughts drifted. Birthdays and anniversaries made him sentimental. And he'd noticed that as he grew older, he got more nostalgic. Though at fifty-nine he didn't consider himself old, he knew that Gitty thought he was ancient. Ah, Gitty — the joy of his life. How he loved that child! Even so, he was disappointed that he didn't have more grandchildren. He wished he had a grandson to carry on the mill after he and George grew too old to run it. But then, he could have had two or three grandsons and none of them might have had any interest in the mill, just as Rebecca's Jason wasn't interested in it.

Strange, he considered, that I fathered three children and ended up with but one grandchild. Conway's thoughts slid to Cath, his little blond darling, who'd run off twenty-one years ago. His eyes grew damp. He dabbed at them with his linen napkin. Thank God he knew she was all right. It would've been unbearable if she'd just disappeared, never letting them know how she was and what she was doing. Fortunately, Cath wrote to Rebecca, and Rebecca shared the letters with him. He'd always hoped that Cath would come back, at least for a visit. Once he'd even asked Rebecca to write Cath and tell her that he'd send her money for the trip to Michigan. Weeks later, when the reply came, Cath thanked him for the gesture, but said it wasn't money which kept her from visiting. Cath claimed to have sufficient money; it was simply time which prevented her visiting Mattigan.

And now Cath had moved even farther away to Stardancer, a gold rush settlement on the far western border of Dakota Territory. Conway sighed. Why had his eldest daughter inherited such a hankering for distant places? He shook his head. Cath had seemed such a normal child, happy, bubbling. At least until...Cath's finding her mother's body had been a horrible experience for a young girl. Ruth's murder and the scandal surrounding it seemed to have bothered Cath more than it had Rebecca. Rebecca had stayed here, married, raised Gitty. She'd earned the respect of the community. In Mattigan she was a well-regarded young matron. During that long ago tragic time Conway and Rebecca had held their heads high. Eventually the gossips had moved on to more recent misdeeds. Why was it that Cath had to run away? It always puzzled Conway.

Nowadays, he could think of his dead wife without becoming bitter. There had been a time when the mere thought of Ruth had drawn his lips tight across his teeth. Eventually he'd come to terms with Ruth's adultery by deciding that the death of Baby John had addled her brain. Even now he could recall the wild look on her face as she swung the ax and burned the cradle. After that she wouldn't allow him to touch her, ever again. That wasn't normal. Then after she secretly turned to The Reverend Campbell for...well, that wasn't normal either. Ruth had been raised in a proper family, excellent upbringing. She...

Enough of this kind of thinking! Going over unpleasant past is useless, probably harmful. Might as well recall good memories! Conway tossed his napkin onto the table and rose. He must get to the mill and finish his work for the day so he'd be free this afternoon to celebrate Gitty's birthday.

The party was to be held here at Conway's house because Jason and Rebecca wouldn't get back from Chicago until mid-morning when *The Henry Leigh* was scheduled to dock. Gitty's parents had gone to Chicago to select new parlor furniture, including a piano, and they planned to bring it back with them. Both Gitty and Rebecca were excited about having a piano of their own. They'd been taking lessons, learning both organ and piano. Now they'd have a piano in their own parlor.

His daughter and son-in-law had been gone for a week, and in their absence Gitty was staying with Conway. He enjoyed every minute of her presence. After many years of living alone he loved hearing voices when he came home. Late afternoons when he arrived home from the mill Gitty usually was in the parlor with one or two girlfriends, pouring over fashion catalogues or reading to each other from novels, blushing and whispering over the romantic portions. Conway usually suggested that Gitty invite her friend for supper. If the girl stayed, that meant a joyful dinner of girlish conversation — such happiness for him after so many years of eating alone. Hearing youthful voices took him back to the days when Cath and Rebecca were young, back before Ruth...

Slipping his arms into his brown woolen overcoat, Conway forced himself to think of something else. He'd have time to get a few hours' work done before going to the wharf to meet Rebecca and Jason's ship.

He took long strides on the six-block walk to his sawmill. Snow was gone from walks and streets, but unmelted dirty gray piles of snow remained at intersections. The northwest wind was cold. A gust whipped his hat from his head, and Conway ran after the rolling hat. As he grabbed the hat, dusted it, he thought of Rebecca aboard *The Henry Leigh*. Unless the lake was perfectly smooth, Rebecca suffered terribly from seasickness. With this gale she must be absolutely miserable.

Every morning as he walked to the mill Conway looked about with amazed satisfaction. Thirty-four years ago when he'd arrived here, Mattigan was only a cluster of log cabins built around a trading post. Now it was a city of fifteen thousand people, a busy lake port and a booming lumber town. From the very beginning Conway's mill had done well. He and George Gordon had anticipated the great need of the tree-hungry West. Six years ago last fall the huge fire in Chicago had pushed them hard to supply the lumber needed to replace the seventeen thousand homes and nearly all the businesses of that city. Within four years Chicago was completely rebuilt. By that time demand for lumber farther west kept the whirring saws of the Carleton-Gordon Mill running at full steam.

Once at the mill, Conway concentrated on the piles of orders and correspondence waiting for him at his desk.

He looked up at the sound of his assistant's voice. "I thought I should let you know, sir," Robert Clarion said after clearing his throat, "that *The Henry Leigh* hasn't yet been sighted from the breakwater. That's why I didn't remind you earlier about getting the buggy ready."

Conway reached into his vest pocket for his gold watch. "Eleven-thirty!" he exclaimed. "They were supposed to arrive around ten."

"Perhaps the heavy seas, sir," the assistant offered.

"Um, yes," Conway nodded. "Well, keep me posted and let me know when she's sighted." He bent, returning to his price quotations, but not with the same concentration as before. Now a nagging finger probed at him, worrying away his serenity.

Finally, at one o'clock he could stand it no longer. He ordered his horse and buggy brought to the office entrance.

At the wharf he found himself in the company of concerned people wanting to know why *The Henry Leigh* was so far behind schedule. Conway knew that Rebecca would be frantic, wanting to be home in time to help supervise final preparations for Gitty's birthday party. The dockmaster shrugged. He'd had no word. He couldn't tell them a thing.

For an hour and a half Conway waited at the wharf, sitting in his buggy instead of milling on the dock with the other anxious people. From the height of the buggy seat he was in a better position to scan the waters of Lake Mattigan for the sails of *The Henry Leigh.*

At last, far off, he made out the outline of slender sails coming through the channel from Lake Michigan. Squinting, he kept his eyes on the sails until, as the boat neared, he saw that it was only a skiff, probably a fisherman. Conway continued to study the horizon, only occasionally glancing at the small boat making its way toward the shipping dock. Strange. Fishing boats had their own wharf, closer to the channel. The shabby, unpainted boat sailed directly to the wharf. The strong stench of fish swept over the dock. With lacy handkerchiefs ladies covered their noses. A man wearing a black India-rubber mackinaw jumped from the fishing boat onto the dock and walked with heavy, angry steps toward the shipping office. In one arm he carried what appeared to be a life preserver. The finger of uneasiness inside Conway prodded him. His mouth went dry as he leaped from the buggy.

"What have you got there, friend?" Conway asked, reaching out and rotating the life preserver so he could make out the writing on it. Large black letters read "The Henry Leigh."

"Where'd you get this?" Conway gasped.

"Out 'bout five mile from the breakwater."

People gathered around them, muttering. Sight of the lettering on the life preserver brought loud gasps of fear.

"This preserver broke loose from the ship during the gale." Conway spoke to the crowd in general. "We shouldn't let ourselves be upset by one life preserver!"

The fisherman's weathered face remained grim. Heavily, he clumped back to his boat and climbed aboard. "This blow loose too?" he asked, his voice harsh. He threw down the arched wooden lid of a steamer trunk. "And this?" He tossed out what appeared to be the top of a table, followed by other watersoaked wooden items.

159

"There was all sorts of flotsam. Rough out there. Down to about six-foot waves now. I come back because bigger boats than mine should go out there and look for bodies. Couldn't be no survivors. Too cold."

The murmurings from the waiting crowd grew louder as the fisherman's words cut through the wall of hope and denial that those waiting for *The Henry Leigh* had built against their fears. Conway heard a strange swooshing sound. Vaguely, he realized it was the sound of his blood rushing through his neck toward his head. He closed his eyes against the pain, and saw brilliant scarlet. How could he bear to think of his daughter lying at the bottom of Lake Michigan, tons of cold water pressing on her? Rebecca! his thoughts cried in anguish. My dark-haired beauty. My little girl. Rebecca!

Suddenly he thought of Gitty. Tragic news travels fast. He must get to Gitty! He wanted to be with her.

Heavily, Conway climbed into his buggy and flicked the reins. The horse moved forward, and Conway directed the buggy toward the school.

Sunday, April 15, 1878

In the attic of her house, the home she'd lived in all her life, Gitty sat crosslegged, going through her mother's possessions. It'd been two weeks since the disappearance of *The Henry Leigh*. At first, Gitty had refused to believe that her parents had drowned. In fact, she wouldn't even believe that the ship had sunk. But then some bodies had washed ashore, and she'd had to face the fact that *The Henry Leigh* had sunk. For days she pretended that her parents had missed the boat and were coming home by train and coach. Yet for them to miss sharing her sixteenth birthday with her — that was hard to believe, unless, of course, some great calamity had befallen them, something horrible — such as their ship sinking, drawn beneath the crashing waves of Lake Michigan.

Yesterday a memorial service was held for Rebecca and Jason McDaniel at the Methodist Church. It had been postponed for awhile because Grandfather had hoped the bodies might be recovered. When it appeared that Lake Michigan was not going to give up many victims of *The Henry Leigh*, the service was conducted without any remains. Gitty thought that maybe the memorial service would convince her that Mama and Papa were truly dead. She sat straight and tall beside Grandfather and listened half-heartedly to the minister's doleful voice explaining the mysterious ways of The Lord.

160

I won't listen! Gitty told herself. If The Lord caused my parents' ship to sink, then I don't want to have anything to do with Him anymore! How could He do that to nice people? Only a cruel god would take Mama and Papa from me!

Now, going through her mother's things, Gitty felt the reality of her parents' deaths more than she had in church. She tried to shake off the feeling that she was being a naughty child, sneaking up to the attic and prying into her mother's personal belongings. Grandfather had asked her to go through her mother's things to see what she wanted to keep. Clothes and items Gitty didn't want would be given to the poor.

Grandfather was going to sell the house and furnishings. Already Gitty had moved her clothes to Grandfather's huge old mansion. She realized she couldn't live here alone, but it hurt to think of strangers living in her home. Papa had built this house before Mama and he married. It was the only home Gitty had known.

Grandfather seemed pathetically eager to get her belongings moved to his house. It was obvious that he was delighted at the thought of Gitty living with him. "This was your mother's room," he'd said, puffing slightly, as he set her luggage down in the upstairs bedroom. "We'll have it redecorated, darlin', however you want it."

Gitty added another packet of letters sent by Aunt Cath to Mama to the growing pile on the attic floor. She knew so little about her aunt — the strange woman who'd fled from Mattigan and kept moving farther west. Hoping she'd learn more, Gitty had decided to take the letters back to Grandfather's house to read.

There, that seemed to be the last of the letters. She reached into the storage chest, fishing. Her hand touched soft material. As she lifted out a blue cashmere scarf, her Grandfather's voice called to her from below.

"Yoo, hoo, darlin'," he called. "Are you in the attic?"

"Yes, Grandfather!"

From the attic stairs his head peeked at her. "Well, for heaven's sake! Did your mother keep that all these years?"

Gitty glanced at the long scarf in her lap.

Grandfather nodded toward it. "Years ago I brought your mother that scarf from St. Louis, along with identical ones for your grandmother and your aunt."

Gitty rose, gathering the scarf and the packets of letters.

161

"Hungry?" Grandfather asked brightly. He was trying so hard to be cheerful these days. Someday, probably, they could be happy again, but now Gitty felt sad. Why shouldn't she? She'd lost her Mama and Papa. She was an orphan.

Gitty would've burst into tears if her grandfather's voice hadn't distracted her. "Where would your mother keep recent letters from your aunt?" he asked. "I want to write to Cath, let her know the terrible news."

Gitty directed him to the dainty rosewood secretary in the parlor where her mother had sat to write letters. She assumed this would be where recent letters were kept. In a pigeonhole of the desk they found two letters, the most recent letter giving Stardancer, Dakota Territory, as Cath's address. Gitty added them to her collection of older letters.

Later that evening, after supper, Gitty dutifully kept her grandfather company for more than an hour. The old letters written by her adventurous aunt beckoned her. Gitty used the excuse of having to do homework to retreat upstairs to the bedroom which had been her mother's as a girl.

Gitty plaited her long copper-colored hair in one braid to keep it from tangling during the night. Slipping into a warm flannel nightgown, she pulled the lamp on the night stand closer to her bed. After climbing into bed, she arranged the letters in sequence. She intended to begin reading the first letter and continue to the newer ones. That way she hoped to get a realistic feeling of her aunt's life. Mama never had said much about her sister, yet she'd always appeared excited when a letter from Aunt Cath arrived. Sometimes, when Gitty asked about Aunt Cath, and why she lived so far away, her mother frowned, mumbling something about Mattigan not being exciting enough for her aunt. Gitty had sensed that there was more to Aunt Cath's separation from her family than Mama let on.

Now maybe she'd find out. Gitty finished lining up the envelopes from the oldest to the newest.

The first letter, written aboard a steamboat on the Mississippi River, said that Aunt Cath was working as a companion to a widow and hinted that she was leading an elegant life, a life much happier than in Mattigan.

In the second letter written months later Aunt Cath gave an address in St. Louis where her mail should be sent. Since she'd be traveling up and down the Mississippi River, she said that she'd pick up her mail at that address every time her boat docked in St. Louis. This was a much longer letter, and Gitty dwelled on it, reading it a second and third time. Her aunt alluded to why she left Mattigan when she wrote, "Oh, Becky, after the thing with Mama, I couldn't bear to stay!" Gitty wondered what "the thing" had been — serious enough, apparently, to make Aunt Cath leave town. Gitty remembered Mama saying that Grandmother Carleton had died before Cath left town. Perhaps grief drove her away. Maybe she felt a change of scenery would help her stop feeling sad. Thoughtfully, Gitty stared into the shadows.

She was especially intrigued by her aunt's description of how she left Mattigan, traveled across Indiana and Illinois to Iowa. Gitty nearly wept as Cath described how she'd cut her blond curls to disguise herself as a boy. That took courage. Her interest in her distant aunt intensified. The letter went on to say, "Becky, dear, my hair is beginning to touch my shoulders again. Before, wearing a bonnet concealed my shorn state. Sometimes I even wanted to wear a bonnet to bed."

Gitty followed her aunt's travels on the Mississippi, to her millinery shop in Sioux City, Iowa, and farther up the Missouri River to Stimsonville. Cath's telling about the Indian uprising made Gitty shiver. She'd studied about the New Ulm massacre in history class. To think her own aunt was nearly involved in it!

The last two letters explained that Cath's employer, Mrs. Stanton, had died, and that Cath was moving her millinery shop to a goldrush boom town in The Black Hills. "I've talked to those who have seen The Hills. Their beauty is said to be spectacular. Fortunes are to be made in boom towns, and I'm going to give it a try."

This last letter was dated November, six months ago. Gitty wondered if her aunt had gotten started on making her fortune.

Gitty bundled the letters together, being careful to keep them in proper order. She set them on the night table and blew out the lamp. Lying in the dark, Gitty thought of all the exciting places Aunt Cath had seen — the interesting people she must have met along the way.

Gitty considered her own life in Mattigan. She agreed with Aunt Cath. There was more to the world than Mattigan. What was to keep her here with Mama and Papa gone?

Every night since the sinking of *The Henry Leigh* Gitty had cried herself to sleep. Tonight she lay awake, drowsily thinking of Mississippi River steamboats and elegantly dressed ladies wearing Aunt Cath's custom-designed bonnets. Gitty fancied the dark tree-covered mountains of Dakota surrounded by pale expanses of buffalo grass waving in the constant prairie winds.

Chapter 15
Kid Called Me "Sir!"

Thursday, June 20, 1878

For two months, ever since Mama and Papa drowned, people had been telling Gitty how fortunate she was to have her grandfather to look out for her. Sometimes these well-meant remarks made her angry. Gitty didn't feel "fortunate." She'd lost her mother and father in a tragic lake disaster. She was without parents, without brothers or sisters. Why was she supposed to be grateful that she had a grandfather?

Gitty shrugged her shoulders and glanced in the mirror. Her green eyes sparkled dangerously. She felt restless. Perhaps it was the heat.

A week ago Grandfather had gone to St. Louis. All that time Gitty had been alone in the house, except, of course, for Mrs. Tarkington, but a housekeeper isn't companionship. Eating alone wasn't fun. Gitty now sympathized with Grandfather for having had to eat alone all the years since Grandmother died.

Through her bedroom window Gitty heard the clopping of a horse and buggy coming down the street. The sound stopped in front of the house. Gitty sauntered to the window. Grandfather! She smiled. It would be good to have him back. She leaned forward curiously. Grandfather had turned and was helping someone out of the buggy. It was a lady — a lady wearing a smart pale green silk gown. Her hair was dark and shiny, almost blue-black. Her grandfather's arm rested possessively around the woman's waist.

Uneasily, Gitty went down the staircase to meet them. Already she thought she knew what Grandfather's first words would be.

As the ornately carved oak door opened, Grandfather and the lady entered. Gitty stood on the bottom step of the staircase.

"Gitty, darlin'!" Grandfather's voice boomed cheerfully, "I have a surprise for you. My wife!" He turned to the dark-haired lady. "Gladys, meet my granddaughter, Gitty McDaniel. Gitty, this is Gladys Carleton."

The lady held out her arms and she embraced Gitty stiffly. "And please, dear child," the woman said, "call me 'Gladys.' I couldn't bear 'Grandmother.' I'm much too young for that."

Fine! thought Gitty. *I have no interest in calling you "Grandmother."* Privately, Gitty thought the woman was plenty old enough to be a grandparent.

Gladys hugged Grandfather's arm. "Oh, do show me the house, sweetheart. I'm dying to see it!"

Apparently Grandfather and Gladys had known each other for years. Gitty never questioned Gladys about her past, and Gladys never mentioned anything other than "I come from St. Louis."

For several weeks Gitty watched this new member of their household. She couldn't figure Gladys out. Gitty's only experience with women was with her mother and ladies like her, or with housekeepers and maids. This Gladys didn't fit into either type. Though Gladys tried hard to act like the respectable matrons of Mattigan, her manners appeared false. Gladys seemed to be acting a role. And Gitty thought Gladys was mis-cast as a respectable matron. Gitty couldn't put her finger on what Gladys did wrong. Her clothes were a little on the gaudy side. She wore a bit too much color on her face. Gitty shrugged. Why should she care?

Tuesday, October 15, 1878

For almost four months Gitty and Gladys kept up the pretense in front of Conway Carleton that they were fond of each other. At the dinner table they were polite to each other. But when Conway left the house, smiles left their faces, and the two women moved about the house ignoring each other.

Gitty thought Gladys a silly, frivolous woman who was using her grandfather for his money. Once, when she was irritated over something, Gladys shouted at Gitty, "You're a spoiled rich brat!" It got to the point where Gitty didn't feel welcome in Grandfather's home anymore. Grandfather seemed happy to have her, but Gitty knew that Gladys hated having her around.

Gitty's classes had been dismissed early today. She strolled slowly homeward, kicking at the scarlet maple leaves covering the wooden walks.

When she arrived home, Gitty headed up the staircase. As she walked into her room, a startled scream rose in her throat when she realized that someone sat on her bed. Then she saw that it was Gladys. Gladys was sitting on her bed, reading the letters written by Aunt Cath to Mama.

"How dare you!" Gitty cried as she snatched the packet of letters from the woman. "Get out of my room and stay out!" she shouted. "Don't you ever come in my room again! If you do, I'll tell Grandfather!"

Gladys's eyes burned at Gitty. "I'll deny it," she sneered. "And who do you think Conway will believe?"

Gitty sucked in her breath sharply as if she'd been struck a blow. She pointed toward the door. "Get out!"

Backing slowly out of the room, Gladys scowled.

That settled it. Angrily, Gitty pulled a leather grip from beneath her bed and dropped the packets of precious letters into it. She opened the tall mahogany clothes press and studied the garments hanging within. It was hard to decide what to take.

Twenty minutes later Gitty struggled down the staircase, the heavy luggage clattering noisily against the oak stair rails. As Gitty pulled open the heavy front door, Gladys came running from the parlor. Her eyes fastened on the traveling case. Gladys screeched, "Where do you think you're going, miss?"

Separating each word to accent her meaning, Gitty said slowly, "Away — from — you!"

Gladys didn't try to follow. Grandfather wouldn't be back from Grand Rapids until tonight. By then Gitty hoped to be on either a train or boat, leaving Mattigan far behind.

By the time Gitty arrived at the sawmill she was puffing from carrying the cumbersome suitcase. When Grandfather's assistant, Robert Clarion, saw how breathless she was, he quickly held a chair for her.

Gitty explained to the young assistant that she'd been summoned unexpectedly to care for her aunt. "Grandfather's out of town and there's no money in the house. Will you give me whatever money is here at the mill? Grandfather will replace it tomorrow when you let him know."

Robert Clarion managed to collect two hundred dollars from various cash boxes about the sawmill, and he even added a twenty dollar gold piece of his own. "I really appreciate this, Mr. Clarion," Gitty thanked him. "And you be sure and tell Grandfather about your own twenty dollars."

The assistant was so helpful that he even had the buggy brought out of the stables, drove Gitty to the wharf, and carried her suitcase aboard the schooner *Evangeline* which was sailing for Chicago within the hour.

Dusk was falling as Gitty stood on deck and watched Grandfather's assistant drive away from the wharf. She hoped his helpfulness didn't cost him his job.

Thursday, October 17, 1878

All the way to Chicago Gitty was terrified. The seas were calm and the bright moon showed an almost cloudless sky —no hint of any storm in the offing. Still, she didn't close her eyes all night long. Each time the vessel rocked, she clutched her reticule, fearing that she was about to share her parents' fate.

Once safely in Chicago, Gitty relaxed. The moment her feet touched the solid wharf, her nerve returned. This was a beautiful Indian summer day, a day to enjoy. After all, she told herself, this is an adventure! Everything had happened so fast. It was hard to realize she'd actually left Mattigan, was truly on her way to Stardancer, where she'd visit Aunt Cath.

Gitty purchased her railroad ticket and took a dark green Parmalee rig to The Grand Pacific Hotel. She was pleasantly surprised to discover that the hotel was but one block from the Chicago and North Western depot where her train would depart the next morning at ten.

Gitty was dazzled by the opulence of The Grand Pacific, a magnificent six-story hotel. After a short nap, she dined on whitefish from Lake Michigan and green peas from New Orleans. Because of her sleepless night aboard ship, she slept soundly, even though alone in a strange hotel room for the first time in her life.

Her train departed on time. Seated beside Gitty was a portly, gray-haired lady who chattered continuously. Most of her talk was boring, but occasionally she interested Gitty. When they passed through Batavia, the woman told Gitty that windmills were manufactured there, and that there were a lot of windmills farther west. They were used on western farms, the lady said, to pump water from wells drilled deep into the earth. "And there's lots of wind out west, dearie," she warned. "Seems like the wind never stops, just blows and blows."

Dixon was the dinner station, but Gitty was too excited to eat. The train crossed the Mississippi at Clinton, Iowa. The bridge, only the second bridge to cross the Mississippi River, the woman said, was impressive. Nine iron spans crossed the west channel and three spans and a draw the main channel. The woman left the train at Clinton, where she was to visit a daughter. Gitty felt sorry for the daughter, having to listen to such constant chatter. Then she reconsidered. She'd rather have a chattering mother than no mother at all. Gitty wondered, would she be on this train right now if her Mother were alive? She knew she wouldn't. She'd still be living with Mama and Papa. She'd never have run off and left them to worry. Grandfather would worry about her, but he was so crazy about that silly Gladys that he'd be all right.

The train chugged on through rolling prairie. When darkness closed in, Gitty leaned against the side of the car and shut her eyes. Grit from the smoke settled on the seat, windows, and even coated her teeth. She awakened when the dark window began to show daylight. They were nearing the Missouri River. Council Bluffs was the western terminus of the railway. Gitty would continue her journey on the Union Pacific Railroad.

✻   ✻   ✻   ✻

When her train pulled out of Omaha, Gitty said a silent good-bye to civilization. Farther on, as they rolled into the Platte River valley, Gitty studied the countryside, a desolate, featureless land. Occasionally plowed earth, rich and black, showed the touch of man. Gitty moved to an empty seat across the aisle on the left side of the train. The silvery Platte River oozed slowly due west between steep, dark bluffs, moving slowly among wide sandy shallows and low islands fringed with willows and cottonwoods.

On the rear platform of the last car, she watched the straight, shining rails recede in the distance. Telegraph wires flanked the rails as straight and uncurving as the iron tracks. Near North Bend a cluster of white Indian tepees attracted the attention of passengers, who rushed to the rear platform to see this uncommon settlement.

Adult Indians stood, arms folded, staring without expression at the passing train. Gitty had seen many Indians around Mattigan, mostly French-Indian loggers. These natives looked nothing like loggers. Their dark hair was braided. They covered themselves with blankets. Women carried their children in a rack on their backs.

Gitty returned to the passenger car. Later, at a village stop, the name painted on the depot said "Schuyler." The entire town was a few

169

houses painted white, a tank house and a tall skeleton windmill, whirling fast in the brisk breeze. A passenger who boarded at Schuyler seated himself next to Gitty.

At the supper station, Grand Island, the sun set. Raised among woods and always surrounded by tall trees, Gitty was awed by the spectacle. The vastness of the sky was overwhelming. When half of the huge sky turned pink, it was breathtaking. It reminded her of when Mama, Papa and she had walked to the sandy beach of Lake Michigan to watch the sun disappear into the dark lake. This treeless land almost resembled a huge body of water.

Next morning the passenger beside Gitty pointed out tufts of buffalo grass. "It don't look like much," he said, "but it's rich. See how it grows in short bunches with crimped leaves?"

His name was Barber and he was going to the Black Hills. The ticket agent in Chicago had advised Gitty to go to Cheyenne and then take the stagecoach to Deadwood. Mr. Barber said he was leaving the train at Sidney because Sidney was the closest railroad point to the Black Hills.

"You'll get there a lot faster, miss," he said, "if you get off at Sidney, as I'm a gonna do, and take the wagon road north to the hills."

Gitty considered his huge beaked nose and wondered.

Buffalo bones were scattered here and there along the way. When Gitty voiced her disappointment at not having seen a live buffalo, Barber replied, "No buff near tracks for three, four years. All gone. You gotta go farther nowadays to find buffler."

As the train neared Sidney the divides grew steeper. Distant hills were dotted with white tepees, a square barracks and some dugout houses. The brass-buttoned conductor announced there would be a twenty minute stop in Sidney. Only twenty minutes to make up her mind. Should she get off here, or continue on to Cheyenne?

People milling around the depot fascinated Gitty. Pawnee scouts bound for the Powder River country wore blue army coats three sizes too large. Men hoping to make their fortunes in the Hills were buying mining supplies in the outfitting stores. These fellows looked as if they'd just arrived from farms. Gitty picked her way along the plank sidewalk past shops, saloons and a small hotel. She smiled at the contrast between the magnificent Grand Pacific Hotel in Chicago and this plain frontier hotel.

Inside, she asked if a room were available. When told one was, she made up her mind. "I'll take it."

As the west-bound Union Pacific whistled its all-aboard warning, Gitty was lugging her heavy suitcase up the bare wooden steps toward her room. Why not? Mr. Barber said it was only 265 miles to Deadwood from here.

Monday, October 21, 1878

The room was pitch dark. Gitty had been sleeping for several hours when a noise awakened her. She lay still, trying to brush sleep from her head. Just as she realized that the sound was a key turning in her door lock, the door burst open. A figure leaped at her. The cold metal of a knife blade pressed against her throat.

"Don't scream or I'll slit your throat," the voice growled. "All I want is your money. Scream and I'll kill you and take it anyway."

Gitty gasped great gulps of air, trying not to scream.

"Money!" the voice demanded. The blade left her throat. "In your reticule?"

A match scratched as the intruder lit the lamp. Gitty squinted at the sudden light.

The robber pointed his knife at her. Gitty stiffened, closing her eyes. When she opened them she saw that the robber, red bandanna tied over his face, was counting her money.

"Is this all?" he demanded.

"Yes," she whispered.

He gave her a hard stare. Did he want more? Would he kill her? Gitty's whole body trembled.

"I'm goin'," the man said. "If you scream, I'll come back and kill you!" He backed out of the room.

When he closed the door Gitty put her head in her hands. What could she do? It was the middle of the night. Everyone was asleep, the streets deserted. If she ran after him, who could help? He'd stab her.

When she stopped shaking, the sobs began, great gulping sobs. Oh, Mama, Mama, she moaned softly. What am I to do?

As the eastern sky grew lighter, Gitty slid into exhausted sleep.

Later in the morning Gitty awakened. Her first thought was that she'd had a nightmare. She threw back the blanket and jumped from bed. On top of her suitcase lay her reticule. Gitty thrust her hand inside. Her fingers closed around her linen handkerchief. Nothing else. Her money *was* gone. She slumped on the edge of the bed and covered her face with her hands. What could she do?

171

Gitty was almost certain that the robber had been Barber, the passenger who'd encouraged her to leave the train at Sidney.

What a fool she'd been. Another greenhorn from the East. Barber had obviously had robbery in mind from the minute he spotted her on the train. There had been other empty seats, but he'd chosen to sit beside her. Gitty stroked the texture of her silk travel dress. Watered silk. Foolish! — advertising that she was a person with money.

By early afternoon she was in Oberfelder's Store, one of the two largest outfitting places in town. She explained to the storekeeper that she'd been robbed of all her money, that she'd like to trade her valise and the clothes in it for an outfit of boy's clothes, including a warm jacket.

At first, the storekeeper claimed he had no use for fancy ladies' clothes, but when he saw the quality of the dresses, he agreed to the trade. "Just one more thing," Gitty added. "I have no money, haven't eaten since yesterday. Would you buy my gold locket?"

The man hesitated, looking at her over his spectacles. Gitty's eyes filled with tears at the thought of giving up the locket which contained tintypes of her father and mother. The tears made the storekeeper relent.

Quickly, Gitty removed the locket from her neck and handed it to him in exchange for coins. "Thank you," she said quietly and turned to leave. Was she to have *nothing* from her past? Impetuously, she turned back toward the storekeeper. "There's a cashmere scarf — old. It belonged to my Mother. Please, could I keep it?"

The storekeeper pawed through the garments. "You mean this?" he asked, holding up the blue scarf.

Gitty nodded.

He tossed it to her. Clutching this one link to her past, Gitty left. Back in her room at the hotel Gitty tossed the boy's clothes onto the bed. She glanced at her wavy reflection in the cheap mirror over the washstand. All she saw was her coppery curls. For a long time she studied herself, then brusquely turned away. If Aunt Cath could do it, so could she.

Quickly, before she lost her nerve, Gitty found a chambermaid and borrowed a pair of shears. Swiftly she cut away at her auburn hair, shuddering each time a handful of curls hit the floor. When all the long hair was shorn, she began shaping the hair around her ears and on her neck. At last she set the shears down on the washstand and looked away from the mirror. It'll grow back, she told herself grimly.

Gitty took off her silk traveling dress and laid it carefully on the bed. She'd leave it as payment for the hotel room. She scrambled into

172

the boy's underdrawers, pants, and the gray shirt and brown sweater. The boots were stiff. Until they were broken in, it wouldn't be easy walking in them. She tugged them on over wool socks. At least the boots were a good fit. She clamped the black felt hat on top of her head and stalked to the mirror. A young boy looked back at her.

Looking around the room, Gitty tried to decide what else she needed to do. The auburn curls on the floor caught her attention. She'd have to get rid of them. For the time being, she stuffed the hair into her pockets. She wound the cashmere scarf around her neck. Somehow, wearing her Mother's scarf warmed her and soothed her. She stroked the soft texture and thought of Mama, Papa and Grandfather.

Tears prickled her eyes. With the back of her hand she rubbed them. Don't think of home! she told herself. Think of Aunt Cath — Adventure!

On the board walk in front of Oberfelder's outfitting store she watched men come out with their newly-purchased goldmining supplies. One by one, she approached them, asking if they needed a helper. Most of them ignored her. A few smiled, "Sorry, sonny."

One clean-shaven, gaunt man stopped and studied her for a moment. "What'ud you do to help, lad?" he asked.

Gitty cleared her throat. "I'd carry things for you, run errands, get firewood. I can cook, too," she added, smiling.

"Drive a team?" the man asked.

"I'll learn," Gitty replied with spirit.

"Sorry," the man said and walked off.

After an hour of similar rebuffs Gitty began to worry. She couldn't just start walking across the desert, heading north. She knew nothing of the dangers, but she was sure there were many. She had to find someone to give her food in exchange for work on the way to the Black Hills.

As her spirits sank lower, a gravelly voice said, "Hey, kid!"

She turned toward the speaker. A fetid stink met her nostrils. She was staring into a black beard crusted with dried food. With shock, she saw that bugs crawled in the man's beard. A cloud of sour stench emanated from him.

"You the kid looking for work?" he growled.

Gitty swallowed. She didn't want to work for such a filthy creature! Then her stomach growled with hunger groans. She asked, "What sort of work is it?"

"Buffalo skinner. Ain't no buffalo in these here parts no more. I'm a headin' north to hook up with a good buffalo hunter. Need someone to cook and work my goddamned mule team. Them damn mules so hard-mouthed it's a job to hook 'em up!"

"Where are you heading?" Gitty asked.

"Black Hills. Couple days out of The Hills I'm a gonna find me couple buffalo and take carcasses into The Hills. Meat costs, there. Lotsa miners."

Never in her life had Gitty been so repulsed by anyone. The insect-infested beard was enough to make her gag. The stench of his body was awful. His bushy black eyebrows shaded small, dark eyes. His deerskins were so encrusted with blood and dirt that they appeared black.

"I ain't got all day," he snapped. "Wanta go or not? I furnish grub. No pay."

"Yes, sir. I'll go." Gitty's voice was a whisper.

"Sir!" the man bellowed. He pulled off his brown felt hat and slapped his thigh with it. "Sir?" He collapsed in raucous laughter.

Gitty's face reddened. Passersby stared at them. Some stopped to watch.

"The kid called me 'Sir'," the buffalo skinner gasped to the gathering crowd as he wiped tears of laughter from his eyes. "Me! — Sir!"

A few watchers laughed with him. As soon as they caught a whiff of his stench, they pinched their nostrils with their fingers and walked off.

"All right, kid!" the man whacked Gitty on her back with the filthy hat. "Git over to the stable and hitch up Buck and Pansy — those hard-mouthed sons-of-bitchin' mules! One o' these days I'm a gonna skin 'em alive and feed 'em to the buzzards!"

Chapter 16
A Human Being—No, an Indian!

Sunday, November 3, 1878

The buffalo skinner and Gitty had headed north out of Sidney until they reached the north branch of the Platte River. There, the skinner followed the North Platte's southern bank. The river's course angled northwest. Gitty's job was to walk alongside the plodding mules. When they showed signs of balking, she flicked them with a switch. The wagon they pulled was empty, so the mules had a light load. Eb — this was the dirty buffalo skinner's name — said that eventually they'd be going through sand hills and that a heavily-loaded wagon would sink to the axles. Gitty wondered if all mules were as cantankerous as Buck and Pansy. Even pulling the light, unloaded wagon, both mules were obstinate and mean. She suspected that after years of Eb's mistreatment, they had become not only hard-mouthed, but ornery. Each morning as she and Eb struggled to harness the mules, Buck tried to bite Eb. The mule's big square teeth would clatter as he tried to bite his master. Eb would give Buck a frightful kick in the belly. The nasty mule and the filthy man went through this routine daily. Gitty was grateful that Buck hadn't yet tried to bite her.

Gitty had been very frightened when they started to cross the North Platte. The river was as wide as any river in Michigan, and she had assumed that like Michigan rivers, it had a current and deep water. As they waded into the chilly water, Gitty's heart beat faster. She was a good swimmer. Papa had taught her to swim when she was a child. But this water was cold and...she glanced apprehensively at the buffalo skinner, who wore his usual indifferent scowl.

As they moved into the center of the river Gitty looked at the cloudy yellow water. They were in the center of the river, and the water had not yet reached her knees! No wonder there weren't any ferry boats!

Gitty flicked her switch over Buck's back to urge him to climb the six-foot bank on the north shore. Buck and Pansy leaned into their harness; the wagon rumbled out of the river bed.

"Huh!" the skinner snorted, as he looked back at the wide river. "The mighty Platte!" he derided. "A mile wide and a foot deep!"

Late morning, they came upon a prairie dog town, where thousands of fat, furry creatures lived in crater-like holes in the sandy ground. The moment Gitty got close to a hole, the grayish-brown prairie dog popped inside his burrow to hide. Animals farther away were braver. They stood on their hind legs, barking shrilly, scolding the intruders.

Two explosive bangs startled Gitty. The skinner had shot two prairie dogs. He tossed the furry animals on the sand at Gitty's feet. He grunted, "Lunch. Clean 'em and cook 'em, kid."

Gitty had watched her mother clean chickens, so she supposed she could clean a prairie dog. Later, when she finally had the two plump little carcasses roasting on a spit over a buffalo-chip cook fire, she felt relieved, and even a bit proud of herself. She squatted by the fire and kept the spit turning. Before long the skinner ambled over. He pulled one of the roasted carcasses off the spit and frowned.

"You skinned it!" he complained. "Don't have to. Fire'd burn off the hair." With that he took an enormous bite. The meat juices ran down into his snarled black beard, mingled with the old food clinging to the whiskers and the insects inhabiting the beard.

Gitty wondered if she could eat a prairie dog. She was very hungry. Walking the miles of prairie each day required energy and gave her a big appetite. After some thought, she told herself to think of it as a squirrel. After all, a prairie dog wasn't a *dog*! It looked more like a squirrel or a small beaver. As she bit into the meat she discovered that it tasted much like the squirrels Papa shot back in the big woods in Michigan. I'll have to watch myself, she thought grimly. Very long out here in these sand hills with the skinner and she'd become like him.

Gitty walked down to the water hole to wash. Her reflection in the clear pool looked back at her. Her appearance no longer surprised her. For so many days now she had concentrated on acting like a young boy that her rough woolen trousers and jacket didn't seem strange anymore. Only when she unconsciously put her hand to her head did she feel the shock of feeling her missing curls. The buffalo skinner never had asked her name. He called her "Kid." Sometimes, as they walked across the hard-baked prairie, she wondered about the future, *her* future. Her parents were dead. Her grandfather had married a cheap, money-hungry woman. All Gitty had were the clothes on her back and her mother's soft warm scarf. If she had a future, it lay to the north, in the Black Hills at Stardancer, with her adventurous Aunt Cath.

On the opposite bank of the water hole she spotted a young cottonwood tree, and strode around the water hole toward it. She needed the brush for screening from Eb, since she felt the need to relieve herself. At first, Gitty had been nervous about going off by herself to empty her bladder and bowels. In this nearly treeless expanse, there were no convenient bushes and woods for modesty. That first day when they'd left Sidney she'd explained to the skinner that she couldn't pee in front of anybody. He'd grumbled "Humph!" and spat on the ground. Since then, he hadn't paid attention to when she went off by herself. He relieved himself wherever he happened to be when the urge struck him. He delighted in putting out cook fires. He watched with fascination as his stream sizzled and steamed on the hot embers.

As they moved northward, Gitty marveled at this treeless country. Only along watercourses could cottonwoods or stunted red cedar grow. Elsewhere, this was a land of pale brown grass or blow sand. They were entering an area dotted with small lakes, which was surprising considering the desert-like countryside.

In late afternoon, as they passed a small lake — really only a water hole — Gitty sauntered over to its shore, and dropped to her stomach, flattening herself to get a drink of water.

"No! *Stupid!* Dumb kid!" the buffalo skinner yelled. He continued with a litany of obscenities.

Bewildered, Gitty scrambled to her feet. Eb continued howling his string of foul words, waving his arms wildly.

At last enough words came through to her. This water hole was an alkaline lake — no good for drinking from. Because there was no vegetation growing on its shores, she should have recognized it as an alkaline wasteland.

She was getting an education in western dangers.

In the heart of the sand hill country Gitty discovered that the whole surface was dotted with conical hills of constantly shifting sand. The hills were topped with craters. The wind whirled in the depressions, scooping out more sand, and leaving strange hollows with circular rims. Yucca plants covered many hills. Their roots protected the hills from being blown away in the wind. In spite of the sandy ground, there was a great deal of vegetation.

The buffalo skinner was surprised and angry that there were no buffalo or antelope grazing among the rolling sand hills. He said this had been one of his best ranges. He climbed to the top of the tallest hill and looked in all directions, hoping to see some edible creature. He stamped down the sand hill, swearing, "Salt pork and beans tonight! Godalmighty! Salt pork in the middle of buffalo country! Shit!"

He stalked to the wagon and reached inside his haversack, pulling out a bottle of whiskey. Gitty shivered. She'd never seen the skinner drink. He was despicable enough, sober. What if he got drunk?

The big man walked back to the sand hill and sat on his haunches, leaning back against the slope. Grunting, he pulled the cork from the bottle with his teeth.

"I'm hungry, kid!" he bawled. "Get cookin'!"

While they ate their pork and bean supper, the buffalo skinner took noisy gulps from the brown whiskey bottle. After each slurping swallow, he wiped his lips with the hairy back of his hand. Gitty's initial uneasiness turned to concern. The cook fire burned low; only red embers were left. She moved out of the small circle of light. Quietly, she lifted her blanket out of the wagon and moved off into the darkness.

Sleeping away from the fire might be dangerous because of wolves. Even so, she believed that the drunken Eb could be worse danger.

Gitty found a scooped-out area on the far side of a conical hill. In the small depression she bundled up in her blanket. She heard faintly the skinner's drunken mumbling and cursing at a distance.

She dozed. When she awakened, she was aware that the crescent moon had risen in the east. Her hiding place was no longer in total darkness.

"Where'sh kid?" the skinner bellowed. "You! Kid! Come here! I need woman. No woman here. Boy better'n nuthin'! Come're, kid, or I'll kill ya'!"

Gitty lay still, biting her thumb to ease her terror. He muttered curses as he staggered about. The obscenities grew louder when he stumbled over the coffee pot and sent it clattering. Once, she saw him reeling unsteadily in the dim pale moonlight. Thankfully, his back was to her hiding place. He lurched in the opposite direction.

Eventually, no sounds at all. Gitty hoped that meant he'd gone to sleep. Or perhaps he'd fallen into the water hole. She hoped that he *had* drowned. Her mind reeled. Never had she wished a person dead. Now she would be happy to see the filthy skinner dead. But if he drowned, in the morning she wouldn't want to drink or wash out of the water hole. And where would she go?

What would she do in the morning — assuming the abominable skinner was still alive? For awhile she considered running off while it was still dark. But striking out on her own might be a fatal mistake. She'd have no water. She had no knowledge of where the water holes and watercourses were. What would she eat? She had no gun nor any way of getting food.

As the eastern sky glowed a pale yellow, Gitty made up her mind. She decided to stay, hoping the skinner wouldn't remember last night. She slipped out of her hiding place and moved silently toward the cold ashes of the cook fire. The tin coffee pot lay on its side. In the dusky light Gitty squinted, looking around for the skinner. Finally, she spotted his hulk under the wagon. He slept with his mouth wide open, snores gurgling from his throat.

Carrying the pot down to the water hole, she filled it with water. Perhaps the smell of brewing coffee would help his disposition. Just in case it didn't, Gitty slipped the paring knife into the pocket of her jacket.

Thursday, November 7, 1878

Eb awakened, groaning, belching, holding his head. "Coffee!" he bawled. She brought him a cup of the strong brew.

After breakfast of fried salt pork and beans, he heaved himself to his feet. He hadn't even taken his boots off to sleep. "Let's harness the mules, kid!" he growled, punctuating his order with a deep belch.

That was three days ago. There'd been no repetition of the drinking. Gitty had no way of knowing if he had more whiskey stowed away.

On the second day after that frightening night, they encountered the remains of a huge buffalo slaughter. A wide valley was strewn with dozens of buffalo carcasses. Massive white rib-cages scarred the prairie, lying bare and bleached, showing that even the strong and the healthy could perish. A dozen wolves prowled the site of the slaughter, or "stand" as Eb called it. One large wolf sat arrogantly on top of a buffalo head. It must have been a huge old bull. The expanse between its wrinkled horns was enormous. In spite of the bull's age and strength, the wolf sat there, howling to the heavens. Crows and buzzards cawed and hopped about, picking at the shreds of flesh remaining on the devastated carcasses.

Now, when they pulled up a rise, a purplish cloud rested always on the northern horizon. Eb said that was the Black Hills. Gitty's spirit rose. Even though the southern edge of The Hills was fifty miles distant, it cheered her to be able to see her destination, the place where she felt sure she'd be welcomed. No more would she be a penniless orphan adrift on a sea of grass with an uncouth, threatening buffalo skinner.

By sundown they had covered another twenty miles. The purple cloud on the horizon was definitely not a cloud any longer. Though Gitty never had seen mountains, she recognized that purple blur as distant mountains.

After he finished eating, Eb wrapped up in his blanket and crawled under the wagon to sleep. As usual, Gitty got as far from him as she could, still remaining in the protection of the campfire. She rolled up in her blanket and fell asleep in minutes.

In the night, her eyes flew open. It wasn't that she heard him. She smelled him — the sour smell of his unwashed body and the rancid food caught in his tangled beard. She rolled over. He was putting his blanket down beside her! Gitty lurched. His hand caught her shoulder. With a painful jerk, he shoved her back down onto the hard ground.

"Don't go fer boys," he mumbled. His hands moved over her body. "Too long, no woman. You gotta do, kid." He grabbed at the waistline of Gitty's trousers and yanked.

Buttons popped off the fly as the trousers and her underdrawers were pulled down. She screamed. Flailed out her arms. The man pinned her tight with one arm. His other arm was removing her trousers.

Suddenly, his big hand stopped moving. He grabbed at her crotch. "A girl!" he screamed. "Kid's a girl!" He howled hysterically. "Whoopee! Old Eb's gonna show you a good time, Kid!"

One last tug pulled the trousers over her ankles. While he was loosening his own trousers Gitty slipped out of his arms. He lunged. Her trousers came off in his hands. Gitty staggered, half crawling, toward the cook fire.

She could hear his heavy breathing as he lurched after her. Gitty grabbed the long butcher knife out of the iron skillet and, naked from the waist down, rolled over on her back to face him. His small eyes glistened. Not for a second did he take his eyes from her private parts. He stared at her nakedness, licking his lips. Gitty heard the harsh whistle of his breathing.

He fell to his hands and knees above her. As the horrid, foul-smelling whiskers moved close to her nose, Gitty plunged the butcher knife into the skinner's belly.

With a drawn-out expulsion of air, he dropped on top of her, motionless.

It was more than she could bear to have that stinking body on top of her. Grunting, sobbing, Gitty fought to wriggle out from under the still body. Shakily, she stood, shivering in the cold. She tossed buffalo chips on the embers of the cook fire. She needed more light. When she found her underdrawers and her trousers she hurriedly stepped into them, though her legs trembled so violently she had to direct them with her hands.

Gitty glanced nervously at the unmoving body. She half-expected him to get up and come after her. The enlarging dark pool of blood under him reassured her. She knew it would be impossible for her to harness the mules by herself. Rummaging in the wagon, she found some rope. A small piece of the rope held up her trousers: the rest she used to pack things on Pansy's broad back. Gitty hesitated to take the skinner's gun. She knew nothing about guns. Then, glancing uneasily at his unmoving body, she worried that if he roused, she wouldn't want him coming after her with a gun. She tied that on Pansy's back, too.

Heading off into the darkness, northerly, she rode Buck, pulling Pansy along by a length of rope. She didn't actually ride Buck; he didn't have a bit in his mouth. She just sat on his back, letting him have his head, relying on a mule's canny ability to preserve his own life by not walking off a cliff.

As Buck plodded onward, the trembling of her body lessened. She had been breathing in huge gulps, almost sobs, but now her breathing slowed. Be calm. You're all right, she assured herself. She shuddered as she thought of the horrid skinner pulling her clothes off.

Out in this wilderness, if she wanted to stay alive, she must be alert, watchful. Renegade Indians might be roaming about. Being taken by Indians could be worse than what nearly happened to her with the skinner. At least, that's what she'd heard: Indians made slaves out of white women and tortured them. Gitty had heard of a white woman who had been captured by Indians a few years back. The woman had borne two children while enslaved. Later, she was traded back to white missionaries. Constantly, she mourned her children, begged to be allowed to return to them. White people were repulsed by her, blaming her for becoming intimate with an Indian. Gitty couldn't remember for sure, but she thought the woman had drowned herself.

After an hour of riding blindly, Gitty decided there was enough distance between herself and the odious buffalo skinner. She stopped. Her trust in Buck had been stretched to the limit. From now on Gitty wanted to see where she was headed.

Friday, November 8, 1878

The sky glowed pink. Dawn was accompanied by a warm breeze from the south. Gitty guided the mules northward, keeping her eyes on the enlarging purple cloud on the horizon, the "cloud" that was the Black Hills. Sometimes she led both mules. Other times, when she grew tired, she crawled up on Buck's warm back. The problem with riding was that Buck had a tendency to head west and periodically she had to get off and correct their course by leading them due north.

By mid-morning the mild breeze blowing against her back was so warm that Gitty took off her jacket. Though she didn't know the exact date, Gitty thought it must be November. This was certainly strangely warm weather!

At mid-day, as they crossed a small stream, Gitty decided to pause to let the mules graze. Besides, coffee and side pork might give her energy. What with so little sleep and the energy it took to keep Buck under control, both arms ached, from her neck to her fingertips.

The steaming black coffee invigorated her. She chewed listlessly on the side pork. It tasted terrible, but she had to keep her strength up. If she hoped to survive, she'd have to stay strong. For courage, she glanced briefly toward the rising hump of the Black Hills.

"I'll be there soon, Aunt Cath!" she called, then felt silly.

While she was throwing sand on the cook fire, a sudden gust of wind blew ashes and sand in her face. Sputtering, Gitty spit the ashes from her mouth. Another blast of wind scattered the dry sand. Gitty shivered. She retrieved her jacket from Pansy's back. In moments, the warm day disappeared. The wind came steadily from the northwest. A dark cloud filled the sky to the north and west. Gitty looked back in the direction from which she'd come. In the south and east the remainder of bright blue sky glimmered.

The mules were balky. Gitty had a hard time getting them to leave their grazing. By the time she'd whipped Buck enough to get him plodding onward, spits of sharp sleet hurled at them from the darkening gray sky.

For an hour Gitty forced the mules northward through the sleet and rain. She was soaked through. Her teeth chattered. She squinted through the sleet, hoping to find something that could serve as shelter: a cave, trees, anything.

With dismay, she saw the sleet turn into flakes of snow. Gitty couldn't believe that weather could swing from balmy to a blizzard in such a short time. She'd heard that the West was a land of extremes. Now she saw how drastic those extremes could be. In a short time the gusty northwest wind covered the ground with two inches of snow. Though Gitty followed no trail, just headed northward toward the looming dark hills, the ground seemed to be rising. Gitty urged the mules up the slope of a hill. When they reached the crest, they slid and stumbled down the other side. She was more conscious of the hills now because of the slipperiness of the snow-covered slopes, but it did seem that they were climbing more than they were descending. Could it be that they were already in the foothills of the Black Hills?

The snow grew deeper. Gitty's shivering was so uncontrollable she could barely walk. Once more, she crawled up on Buck's back to ride awhile. As she shielded her eyes from the blowing snow, she thought she saw the darkness of a woods ahead, though her vision was blurred by the pelting white flakes. Yes! She was right! It *was* a woods: pine trees, with needles and branches for shelter.

Soon she rode into the protection of the woods. She followed a cleared trail through the forest. A rocky cliff rose on her left. Pine trees crowded the path on her right. The wind whistled in the pine needles far above her head.

Suddenly, from up on the cliff came a bloodcurdling scream. Seconds later, an echoing shriek came from Pansy. Buck lunged sideways. Gitty pitched head first over his back. Dimly, she sensed being thrown through the air. When her body smashed heavily into the hard rock wall, the pain was dull and pounding rather than sharp. For a moment, Gitty saw nothing but blackness. With enormous effort, she shook off the fuzziness. A horrible snarl came from where Pansy had been. Gitty struggled, pushing up to hands and knees, looked back. A giant cat stood on top of Pansy, who lay unmoving, on her side. The cat had chewed a huge hole in the mule's throat. Even through the thick white snow, Gitty could see that the mule's gray coat was blood red. Growling, slurping sounds came from the cat as it hungrily devoured Pansy. Buck was gone. The rope binding him to Pansy had snapped when he'd lunged forward to avoid the mountain lion.

Eyeing the monstrous cat warily, Gitty moved off down the trail away from it. The cat, intent on eating, didn't watch her. Briefly, Gitty thought of the gun tied to Pansy's back. With the cat crouching on top of the mule, there was no way to get the gun. Even if there were a safe way to retrieve it, Gitty didn't know how to load or fire it.

Once out of sight of the horrible cat, Gitty began to run, sobbing and retching. Fear put her beyond feeling. When she touched her forehead her hand came away red. She was bleeding from a cut on her head. Gitty stumbled on, gasping and sniffling.

Suddenly, she slowed her pace. What was it? Something tweaked at her brain, warning her to take notice. She stopped — stood absolutely still, peering into the falling snow. All she saw was more forest. Then she sensed something different. Gitty sniffed. That was it! The smell of wood smoke. Not far away, someone was burning logs. That meant a cabin. Oh, thank God! Human beings! Safety! Warmth!

Gitty stumbled on, sniffing the air like a dog. The pungent odor of burning wood grew stronger. She was getting closer! The path curved left. Gitty pressed on. A gust of swirling white snowflakes blew across the trace. When it cleared, Gitty stopped short.

She blinked, shook her head in horror. No! It can't be! Before her was a single tall, pale, animal-skin tipi. Climbing out of the flap doorway was a man. The wind tossed his black, straight hair across his face. He held out an arm to Gitty in a gesture of welcome. An Indian.

Gitty crumpled to the snow in a heap, sobbing hysterically.

Chapter 17
Doe Eyes

Gitty struggled to regain her wits. When would this nightmare end? She smelled wood burning. There must be a cabin nearby. Gitty opened her eyes and saw that the Indian was still standing beside the tipi. Gitty shuddered and closed her eyes.

"Don't be afraid," a voice said in perfect English. "I won't hurt you." Gitty felt a touch on her shoulder. She flinched. Lying on the snowy ground, she trembled as she awaited the agony of being scalped by the savage.

"Come inside my tipi," the low voice persisted. "Cougar not far away. You are wet, you will freeze." He put both hands under her armpits and forced Gitty to a sitting position. "Come," he said. He pulled her to her feet.

As the Indian tugged Gitty toward shelter, her legs buckled. She would have fallen if he hadn't caught her. After that, she leaned heavily on him as he guided her to the open flap of the tipi. She crouched, ducking her head, and stepped inside. Warmth from the cook fire in the center of the tipi fell upon her like a welcome cloak. She shivered.

"Out of wet clothes," the Indian said. "Lung fever if you don't." He rummaged through a cream-colored doeskin bag hanging from a tipi pole. "Wear my clothing until yours are dried out." He thrust an armful of buckskin garments toward Gitty.

Gitty's heart pounded in her chest. For the first time, she raised her eyes to look into his bronze face. His dark eyes gleamed warm — not like the wild eyes of a savage.

"Into dry clothes," he persisted, "or you become sick. Dry your skin before you put on the fresh clothes."

He dropped an armful of feathery wisps at Gitty's feet. They looked like the fluffy seeds of milkweed pods.

Gitty's face reddened at the thought of undressing in front of an Indian.

He seemed to sense her embarrassment.

"I turn my back to give privacy. While you dress I fix willow-bark tea. It warm you and give you strength." He turned away and knelt in the center of the large tipi beside the fire.

Her hands trembled so much that she had difficulty pulling off her soaked wool jacket. The wet wool smelled terrible. She almost giggled, but it turned into a strangled sob. Here she'd always heard how bad Indians smelled, and now *she* was stinking up this Indian's home with her dirty wet clothes.

Before slipping out of her drawers, Gitty took a deep breath. When she stood naked in the warmth of the tipi, she shivered. How she wished this was all only a horrible dream! At least the Indian was keeping his word. He remained kneeling with his back to her. With the fluffy milkweed seeds she rubbed herself until her skin stung. She slipped into the soft doeskin shirt and pants. The sleeves and pant legs were much too long for her so she rolled them up.

Gitty cleared her throat. She had not yet spoken to the Indian. "Thank you for the dry clothes," she said. Her voice wavered and cracked.

Gracefully, the Indian rose. He turned, handing her a curved animal horn — she thought it was a buffalo horn — filled with steaming hot liquid.

"Tea made from willow bark. Kills pain, soothes spirit," he explained. "You are traveling alone, or did something happen to your companions? Are there more people out there caught in blizzard?" He leaned toward her, his brown eyes gleaming as if concerned.

Gitty's hands trembled as she took the tea-filled horn. Her mind raced furiously. Would she be safer if he thought there were others nearby? Or would that make him feel threatened and more inclined to harm her? She just didn't know.

Gitty swallowed. "Last night my partner and I had a disagreement, and we parted company. That was a day's travel ago, and I don't know which direction he would have gone after I left him." Gitty's voice choked off. Her terror at being captive of an Indian made her nearly speechless. When she gulped a mouthful of the hot brew she could feel it sliding down to her stomach and soon her whole body warmed. Her uncontrollable shuddering lessened.

While Gitty continued to sip the steaming tea she looked about her, studying the tipi. She was impressed with how roomy and warm the tipi was. It was larger than many log cabins, and because the fire was in the center, the whole tipi was warmed by it. To think of how afraid she'd been just a short while ago when she saw that her rescuer was a savage! The Indian was acting like a kind and gentle human being. Gitty acknowledged to herself that she just might better off with this Indian than with some old prospector in a log cabin. A lonely white prospector might have turned out to be like the horrible buffalo skinner.

"My name is Doe Eyes," the Indian said as he inclined his head in a regal gesture.

Gitty looked into his brown eyes. She could understand why he had been named "Doe Eyes." His intense eyes did look like the large innocent eyes of a young doe. The Indian looked at her expectantly. Then she remembered. "I'm forgetting my manners, and I'm sorry," she gave a nervous laugh. "I'm George McDaniel," she lied.

The Indian studied her intently, his eyes probing into hers. She wondered if he believed her.

"How old are you, George?"

"Sixteen." Her voice was a whisper, but she told the truth.

"Your destination?"

"I'm on my way to join my aunt at Stardancer in the Black Hills."

"I don't know of Stardancer," the Indian said.

"I think it's a new place. A gold mining town." She paused, and for the first time she looked without fear at the dark-skinned man. "Do you live here all the time?" she gestured with her hand, sweeping around the tipi.

The man chuckled. He looked much younger when he smiled. Gitty had thought of him as perhaps in his forties or fifties, but now that he smiled she could see that he probably was much younger.

"No," he answered. "I usually live with my people on reservation. I'm out here to meditate and to make strong my spirit. I'm a shaman, a religious leader to my people. Time to time I stay in solitude to pray and think."

"I'm sorry I broke into your solitude," Gitty apologized.

The man's eyes crinkled kindly. "Glad I was here. Not another human being for miles."

187

Gitty shuddered as she realized how close she'd come to being mauled and eaten by that mountain lion! And if this Indian hadn't been here with his warm tipi, she would have frozen to death.

The Indian had re-filled her horn cup with more willow bark tea, and she continued to swallow the pungent liquid. Now that she was no longer convulsed by shudders and shakes, her body began to relax. She yawned.

"You tired," the Indian said sympathetically. "Willow bark tea helps sleep come." He had been sitting cross-legged on the hard earth, but he stood quickly, his ankles still crossed. "I get you bedding and blanket."

The man produced several colorful blankets with which he made up a pallet. From another side of the tipi he pulled out what looked to be a bedroll. As it was unrolled Gitty saw that it was a furry buffalo robe, complete with tail. When the Indian got it completely unrolled he lifted one side of it proudly. "This all blanket you need. Roll up in it anywhere. You stay warm."

Gitty took the buffalo robe from the Indian. She was surprised how heavy it was. The fur was soft, more like the wool of a sheep than the hair of a horse.

With a tired sigh she lay down on the pallet the Indian had made for her and pulled the buffalo robe over her. A part of her brain warned her that she should beware and not become too trusting of this Indian, but she was so very tired. Now that she was warm, she just wanted to sleep.

She didn't know how long she had slept, but she suspected it had been hours. When Gitty woke she was shaking uncontrollably. Her teeth chattered. She coughed, and the tight pain in her chest was terrible. Again, she coughed. She could hardly get a breath.

She was only vaguely aware of the Indian's palm pressing on her feverish forehead.

✳   ✳   ✳   ✳

Doe Eyes threw more wood on the fire. When the new logs crackled with flames he placed five round stones in the middle of his camp fire. From a hanger on the tipi wall he removed a rawhide container. Ducking under the flap protecting the doorway, Doe Eyes went outside where he filled the container with water from the creek trickling downhill behind his tipi. He reached over his head and broke a snow-encrusted bough from a slender cedar tree. Once back inside, he set the rawhide bucket near the fire. He dipped his hand into the chilly water and then flicked his wrist over the heating stones. The water droplets bounced and sputtered as they hit the hot stones. He grunted to himself. The stones were hot enough.

He plunged the green cedar bough into the bucket of water, and shook the dripping branch forcefully over the heated rocks. As the drops of water hit the stones, great clouds of steam rose, filling the tipi with pungent warm dampness. Again and again Doe Eyes dipped the branch and shook it over the fire, each time bringing up a fresh pine-smelling steam cloud.

Every so often he walked over to the white boy's pallet and felt the brow of the sleeping youth. Sad lines creased around Doe Eyes's lips; he shook his head mournfully. The boy was not getting better. His fever was bad. What should he do? Doe Eyes thought of his mother and her "skin-to-skin" treatment. When nothing else seemed to break a fever, she'd said, "Let the sick one soak the healthy spirits from your body." No clothing could interfere. Quickly, Doe Eyes stepped out of his pants and pulled his shirt off over his head. Once more he shook the wet cedar bough over the rocks, then turned to the flushed youth. The shirt was so big for the slender boy that Doe Eyes had no trouble working his limp arms out of the sleeves. Gently, Doe Eyes pulled the doeskin shirt over the tousled auburn head. For one moment Doe Eyes touched the curly copper-haired head. Such strange color for hair!

Doe Eyes turned back the buffalo robe in order to remove the boy's pants. His eyes widened as they fell on the boy's chest. Two round breasts curved out from the chest. Doe Eyes blinked. For a moment his mind tricked him, trying to tell him that perhaps white men had breasts when they were young. Slowly and with a troubled frown, Doe Eyes began to pull down the pants. This fearfully ill intruder was a young girl! He closed his eyes as a wave of discomfort swept over him. Muttering a quick prayer to The Great One, he asked that he be helped to remember his vows of celibacy.

With an agonized sigh, Doe Eyes crawled beneath the buffalo robe. Gently, he turned the girl on her side facing away from him, and he enveloped her naked skin with his own. The soft skin of her back and buttocks was hot and dry. At each breath deep rasping sounds rattled in her chest. Doe Eyes lay still and concentrated, willing his strong spirits to enter the girl's body. His spirits should be strong. For more than ten sunsets he had been here, away from his people, praying and meditating. Doe Eyes intensified his concentration until he could feel the healthy spirits seeping from his skin and entering the feverish body of the girl.

Eventually her skin began to feel damp. When at last she was actually perspiring, he slipped out from beneath the buffalo robe. Quickly, he stepped into his doeskin pants and pulled on his shirt. In case the girl should awaken he wouldn't want to frighten her with nakedness. Such a young little thing. He wondered why her hair was so short. He was quite sure that white women, like Indian women, prided themselves on a head of long hair.

Doe Eyes resumed sprinkling water from the cedar boughs onto the heated rocks, and once again the tipi was filled with pungent steam.

Every so often the girl's body heaved with spasms of coughing, but with each coughing spell the cough was more moist and loose than before.

※　　　　※　　　　※　　　　※

A long session of coughing and spitting up wakened Gitty. Groggily, she raised herself to one elbow to ease the pain in her chest as the coughing spasms continued. When she moved to sit upright she suddenly realized she was naked. She slid back under the buffalo robe, her cheeks reddening. I'm not wearing any clothes! How did I get like this? Water sputtering on the fire drew her attention to the center of the tipi. Oh, Lord, *no*! The Indian is still here! He was shaking a branch over the fire and watching her. Was it some Indian ritual or incantation?

Her body ached. She felt weak. She doubted if she could stand up. How long had she been sleeping? Why did she feel so terrible? For several moments a fierce spasm of coughing shook her.

The Indian explained without being asked. "You had lung fever. You very sick. My healthy spirits entered your body. Fought sick spirits. You look better.

"I make pemmican broth. Help your spirits grow strong." He knelt at the fire and began collecting cooking equipment. He was preparing to make the broth in a heavy iron skillet. Surely, that was a white man's utensil.

Gitty studied the lean man's back. His black hair was drawn severely into two braids interlaced with strands of nearly white buckskin.

190

Who was this Indian? Uncomfortably, she realized that the Indian must have undressed her while she was out of her head with fever. That meant that he had discovered that she was female. Somehow his attitude toward her didn't seem any different from when he thought she was a boy. Still...Gitty didn't trust him. She'd heard too many horrifying stories about Indians and how they treated white women.

As her mind cleared, she decided she'd feel more comfortable with clothes on. Beneath the heavy buffalo robe, silently, almost secretively, she began to wiggle into the doeskin pants. Because of the weight of the heavy robe it wasn't easy, and by the time she pulled the pants up to her waist Gitty lay perspiring and exhausted. She had become terribly weak.

Some time passed before she felt strong enough to struggle into the shirt. The exertion of doing that wore her out. She lay still, breathing heavily. At least she was no longer naked. When the pemmican broth had simmered long enough to suit the Indian's satisfaction, he filled a buffalo horn with it and brought it to Gitty on her pallet. With effort, she struggled to sit. She reached for the horn. Her hands trembled so much that the steaming broth spilled from the horn, and the Indian retrieved it from her hands.

"Still weak," he said. "That why your hands shake. I'll hold it." As if he were feeding an infant, Doe Eyes patiently held the hot broth to Gitty's mouth and then leaned back, waiting for her to swallow and rest before he moved the horn back toward her lips once again.

After a week, or "seven sunsets" as Doe Eyes called it, Gitty was well. She had to laugh now when she recalled her initial terror of the Indian. Never had she encountered a more gentle or tender person than this tall Indian. Even her own mother could not have nursed her more thoughtfully or efficiently. Gitty peeked shyly from beneath her lashes toward the far side of the tent where Doe Eyes had retired to meditate.

He sat cross-legged, arms folded, eyes closed. Gitty thought of those warm brown eyes and smiled. His prominent cheekbones and straight nose framed expressive eyes. His nut-brown skin glowed in the flickering firelight. Gitty sighed. It gave her pleasure just to look at him, his face serene in his meditations.

Doe Eyes told her he had always been a shaman to his people, beginning study under his mother's brother when "the teeth of manhood emerged from his gums." He married young, and his beautiful wife gave him two fine sons. For many years his group of Dakota Indians had camped near a white settlement. As a boy, Doe Eyes had learned the English language and become the interpreter between the white community and his people. The Methodist minister in the town had grown fond of Doe Eyes. He spent hours teaching the young shaman the finer points of English and trying to explain Christianity to Doe Eyes.

Doe Eyes was impressed with the teachings of this white man's religion and came to the point where he explained Christianity to his wife and small sons. Though he hardly admitted it to himself, one part of his mind actively considered converting to Christianity.

Cruel violence changed his mind. Some traveling white people who said they were missionaries came to the Indian camp. They traded colorful woolen blankets for furs. Small One, Doe Eye's wife, received a bright blue-and-red blanket in exchange for a fox fur she had meticulously tanned. The so-called missionaries left. Not long afterwards, Small One and the two sons of Doe Eyes suffered chills and severe pains of the back and legs. Soon they were vomiting uncontrollably. When red spots appeared on their skin, Doe Eyes feared the worst: his wife and children were stricken with the dread white man's disease, smallpox. The Dakota people had no tolerance for the devastating disease. First the youngest son died; within twenty-four hours Doe Eyes lost the rest of his family. In all, in the Indian encampment, one out of every three people died. When Doe Eyes told Gitty about this tragic time in his life, his mouth turned downward in uncharacteristic bitterness.

"I think," he said, "those evil people on purpose gave us sick blankets. I think they were blankets that had warmed people sick with smallpox." He sighed and closed his eyes. "Many people want my people to disappear."

After the death of his family, Doe Eyes withdrew from contact with whites. He wanted nothing to do with them. Gitty was the first white person he had spoken to in many years.

Across the tipi, Doe Eyes stirred and opened his eyes. Apparently, his meditation was over. Gitty never minded the time he spent in silent contemplation. She loved sitting quietly and, unknown to him, studying his handsome features.

In a smooth movement, he rose and raised his arms overhead, stretching, turned toward Gitty. When he caught her looking at him his lips parted. He gave her a broad smile. "Perhaps it is time to eat?" he asked. "We cook the rabbits I snared this morning." In three long strides he reached the doorway and opened the flap. "I keep them in the snow," he added as he reached outside.

Smiling softly, Gitty watched his every move. It was really curious. Here she was, lost in the wilderness, snowbound in a tipi with an Indian medicine man, and she was not afraid. She watched Doe Eyes carry the skinned rabbit carcasses toward the cook fire, not understanding her feelings at all. With Doe Eyes, she felt safe and cared for. And she had always thought of Indians as savages.

It was Eb, the buffalo skinner, who was the savage. She shuddered at the thought of him. She wondered if she had killed him. To kill a human being was a terrible thing. *Thou shalt not kill* is one of the Ten Commandments. Somehow, Gitty didn't feel guilty. She had been defending herself. Besides, the skinner hardly seemed human.

Doe Eyes touched her arm. "Something wrong? You feel pain?"

At his touch, Gitty broke into a happy smile. How warm she felt here! Doe Eyes knelt beside her; his eyes gleamed with concern.

"No," she shook her head, placed her hand on his doeskin sleeve. "I was thinking of an evil man who frightened me very much."

"He can't hurt you here," Doe Eyes spoke softly, his voice a caressing whisper.

Their faces were close, his brown eyes probed deep into her green ones, seeking. Doe Eyes raised his brown hand and lightly touched the side of Gitty's face. "You are lovely, my copper-haired lady."

Gitty leaned toward the searching dark eyes. Softly, Doe Eyes's lips touched hers. A thrill shivered throughout Gitty's body. As his lips pressed firmly against hers, she reached up to touch his neck, stroking the soft skin there.

Doe Eyes's warm hands stroked her cheeks, the tips of his fingers grazing across her skin. For a long time they exchanged a lingering kiss.

Suddenly, Doe Eyes groaned — a harsh, desperate sound. He pressed Gitty back down onto her pallet, moved his body from a kneeling position to where he lay on his stomach beside her. Reaching across her shoulder, he tipped her face toward his. His lips were moist, more insistent than before. Gitty returned his kiss.

His hand slipped under her doeskin shirt. She caught her breath. Her body tensed. Then, as he gently stroked her breasts she relaxed. Gitty let herself slide into a new world promising pleasure.

Chapter 18
Don't Look Back

Fierce storms and heavy snows battered them off and on all winter. For a while, Gitty marked off the days by dabbing a piece of charcoal on a parfleche packing case Doe Eyes gave her to hold her belongings: the boy's clothes she'd arrived in and her mother's blue cashmere scarf. She couldn't be sure when Christmas Day approached and passed. Doe Eyes called December "The Moon of the Popping Trees," and January was "The Moon of Frost on the Lodge." The present moon, he said, was "The Moon of the Dark Red Calf," and the next moon was of Snowblindness.

Doe Eyes was a good hunter, skilled with bow and arrow. Game had been plentiful; they always had enough meat. Gitty tried to be grateful for Doe Eyes' hunting skills, but often she yearned for vegetables, jams and wheat bread. Occasional dried berries were a treat. Doe Eyes had brought the berries with him from the reservation so that even in wintertime he could make pemmican. Every day they drank spruce tea. Doe Eyes said this would prevent them from losing their teeth during the winter months when fresh fruits and berries weren't available.

On days when it wasn't too cold Gitty accompanied Doe Eyes while he checked his snare lines. They giggled and threw snow at each other, tussling like children in the clean snow. He taught her how to shoot arrows from his bow, which he had made out of ash and strung with two buffalo sinews twisted together. Doe Eyes said Gitty was good with the bow — better than some of the braves, he admitted ruefully with a lop-sided grin. Gitty's heart swelled. Doe Eyes was a handsome man. His hooded eyes were spaced wide over high, curved cheek bones. His nose was straight, lips full.

One day around the middle of January the temperature rose to almost spring-like warmth. Gitty and Doe Eyes walked far that day, enjoying the balmy air. They were an hour's walk from their tipi when Doe Eyes grunted and knelt, studying the ground. He picked up charred ashes and ground them between his fingers. He walked in a small circle, examining the earth. After awhile he straightened. "Nine or ten Dakotah camped here overnight," he announced.

"How could you tell?" Gitty asked skeptically.

"Horse droppings, size of holes left by lodge pins. They built sweat lodge. That means they camped overnight. Their moccasins are sewn with thread instead of sinew. All signs are left to read," he answered, grinning with pride in his ability.

When the screaming winds roared down from the mountains and snow swirled thick through the air, Gitty stayed in the warm tipi when Doe Eyes went out to hunt. Housekeeping in a tipi was simple. Buckskin bags hanging from the walls of the round dwelling held pipes, food, fire-making tools, medicines, tobacco and sewing tools. There wasn't much to get messy or dirty. She learned how to adjust the flap for the smoke hole near the top of the tipi so the smoke from the fire would go up and out, and not fill the tipi. The hole faced east, away from the prevailing wind.

On fierce, wintry days when Doe Eyes returned from his hunting trips, he was shivering with cold. While he was out hunting, Gitty always kept a pot of spruce tea simmering on the edge of the cook fire so she could hand him hot tea the minute he stepped inside the tipi. After he had downed the tea, it became a ritual for Gitty to undress Doe Eyes, slowly peeling off the chilly layers of buckskin. When he was completely undressed, she led him to the brown buffalo robe bed and pressed him down onto the soft fur. While his eyes glowed with passion, she slowly took off her pale doeskin garments, never taking her eyes from his. Then, slowly, she lowered herself to the fur and covered his cool body with her warm, soft skin.

After making love, they dozed for awhile, bodies and legs enwrapped. Waking, they lay on the buffalo robe bed and talked. Doe Eyes taught Gitty some Dakota words. She learned that "sapa" was black, that "ska" was white, and "sa" was red. Doe Eyes said he was called a "wicasa wakan," a holy man who can cure illnesses, prophesy the future, commune with stones and herbs, conduct the sundance, and change the weather. Each time before conducting the sundance, he had to do a hanblechia, a vision quest in which he stayed in a pit four days and nights with no food or water.

Sometimes, during the dark hours of the night, when the fire had burned low, Gitty awakened. Raising herself on one elbow, she'd quietly study Doe Eyes' sleeping face, dimly visible in the glow of the embers. Gitty no longer thought of Doe Eyes as an Indian. He was a dear man, a man who had saved her life and who treated her lovingly and kindly. Gitty took pleasure in stroking his hairless brown skin and watching his lips spread into a smile of delighted pleasure. When they had first become lovers, Gitty was so thunderstruck by the newness and the power of her sensual emotions that she'd given no thought to her lover's background. But, once, while Doe Eyes was doing his daily meditation, the awesome thought came to Gitty: What am I doing here? In a tipi, making love with an Indian? Goose pimples rose on her arms. What would Mama think? She shuddered and bit on her lip to keep from sobbing.

One night, she awakened and studied Doe Eyes' features in the faint firelight. He is handsome, she smiled to herself, and kind, and loving, and...but she couldn't say, "everything a girl would want in a husband." Doe Eyes was an Indian medicine man, dedicated to the nurturing of his people. This was the moment she began to think about their future.

She got into the habit of awakening in the wee hours to study Doe Eyes and ponder their future. At last she came to the realization that they had no future. There was no such thing as *our* future. Doe Eyes and she each had a future, but it could not be together. When winter ends, Doe Eyes would return to his people. She would not, could not go with him. Tears trickled down her cheeks, blurring her vision.

She wanted to be with Doe Eyes. She couldn't bear the thought of being parted from him. But she would not spend her life with a strange people. She wouldn't make his people, *her* people. She wanted her Aunt Cath. She was a white woman, used to modern conveniences. She wouldn't live out her life in a tipi, not even with Doe Eyes.

Gitty jumped at the sound of Doe Eyes' voice. She hadn't realized he had awakened.

He lifted a brown arm out from beneath the buffalo robe and stroked her cheek. "What are you fretting about, my Little Flame?" His eyes sought hers, begging to understand.

"What is to become of us?" she whispered.

A shadow of pain hurried across his face. He stared up at the air vent, then turned to look at her. His dark eyes filled with tears and spilled down his temples. He closed his eyes for a few moments, then heaved a shuddering sigh. "I must go back to my people," he said.

Gitty nodded. "I know."

Their eyes held for a time until Gitty turned her face toward the glowing embers. "I can't go with you."

There was a long moment of silence. "As my wife, you could."

His wife. To live with him, sleep with him for the rest of her life. For Doe Eyes, that would mean giving up being a medicine man, since he would not be celibate. Gitty turned back to the dear face. His eyes begged her not to abandon their love.

She touched his chin with the tip of her finger. "You say that I could, my dearest," she whispered, "but the problem is that I will not. I want to go to my people."

Doe Eyes clutched Gitty's hand close to his neck. For a long time, they stared into each other's eyes.

"I understand," he said at last. "Our love is impossible. I have my destiny, you, yours. It was good fortune to share a part of the road as we walk to fate." He smiled, wiped a tear from her cheek. "Let us not weep. Instead, rejoice that we are together in this warm place while the winter wind blows. We celebrate our days together instead of thinking about our time apart. Come to me, Little Flame." With both arms he encircled her body and pulled her across his chest.

Gitty nuzzled his warm neck and forgot about the future.

❊   ❊   ❊   ❊

As Gitty knelt by the fire preparing tea a nightmarish high-pitched scream echoed outside the tipi. She recoiled. Boiling water splashed on her hand. As she pressed her burned fingers against the cool doeskin of her shirt she stared at Doe Eyes.

"What was that?" Her eyes were wide.

Another scream pierced the silence of the woods. This time it was farther away.

"Cougar," he answered, his voice harsh. "I feared this. For two days my trap lines are empty, cat paw prints around them. Cougar eats all the game I snare."

With a sigh, Doe Eyes stood and reached for his fur-lined hunting shirt.

"Don't go out there!" Gitty cried. "That awful creature might hurt you. Please don't go out, Doe Eyes!" Her eyes beseeched him to stay inside with her.

"He takes our food." He frowned, creases wrinkling his forehead. "I must kill him, or we starve before spring." He took the large copper-headed tomahawk from its parfleche and picked up his bow and arrows. "I won't go far, Little Flame." He stroked Gitty's cheek, turned and opened the flap. A gust of cold air rushed into the tipi as he moved through the doorway. When the flap closed behind him, Gitty shivered so hard her teeth chattered.

She was trembling with fear. How could she bear to have Doe Eyes out hunting that giant cat? What if something happened to Doe Eyes? Whatever would she do? Then she remembered that once warm weather made it safe to travel, they would be going their separate ways — he to his reservation, and she on to Stardancer. Thinking of Aunt Cath took her mind off the danger lurking outside. Gitty put her mind to picturing what Aunt Cath must look like. If her Mother were alive, she'd be thirty-seven. Aunt Cath was two years older, so that would make her thirty-nine. That was getting up there. Actually, her Mother had looked quite beautiful, so perhaps Aunt Cath had aged gracefully, too. Grandpa said Aunt Cath's hair had been like spun gold...

Her thoughts froze at the sound: a sharp grunt, followed by a hiss. Gitty sat still on the buffalo robe, not blinking. Was it the cat? Long moments passed with silence. At last, her ears picked up a crunching sound on the snow. Something moved in the snow outside the tipi. The hair on Gitty's neck prickled.

A shrill scream rent the air. It was close — just outside the tipi skins! Gitty looked about wildly for something with which she could defend herself. Doe Eyes had taken both bow and tomahawk. What could she use? In desperation, she snatched a burning stick from the fire. Just as she brandished the burning weapon, pointing it in the direction of the scream, the cougar gave another shriek and took a swipe at the tipi with his claws.

The tipi skin shredded away in a two-foot gash. A second slash of the cat's claws just below the first opened a wide gap in the skin-wall. The cougar's almond eyes glowered at her. For a moment they stared at each other. A snarl came from deep in the cougar's throat just before he leaped at the hole. Gitty thrust her burning stick toward the cat and screamed.

At that moment Doe Eyes, yelling and waving his tomahawk, burst through the tent flap. In a blur of speed, the tomahawk flew through the air toward the cat. With a thud, it imbedded itself in the cougar's jaw, beneath the left ear.

"Get over!" Doe Eyes yelled at Gitty, pointing to the far edge of the tipi.

The cat fell on its side, its legs kicking convulsively. With a mighty lurch, it rolled to its stomach and struggled to rise, staggering into Gitty's lap. She threw her arms over her face and cowered against the skin wall.

A thud, a grunt, a terrible scream filled the tipi. At first Gitty thought the cry came from the cat, but as she took her arms away from her face, she realized that it was Doe Eyes who had screamed. He lay atop the cat, which lay unmoving. Scarlet blood seeped from Doe Eyes' belly, soaking his buckskins.

"I thought it got you," he gasped, his dark face contorted.

"What can I do?" Gitty cried. She stroked his temple, helpless.

"Pressure on wound. Keep cuts clean." Each word was said slowly, punctuated with grunts of pain.

"Is something in your medicine bag for pain?" Gitty asked.

He pointed.

Gasping, heaving, Gitty managed to pull Doe Eyes off the cougar and over to their fur skin bed. She jumped up and lifted the medicine bag down from its hanger.

Doe Eyes grimaced. Through clenched teeth, he said, "Small, dark red balls."

Her hands shook so badly Gitty had trouble opening the small drawstring pouches. At last, she found one containing dark red round seeds. "How many?" she asked.

Feebly, he lifted one finger.

Gitty placed a red seed between his lips. He chewed it.

"I grow very cold," he groaned. "Keep me warm."

※   ※   ※   ※

The three weeks following the cougar's attack were a nightmare, but Gitty managed to keep Doe Eyes and herself alive.

Using her experience in dressing out the prairie dogs when she was with the buffalo skinner, she cleaned the cougar's carcass. She even figured out that she should get rid of the inedible parts, disposing of them far from the tipi, since it might attract wolves or even another cougar. After cutting the carcass into chunks, she suspended them from nearby trees to keep them safe from wolves and foxes. She mended the torn tipi. It didn't look neat, but it kept the frigid winds out.

Most of all, she cared for Doe Eyes. The first ten days, he was out of his head most of the time, from the seeds he demanded for his pain.

One day, when his eyes appeared more clear, he rasped, "Don't give me red seeds as I ask. I ask, but spread them out. Must get away from them. Not good." His face contorted in agony, then smoothed out. Weakly, he asked, "Do you carry my seed? I have not seen you attend to your moon bleeds."

Gitty swallowed. "You just haven't noticed," she answered and moved to stir the soup bubbling on the cook fire.

After that, she did as instructed, even though Doe Eyes begged and sometimes raged at her for denying him the relief from pain. Gitty decided that the seeds were bad, for they brought out a nasty, demanding side of him that was not like her gentle lover.

Whenever Doe Eyes came out of his stupor for a few moments, Gitty held a horn of hot cougar meat broth to his lips. One day, when he was particularly lucid, Doe Eyes asked what sort of broth it was.

"Made from the cougar you killed," she told him.

Doe Eyes grunted approval. "Good. Cougar's strength will flow into me, the victor."

Gitty hoped he was right. Actually, she was using the cougar meat because that was the only meat available.

The stench in the tipi was awful. Doe Eyes had suffered four deep wounds in his belly from the dying kick of the cougar. One of them, deeper than the others, had gone all the way through the abdominal wall, into the bowel. Though Gitty worked constantly at keeping the wounds clean, the deeper one was impossible. Fecal matter oozed out. She dabbed and blotted at the foul-smelling material. When she went outside to get firewood or more cougar meat for broth, she gratefully filled her lungs with crisp, fresh air. Usually, she remained outside for several minutes, walking about, stretching her legs. She was careful to never get too far from the tipi in case Doe Eyes called her. When he did, and he usually did after five minutes of her absence, Gitty had to force herself to lift the flap and go back into that foul-smelling cage inhabited by the desperately sick man who needed her care.

✳   ✳   ✳   ✳

Spring was definitely upon them, though the nights were still crisp and cold enough to freeze water standing in puddles. Some time in the past few weeks, she knew, there had been a day which had been her seventeenth birthday. She had lost track of the days, though Doe Eyes knew exactly where they were in his calendar of moons.

Doe Eyes had regained his strength. Though he was thinner and his face had added creases beneath his cheekbones, his appearance was much the same as before his encounter with the cougar. With his clothes on he seemed the same, but his hard, brown belly never would be. The four, parallel wounds had healed and were now dark red scars. The deeper wound had developed a hole with a tract leading into the bowel and fecal material continued to ooze out of the hole and onto Doe Eyes' belly. He kept skins on the hole, and Gitty knew he tried to keep it clean, but even so, there was an odor of bowel material about him all the time. Outside, in the fresh air, sometimes she didn't notice it, but a whiff of breeze could bring the distasteful smell to her nose.

Doe Eyes was aware of her revulsion. Never once since he had recovered had he made a physical advance, or even touched her. While he was so desperately sick she had made a pallet for herself a few feet away from their bed, upon which Doe Eyes lay. After his recovery, she continued to sleep away from him. Sometimes, in the evening when they sat talking in the light of the campfire, Gitty saw the old familiar warm, loving glow build in his eyes. She knew that with any encouragement at all, he would take her into his arms. She didn't want that. She couldn't bear it. She loved him, really loved him, but in a special way. She could never recapture the passions and delights of the winter. Then, she had been like a butterfly coming out of its cocoon, fanning its wings to dry. Now her wings were no longer damp, her debt to Doe Eyes for saving her life was repaid. Gitty was ready to get on with her life. Only the fear of getting caught in a springtime mountain snowstorm kept her here.

Doe Eyes came out of the tipi to join her. She knew he had been cleansing his wound again. She gave him a quick smile.

"Anxious to move on, my Little Flame?" he asked.

"I've never seen my aunt," Gitty answered, shuddering at the whine she heard in her voice.

202

"Of course," Doe Eyes agreed, a bit too heartily. "I must return to my people. They expect me long before this." He frowned. "You should travel as a boy into the Black Hills. The miners, many of them are rough. Your hair is too long. I will shorten it."

With a razor-sharp stone blade, Doe Eyes cut Gitty's copper-colored hair until once again she resembled a boy. Though Gitty didn't notice, Doe Eyes carefully set aside a lock of her auburn hair. He brought out doeskin pouches of pemmican which he had made for them to eat while traveling, each in their separate directions.

Just before sunup Gitty awakened to the sound of Doe Eyes adding kindling to the cook fire. When he saw that she was awake, he said, "I want you to get an early start. I wish you to be on your way as soon as it is light."

The woolen clothes felt strange against her skin after so many months of wearing soft doeskin.

Doe Eyes grinned when he saw her standing awkwardly in the white boy's clothes. "Somehow, Little Flame, you don't look as much like a boy as you did when you arrived. There is a woman-look in your eyes."

Gitty blushed. But she knew he was right. She felt like a woman, not the naive sixteen-year-old of last November. She'd given her love and her body, and in return she'd been loved. Perhaps some people never experience this in their whole lifetime — never once a mutual, loving relationship.

After they had eaten, Doe Eyes rose abruptly. "It is time for you to go. The sun stretches up over the earth to wish you a safe journey. My prayers go with you, Little Flame."

He led her to the edge of the small clearing beyond the tipi and pointed north along the trail. "There are many trails, and you must ask for Stardancer at mining camps and settlements you come to."

He put both his hands on her shoulders and looked into her eyes. "I thank The Great Spirit for sending you to me. Your memory I keep in my heart for my life. Whenever I wish, I lift the memory of you from its special place and stroke it." He leaned forward and pressed his lips gently to her forehead.

Tears brimmed out of her eyes as she stood before this gentle man with his lips touching her skin. As the tears slid down her cheeks, her resolve to leave weakened. How could she leave this good and loving man?

Doe Eyes dropped his arms. He saw her eyes streaming with tears. His face softened. "Don't cry, Little Flame. This day has to be — ever since the day you stumbled to my tipi. We not meant to be man and wife. Our journey together was only for a few moons, and long enough for us to save each other's life. Leave now, little one. Hold a place for our time together in your spirit."

"Oh, Doe Eyes!" Gitty threw herself into his arms. "How could I *ever* forget you?"

As she rested her head against his buckskin shirt the stench of fecal matter wafted up to her nose. Her body stiffened.

Gently, Doe Eyes moved her away from him. "Go, little one," he ordered. "Don't look back. It just make worse our pain." He gave her a light shove toward the path.

Lifting her shoulders, raising her chin, she started off at a brisk walk. At the top of the first rise she stopped, turned. The tall white tipi was small in the distance. Standing in front of it was the far-off figure of an Indian in golden buckskins. Gitty raised her arm straight over her head and waved it slowly, back and forth.

The distant shape raised his arm in answer.

She turned and headed down the incline, blinking away the unwanted tears.

Chapter 19
Cath's Millinery Shop

As Gitty climbed ever higher in the Black Hills the scenery grew more spectacular. Tiny wildflowers with purplish furry petals peeked from the rocky earth, adding their color to the pink wild roses and the greening springtime grasses. The trees were leafing out in delicate shades of yellow and green. Dark Ponderosa and spruce pine towered over them. Massive distant peaks wore white caps of snow. The trail angled along a rocky ridge that bordered a wide, deep canyon in which flowed a mountain freshet. Across the canyon, spire-like granite fingers pointed heavenward.

Gitty took a deep breath. What rugged grandeur! Doe Eyes said the Black Hills region was sacred to the Dakotah. He said the Indians were angry when white men trespassed upon their holy ground and cut gold from its breast.

As the trail wound hairpin-like around another mountain, Gitty wondered why these were called the Black "Hills." They seemed high enough to qualify as mountains. Though she had never seen a mountain, she'd seen pictures of the Adirondacks in the East. She thought these hills were much taller and grander than those. The Black Hills seemed to be doubly mis-named. From fifty miles away, they appeared purple. From her winter camp with Doe Eyes they'd seemed black, but now that she was in their midst Gitty thought of them as the "Green Hills," or even the "Green Mountains."

Many of the tracks she followed were lined with ditches and sluice boxes apparently left behind by miners who had panned for gold there. Sometimes she came upon abandoned campsites, swarmed over by scavenging magpies, bickering noisily among themselves.

Four days after leaving Doe Eyes, Gitty trudged up a steep track toward a settlement she thought would be Stardancer. Twilight was settling on the mountain when she spotted buildings ahead. A cedar fence post on the side of the wagon trail bore a lopsided, weather-bleached board upon which was painted, "Stardancer." Gitty paused to catch her breath. At last, she was here! Now she would find Aunt Cath and have a warm and safe bed tonight.

The first building she came to was a livery stable. Gitty sniffed. Along with the strong smell of horse manure, there was a familiar odor — unmistakable: new-sawn lumber, a common smell back in Mattigan with all the saw mills. Aunt Cath had written that Stardancer was a new gold rush town. That made it reasonable that all the buildings would be new. The unpainted pine siding forming the stable walls was nailed on sloppily. Many boards were crooked, as if the builders had been in a terrible hurry to finish.

Gitty stepped inside. It took a moment for her eyes to adjust to the dim light. A stableman was pitching hay into mangers.

"Excuse me, sir," Gitty began. "Can you tell me where I might find Miss Cath Carleton who has a millinery shop here in town?"

The man stopped throwing hay and leaned on his pitchfork. "Ain't never heard of any Carleton here, and don't know what a mill...milly...whatever you said, is."

"A shop that makes bonnets," Gitty prompted.

"Don't know of no sech shop."

"But Miss Carleton *has* a millinery shop here! I know she does," Gitty insisted.

The man shrugged and returned to pitching hay.

Gitty went out on the street and moved on, though now her shoulders drooped. When she found an inn, she entered. A tall man with a large black moustache approached, wiping his hands on his white apron.

"Do you want to eat, lad?" he asked.

"No, sir," Gitty replied. "I need directions. I'm looking for Miss Cath Carleton, who has a millinery shop here in Stardancer."

The man frowned, thinking, as he continued to wipe his hands on the ankle-length apron. "I don't know of no millinery shop here, sonny. Why don't you go down the street to The Lucky Pearl? The gals there gets lots of dresses and hats so's they might know your aunt."

Grateful, Gitty thanked the man and headed down the street looking for The Lucky Pearl. It wasn't hard to find. The grandest building in town, The Lucky Pearl was a two-story structure wearing a fresh coat of glossy white paint. Suspended from the second story level and hanging over the boardwalk was a huge ball, its surface covered with a milky iridescent substance. It looked like a huge pearl.

Standing before the opaque panes of glass in the front door, Gitty hesitated, wondering if she should knock or just enter, the way you walked into a store. Feeling suddenly shy and a little frightened, she knocked. The door partially opened. A dark-haired girl peered out.

"Sorry, sonny. Kids aren't allowed here." The door began to close.

Just then two men came up behind Gitty and pushed open the door. The taller of the two boomed, "Marcelle, baby!" He caught the brunette in his arms and whirled her. When he set the grinning girl down she caught sight of Gitty standing in the open door.

"Hey, kid, beat it!" she shouted.

"Oh, please," Gitty pleaded, "I'm looking for Miss Cath Carleton who's a seamstress. She has a millinery shop here in Stardancer. At the inn they told me you had dresses and hats made and that you'd know where she is. I've come all the way from Michigan to find her." Gitty's eyes filled with tears.

Whether it was the tears or the sincere misery in Gitty's voice, the girl invited her in. "Pearl knows lots of people around The Hills. We'll see."

A blond, slightly plump woman with rouged cheeks came into the hallway. "Hello, son." Her voice had a melodic ring. "Marcelle says you're looking for someone who is a seamstress. Is she supposed to have a business here in Stardancer?"

Gitty nodded.

"I'm afraid you're mistaken. Mine is the only business in Stardancer run by a woman."

"No, ma'am," Gitty shook her head. "I'm not mistaken. She's Miss Cath Carleton."

The blond woman's face blanched. Harshly, she whispered, "Cath Carleton?"

"Yes, ma'am," Gitty replied. Her heartbeat quickened. The woman's dismayed look frightened Gitty. What was the matter? Had something terrible happened to her Aunt Cath?

"Who are you?" the woman demanded. "How do you know Cath Carleton?"

"She's my aunt," Gitty repeated. "My mother's sister."

The woman frowned. Color seeped back into her cheeks. She retorted, "Rebecca had only one child, a daughter!"

"That's right. That's me. I'm a girl." Gitty pulled off her cap and tousled her hair with her fingers. "I just cut my hair and wore these clothes because it seemed safer to travel if I looked like a boy."

"Good lord!" The plump woman leaned against the door jam.

"Please, ma'am," Gitty insisted, "do you know where I could find my Aunt Cath?"

A faint smile crossed the woman's face. Two red spots appeared in her cheeks. "Yes, yes. That's *me*, child. It's been so long since I've been called 'Cath' that I can scarcely remember. Everyone calls me 'Pearl.'"

The woman put her hand under Gitty's chin and looked into her eyes. "Are you really my little Gitty?"

Gitty swallowed, trying to adjust to this new information. "I'm Gitty McDaniel."

"Your father's name?"

"Jason McDaniel, and my mother was Rebecca McDaniel."

The woman threw her arms about Gitty and squeezed her against her soft body. "Oh, child! I've been so worried ever since I got Papa's letter saying you had run off to find me! Once the winter snows started I gave you up for dead!" She leaned back and looked up at Gitty, who was several inches taller. She touched a lock of Gitty's bright hair. "You look like your mother, but you have your father's coloring." She paused, tipping her head to one side. "But then, of course, your grandfather has auburn hair, too."

Gitty blinked. She'd thought of Grandfather as having gray hair, oh, maybe some auburn, but mostly gray. Then she remembered how long it had been since Aunt Cath had seen Grandfather.

Cath reached out and stroked the blue cashmere scarf tied loosely about Gitty's neck.

"My mother's," Gitty said.

"Yes," Cath replied, a distant look on her face. "I remember when Pa brought them to us."

A group of boisterous men pushed past them through the hallway. Several called out, "Hiya, Pearl!" as they moved past her into the house. Music began. From two fiddles and a piano came a lively ballad.

Absently, Cath responded, "Hiya, boys!"

"Come, child, let's go to my rooms," Cath said, grasping Gitty's arm. "You look dead tired. Are you hungry? Well, of course, you are! But first, a hot bath. Wouldn't that feel good? Then you can eat."

Cath led the way through a maze of parlors, small dining rooms, even through a large kitchen. Gitty was thinking furiously. What sort of place was this? Obviously, no millinery shop. Men, music, gambling, dancing, pretty girls. In Mattigan she and her friends had giggled and whispered about the notorious houses of ill repute said to be frequented not only by lumberjacks, but also by respectable Mattigan businessmen. This appeared to be that sort of place. Gitty could understand why Aunt Cath wrote to her father and sister that she had a millinery shop.

"My rooms are at the back of the house," Cath explained, "away from the noise and music."

Cath's quarters were two spacious rooms: a parlor and a bedroom, filled with massive furniture — a large piano, a Chippendale highboy and a block-front secretary, a Duncan Phyfe sofa coupled with a pair of Phyfe side chairs. The papered walls were decorated with large oil paintings in gilt frames. Oriental rugs covered the floors. The rooms were elegant, yet comfortable. Gitty was amazed to find this much civilization in these newly-inhabited mountains.

Cath picked up a silver bell, walked to her open doorway and shook it.

A small Oriental man came to the doorway. "Yes, missee?" he said.

"Come in, Won-Tu," Cath waved to the man.

"Gitty, my dear," she said, "meet Won-Tu Hung, my right arm and half of my left."

"How do you do?" Gitty stammered as the tiny man bowed low.

"Good lord, Won-Tu, cut the houseboy act!" Cath sputtered. "This is my niece!"

The man's hooded eyes looked at Cath; his face broke into a toothy grin. "He really is niece, one you thought was lost or worst?"

"She sure is, and a welcome sight she is!" Cath smiled. "We'll get her looking like a girl again, don't worry. But she's carrying about an inch of Hills dust on her and wants a bath. I know it's a bad time. Could you free a couple of the maids to bring a tub?"

"Right away," Won-Tu said and turned to go.

"Won-Tu," Cath added sternly, "I don't mean for *you* to get it. Get two maids to take a few minutes."

After the Oriental disappeared, Cath sighed. "That man! He'd cut off his head if I hinted that I might want that! I purposefully built a separate house for him after we got here because he's got a fourteen-year-old son who shouldn't — well, never mind. Anyway, Won-Tu is always here. I don't know when he sees his wife and son."

"Now, tell me," Cath went on, "Where have you been? What kept you from getting here last fall?"

Gitty's mind raced. Her first impulse was to make up some respectable story. Then she remembered the baby growing in her womb. Just within the last week she'd felt the light tapping of wee feet and fists. Her belly was beginning to stretch. Before long she would have to admit her condition.

She decided to tell the story of her travels from Mattigan to Stardancer pretty much as they actually happened. The one exception was that she transformed Doe Eyes and his tipi into a gentlemanly mountain trapper and a log cabin.

Aunt Cath eyed her thoughtfully, chewing on her lips, apparently pondering what the relationship with the trapper had been, when two ruddy housemaids appeared in the doorway carrying a galvanized tin tub half-filled with steaming water. Behind them came Won-Tu, burdened by a wide shoulder yoke with pails of hot water. With a grunt, he set the buckets down on the carpet. From a huge pocket in his tunic, he pulled out a fluffy white bath towel and a bar of brown soap. These he deposited with a flourish on the Oriental rug. He bowed, escorted the housemaids out of the room and carefully closed the door.

"Are those the only clothes you have?" Cath asked, nodding toward Gitty's grimy pants and jacket.

"Yes."

Cath studied Gitty's figure. "You're about Lillian's size," she said. "While you bathe I'll see if I can borrow something from her. I'll be back to scrub your back and help you rinse off." With a rustle of blue silk, Cath left.

Over the next few days, Gitty grew acquainted with The Lucky Pearl. There was a large room containing faro tables, a roulette wheel, and several tables for poker. Past the casino was a large ballroom for dancing. Against the walls were comfortable velvet settees. A small raised stage at one end was used by musicians or other performers. The upstairs was where "the boarders" slept and entertained any gentlemen wishing upstairs service. At first, Aunt Cath tried to carry on the pretense that The

Lucky Pearl was a boarding house for young ladies who, in the evenings, danced with men. Finally, she admitted, "This is a leisure house, a place to gamble, dance, drink and relax. It's like a club. My girls aren't common whores like you'd find in the red light district. I'm not saying they're innocent, wide-eyed ladies, you understand." She tapped Gitty on the wrist.

"I've never taken inexperienced girls. That would be nothing but trouble. No matter what men say about wanting a virgin, it's all talk. They really want a woman who knows what pleases a man!"

Appreciating having someone to talk to, Cath expanded. "My girls don't have clownish names like 'Hog-Eyed Kate' or 'Bulldog Betsy' like whores in Deadwood. On Main Street in Deadwood there's a house of pleasure called 'The Green Front.' It's famous all over the West, but doesn't have quality girls like I do. Do you know, child," she looked up at Gitty with a shining smile, "when I got to Stardancer with my crew, the people on the street applauded when we got off the stage. If they'd had a band, they would have played a welcome. One of the fellows said, 'Now all we need is a shoemaker.' With my arrival, civilization had come to Stardancer."

The Lucky Pearl was outfitted elegantly, a practice Cath said was important to cut down rowdiness. "Treat them like gentlemen, and they're more likely to behave like gentlemen," she said. Heavy burgundy velvet draperies hung from the tall windows: oil paintings of voluptuous nude women decorated the walls. Spittoons, some brass and some hand-painted china, were everywhere. The whole effect was toned to be pleasing to gentleman customers.

Gitty learned that Cath was a top-notch poker player, though she used this talent only with certain gentlemen and then only for high stakes.

Not long after Gitty found her way to The Lucky Pearl, a new recruit arrived to join the "boarders." She was a gorgeous little thing, all golden curls and tawny eyes. Her name was Flora. She spoke in a strange accent typical of an upbringing somewhere on the Eastern seaboard. But Cath didn't care about Flora's disagreeable voice because the girl had a magnificent talent: She played a huge, golden harp. Immediately, Cath installed her in a corner of the ballroom. Behind Flora were hung two plate-glass mirrors framed in bird's-eye maple. As the beautiful girl's arms gracefully moved up and down the strings of the harp, her swaying reflection was sent about the room from the two mirrors. It was a lovely sight. Every evening, the list of gentlemen waiting for Flora's upstairs favors grew longer.

One of the first things Gitty noticed while she browsed through The Lucky Pearl was the presence of several gold scales. "Most of the miners expect to pay in dust," Cath explained. She showed Gitty how a blower was used to separate dross and sand from the gold before placing it on the delicate scales.

As Gitty became acquainted with the town of Stardancer, she grew accustomed to seeing gold scales everywhere. All businesses had a pair. The miners carried their gold in a small bottle or a buckskin sack. Often, purchases or debts were settled with a pinch of dust.

Stardancer's business district was five blocks long. Signs on the stores showed a blacksmith, bakery, hotel, ladies' emporium, dry goods, real estate agent, groceries and produce, gents' furnishings, butcher and photographer. Cath said that Deadwood was larger and livelier than Stardancer, but that The Lucky Pearl drew quality gentlemen. "The unwashed miners and those who just want to elbow-bend go into Deadwood," Cath sniffed, dismissing their trade as unwanted.

Gitty was surprised to discover that Sunday was the busiest day in Stardancer. That was the day miners came to town for supplies, to pick up mail and to spend money. Back in Mattigan, everything had shut down on Sunday, the Sabbath being a day for church and quiet family dinners.

It was Mr. McDonald, the grocer, who told Gitty how Stardancer got its name. "It was called Clayville at first," he said, "after the first miner who arrived. But then there was this Indian gal who climbed that cliff over there and danced at night under the stars. The Indians said she was loco. Anyways, people called her 'Stardancer,' and miners come into town at night just to see that crazy squaw dance. They said they was going to see Stardancer, and purty soon that was the town's name."

Cath kept a retinue of twenty girls at The Lucky Pearl. "We started with eighteen back in '62," she said. A far-off look glazed her eyes. Then she shook her blond curls. "It's hard to keep these girls," she chuckled. "They keep getting married on me. Only Vera's been with me from the beginning," she reminisced, "seventeen years."

"Vera?" Gitty choked. Vera, the bookkeeper, who parted her hair in the middle and drew it into an unbecoming bun?

"Surprised?" Cath laughed. "Well, Vera didn't have her heart into entertaining. In fact, she was miserable. That's why I made her my bookkeeper. A damn good one she's been, too!"

Early in June, Cath confronted Gitty about her growing waistline. "Who's the father?" Cath wanted to know.

Gitty hung her head. "I got it along the way."

"It was that damnable mountain trapper, wasn't it?" Cath raged. "If I could just lay my hands on him..."

"It wasn't his fault, Aunt Cath. We were trapped in that cabin together all winter. Don't forget, he saved my life when I had lung fever."

Cath muttered, but all Gitty heard was, "If Papa ever found out!"

Actually, Gitty didn't feel ashamed. For her, the baby was a symbol of her love for Doe Eyes and his love for her. Always, because of this child, she would have a piece of Doe Eyes. At the same time she and Doe Eyes parted, Gitty was almost positive that she was with child. She hadn't wanted him to know that he was losing not only her, but a child. He'd lost two sons to smallpox. It would have been a terrible thing for him to bear— the knowledge that he had again lost a child.

Once Gitty's pregnancy showed, Cath insisted that she no longer go out into the streets. "If we're going to find you a decent husband," Cath insisted, "we must keep the baby a secret."

Cath moved the live-in cook out of a downstairs room near her own and installed Gitty. At first, Gitty felt terrible about dislodging the cook, but one of "the girls" told her that the cook was delighted. The cook had a gentleman friend who wanted to visit her, but she had not dared let him slip into the house when her room was so near Cath's.

With Gitty's arrival at The Lucky Pearl, Cath's life took on new zest. Not since Wade was alive had she felt in such good spirits. It was as if Gitty became the daughter she'd never had. It seemed right that Gitty had come to her, now that poor Rebecca was dead. Since Rebecca could no longer be mother to this lovely girl, Cath was delighted to substitute.

In all her life Cath had been close to only two people — her father and Wade. She'd never had a close relationship with a woman. Though she and Rebecca had never been at odds, they hadn't been truly close, as some sisters are. She welcomed wholeheartedly this child of her younger sister. Cath felt maternal toward Gitty. Because her own mother had been so aloof, Cath found herself playing the role of mother the way she thought a loving mother should be.

Last winter, Cath had written a long letter to Rose Henright in St. Louis, describing the great success of her new business. In a moment of silliness, not meaning it seriously, she mentioned that she lacked only a good mouser for complete happiness. "Cook complains of always having to sift the flour because of mice in the flour barrel," she had written.

Late June a bull train arrived in Stardancer, delivering, freight collect, to a startled Cath, several crates containing fifty-eight cats. Glued to one of the crates was a letter from Rose Henright telling Cath about a party she gave. "I was telling my guests," she wrote, "about your need for a mouser. One of the gentlemen, who had enjoyed several pourings of Burgundy, suggested that the gentlemen engage in a cat-hunt, with the most successful hunter being paid twenty dollars by each gentleman who caught fewer cats. In no time, my dinner party turned into a ladies-only affair. Within an hour, the gentlemen returned, carrying every description of feline creature. Some of the gentlemen, I might add, bore wounds testifying to the ferocity of their cat hunt.

"At any rate, dear Cath, we had a marvelously good time at my dinner-party-turned-cat-hunt. I do hope you can find a decent mouser out of this motley collection. As always, Rose Henright."

Cath kept two of the cats. One gray male appeared to be a good mouser. The other, an emaciated all-white tabby, captured the girls' hearts, so Cath let them keep her as a lap pet. She sold the remaining fifty-six cats for ten dollars apiece, which left Cath with a neat profit over and above freight charges. When she sold the last cat she chuckled, thinking how Rose thought she was being so clever and crafty, sending the cats *freight collect.* Cath reminded herself to write Rose and thank her for sending such a profitable shipment.

From mid-July on, Gitty's only exposure to the outdoors were twice-weekly buggy rides, which she enjoyed immensely. With Won-Tu handling the reins, Cath, Gitty, Won-Tu's wife, Ten-Fu, and his son, Henry, headed off at mid-morning to explore the nearby hills and valleys. There was a hint of autumn in the crisp mountain air. The leaves of the paper birch on the high slopes already had faded to yellow, their color glowing brightly against the white spruce. Once, they journeyed far enough to get a close look at Harney Peak, an immense mass of pink granite. As Gitty gazed in awe at the massive rock face, it made her dizzy. It was hard to focus on the seemingly near, but actually far-off, rocky eminence. Black pine grew thick in the ridges, and mica, imbedded in the rocks, flashed glassy reflections in the sun.

At noon, they spread the picnic lunch the cook had prepared. There was crisp fried chicken, fresh carrots from The Lucky Pearl's garden, biscuits smothered with chokecherry jam, lemonade, and half of a chocolate cake. They had stopped next to a bubbling mountain stream. The foaming water roared as it dashed against the boulders on its rush down the steep slope. Goldenrod and tall sunflowers bloomed in the moist soil near the bubbling brook.

"Look!" Won-Tu pointed. A magnificent elk paused majestically on the far side of the canyon, his long, branching horns silhouetted against the salmon-colored granite.

Gitty glanced sideways at Ten-Fu and caught the tiny Oriental woman looking at her. Ten-Fu colored, but then recovered, asking timidly, "You feel all right, missee?"

Smiling, Gitty patted the woman's small hand. Ten-Fu was an experienced mid-wife, and she would deliver Gitty's baby. Gitty had grown fond of this self-effacing, quiet Chinese woman. She leaned back and inhaled the fresh air. With Ten-Fu helping, she was sure that when her time came, it would go well.

Toward the end when her belly was swollen huge and tight and her puffy ankles throbbed, Gitty spent most of her days propped in a chair with her legs raised on a footstool. Nearly everything she ate caused a burning indigestion. She didn't sleep well because of the weight of the child in her womb.

One day in Cath's parlor Gitty burst out petulantly, "Oh, Aunt Cath! I feel so miserable! Do you suppose it's always like this?" She laid down the infant nightgown she was smocking. Looking thoughtfully at her aunt, Gitty asked, "Did you ever want to have a baby?"

Cath's thoughts leaped back to that brief time when she feared she was carrying John McAffery's seed, and she shuddered. The unwanted baby had been like a bloodsucker in her womb — nothing she wanted. What a blessing it had been when the bleeding started! No, Cath thought, I never wanted a baby. I don't know why. Perhaps Wade was all the love I ever wanted.

Gitty seemed to be anticipating the birth. Apparently this was a wanted baby. Cath wondered if her niece felt something for her baby's father. She looked up to find Gitty regarding her curiously. "What did you ask, child?"

"I wondered if you ever wished for a child of your own."

Cath gave one of her hearty chuckles. "Land sakes, no. What would I do with a baby in these surroundings? A gaming house and dance hall isn't proper surroundings for bringing up a child!"

Gitty's head jerked. "What will become of *my* baby, then?" she asked. Her voice trembled.

"I'll find a wet nurse."

"You'll bring the wet nurse here?"

"No, child!" Cath retorted. "Use your head! We can't have a baby here! How long would I keep my customers if they heard a baby crying?" Cath stood and crossed the room where she could squeeze Gitty's shoulder. "The baby will live with the wet nurse, but you can visit whenever you wish."

Through tear-filled eyes Gitty gazed at her aunt.

"It's the only way," Cath said.

Gitty gave a resigned sigh. Her head throbbed. The eager sparkle of youth left her eyes.

Chapter 20
The Arrival of Dawn

Sunday, September 28, 1879

The first hint that she would soon have the baby was a cramping pain low in her belly. If she hadn't known better, Gitty would have thought she had summer complaint. The cramps began mid-morning, but Gitty said nothing about them. At lunch time when she refused anything to eat Cath looked sharply at her. "Is it your time?"

"I think so, but I'm sure it's a long way off. I'm not uncomfortable yet."

"Nonsense!" Cath exclaimed. "You know nothing of such matters, child!" She jumped up from the long, linen-covered table where she and her girls ate their meals. "I'm going to fetch Ten-Fu!"

The girls of The Lucky Pearl stared with awe at their madam's niece. A baby was going to be born.

When Cath returned with Ten-Fu, the Oriental woman persuaded Gitty to go into Cath's room so she could check the progress of the birth. Cath had insisted that the baby be born in her bed. "I will not have my great-nephew or niece born on that little cot you sleep on. He shall be born in a proper mahogany bed!"

Ten-Fu's examination found that the baby had not yet turned into the proper head-down position. She agreed with Gitty that birth was some time away. Gitty felt more comfortable walking around the room than she did lying in the big bed.

"That all right. That all right," Ten-Fu assured the fussing Cath. "She stay up, maybe baby go down sooner. Indian ladies squat: baby drop out easier. Less pain." She shrugged, giving approval to the squatting position.

For awhile Gitty paced the floor. When she grew tired, she lay down to rest. The pains became increasingly more uncomfortable. Each hour passed slowly. Every few minutes a girl peeked in the door and asked about progress. Cath had closed The Lucky Pearl down for the night, fearing that Gitty might cry out and the visiting men might discover that a baby was being born. She had warned her girls, upon penalty of everything short of death, not to tell why the house was closed tonight. "Just say we're having a special birthday party," she told them.

Long after midnight, a great cramping pain twisted Gitty. She grunted without meaning to. That strong contraction was followed a few minutes later by another. Ten-Fu examined the position of the baby. Her delicate face twisted with worry.

"Baby want be born. But head *up*. He trying to come bottom-first. Hard for mother, hard for baby." The wrenching pains went on for fifteen minutes before Ten-Fu made her decision. "I try turn baby," she announced.

With one hand inside Gitty's body and the other on top of her belly, tiny Ten-Fu exerted pressure, twisting, pressing on the unborn child to turn its head toward the birth canal. Each time Gitty's abdomen hardened with a contraction, Ten-Fu relaxed and waited, then resumed her manipulations.

"Ah ha!" the Chinese woman cried, a relieved smile spreading across her face. Baby turns."

Soon after the infant's head entered the birth canal the contractions of the womb increased in intensity. Within ten minutes, Ten-Fu announced that she could see the top of the baby's head.

When a new contraction began, Gitty felt as if a giant fist had her abdomen in its grip. It was squeezing, squeezing. Without having to be told, she pushed, grunting with the strain.

"That right, missee, push. Push!" Ten-Fu encouraged.

With a sucking, swooshing sound, the infant left Gitty's body and slid onto the bed sheet. Quickly, Ten-Fu cleared the tiny nostrils and mouth of mucous. Then, grasping its slippery ankles, she suspended the baby upside down.

She gave two stinging slaps to the tiny bottom, but there was no sign of breath. Deliberately, Ten-Fu inserted her index finger into the infant's rectum. The result was immediate: a sharp intake of breath, followed by a healthy howl.

Gitty sighed with relief. She raised her head off the pillow and saw that her child was a girl-baby. Good! she thought. Alone, she could do better raising a daughter.

Looking out the window, Cath observed, "Dawn is here."

"Dawn is here," Gitty echoed. "The baby arrived at dawn. Dawn. That's a nice name. Her name will be 'Dawn.'"

Cath was ecstatic. "A great-niece! I'm a great-aunt!"

Lillian stuck her head in the door.

"It's a girl! The Lord be praised!" Cath was beaming.

"The Lord be praised!" Lillian responded.

"Break out the brandy," Cath instructed. "We'll toast the new arrival!"

Lillian disappeared to spread the word.

Ten-Fu cleaned the baby. She giggled, covering her mouth shyly with her hand. "Baby look like my Henry W. Longfellow Hung," she snickered.

Cath looked closer at her great-niece. A cold finger of uneasiness prodded at her. She studied the hooded eyes, the dark skin, the straight black hair. The infant looked like an Indian papoose. Cath shuddered. Could it be that Gitty had been raped by an Indian? Her niece wouldn't talk about the baby's father. Cath shivered. As soon as possible, she must find a wet-nurse, foster-mother for this child. Cath would have to go through the motions of celebrating with her girls, but her joy had evaporated. This great-niece presented a problem.

Cath took a deep breath. Soon she must find a suitable husband for Gitty. Then Cath would have legitimate great-nieces and nephews to be proud of, ones she would acknowledge.

Looking again at the dark, wriggling, wailing infant, Cath shook her head. It looked no more like Gitty or anybody in the Carleton family than a wet kitten.

Cath watched as Gitty raised herself on one elbow to study her daughter. Softly, to herself, Gitty murmured, "She looks like him." The infant raised a trembling, uncoordinated fist and stretched her tiny fingers.

"Yes," Cath sighed. To herself, she added, "more's the pity."

✳   ✳   ✳   ✳

With quivering lips, Gitty wrapped her baby in the pale yellow blanket Aunt Cath had knitted during the months while they waited for

Dawn's birth. Though she was dry-eyed this morning, Gitty's eyes were puffy from a long night of sobbing. A huge lump filled her throat, making it hard to swallow. At some point in the dark hours of the night, she had convinced herself that parting with little Dawn was inevitable — something she had to do if she or her innocent daughter were ever to achieve the good things in life. The thought of Dawn being called a bastard made Gitty's skin crawl. She must protect her child from ever hearing that word. And money and success were the keys to safeguarding her reputation and that of her daughter. During the long night, Gitty lay sleepless, staring into the darkness, figuring how she could become wealthy — *really* wealthy. Finally, she came to the same conclusion Aunt Cath had preached at her for weeks. She must marry well: find a wealthy, generous man. "And," Aunt Cath warned, "you won't find that sort, not toting a bastard child on your hip, you won't!"

A few days after Dawn's birth Cath found a French-Indian woman in the foothills outside of Stardancer who had given birth to a stillborn child. Cath went to see the woman, called "Walks Softly."

"She's a fine woman," Cath later assured Gitty. "She's gentle, kind. Her eyes filled with tears of gratitude when I proposed that she wet-nurse and care for Dawn. Her living quarters are primitive, but I'll see that they're improved. The woman speaks good English, but with a pronounced French accent."

"Is there a husband?" Gitty wanted to know.

"Apparently, there was a miner who said he would marry her, but disappeared."

Good. She wouldn't have to share her baby with a foster-father; only the mother.

When Won-Tu pulled the buggy up in front of The Lucky Pearl, Cath held open the front door for Gitty, who carried the baby.

While Cath fussed over Gitty's comfort and made sure the baby was well-covered, Ten-Fu came running, her cloth slippers shuffling softly on the wooden walk. "I come, too, please?" she asked plaintively. Ten-Fu had taken a proprietary interest in little Dawn since the difficult delivery.

As the buggy bounced and rattled down the wagon trail Gitty tried to keep her mind blank. It was agony to face the thought that this afternoon she would return on this same road, but without little Dawn in her arms. A stranger would cuddle and feed her baby. Gitty shuddered. The knot in her throat swelled larger.

Ten-Fu kept reaching across Cath's lap to pat Gitty's knee.

For more than an hour, the passengers in the buggy jostled and swayed along the rocky trail. For some time, Gitty had noticed a plume of smoke coiling upward. When she pointed it out, Cath said that it was the smoke from the home of Walks Softly. Eventually, Won-Tu drew up in front of an isolated log cabin.

The front door burst open and a tall, bronzed woman strode out. "The baby?" she cried, holding her arms out.

Gitty looked hard at the woman who was to take her place. This woman would receive Dawn's first smile, would celebrate the cutting of the first tooth. The woman soberly returned Gitty's appraising look of inspection, but her dark eyes kept swaying to the small figure in the blanket. Walks Softly repeated, "The baby? Please?"

Slowly, Gitty unfolded her arms and handed the baby to the Indian woman. "Come inside," Walks Softly said. "I have tea ready. Long time I heard you coming."

Without waiting for Won-Tu's help, Gitty slid off the wagon seat and followed the woman inside the cabin. The moment Walks Softly stepped into the warmth of the cabin, she began unwrapping the layers of blankets from the baby. A look of rapture spread across her face as she saw the infant for the first time. "Oh," she sighed. "She is beautiful. Beautiful."

Gitty studied the woman's dark face. The high cheekbones showed her Indian heritage as did her dark, straight hair. Her eyes were a hazel brown. There was an intense, yearning glow in them as Walks Softly looked at Dawn. The tightness in Gitty's stomach eased a little.

The only seats in the small cabin were two pine benches on either side of a scarred plank table. Walks Softly motioned for them to be seated as she poured tea, all with one hand, since she cuddled the sleeping baby in the crook of her left arm.

While they sipped their steaming tea, the Indian woman explained to Gitty that her father was a French-Canadian boatman on The Missouri and her mother a Cheyenne. Walks Softly smiled, shrugged. "I am what they call 'a half-breed.'" She looked down at the infant in her arms. "Like this baby, oui?" she asked, raising her hooded eyes and looking pointedly at Gitty.

Gitty's face grew flaming hot. For a moment, she returned the woman's curious look with a defiant glare. Walks Softly continued her cool, questioning gaze. Finally, Gitty lowered her eyes and looked down, staring in misery at the amber tea. Gitty dared not look at either Aunt Cath or the Chinese couple. What must they be thinking?

The awkward moment was broken by the sudden fretting of the baby. The initial squeaks quickly turned into demanding wails.

"She's hungry," Gitty said. "She slept all the way here." She held her arms out, intending to nurse her baby.

Walks Softly hugged the crying baby possessively, looking hard into Gitty's puzzled eyes. "I *must* feed," she said. "It be some days since my milk was suckled. If I go dry, baby not eat." The Indian woman looked fiercely at Gitty. "*I* must feed baby."

After a long inner struggle, Gitty nodded and looked away. She heard the rustling of Walks Softly's shawl as the woman bared her breast for Dawn. The noisy, wet sounds of the baby's sucking ended the silence in the one-room cabin.

A roaring noise filled Gitty's head. She took a deep breath. For an awful moment, she feared she would be sick. Another deep breath, and she felt herself begin to relax. She must stop fighting this woman! Gitty realized that even though she had brought the baby here, she'd been resisting. Now she had to face it: Recognize that it was here she would leave her baby. In this shabby hut, with this strange woman. When Gitty finally raised her head she saw Dawn's tiny cheeks screwed up as she fastened her pink lips to the brown nipple. The woman's exposed breast was the color of the baby's own skin. At the sight of her baby suckling another woman's breast, Gitty felt her own breasts tingle and throb. As hot tears poured from her eyes, warm milk trickled from her nipples, soaking through and wetting the bodice of her dress.

Walks Softly's brown eyes took in the spreading dark stain across the front of Gitty's dress, and a wave of sympathy crossed her face. She recognized that this sorrel-haired girl was suffering just as she, Walks Softly, had suffered since the death of her new son. Walks Softly reminded herself to be kind. The white lady was actually paying her to care for a beautiful baby. The empty spot in her soul left by her own baby's death filled now with love.

Walks Softly sighed and closed her eyes. It was wrong for her and the white woman to fight over the baby. The white lady cannot keep her baby with her. This is my good fortune, Walks Softly thought, for I have need of a baby to love. She smiled to herself. There is room in this girl-baby's life for two loving mothers.

Cath announced it was time to head back to Stardancer. As they walked toward the cabin door, Walks Softly gently touched Gitty's sleeve. When Gitty faced her, the Indian woman placed the baby in Gitty's arms.

"Come often," Walks Softly said. "No baby can have too much love. We will give this baby all the love she can hold."

✳ ✳ ✳ ✳

Like a caged beast, Gitty paced Cath's parlor. It had been a week since she visited Dawn and Walks Softly. Until now she had gone to see her baby twice a week, but six days ago a roaring blizzard had swept down from the northern plains. Any travel into and out of Stardancer was impossible except on snowshoes.

Cath looked up from the sampler she was cross-stitching. "It's time you had a lesson in beauty care," Cath said. She laid down her handwork. Anything, she thought, to get the child's mind off her baby. Cath was anxious to turn her niece's thoughts toward the opposite sex. Her thoughts and worries centered on figuring out who would be an eligible husband for Gitty. Come spring, the girl would be eighteen, plenty old enough to marry. She was at her prime.

"You're a lovely girl, Gitty, but we can enhance your beauty. Plus," she paused, "and this is very important, child, the West is cruel to a woman's skin. The dry air constantly sucks moisture from our skin. We could look like wrinkled hags by the time we're thirty. If you stay here, you'll have to take good care of your skin. Darker complexioned people have tougher skin, but you and I are fair. Our skin is thin and delicate."

Cath stood and moved toward her door. "I'll get some things, and we'll start our beauty lessons."

She returned with a colorful carpetbag. The first item she removed from it was a fresh lemon. Gitty shook her head. "Aunt Cath! How on earth did you come by a lemon in the middle of winter in Dakota Territory? You are truly a magician!"

Cath cut the lemon in half and scooped the pulp from one of the halves. Carefully, she turned the peel inside out. Next she took a small bowl and whisk from her bag and set them ceremoniously on the tea table. She broke an egg white into the bowl, keeping the yolk in the eggshell. After beating the egg white into a frothy mixture she poured it into the inside-out lemon peel. "There!" she exclaimed. "Now it must set for awhile so the lemon oils can combine with the egg white. Then we'll rub the mixture over your skin to keep it soft and moist."

For two hours, Cath dispensed beauty secrets. She instructed Gitty to rub sour milk or buttermilk on her skin at night to act as a bleach to keep her skin creamy white. Cornstarch was to prevent a shiny nose. Cath opened a glass vial and Gitty peered into the red liquid.

"Beet juice," Cath explained. "To make your cheeks rosy."

✳   ✳   ✳   ✳

The winter of 1879 was a hard one in the Hills. Long periods went by when Gitty was unable to see Dawn. Once the warm temperatures of spring melted the snowdrifts Gitty was obsessed with seeing her baby every other day. This put a burden on Won-Tu's time and tied up the buggy three days out of each week. Cath's solution was to buy a handsome sorrel mare for Gitty. The stable behind The Lucky Pearl and next to Won-Tu's home presently housed only the buggy and Ben, the faithful gelding who pulled it. There was plenty of room for another horse.

"A horse of my own?" Gitty squealed. "Oh, thank you, Aunt Cath!" she cried. "When can I see him? Where is he?"

Clutching her aunt's hand, Gitty practically pulled Cath out to the stable. In a box stall next to Ben's stood a beautiful sorrel mare. Huge brown eyes gazed with interest at Gitty.

Whirling, Gitty threw her arms around her aunt and lifted her in a grateful hug. "Aunt Cath, I love you! She's a beautiful mare. Now I can visit Dawn whenever I want to!"

"That is precisely the idea," Cath gasped as Gitty released her. "Come see your saddle."

The aroma of well-oiled leather filled the tack room. A light tan double-cinch saddle with huge pommel rested on top of a colorful saddle blanket draped over a wooden saw horse. It had a high cantle, and the skirts were lined with sheepskin. One eyebrow raised, Gitty looked at her aunt.

"What's the matter, child? Don't you like it?"

Gitty stammered, "It, it's not a sidesaddle!"

"I should say not!" Cath replied. "The sidesaddle is an abomination invented by the devil himself to endanger the lives of ladies! I'd like to see gentlemen canter safely while riding sidesaddle! Ridiculous!" she snorted.

224

"But what will I wear?" Gitty persisted.

"Come to the house," Cath motioned. "I'd hoped your riding costume would be ready for your birthday, but that late spring storm blocked the roads. Only yesterday it came in with the bull train."

The riding costume was a ruffled long-sleeved blouse with matching pale tan, form-fitting trousers. Tiny buttons closed the sleeves from wrist to elbow, and on the trouser leg, the same small buttons fastened from ankle to half-way up the calf. An ankle-length green frock with split tails formed the outer layer of the costume. Gitty saw that when she was walking, the fullness of the coat gave the illusion that she was wearing an ordinary dress. However, once up on the back of the horse, the coat would billow behind, out of the way. Gitty shrugged. Who was to see her out in those deserted foothills on her way to Walks Softly's cabin? She agreed with her aunt that a regular saddle would make an easier and more enjoyable seat. Gitty never had liked sidesaddles. She'd just thought there was no escaping it. Gitty grinned. She should've figured her Aunt Cath would not accept a hobbled position, not for herself, and not for her niece.

Impulsively, Gitty grasped her aunt's gloved hand. "Aunt Cath, why don't you get a horse for yourself? We could go riding together!"

Cath's face paled. She gave a polite cough. "I'd rather pet a porcupine! My dear, I hate horses. I absolutely despise them, and the feeling is mutual. Horses hate me. All my experiences with them have been bad. Do me a favor and keep your horse away from me. I have occasionally driven the buggy, but I'm not comfortable or confident with the reins. I much prefer having Won-Tu drive me. Perhaps someday someone will invent a horseless carriage. Then, with no horses, I should feel quite comfortable driving such a contraption. But horses!" she snorted her disdain.

The next morning Gitty awakened early before any of the girls or Cath were stirring. She got into her strange new riding costume and left a note for Cath, telling her she was going to visit Dawn.

The mare snorted a welcome when Gitty entered the stable. The horse offered no resistance when Gitty placed the curb bit in her mouth and stretched the split-ear headstall around her ears. It seemed to be a well broken horse. Gitty smiled. Of course it would be. Knowing Aunt Cath, the mare was probably the best-trained horse in Dakota Territory. The saddle was heavy, but she managed to swing it up onto the broad back of the mare, which she'd decided to name "Moonbeam." The sorrel's lush, flowing white mane and tail made Gitty think of moonbeams. After fussing with the saddle blanket she tightened both cinches and led the mare out of the stable.

Gitty swung up into the saddle and positioned her boots in each stirrup. What a confident feeling to have *both* feet in a stirrup, so different from the sidesaddle position she was accustomed to with only one stirrup. She loved the confident sensation. As she rode out of town Gitty breathed the clear mountain air and smiled. Around her the world was verdant, the lush vegetation a product of the moisture from the melted snow runoff from higher slopes. A year ago when she'd trudged into Stardancer seeking her aunt, the grass and brush had appeared much the same. While at Stardancer she'd learned the cycle of the seasons, and how, as the months moved farther past spring, the countryside green seared into a crisp brown.

Moonbeam's hooves clicked against rocks on the angling trail. Gitty chose shortcuts now that she was on horseback, trails that couldn't be negotiated by a buggy. When she arrived at Walks Softly's cabin she swung down from the mare. The cabin door was open, coaxing inside the warmth and sunshine. The Indian woman appeared in the doorway, and stepped outside to greet Gitty.

Surprised at seeing the sorrel mare instead of the usual horse and buggy, Walks Softly stopped short. Her lips formed a round hole, and she gave an admiring gasp. "Beauty!" she exclaimed as she walked around the mare. "Yours?"

"Yes!" Gitty bubbled. "Now I can come see Dawn more often." She paused. "At least if it's all right with you."

The French-Indian woman gave Gitty a piercing look. "I told you. You can move in if you wish. *Our* Dawn cannot have too much love."

Relieved, Gitty sighed. Walks Softly always assured her that she was welcome any time. Gitty looked at the Indian woman, who was regarding Moonbeam with a longing expression.

"Do you like horses, Walks Softly?" she asked.

"Do I like to breathe?" the woman replied.

"Would you like to ride her?"

Walks Softly's eyes darkened a shade, taking on an iridescent glow. "Could I?"

"Take her for an hour or two. I walked her most of the way up here, so she's not hot or tired. I'm trying to get used to the man's saddle, which is new for me."

Walks Softly was staring at Gitty. "You're going to let me ride her? Now?"

"Why not?" Gitty laughed. "It'll do you good to get away from the cabin and the baby for awhile."

The woman moved quickly to the mare, her fingers working swiftly to unbuckle the cinches. Before Gitty realized what Walks Softly intended, the woman had removed the saddle and swung it to the ground. Walks Softly pulled off the saddle blanket, folded it, and laid it on top of the saddle.

The Indian woman swung herself onto Moonbeam's back. With a cluck and gentle pressure from the heel of her moccasin she turned the horse. Horse and rider disappeared around a rocky bluff.

Gitty skipped into the cabin. This was the first time in seven months that she'd been alone with Dawn. During Gitty's visits Walks Softly thoughtfully busied herself with household duties while Gitty played with Dawn, but the other woman's presence was a shadow. Sometimes Dawn would get distracted from the games Gitty played with her. Her eyes would dart about the cabin, searching, until she spotted Walks Softly. Dawn knew Gitty and never showed any sign of thinking Gitty a stranger, even when as long as two weeks passed when Gitty was unable to get through the snow. Still, it was obvious that the baby's "real mother-person" was Walks Softly, the one who cared for her day-to-day.

It could be no other way. Gitty realized this. It was the price she must pay for allowing another to rear her child. Though Dawn was sleeping, Gitty touched her chubby cheek to awaken her. She didn't want to waste a single moment of being alone with her daughter. The child's eyelids fluttered and opened. When at last they focused upon Gitty's smiling face, the tiny mouth broke into a happy smile. The chunky round arms flew up, begging to be picked up. Gitty's heart ached with the love she felt for this child, this product of impossible love. For one moment Gitty thought of Doe Eyes, wondering where he was, what he was doing. But then she brushed the thought away. As she picked up the warm child she reminded herself that Dawn was real. Dawn was here, now.

"You are my life, my lovely child," she whispered, as she bent her head, pressed her lips against her daughter's bare round belly, and nibbled playfully. The baby gurgled with delight.

Chapter 21
The Biggest Fish in the Lake

While Walks Softly was riding Moonbeam, Gitty wallowed in the joy of playing with her daughter. With the baby chuckling happily, Gitty counted each of her tiny brown toes, savoring the ever-so-perfect nails. Dawn loved playing peek-a-boo, especially when Gitty covered her own eyes and asked, "Where's Mama?" then flung back her hands crying, "*Here's* Mama!" When Dawn fretted with hunger, Gitty dipped small pieces of cornbread into water and popped the softened bread into the baby's mouth. Dawn squealed her delight as she gummed each mealy morsel.

For two hours Walks Softly remained away. When she returned, Gitty suspected that Moonbeam had been galloped hard. The Indian woman worked for a long time rubbing down the sweating mare. Gitty wondered if Walks Softly had raced Moonbeam out of high spirits, or whether she'd worked off frustration or anger. It was impossible to guess. The Indian woman always wore an unreadable expression, much as Won-Tu and Ten-Fu did. Gitty felt compassion for this woman who was mothering her beloved Dawn. Within the past year, Walks Softly had been deserted by her man and lost her baby. Gitty studied the woman whose strong brown arms rubbed Moonbeam's damp coat. She liked and respected Walks Softly. Aunt Cath had made an excellent choice. Deep inside, crowding near Gitty's soul, was the knowledge that this woman was an important part of Dawn's life, not only now, but forever. With this being so, Gitty accepted Walks Softly as a significant influence in her own life.

Gitty ate fresh greens and deep-fried squaw bread with Walks Softly before starting back toward Stardancer mid-afternoon. Because she had plenty of time before sundown, Gitty decided to try a different trail, one which led across a gently rolling, green highland prairie. Several times when she'd traveled up here in the buggy she'd noticed in the distance a strange-looking butte. It seemed to be composed of varicolored sandstone. Now, because of the freedom offered by her horse, she guided the mare toward the conical hill which rose abruptly from the flatlands. The colors of the butte were unusual, ranging from velvet purples, to reds, reddish-browns, and yellows.

The beauty of her surroundings was marred only by the incessant buzzing of the black deer flies, which bit at Moonbeam, causing the mare to sidestep nervously.

Directly ahead of her appeared a small lake, surrounded by birch and quaking aspen. Its surface was glassy-smooth. Gitty reined in and climbed off Moonbeam. Leading the mare down to the water's edge, she fastened the reins loosely to a willow. Using fistfuls of dried weeds as a sponge, she poured cool lake water over the mare's sorrel coat. "There!" she patted Moonbeam's flank. "That should chase off the deer flies for awhile."

The horse's muscles twitched in response.

Squatting, Gitty splashed her fingers in the clear water. She'd expected it to be colder. Having grown up accustomed to the frigid waters of Lake Michigan, Gitty thought this mountain lake temperature quite enticing. Impulsively, she slipped off her green riding cloak, laying it carefully across an elder bush. Her blouse and trousers followed, and she paused only a moment before wriggling out of her cambric drawers and chemise.

She waded into the lake up to her knees, then dived, cutting smoothly through the water. As she surfaced, she threw back her head, tossing wet hair from her face. The cool water made her body tingle.

A surface dive slid Gitty toward the bottom of the pond. The lake must be a dozen feet deep, but even at that depth she could see perfectly the smooth rocks on the bottom. Lake Michigan's sandy bottom kept its water murky, nothing like this crystalline water.

When she climbed from the pond she used her chemise for a towel, blotting herself dry. Her skin glowed bright pink from the cool water and from the brisk patting of the cambric material.

As Gitty stepped into her trousers Moonbeam snorted. For a moment Gitty thought she heard the nearby answering snort of a horse. After tossing her dripping hair back and wringing it out once again, she decided she was mistaken. Later, as she finished buttoning her boots, Moonbeam snuffled again. This time a replying snort answered from close by. The sound of hooves striking stones came from a stand of white birch and spruce. Gitty turned toward the noise. Dramatically framed by white birch trunks, a magnificent black gelding appeared. As he approached, his mane and tail gleamed like ebony in the afternoon sun. The rider was dressed in black, from shiny Wellington riding boots to his Stetson. Only a white shirt and red silk scarf broke the solid black image of rider and horse. Even the man's hair and moustache were black. Gitty blinked. Was it a mirage?

Man and horse advanced toward her. Gitty straightened, staring, feeling foolish. Why did they seem unreal — more like an apparition than human and beast?

"Good afternoon." The man dipped his head and swept off his broad-brimmed hat. "Did you have a nice swim?"

An Englishman! His clipped accent left no doubt about that.

"My name is David Dunnington," he introduced himself, half-standing in his stirrups, making a bow from the saddle.

Speechless, Gitty stared, not realizing that she held her damp chemise in her fists, wringing it like a sponge.

"I don't believe I've had the pleasure?" the man prompted.

He moved his horse close to Gitty. She stared up into the blue, blue eyes of an incredibly handsome man.

Gitty recovered her wits. "I don't believe so," she answered, giving a slight unintentional curtsy. She felt a blush flood her face. "I am Gitty McDaniel, presently visiting my aunt in Stardancer."

"Ah, my dear, how nice! And who is your aunt, if I may ask?"

"Cath Carleton."

"I don't believe I know a Mrs... er, Miss Carleton?"

Gitty gave a light-hearted laugh. "Most people call her 'Pearl,' of The Lucky Pearl."

"Ah, yes," he said, rubbing his dark moustache thoughtfully. He studied Gitty hard for some moments before asking, "And what are you doing out here today?"

Gitty hesitated. She couldn't say she was visiting her daughter. "Yesterday my aunt gave me this beautiful mare. Today, she and I are getting acquainted." Gitty smiled happily as she reached over and patted Moonbeam affectionately on the neck.

Suddenly, it occurred to her that the Englishman was asking all the questions. "And, sir, if I may, who are you, and what are *you* doing out here?"

He grinned, deep dimples slashing into each cheek. "Well put, my dear!" He slid from his horse and stood facing Gitty. Though she was tall, she had to tip her head back to look at his face. He was well over six feet.

"As I said before, I am David Dunnington. This," he said, and swirled his hat in a complete circle, "is Calico Butte Ranch, named for that strange-looking butte over there. I run cattle under the Ball-4 brand. I take it you haven't heard of me, but I'm sure your aunt has."

"Do you know my aunt?"

"Everyone in The Hills knows of your aunt." He studied her closely.

"I guess what Aunt Cath does *is* rather unusual for a lady," Gitty observed, almost to herself.

At that remark, the tall Englishman pulled himself up taller. Almost to himself, he mumbled, "Yes, a *lady*." Dimples creased his cheeks. "Would you like to see my ranch house? It's not far. I'd be pleased to show it to you. It's a bit different, you know, my being English and all that." He paused. "Chaperones, I promise you. My cook, my laundress, and Uncle Volney, who thinks I can't scrub my teeth without his help."

Gitty burst into a giggle. "I wonder if Uncle Volney is anything like Aunt Cath's Won-Tu."

"Let's find out," the Englishman proposed.

Side-by-side, they trotted their horses through the tall grass of the highland prairie. When they came to a tortured, twisting trail, the Englishman led the way and Gitty guided her mare behind the black gelding. Gitty asked herself what she was doing out here in this wilderness, following a stranger into heaven knows what? Each time, just as her doubts began to overwhelm her, the man turned in his strange, small flat English saddle and gave her an encouraging grin. How could anyone resist those eyes, the color of a summer sky? Or the creases in his cheeks which coaxed one to touch them?

The ranch house looked as if it had been added to at the whim of a moment whenever another room was needed. Perhaps the Englishman had said, "I have no place to hang these horns. Build a room for them." The dining room was impressive, the long mahogany table covered with a delicate Irish lace tablecloth, the places set with bone china and silver flatware. Linen napkins were rolled into silver napkin rings. The centerpiece was an elaborate crystal candelabrum. On the walls hung oil portraits of bearded men and ladies in old-fashioned dresses, apparently ancestors of David Dunnington.

Uncle Volney proved to be as protective as the Englishman had said. A wiry, gray-haired former trail hand, Uncle Volney had decided that David Dunnington needed a mother, and he had voted himself into the office. With a wry smile, Gitty acknowledged that Won-Tu and Uncle Volney bore similar traits. Indispensable to their employers, their domineering presence couldn't be ignored.

By the time Gitty finished touring the house and part of the vast expanse of Calico Butte Ranch, the sun hung low in the sky. She realized she'd stayed too long.

"Oh, dear," she breathed, "I've been so fascinated, I've overstayed my time. My aunt will be worried frantic, especially since this is my first day out on a new horse. I should've started back long ago. Forgive me for taking my leave so quickly, but I must hurry back to Stardancer."

"I won't hear of it," the Englishman overruled her. "I shall drive you back. It won't do for you to ride back alone."

Gitty opened her mouth to protest, but it was obvious that it had all been arranged, even before she began to worry about the late hour. The buggy appeared, Moonbeam tethered behind, and Uncle Volney handed the Englishman a picnic basket. "Your dinner, sir," he said.

The sky turned from light crimson to rose as the Englishman guided the buggy down the trail toward Stardancer. Letting the horse have his head, he opened the wicker picnic hamper.

"What do you suppose Cook and Volney have put together for us?" he said, raising an eyebrow. Inside were baked grouse stuffed with wild rice, leeks, even a bottle of French wine and two dainty goblets wrapped protectively in Irish linen. Gitty wondered if this was a typical English picnic, or if perhaps the Englishman and his Uncle Volney fellow were a bit eccentric.

As their buggy creaked along in the twilight, David Dunnington told her that he was the second son of a prominent English family. His parents and older brother had sent him to western America to make his own fortune, since the family wealth would pass to the eldest son, by English law.

"My family is strong on bloodlines," he said ruefully, "but not heavy on making or saving money. They financed a small nest-egg for me when I started these cattle operations, but now they count on me to support them in the manner to which they've grown accustomed. There's money in American cattle-ranching, if you're good at it. Luckily, I seem to be. Already, I've repaid their initial loan. Now I'm sending them quarterly dividends."

Many Englishmen, he said, who came to this western cattle country did not succeed. People called them "remittance men," because they were supported chiefly by remittances sent to them from families in England. David Dunnington smiled. The delightful dimples pierced his cheeks. "Neither breeding, brains nor money counts for much in cattle ranching," he said. "That's all many of the poor blokes have. Raising cattle is relying on your instincts." He chuckled. "If your instincts are good, and thus far, mine have been good, things go well." He glanced sideways at Gitty with an appraising glance.

When the buggy pulled up in front of The Lucky Pearl several noisy customers were causing a disturbance in the front hallway of the gambling house. "Wait a moment," Gitty said, placing her hand on the soft tweed of the Englishman's sleeve. "Someone will put a stop to that."

Won-Tu's small figure appeared. The rowdy customers were turned away.

"Please come in and meet Aunt Cath," Gitty said. "You've been so kind. I'd like you to meet her."

"Of course."

The Englishman wrapped the reins loosely around the white hitching post. "Follow me," Gitty said, catching his gloved hand. "We'll go in the private entrance." She giggled. "It's nothing special. It's where they deliver the meat and produce."

Gitty led the Englishman through the large kitchen and on to Cath's quarters. Lightly, she tapped on her aunt's door.

"Aunt Cath, I'm back."

Cath's door flew open. Lamplight nearly blinded Gitty. "Are you all right, child?" Cath cried. "I was so worried! I just knew that damn horse..."

Gitty squeezed her aunt's arm. "Please, Aunt Cath, Mr. Dunnington brought me home safely. He was kind enough to show me his Calico Butte Ranch. I wanted him to meet you."

Puzzled, Gitty watched her aunt's face change from a worried expression to a giddy look. Cath stared up at David Dunnington with unabashed rapture.

"Dunnington," Cath whispered. "I've heard of you, but I've never met you."

"To my disadvantage, madam," he said, dipping his head.

A far-off smile appeared on Cath's face. She continued to gape at the tall Englishman while Gitty stared at her aunt in amazement. Gitty had no way of knowing how much David Dunnington resembled Wade Stanton. Except for the color of their eyes, and their heights, the two men could have been brothers.

It was Gitty who rang the bell to summon tea. Won-Tu appeared so quickly that he must have been hovering close by. When Cath introduced David Dunnington to the Oriental, the little man stiffened. Later, when he brought the tea service, Won-Tu set it down hard in front of Cath, causing the china cups to rattle against the saucers. Gitty was surprised at Won-Tu's rudeness. Usually, he fussed over Cath's guests.

After Won-Tu left the room, Gitty nodded toward the empty doorway. "That's *our* Uncle Volney," she smiled. Dunnington chuckled in understanding.

After the Englishman left, Cath collapsed onto her settee, her voluminous flesh-colored silk frock rustling about her. "Land sakes, child, when you go fishing, you bring home the big one! That magnificent specimen of manhood has got to be the best catch this side of the Missouri River! And a rich Englishman, son of a baron, to boot!"

Gitty blushed. She hadn't thought of him as "a catch." He was just a handsome man who had treated her in a gentlemanly and hospitable manner.

"Why did Won-Tu act so peculiarly toward him?" Gitty asked.

Cath bit her lower lip. "I wondered about that. Then I remembered how Won-Tu hates the British. He says they purposely brought opium into China to make addicts out of the people, so they could take over the country."

It wasn't until later when Gitty lay in bed, thinking over the events of the day, that the thought occurred to her: Before Dunnington rode out of the stand of white birch after her swim in the lake — how long had he been there? She tried to remember when Moonbeam had first whinnied. She couldn't recall. Was it possible that he'd been there all the time, watching her disrobe, get into the water?

Her body tingled at the thought. It had been more than a year since she'd felt such sensations.

Over the next three weeks, there was only one day when Gitty and David Dunnington didn't spend time together. Within a few days after they met, Gitty became aware that the Englishman was infatuated with her. He found excuses to touch her arm, hold her hand. Gitty appreciated the attention. It was flattering to be admired by a handsome and powerful person.

They took long rides through the foothills. Usually, David used a western saddle. On occasion, he'd cinch on his flapjack English saddle, "just so I don't forget how," he'd laughed, shrugging.

They discovered their amusing language variations. David insisted that the elk horns hanging over his great stone fireplace were the horns of wapiti.

"Elk!" Gitty protested.

"What can you expect," the Englishman moaned, "from people who call thrush 'robin' and speak of grouse as 'partridge'?"

Gitty shook her head when he spoke of elk bulls as "stags," and elk cows as "hinds."

One afternoon, after a long ride, Gitty sat quietly in his parlor. She glanced casually at the elegant furnishings. Green brocade Queen Anne wing chairs flanked the fieldstone fireplace. Absently, she stroked the soft calf-skin leather of the sofa. The room was a strange combination of decor. It seemed to blend English aristocracy with the hominess of a western ranch house. At one end of the large oak-panelled room hung a monstrous pair of gray longhorns. The horn tips spread six feet across. David's black Stetson hung jauntily from the tip of one of the horns.

"Sorry, my dear," David apologized as he returned. "The foreman had a bit of a problem, but it's taken care of."

He seated himself beside her on the sofa and picked up her hand. He cleared his throat. "I've grown exceedingly fond of you in the short time we've been acquainted. I'm wondering if the feeling is mutual?"

"Why, of course, David," Gitty replied, smiling. "I'm very fond of you. But.." She paused, and her face grew long and serious.

"But what, my darling?" he cried, leaning toward her, distressed.

Gitty regarded him for a long moment, shaking her head sadly. Solemnly, she shook her head. "I hate leeks."

After a moment of silence David assimilated this, and when he did, he exploded in a bellow of laughter. Jumping up, he pulled Gitty to her feet. "You little minx!" he cried as he folded his arms around her waist. "You had me frightfully worried!" His lips came down hard on hers. Unconsciously, Gitty lifted her arms and circled his neck. As her breasts crushed against his chest she closed her eyes and surrendered to the waves of silky passion flowing throughout her body.

When David released her, Gitty's knees felt weak. She sank onto the sofa.

David dropped to one knee on the carpet in front of her. "Will you marry me, my darling?" Blinking, Gitty looked directly into his glittering blue eyes.

"Yes, David," she gasped, touching his cheek, caressing the dimple. "But you must get my aunt's permission, of course."

That evening, after David had returned her to The Lucky Pearl, Gitty sought out her aunt. She wanted to get Cath's feelings about David and what marriage to a wealthy English cattleman would offer. Cath was ecstatic.

"My child, you have hooked the biggest fish in the lake!" Cath gloated. "He is handsome, rich, powerful. He has brains and breeding. What more could any girl want?"

Gitty winced over her aunt's choice of the word "hooked." She felt no guilt along those lines. She'd used few feminine wiles on David Dunnington. If, going along with Aunt Cath's metaphor, David had "taken the bait," Gitty knew that she had spent little time choosing an enticing lure or setting the hook.

"The problem is, Aunt Cath," Gitty paused, taking a deep breath, "I don't love him."

"Fiddlesticks, girl!" Cath shouted. "Maybe you don't love him now, but if you can't learn to love David Dunnington, you've got a keg of nails where your heart is supposed to be. Migawd, he can put his boots beside my bed any night!"

"Aunt Cath!" Gitty protested. She knew Cath was teasing her. Still, she suspected that Cath was smitten with the handsome Englishman.

In a softer voice Cath asked, "What do *you* want, Gitty? If the baron isn't right, who *are* you looking for?"

"I'm not looking for anyone," Gitty answered quietly. "I already found him. It was an impossible situation."

"Dawn's father?"

"Yes."

"My dear, for heaven's sakes, I beg of you, forget —"

237

"I know I shouldn't dwell on the past. It's just that David doesn't, well, I don't have the same feelings toward him that I do, ..ah, *did* for the other."

Cath took Gitty's hand and looked intently into her eyes. "Let me tell you something: I carried a false love in my heart for more years than I care to remember. This young man worked in Papa's mill, and I thought I was in love with him. He disappeared into the prairies. Meantime, I met a wonderful man who loved me very much, but I brushed off the love, or maybe just took it for granted. I spent all my energy trying to find my false love. When I eventually did, it was a disaster. He was a self-centered fool. I finally made my way back to the wonderful man, who was loving enough to take me back. And I thank God every day of my life for the years we had together. I shudder to think how close I came to losing him because of my false yearnings."

Cath released Gitty's hand. "What I'm saying is, don't be stubborn in thoughts about love. Don't get caught on the hopeless shoals of but-I-love-someone-else. If the situation with Dawn's father is an impossible one, then forget him. You have Dawn. Now build her future and yours."

"Should I tell David about Dawn?" Gitty asked.

"No!" The answer was instant. "Not now. The day may come when you can. I hope it does. But right now he's a lovesick suitor. Worldly complications would not be welcome. He's in love with a beautiful, fresh young girl. Give him what he wants — a loving adoring sweetheart."

Chapter 22

David wanted to have the wedding the very next weekend. "No matter how far off we schedule the ceremony, my family is too far away to come," he said. "You're our family, Miss Cath, you're all we need!"

Cath insisted that she needed time to have a suitable wedding gown made for Gitty.

"A girl's wedding day, David," Cath reproved him, "is the most special day of her life. Surely you want your bride to have a lovely gown."

David smiled sheepishly and nodded in agreement. Cath judged that planning the ceremony for June 26 would allow enough time for the seamstresses to make the bridal gown. She also needed time to order and have shipped in a supply of suitable champagne, Mumm's extra dry and smoked oysters and terrapin.

Won-Tu refused to have anything to do with Gitty's wedding to "that English." He wouldn't help Cath with ordering the food, nor would he attend the ceremony.

"Give him time, honey," Cath reassured Gitty. "After he gets to know David, he'll forget his prejudices against Englishmen."

The girls of The Lucky Pearl were beside themselves with excitement over the idea of a wedding to which they were all invited. Some of them had never attended any sort of wedding, and the more worldly ones who had seen a bridal ceremony said that this one would be extra special because the groom was "practically royalty."

The wedding was held at the Calico Butte ranch house. Cath had hired an itinerant Methodist preacher to perform the ceremony. The preacher was delighted. The fee Cath paid him was more than his collection plates gathered in three months of hard travel and pulpit-pounding.

Before noon the girls from The Lucky Pearl began arriving. Gitty peered out the window of the upstairs guest room as the excited guests rattled up in a long caravan of buggies and farm wagons. She was surprised to see how little coloring the girls wore today. They looked chaste and ladylike. Gitty wondered if this was due to instructions from Cath, or if the girls were interested in attracting ranch hands in a matrimonial way.

Looking uncomfortable in their stiff boiled shirts and boots unaccustomed to such a waxy shine, the cowhands filed into the parlor and gathered in a corner, standing uneasily, shifting their weight from one foot to the other.

Polly, one of Cath's girls, played suitable wedding music on the big square piano, which was festooned with wildflowers. At the proper signal Cath opened the guest room door and walked ceremoniously down the open stairway toward the parlor. All eyes turned and faced the staircase as Gitty followed her aunt. The heavy slipper-satin gown swooshed as she walked, and Gitty felt the drag of the heavy train. As she neared the makeshift, sheet-draped altar, Gitty looked up. Through the lacy pattern of her bridal veil she saw David, tall and handsome, standing to one side of the altar. Uncle Volney, his best man, stood beside him. She caught her breath as David moved to stand beside her, his upper arm brushing lightly against her satin-draped shoulder.

Gitty heard the short service through a haze. She just couldn't believe this was her wedding day. It didn't seem real. Always, she'd imagined Papa walking with her down the aisle in the Mattigan Methodist Church, with Mama sitting in the front pew, sniffling sentimentally. Never would she have dreamed that she'd be out on the frontier marrying an Englishman!

After the ceremony the guests dived into the tasty food set up on the sideboards. Champagne corks popped with regularity, though the ranch hands preferred the beer keg set up outside under the tall cottonwood tree. Gitty could tell that many of the hands felt uncomfortable in the parlor. They were men who spent their lives under the sun and the stars. A crowded, smelly bunkhouse was their idea of home.

In the early evening Cath herded her girls into their buggies, saying it was time for them to get back to Stardancer. David's cowhands drifted off to their poker games.

240

"I'll be saying good-night now," Uncle Volney said, as he stood rocking uneasily in the kitchen door. "I'm a-going to play cards with Tal tonight. He said I could bunk with him. See you tomorrow." He spun on his boot heel and was gone.

"And that, my dear," David grinned down at Gitty, "means we're alone in the house. I had no idea old Volney was capable of such tact." He flashed her a wicked grin.

Gitty returned an uneasy smile. She had to remember to act like a virgin!

Seeing her disquieted expression, David put his arm around her shoulders. "Please don't be afraid, dear. I love you. I won't hurt you." He took her hand and led her into the kitchen.

"I shall concoct a nightcap for the nervous bride," he announced, reaching into a high cupboard. "It's a new drink, very popular in London, my family writes me." He brought down a bottle of imported scotch whiskey. "This is the base," he said, as he poured a generous amount of amber fluid into two round goblets.

He pulled a shiny ebony japanned tray toward him, and Gitty realized that the ingredients had been set out. On the tray was a small silver pitcher of milk, two eggs, and a bowl of sugar. Beads of sweat clung to the pitcher. The milk was still chilled. Gitty smiled, supposing that Uncle Volney must have been instructed to set out these supplies before he left.

"And now, to the beautiful brown fluid from Scotland," David said, "I add a little hen fruit." He broke an egg into each of the goblets and stirred the egg into the whiskey. "Next a bit of saccharine substance," he sprinkled a bit of sugar into the mixtures. "Finally," he picked up the silver pitcher with a flourish, "I shall add a bit of lacteal fluid, and *voila*! — our matrimonial toast, called not too imaginatively, a 'Tom and Jerry'!"

David picked up both goblets and handed Gitty one. "To our long and happy life together!" he toasted. Tears rushed to Gitty's eyes as she touched glasses with her new husband. Ringing in her ears were the minister's words, "Till death do you part."

"Cheers!" David grinned. "Bottoms up!"

After they drained their glasses, David caught Gitty's hand in his. "Come," he said softly, leading her toward his bedroom on the first floor. Gitty never had seen his room. She was impressed with its comfortable masculinity. The floor was covered with two dark brown bearskin rugs, and several steer hides, tanned with the hair on. Gitty had

241

the sudden urge to kick off her shoes and silk stockings and stand barefoot on the bear rugs, wriggling her toes.

"David," Gitty said softly, "I'm afraid you'll have to unbutton the back of my dress. It's impossible for me to reach."

"My pleasure." He fumbled with the tiny and slippery satin-covered buttons. When he finished with the last button, he turned Gitty around to face him. "Would it help you be less nervous, darling, if I told you that I've already seen you unclothed? That day by the pond..."

In mock horror Gitty shrieked, letting the white satin gown fall to the floor at her feet. She leaped high toward David, throwing her arms about his neck and wrapping her long legs around his waist. She pressed her forehead against his, as she whispered hoarsely, "You beastly creature, you! You were spying on me!"

David grinned. "Only a fool would turn his back on such a lovely sight!" With Gitty's arms and legs still wrapped around him, he moved toward the bed, and the two of them fell onto it.

There was a loud splitting sound of breaking wood as a slat broke. Springs and mattress clattered to the floor. Gitty and David tumbled into a pile, gasping and laughing.

"It's a good thing Volney's out of the house," David choked, "or he'd be in here to see what's going on." He stood up and surveyed the wreckage. "Well, we're not sleeping in that bed tonight!"

"I'll fix a substitute," Gitty said. "Here, let's pull the mattress out of that mess and drag it over to the corner."

They tugged and heaved the unwieldy mattress into a corner of the bedroom. Humming a silly tune, Gitty skipped around the bedroom snatching up steer hide rugs. She laid these on top of the mattress and covered them with the two huge bearskins. "There!" she said as she arranged the last furry rug. "A bed fit for a king — a king of the Eskimos!"

Taking off his jacket, David studied his bride, who sat cross-legged on her furry creation, wearing only a thin chemise and drawers. There was a new look of appreciation in his eyes. Gitty looked back at him saucily. When he had stripped down to only his drawers, she held out her arms.

❋   ❋   ❋   ❋

During their first week of marriage, Gitty and David spent a considerable amount of time together in spite of the fact that roundup

242

time was upon Calico Butte, the busy time when calves must be caught and branded with the Ball-4 brand. When David was out supervising operations, Gitty got acquainted with her new surroundings.

To the northwest, Calico Butte towered over their little group of buildings. Between the butte and the ranch house ran a small creek called Cottonwood Run. Directly to the east, across the dusty road to Stardancer, were the ranch outbuildings, the bunkhouse where the hands slept and ate, the stable, the blacksmith shop, and the storehouse. Beyond the stable was the square paddock where cowhands broke unruly horses, or where an ailing animal could be kept. A smaller enclosure next to the paddock housed two milk cows. The chicken house was on the far side of the paddock. David believed it was important to have fresh milk, butter and eggs, so he kept the cows and chickens, though he refused to have pigs. "I'm not a farmer," he insisted stubbornly. "I shall buy my bacon and hams as well as my mutton."

One day Gitty's curiosity led her to the spacious kitchen. As she opened a cupboard door she was stopped by Cook, the portly wife of Tal Frude, the ranch foreman.

"No need to bother yourself about the kitchen, ma'am," Cook objected. "I run a good kitchen and set a good table. I'll not have interference."

Gitty closed the cupboard door and regarded the blue eyes snapping with challenge. "Who, then, decides upon the menu?" Gitty asked.

"Oh, sometimes the boss gives me a suggestion, like 'twould be nice to have some mutton one of these days.' But I decides upon the menu, and I buys the necessaries for the kitchen and dining room. I also buys the food for the hands and the chuck wagon." Cook wiped red, beefy hands on her flour-sack apron. "It's a big job, it is. And I'll not have interference from anyone!"

"I don't mean to interfere, Cook," Gitty spoke softly. "But I'm now the mistress of this house, and I assumed that I should..."

"If you interfere in my kitchen, I leaves. And if I leaves, my husband leaves. It's your choice, ma'am."

With a curt nod Gitty swept out of the kitchen. She didn't have much choice but to stay out of food matters.

Since David would probably be out with the hands for some time yet, Gitty thought she might have time to pay a quick visit to Dawn. She hadn't seen her since two days before the wedding.

She saddled Moonbeam and at a smooth, loping canter headed across the rolling prairie toward Walks Softly's cabin. Gitty was delighted to see that Dawn had learned to crawl since she last saw her. The chubby girl scooted about the cabin, getting into everything. Dawn even noticed Gitty's new gold wedding band and tried to chew on it.

On her way back to the ranch house, Gitty was trotting along, her mind on the sweet smile and wave her daughter had given her, when suddenly David was at her side, his black gelding snorting a welcome to Moonbeam.

"Where've you been, love?"

Gitty hesitated. She hadn't planned yet what she would say. "Oh, just out for a ride. Cook won't let me have anything to do with the kitchen, so I guess I rode off my irritation."

David stared at her for a moment, a slight frown creasing his forehead, then he smiled. "If you really want to spend your time ordering supplies, keeping inventory of foodstuffs, and planning menus, I'll let Cook go. I just wouldn't think you'd want to spend so much time on dull accounting chores."

"If Cook goes, she said the foreman would go, too."

"Hum, yes, I'm sure he would, but I can find another foreman. That's no problem."

In the end Gitty decided she would keep her time free and let Cook retain command of the kitchen.

A few days later when Gitty thought David was out rounding up calves, she decided to visit Dawn. As she strode briskly toward the stable, David called from the blacksmith shop, "Where're you going, darling?"

Gitty's heart sank. "I thought I'd pay Aunt Cath a visit," she lied. David walked toward her, brushing dust from his coat sleeves.

"Good, we can go together. I need to check on some freight. Should we take the buggy or ride? Come to think of it, perhaps we should take the buggy. If the Spooner horse-collar I sent for has come, I'd like to bring it back with me."

David dropped Gitty off at The Lucky Pearl while he went to do his errands. The minute he walked out the door Gitty fumed to her aunt, "How am I ever to spend time with Dawn? It's so hard for me to get away! I'm afraid David will eventually catch me in a lie, or suspect me of meeting someone in rendezvous. Oh, Aunt Cath!" she cried. "I never should have married!"

"Now, dear, don't be upset," Cath calmed Gitty. "Let me think. If we use our heads, we can fix this problem." Cath leaned back on the settee and closed her eyes, massaging her temples with her fingertips.

Later, when David returned to pick up Gitty, he had tea with Cath and Gitty. The three of them were chatting about nothing special when Cath said, "David, there's something I've been meaning to speak to you about. I meant to talk to you before the wedding, but we were all so busy!" She leaned forward and her eyes fluttered.

"It bothers me," she went on, "that my niece is out there on your ranch with no maid, no one to care for her clothes and bathing needs. Gitty has said nothing to me, I assure you, but I'm telling you that she should have a woman to help her with her hair, and to keep her frocks fresh, mended, and pressed. She has to do this herself now."

David fingered his moustache lightly. "I see, I never thought of it. What sort of person would you want? I'm afraid a young maid wouldn't stay long. She'd be married to one of my cowboys in a fortnight." He turned to Gitty. "Do you have someone in mind, dear?"

As Gitty blinked in confusion, Cath rushed in. "*I* have a woman in mind. She would be very good in that position, and a good companion for my niece. She's a widow, a half-breed. I don't think your cowhands would fall over themselves wanting to marry her. But there's one problem. The woman has a baby. Would that bother you, dear?" Cath leaned toward Gitty, peering innocently at her niece.

Everything was moving too fast for Gitty. She swallowed and stammered, "Oh, no, that wouldn't bother me. I love babies!"

David frowned. "But I don't see how a woman burdened with a baby..."

"Nonsense!" Cath fairly roared. "Only a man would say such foolishness! No woman is *burdened* with a baby. A baby brings a woman alive and makes her energetic!"

Gitty bit her lip. Her childless aunt was spreading it pretty thick.

Later, as the buggy rocked along the trail toward Calico Butte, David questioned Gitty. "Would you really like to have this woman as a servant? — even though she has a child?"

"Oh, yes, David," Gitty squeezed his arm. "More than anything! I'd so love another woman to talk with when you're not about. And a baby...Oh, David, please."

David shook his head. It was hard to figure women.

245

Within a week Walks Softly and Dawn were moved into the guest room upstairs. Gitty was deliriously happy. The last time she was so contented was back before her parents drowned. When Gitty carried the brown little half-Indian child around the grounds on her hip, no one at Calico Butte Ranch even considered for a moment that she was holding her own child.

✳   ✳   ✳   ✳

It was late to be still branding calves, but some of the outriders had discovered a good-sized cow-calf herd in the valley in the southeastern section.

"Why don't you ride out with me today, sweetheart?" David asked Gitty. "You can see how we account for the increase in our herd each year."

It was a gorgeous day late in July, not a wisp of cloud in the sky. Mid-morning David and she rode up on a large herd of cattle contentedly grazing in a small valley.

Amid clouds of dust, riders on cutting horses separated a bawling calf from its protective mother. Deftly, a cowhand tossed a rope about the calf's neck. Another hand quickly caught the rope near the neck of the animal and reached across its back to take a handful of the loose skin under its body. As the calf jumped, the man shoved his knee under it, tripping the animal and causing it to fall heavily. With its breath knocked out, the calf lay still long enough for the cowhands to get another rope on its hind legs. Now it was helpless, stretched out on the ground. The brander came forward with his red hot branding iron, and touched it to the calf's flank. The moment he finished, the cutter castrated the bull calf and notched its left ear. Just as the cutter began his work, the stench of burning hair, blood, and tissue reached Gitty. With no warning she felt her breakfast rise in her throat, and with a gasp, she rushed away from David, being able to move only a few yards before vomiting.

Immediately, David was at her side, presenting his spotless linen handkerchief. "I'm so sorry, love, I didn't think — please forgive me. I'll take you home right away."

Gitty shook her head, dabbing at her mouth. How embarrassing. The wave of nausea had passed. She felt only a little shaky. "I think I'm all right now," she whispered, patting his sleeve.

246

She was fine until noon when the chuck wagon rolled up. At the first whiff of strong coffee and frying side pork, Gitty's stomach lurched. Cold perspiration broke out on her forehead. She insisted that she could make it back to the ranch house by herself, but David wouldn't hear of it. He accompanied her back and turned her over to the tender care of Walks Softly.

During her first pregnancy Gitty hadn't suffered a bit of nausea. She had felt robust and healthy until the final month when her ankles had swelled. This time, the nausea was almost constant, and it had started so early! For three weeks Gitty refused to be anywhere near food. She couldn't bear the smell. Occasionally, she could be coaxed into nibbling on a soda cracker. She lost weight. Dark shadows appeared under her eyes, hollows showed in her cheeks.

In desperation, Walks Softly persuaded David to send for Ten-Fu. The little Oriental woman shuffled silently into the bedroom where Gitty lay propped on several down pillows, her face pale and wan.

Ten-Fu clucked, spouted and shook her head. She patted Gitty's arm, said, "I fix you up, missee, no time."

Clutching the huge carpetbag she had brought, Ten-Fu asked to be shown to the kitchen. Walks Softly, with Dawn slung on one hip, stepped forward. At the sight of little Dawn Ten-Fu rushed to the baby and tickled her round cheeks. "So pretty, little one," she smiled.

"There is a problem to use the kitchen," Walks Softly told Ten-Fu. "Can't Cook fix what you need?"

Ten-Fu threw Walks Softly such a ferocious look that Walks Softly understood the answer.

Soon from the kitchen Cook's loud shrill shouts and Ten-Fu's sing-song voice mingled with banging pots and pans. If Gitty had been able, she would've gone to the kitchen. When she thought of huge, round Cook, and poor little Ten-Fu pitted against her — what chance did the Chinese woman have?

In ten minutes Ten-Fu, trailed by a grinning Walks Softly, returned to Gitty's bedroom, carrying a tray bearing a teapot, a cup and saucer.

"I suppose Cook has gone," Gitty sighed weakly.

"No," Walks Softly laughed, shifting the child to her other hip. "Cook was interested. Cook was told that only bad cook would ignore suffering of baby-sickness in her mistress. Cook learned how to make special mint tea. Cook doesn't want to cause loss of her boss's child because of lack of knowing medicinal cooking."

While Walks Softly related the conversation that had gone on in the kitchen, Ten-Fu steadily spooned steaming mint tea into Gitty's mouth. Soon, the soothing effects of the hot herb quieted the nausea and Gitty gave Ten-Fu a faint smile. "I feel better, Ten-Fu. Thank you."

Ten-Fu gave Walks Softly a hard look. "Each time she feel bad in stomach, she must have mint tea to settle stomach. Like I told fat cook." Her dark eyes locked with Walks Softly's. "Can you see cook has tea ready, or do I move in to see this child has good care?"

For a moment a dark flush crossed the Indian woman's face at this intimation that she had been neglecting Gitty's care. "I take care of Cook," Walks Softly muttered.

David was delighted that he was to become a father. He sympathized with Gitty and her delicate stomach. He missed their playful bedroom tussling and their wild horseback racing out on the flats. But, adaptable fellow that he was, he assumed that his bride's delicate condition was temporary. He was prepared to be patient.

Gitty figured the baby should arrive about the first of April. When she told him, she giggled, "I think I must have gotten it on our wedding night."

"Conceived on a bear rug," David chuckled. "Then I suppose the child will be born bare?"

"Oh, David," Gitty groaned, holding her nose, and fanning her face with her other hand. "That's terrible! Only you British would dare make such awful jokes!"

Ten-Fu's medicinal tea helped battle the once overwhelming nausea. Even so, Gitty felt tired and, though not in pain, generally uncomfortable. It was almost as if the unborn child fought her from the beginning. Sometimes, Gitty wondered if the baby found her womb distasteful and chose to make them both uncomfortable. Other times, Gitty felt she was carrying an unrelated baby within her womb. Though she would never admit it to anyone, and she could hardly face the truth of it, Gitty felt no anticipation for the arrival of this baby, except that this uncomfortable pregnancy would be ended.

Just after her first birthday in September Dawn mastered the ability to walk. On warm autumn afternoons the little girl loved toddling around the yard, though she had to be watched, as she tried to taste sticks and fallen leaves. Dawn loved to watch the chickens pecking feed from the ground. She made clucking noises in imitation of the hens. Most of all, Dawn loved riding on Moonbeam's broad back in front of either

Walks Softly or Gitty. For over an hour the child would sit contentedly while one of them rode her around the ranch grounds.

In November both Gitty and David received surprising letters. David's letter came first. It was from his mother, Lady Dunnington, who wrote that she was planning to visit them the following May, and that she would bring with her their wedding gifts. "I don't trust the rails to deliver them safely," she wrote. A small shiver crossed Gitty's spine. The woman didn't say, "I want to see you, my son, or I want to meet your bride." She just indicated that she was delivering wedding gifts. Nothing was said about seeing her grandchild, though perhaps David's letter telling of the expected baby hadn't arrived in England before this letter was written.

Exactly one week later in the next arrival of overland mail Gitty received a letter from Conway Carleton. Gitty sat down hard on the divan when she read that Grandfather planned to visit her and Cath in the spring, sometime in May.

Gitty was delighted. How wonderful it would be to see Grandfather again, to have him meet David, and see this beautiful country!

The following day, Gitty rode Moonbeam into Stardancer to tell her aunt the wonderful news. When she showed the letter to Cath, she hadn't expected anything like her aunt's reaction.

"He can't come here!" Cath screamed. "I won't have it! He can't. I'd die if he knew what I do! And he'd have apoplexy! Pa can't come to Stardancer!"

When Cath finally quit storming, Gitty offered a solution. "The baby will be here by the time he arrives. During his visit you can move in with us out at Calico Butte, and we'll say that you've sold your millinery shop, retired, and that you plan to help me raise my baby. We'll keep him away from Stardancer as much as we can, but hardly anyone there thinks of you as Cath, you know. You're 'Pearl' there. Won-Tu can manage The Lucky Pearl during the time."

Gitty squeezed her aunt's hand. "Oh, Aunt Cath, it'll be fun! You'll see! It'll be like a vacation for you to be away from the casino for a few weeks. And think of all the talking you and Grandfather have to make up for!"

Chapter 23
The Buffalo Skinner Returns

With the help of Ten-Fu's mint tea, Gitty felt well enough to keep riding Moonbeam throughout the fall, though she avoided trotting for fear of injuring her unborn baby. Nearly every day she rode out with David to look over the herds. As Gitty's judging eye grew more experienced, she could tell a blooded calf from a rangy longhorn's offspring.

When David had first started raising cattle he'd purchased $100,000 worth of Shorthorn bulls to service his nine thousand long-legged, stringy longhorn cows. One bull was needed for every twenty-five cows. David had been disappointed in the quality of the Shorthorn bulls delivered to him. The best sires were in such demand in the East that only the poorer bulls, culled out as range bulls, were available. Even so, two years later, the addition of the Shorthorn blood could be seen in the blocky bodies of many of the calves.

"A crossbred Shorthorn two-year-old will dress out three hundred pounds heavier than a longhorn dogie," David told Gitty.

Last spring, just before their marriage, David had been able to purchase some top grade Hereford sires. These strange-looking animals with the red hide and white face, promised to upgrade considerably the quality of the Ball 4 beef. "Come spring calving," David explained, "we'll be able to tell how busy our Herefords were last summer. They say every calf sired by a Hereford will have a white face. That way we can distinguish the Hereford-sired calves from others."

David's long-term goal was to breed out the original Texas longhorn blood. Longhorn cows were lean and vicious, wild as deer and difficult to handle. The meat from blooded cattle was more tender and would bring more money at the stockyards.

Even by late November there had been very little snow and Gitty continued her daily rides with David.

One day as they moved through a dry coulee they heard a steady boom of distant guns. "Must be buffalo hunters," David said. "Notice the nearly constant shooting? That means they've got a stand going. The buffalo are confused. They just mill about, grunting and nuzzling the fallen animals. The hunters keep a sharp eye on the animals. Any buffalo that looks as if it might bolt gets the next shot. They don't want one to break loose and run off, or the whole herd would follow. They have to keep them milling around in confusion."

Gitty shuddered, thinking of the buffalo skinner. What if he had survived her knife, and was out there, just over the divide, skinning a dead buffalo?

"Let's go home, David," she said. "I feel chilly."

It wasn't a hard winter as Dakota winters went. Two severe blizzards roared in from the northwest, one in January and the second in February. When Gitty looked out the frosty window at the whirling snow she thought of her snowed-in winter with Doe Eyes. A thoughtful look stole across her face as she remembered their tussles in the snow, followed by languorous lovemaking on the buffalo robes. Off to the southeast, across the white rolling prairies, was the Pine Ridge agency, the reservation which was home to Doe Eyes. He was out there, somewhere, with his people. Tears formed in the corners of her eyes. When you watch this raging blizzard, Doe Eyes, do you think of me? Do you wish you could stroke my hair? You loved my hair so much. Do you think of buffalo robes and damp skin? A quiet smile crossed her face.

"What are you thinking of, love?" David asked.

Flustered, Gitty blushed. To gain time, she asked, "Why do you ask?"

"You had such a contented, happy look on your face."

Gitty shrugged. "I was just trying to think of suitable names for our child. We haven't discussed it, and my time is only a month off. Do you have any suggestions?"

"I rather fancy the name 'Crystal' for a girl," David answered. "I don't know why. I've never known a 'Crystal.' Perhaps that's why I like it. As for a boy's name, I haven't thought. Only, please, not David. I think each person in a family should have his own name."

"I agree. I'm not keen on naming a child after a grandparent, either," Gitty said. "I've always liked the name 'Peter'. What do you think?"

"Nice name. Then it's settled, is it? Crystal, if a girl, Peter, if a boy?"

Late in the morning of March 21 Gitty went into labor. David hitched up the buggy and hurried off to Stardancer to fetch Ten-Fu. He had wanted to engage a doctor to deliver the baby, but the howls of protest from Cath and Gitty changed his mind.

Within a half hour of her first pain, Gitty found herself bearing down and grunting with each contraction. She couldn't help it.

"Lie down on the bed so I can look!" Walks Softly ordered. "Your time is near."

"But with Dawn I labored for hours and hours!" Gitty protested.

"First one's hardest." Walks Softly tugged at Gitty's underclothing. "Let me look. *Mon Dieu!* I see the head!"

When David and Ten-Fu rushed into the bedroom they were flabbergasted to see Gitty propped up in bed, sipping tea, blanket-wrapped bundle beside her.

David rushed to the bed and knelt. "It's over? The baby's here?" he cried.

Gitty rested her cup and saucer on the counterpane, unwrapped some of the white blanket swaddling the infant. "Meet your daughter, Crystal."

David's blue eyes glowed as he gazed at the baby. With his index finger he tenderly stroked the infant's round cheek. From across the room came the shrill noises of Ten-Fu chattering excitedly with Walks Softly, questioning her. Ten-Fu couldn't believe Gitty had given birth without her help.

Beginning with the day of her birth, Crystal was an aloof baby. A small, fine-boned infant, she seldom fussed. She slept long hours. Even when awake, she lay silent, regarding her surroundings with a sober expression. At six weeks, the infant had not yet smiled. Gitty worried that she might have given birth to an idiot.

Cottonwood buds were bursting into miniature leaves when Conway Carleton arrived in Stardancer on the Cheyenne and Black Hills stagecoach. Gitty and Cath waited excitedly with David outside The

Mason House, the stage stop for Stardancer. A rumbling from south of town grew steadily louder, announcing the approach of the stage. The drivers always galloped the horses into town, making a terrible clatter. The noise served to announce to the whole town the arrival of the stage from Deadwood.

The red Concord stagecoach rumbled into sight. The horses pounded down Main Street, snuffling and rattling their harness. A cloud of dust rose, encircling the waiting crowd as the flashing yellow wheels skidded to a stop.

Gitty was so excited she had to contain herself to keep from jumping up and down. Cath gripped Gitty's hand so hard that it hurt.

Two strangers climbed from the stage before Conway Carleton stepped off. "That's him," Gitty squealed as she half-pushed her aunt toward him.

"Oh, *Pa!*" Cath cried as she fell into his arms and burst into tears. Conway's shoulders shook convulsively. He, too, was crying. After a while Conway held Cath away from him as he reached into his pocket for a handkerchief. He blew his nose noisily and wiped his eyes. "My little golden-haired darlin'. I was afraid I'd never see you again!"

At this Cath burst into fresh tears. Against his chest, she sobbed, "I'm so glad you came, Pa!"

Gitty reached up and with gloved fingers dabbed away the tears slipping from her eyes. She looked up at David and saw that he was watching the reunion with a look of fascinated awe.

At last, Conway glanced over Cath's shoulder and spotted his granddaughter. "Gitty, my darlin'! Come give me a hug, though you may have to reach around your Aunt Cath!"

After hugs and tears, Gitty was able to introduce David to her grandfather and the two men turned to gathering Conway's valises and trunk, which they loaded onto the waiting buggy.

As they bounced along the rough trail to Calico Butte, Cath sat beside her father, clutching his hand possessively. "It's been twenty-four years, Cath," he said. "Twenty-four years since you left for the West. Why in tarnation did you come out here? It's beautiful country, but it's at the end of the world!"

David chuckled. "We British say that if hell lay to the west, Americans would cross heaven to get there."

"It's a far piece," Conway murmured. "It *is* beautiful. You know, they say the city belongs to man, but the country belongs to God."

Gitty studied her grandfather. It had been not quite three years since she'd last seen him. His hair had whitened considerably, but he hadn't aged much. Gitty counted. He must be sixty-two now.

"How's Gladys?" Gitty felt obliged to ask.

Conway's mouth twisted in a wry smile. "She took off months ago. And good riddance! That was a mistake. I guess there's no fool like an old fool."

"Oh, Pa," Cath said, "you're not an old fool."

When Gitty pointed out the towering Calico Butte to her grandfather a broad grin spread over his face. "It's aptly named, darlin'," he said. "Looks as if some giant hand has spread a cloak of calico cloth over it."

As the trail wound through Calico Butte land, David pointed out the new white-faced calves. "See how they all look alike, how they stand out from the others? It's easy to see exactly how many half-blooded Herefords we have."

"Are you just getting into Herefords?" Conway asked.

"Yes. At first I introduced Durham bulls, but they weren't top-of-the-line stock. A year ago I brought in some excellent Hereford bulls, and these are our first calves. I'm trying to breed out all the scrub stock and the longhorns."

Conway scratched his moustache thoughtfully. "It's hard for me to believe — all this land and no trees. No trees! To me, trees are money, success. It's difficult for me to grasp the idea of land which can be profitable without trees."

David smiled. "I know the feeling. When I first arrived here and saw how poor in timber and water the country was, I had my doubts. An old-timer told me that the land offered superior soil and grass. He said out here men just had to learn how to build houses without timber and how to burn fires without wood."

Once at the ranch house Conway couldn't wait to see his great-granddaughter. As they entered the parlor Dawn trotted up, her sturdy legs churning in a rolling gait. She held her arms out to Gitty, silently begging to be picked up. Laughing, Gitty lifted the little girl high in the air, and the child shrieked with pleasure.

"And who's this?" Conway asked, puzzled over the familiarity the child was showing to his granddaughter. It was obviously an Indian.

At that moment Walks Softly came out of the bedroom. "Walks Softly, meet my grandfather, Mr. Carleton," Gitty introduced them. "And this is Dawn, Walks Softly's absolutely delightful daughter." Gitty rubbed noses with the little girl and set her down.

"How's Crystal?" Gitty asked as she removed her bonnet. "Quiet, as usual, I suppose?"

Walks Softly nodded.

Gitty led her grandfather into the large bedroom, where the baby Crystal lay awake in a ruffled, beribboned basket. Conway leaned over the basket to examine his great-granddaughter. The baby gazed up into his eyes for only a moment before her face broke into a wide smile. Deep dimples appeared in the tiny cheeks as she puckered into a grin.

Gitty gasped. "She smiled! Walks Softly! The baby smiled at Grandfather!"

"May I pick her up?" Conway asked.

Quickly, Gitty scooped up the baby and placed her in Conway's arms. Once again, little Crystal gave Conway a heartwarming smile. Gitty shook her head ruefully. Here she'd been worried that the baby might be defective. Maybe Crystal was the sort of baby who preferred men. Perish the thought! What a nightmare it would be to raise a daughter who was partial to men!

Conway presented Gitty with several Irish linen tablecloths and napkins. He'd brought all sorts of baby clothes and little girls' dresses which wouldn't fit Crystal for another three years.

"I brought things which wouldn't get broken along the way," he explained. Gitty gave him a grateful kiss on the cheek. "Everything is perfectly lovely, Grandfather," she said. "But having you here is the most important thing!"

That evening Gitty, Cath, Conway and David seated themselves at the dinner table. David raised his glass of amontillado and gave his usual blessing, "God bless the grass."

Cath gasped. "Oh, Pa! That makes me think back! Remember how you used to say "God bless the trees?"

Conway took a sip of wine. With a smile he commented, "One could hardly ask The Lord to bless what isn't here. I can see why David says 'grass'."

"Grass is money to the rancher, Mr. Carleton. Every blade of that buffalo grass out there gets turned into beef. No one would buy the grass, but they surely pay well for what my cattle do with grass."

David and Conway got along fine. They enjoyed each others company. Once Conway got the idea of cattle ranching, he understood and respected the Englishman's business acumen. The two men were similar in their single-minded appreciation for a special kind of business.

As the time neared for the arrival of David's mother, Gitty found herself growing nervous. She confessed this to David.

"Nonsense, darling!" he protested. "Just be yourself."

David went alone into Stardancer to meet his mother's stagecoach. She had written that she was bringing her niece, Aimee, plus several steamer trunks. David said they'd need all the buggy-space for hauling the trunks.

By the time Gitty heard the familiar rattle of the returning buggy, her armpits were damp. She worried whether the moisture showed through onto her bronze watered-silk.

Gitty looked out the window as David helped his mother out of the buggy. Gitty was surprised to see that Lady Dunnington had black hair, as black as David's, with not a touch of gray. That was unusual, as the woman had to be in her late fifties, she figured.

Lady Dunnington swept into the parlor, her brown silk skirt rustling in what Gitty thought to be regal tones. "Good afternoon, my dear, you must be David's Gitty. So nice to meet you," she said. She presented a wrinkled cheek for a kiss. A hint of lavender hovered in the air surrounding Lady Dunnington. Her complexion was ruddy.

David's cousin, Aimee, was introduced. The girl was near twenty years old, David had said. She looked younger. Her pale brown hair was brushed up, almost concealed by a dowdy bonnet which would have been better suited to a middle-aged matron. Aimee seemed to melt into the shadows, perhaps because of Sybil Dunnington's take-charge manner.

"Well, David," Lady Dunnington said as she scanned the room, "it's a bit rustic, but what else could it be in this godforsaken land? Now, where is my granddaughter?"

Gitty led her mother-in-law into the bedroom. The moment Lady Dunnington looked down into the basket, her face broke into a rapturous smile. Deep clefts appeared in her cheeks. The baby Crystal looked up, and when her eyes focused on her grandmother's face, her mouth widened into a smile, with identical creases appearing in her cheeks. Gitty's hand slid to her throat. Crystal looked like her Grandmother Dunnington!

At that moment Dawn came screeching into the bedroom. Pursuing her was Walks Softly, gliding silently in her leather moccasins. Dawn held her arms up, begging Gitty to pick her up. As Gitty gathered the little girl into her arms, Sybil Dunnington exploded, "Why, that's an Indian child! Whatever is she doing here?"

"Dawn is Walks Softly's daughter, Lady Dunnington," Gitty said. "Walks Softly is my maid and companion."

Sybil Dunnington studied the French-Indian woman the way she might appraise a side of mutton. Walks Softly stared back at the Englishwoman, holding her head high.

"Humph," Lady Dunnington snorted. "An attractive woman. Are they all that attractive?"

"No," Walks Softly replied. "They are not."

"She speaks English! How nice!"

"She also speaks French," Gitty added, wondering why she felt it necessary to defend Walks Softly.

"Oh?" Lady Dunnington raised her eyebrows. "You have an education then? Where did you study?"

Walks Softly smiled softly. "I learned French from my father, a Frenchman."

"Yes, of course." Lady Dunnington turned back to her granddaughter in the basket. Her interest in Dawn and Walks Softly had evaporated.

Lady Dunnington's wedding gifts were lavish. She presented to David and Gitty an antique tea urn made in Edinburgh nearly one hundred and fifty years before. Silver snakes formed handles on both sides. Gitty thought it quite ugly. There was a sterling silver cup for Crystal and a huge silver soup tureen on a magnificent sterling platter. The gift Lady Dunnington was most proud of was a stained glass window from Tiffany's. It had been crated protectively in four sections. Amazingly, it arrived unbroken.

David groaned. "Mother, do you know how many cows I could've bought with what you must have spent on that window?"

"Don't be crude, David. That's all you write about is cows, cows, cows. You need some elegance in your life!"

The evening dinner was extravagant. Gitty wondered if this was Cook's idea of a feast for visiting near-royalty, or if David had made one of his "suggestions" to Cook. Wine flowed freely. They had amontillado with the soup, burgundy with the terrapin, Mumm's extra dry with the venison, madeira with a choice of desserts, and cognac with the after-dinner coffee.

When they arrived at the dessert course David said, "Mother, this is the way we dine at the Cheyenne Club. Top drawer — we wear dinner jackets, which the Americans call 'Herefords', and we dine on pickled eel and drink Champagne Perrier Brut. I've learned to enjoy the best of both the Old World and the New World. I enjoy English dinners, but I eschew the abominable English customs of hard beds and cold baths. Here at Calico Butte Ranch you will be treated to warmed beds and heated bath water."

Lady Dunnington told of her long train ride from New York City. "Once in America," she said, "the fact that one is in a democratic country is constantly pressed upon one. There seems absolutely no exclusiveness. Pity. I must say, with apologies to you natives, that I find American table habits revolting. They gobble their food. Their elbows are a menace." She pressed the linen napkin to her lips. "One cause of these obnoxious habits is that American table knives are dull. No wonder the poor souls have to pull and tear at their food! If they had sharp knives, they could slice their food and use their fork merely to carry the morsels to their mouths."

Sybil Dunnington must have thought she was being entertaining as she regaled them with the stories of her travels. Even so, Gitty was offended by the woman's constant criticism of everything American. Lady Dunnington went on and on, describing the revolting food she'd been forced out of hunger to eat. She complained that for this terrible food she was asked to pay three shillings.

Lady Dunnington was smitten with her granddaughter. She spent hours holding the baby and gazing at the small face, so like her own. Wistfully, Gitty wished that her mother-in-law had taken a similar liking to her. With her own mother dead, Gitty would've made a real effort to grow close to David's mother, had she been given any encouragement.

Grandfather and Lady Dunnington got along splendidly. They even developed a private joke about "our mutual descendent."

On Lady Dunnington's second morning at the ranch she kindled deep indignation in Uncle Volney. She was rocking little Crystal when Uncle Volney, carrying an armload of firewood, came into the parlor to refill the log-holder beside the fireplace.

"Is your master busy?" Sybil Dunnington asked him.

Uncle Volney dropped the logs into the metal box with such a clatter that Crystal jumped and began to wail. "No, ma'am!" Volney retorted. "The son-of-a-bitch ain't been born yet!" He stomped from the parlor.

Later, when Lady Dunnington complained about Volney's language to David, he had to explain to his mother the touchiness of Americans and their hatred of master-servant roles.

"He's my employee. I'm his boss," David tried to impress his mother. "Not, I'm master, he's servant. Mother, this is important. This is America, not England."

One warm June day when Sybil and Aimee Dunnington had been visiting Calico Butte Ranch for a fortnight, they decided they'd like to go to Stardancer to get some needlework floss. Aimee needed a special shade of green, and Lady Dunnington wanted a new shade, a delicate yellow called "chicken down." Gitty doubted that the general store would have any new fashionable shades. But it was a gorgeous day, and Cath had been wanting to get to town to check with Won-Tu about how things were going at The Lucky Pearl. Though Cath enjoyed her long chats and walks with her father, Gitty suspected she missed the excitement of The Lucky Pearl. Her girls and the Orientals were really Aunt Cath's family.

Their plan for the day was that Gitty would drop Cath off in front of the gents' furnishings shop, and Cath would slip over to The Lucky Pearl after Gitty drove off. Cath would join them later at the general store.

Gitty clucked to the horse, flicking the reins easily, and the buggy moved forward. Sybil Dunnington expounded for awhile on the country's pitiful lack of trees. Aimee was silent, as usual.

Near the outskirts of Stardancer, Gitty noticed a lone traveler walking toward them on the trail. This was unusual. In the West, no one went anywhere unless he was on a horse or being pulled by a horse. Gitty supposed the man had been thrown, and his horse had run off.

As the buggy drew nearer, a strange feeling of uneasiness crept over Gitty. Her body tensed as the bearded man neared.

The man raised his arm as if to hail them, and in that movement he grabbed the reins beside the horse's head. The horse stopped abruptly.

Gitty made a choking cry. It was Eb, the buffalo skinner she'd stabbed out on the prairie! At the sound of Gitty's gasp the bearded man's small, close-set eyes darted to her. He squinted. His eyes grew hard. He recognized her!

"It's you! It's the kid!" he snarled. "You damn near killed me! Get down here, you bitch! I've got a score to settle with you!"

Gitty jerked the horsewhip from its holder. The skinner took a step toward the buggy, and Gitty swung the whip at him.

With a nasty laugh he grabbed the end of the whip as it came at him and gave it a mighty yank. The wrench pulled Gitty forward. She lost her balance, tumbling out of the buggy head first. The fall knocked the wind from her. As she lay in the dust trying to catch her breath, Cath screamed.

Gitty's cheek pressed into the hot, sandy road. The skinner stood directly over her. His scuffed boots were right in front of her eyes. With a high-pitched, furious howl, he pulled off her bonnet and flung it away. One filthy hand grabbed a fistful of her hair. He jerked her to her feet. Pain shot through Gitty's scalp.

When the skinner's fist crashed into her cheek there was a blinding flash of light before she collapsed onto the dusty trail, only vaguely aware of grunting and scuffling sounds and screaming. Painfully, Gitty raised her head and peered toward the commotion.

Lady Dunnington was swinging her right arm again and again at the filthy skinner, who flinched and howled at each swing.

The skinner lurched away, running off toward a thick stand of pine trees. Immediately, Sybil Dunnington knelt beside Gitty. In her hand, she clutched a long, bloody hat pin. Even through her pain, Gitty felt a flicker of amusement when she realized that Lady Dunnington had attacked the buffalo skinner with a bejewelled hat pin.

"Help is on the way, my dear," Lady Dunnington said. "With the noise Miss Carleton has been making, I am sure aid will be here shortly." Hardly had she finished speaking when two horses appeared in the distance, galloping out of Stardancer. As the horses drew nearer, the women could see that the riders carried shotguns and wore gun belts.

Neither a hastily formed posse nor David Dunnington and his ranch hands were able to hunt down the skinner. The hunted man, in the western man's mind, had committed an unforgivable crime. He had attacked a lady with his fist. This was even more atrocious than if he'd shot Gitty.

At first Gitty denied knowing who the skinner was. But once she was home in her own bed, her battered, swollen face being bathed by Walks Softly, she decided to tell the truth. David and her grandfather were both sympathetic and praised her for her bravery and presence of mind in escaping from the skinner.

After learning the truth and realizing how the skinner wanted vengeance, David intensified his efforts at hunting down Gitty's attacker.

Now he knew that it was not just a crazed fellow who had attacked a lady at random, but someone who hated Gitty and wanted to kill her.

Conway Carleton stayed on two weeks longer than he'd planned so that he could join David and his riders in trying to root out the skinner. Every evening the men of Calico Butte rode in, tired and frustrated from another day's fruitless searching.

When at last Conway Carleton had to return to his lumbering business in Michigan, David, Gitty and Cath put him on the stagecoach for Deadwood. It was the first time Gitty had left the ranch since her encounter with the skinner. She felt vulnerable and uneasy. Cath was tearful. When the driver called, "All aboard!" Cath began sobbing.

Conway held her hands. "Now, darlin', *you* must come visit me," he told Cath.

"Oh, Pa," Cath gulped between sobs. "I just can't! I don't ever want to see Mattigan again!"

With a sigh, Conway kissed Gitty and Cath and then climbed aboard the scarlet coach.

When the coach sped off, a cloud of dust billowed out, and Gitty turned her back. Why, she wondered, was her aunt so bull-headed about never returning to Mattigan?

Chapter 24
He Be Dead

In July Sybil Dunnington reluctantly prepared to leave for England. During her eight-week visit at Calico Butte Ranch she had grown inordinately fond of her tiny granddaughter. Since she prided herself on her ability to suppress any show of emotion, no one could have guessed the depth of her love for this granddaughter who had inherited her facial features.

In front of The Mason House, as Sybil Dunnington prepared to board the stage, she presented her cheek first to her son and then to Gitty. Suddenly, she brought a frothy lace handkerchief to her nose. Her eyes filled with tears as she murmured, "A huge continent and the width of the Atlantic Ocean between us!"

David knew that his mother was not bemoaning the distance between him and herself. "You must come back again to see her, Mother."

Lady Dunnington lifted her chin, her face brightened. "Perhaps you'll let her visit me," she said, "when she is a little older, of course."

After her mother-in-law boarded the stage, Gitty shuddered. How could she bear to let her daughter go thousands of miles away?

Throughout the summer, Gitty remained fearful of being set upon by the buffalo skinner. At night she had terrible nightmares that he was stalking her. She went riding only when David could ride with her. Walks Softly tried to persuade Gitty that she would be protection enough; that she and Gitty could ride safely together. "That filthy man show his eyes around me, I pop his eyes out!"

But Gitty wouldn't go without David. Though she suspected that Walks Softly would be a fearsome opponent, nevertheless, she was only a woman. And maybe the skinner had hired someone to help him.

Because of her self-imposed captivity, Gitty saw more of Dawn and Crystal that summer. Crystal had filled out into a chubby baby. Her hair grew long and softly curly. It appeared that her hair would remain light brown instead of becoming black like her father's and grandmother's. The infant's strange yellow-brown eyes observed her surroundings soberly. Few toys or playful games could make her laugh. At the end of each day, David made it a point to play with Crystal before her bedtime. Gitty marvelled when she heard throaty giggles coming from her daughter while David bounced her on his knee. Wistfully, Gitty wished she could get half that much response from Crystal. It was almost as if the child disliked her. But that was ridiculous. How could a mere baby form a dislike for its own mother?

The fall beef roundup was at hand. Since extra cowboys were brought in to help, Cook was hard-pressed. Even so, she refused Gitty's help. On the second day, the noon dinner was late and skimpy. Angry, David employed two hired girls and told the stubborn cook that they were temporary help for roundup.

The three-year-old, grass-fattened steers were cut out of the herd and headed for the railheads which would deliver them to eastern markets. David said he was getting between $25 and $30 a head. "Profits are excellent," he said, with a satisfied grin. "They've run between 25 and 40 percent ever since I started. It costs from $6 to $10 to raise an animal to age three, and the rest is profit!"

David told Gitty that now, with the new process of being able to refrigerate beef, western beef was being shipped all the way to England. "By the end of this year, about 110 million pounds will go to England alone."

After the beef roundup came the bull roundup. The valuable blooded bulls were herded in closer to headquarters where they could be watched and fed hay during the hardest winter months. Because these animals were costly, David didn't want to lose any in winter-kill. This also served to keep the bulls away from the cows during the winter months so the calves would be born in late spring. Out on the plains, calves dropped during the frigid months had little chance of surviving.

David took to wearing a rattlesnake skin complete with rattles as a hat band on his black Stetson. "Volney says it wards off heatstroke and headache," he laughed. "I don't care what it does, I think it looks pretty 'salty', don't you?" He posed for Gitty, tipping the hat to a rakish angle. His dimples cut deep into his cheeks, and Gitty grinned back. What a handsome man he was!

Seeing the flashing admiration in his wife's eyes, David took Gitty in his arms and placed a long, sensuous kiss on her moist lips. Gitty returned the kiss, trying hard to put feeling into it. Why, she asked herself, why can't I be thrilled by David's loving gestures? He's handsome and thoughtful. What more do I want? Hiding in the shadows of her mind was a brown, smooth, hairless face, hooded eyes regarding her sadly.

In the spring of 1882, one hundred thousand cattle arrived in the area of the Black Hills to be fattened on the nutritious grasses. Gitty learned from Uncle Volney that David was not like other English remittance men in the region. Volney claimed that most of the Britishers spent two weeks at the luxurious Cheyenne Club in early spring, after which they paid a brief visit to their respective ranch headquarters. Then off again to the Cheyenne Club and after the first frost, back to the East or England or the Riviera. To have an English owner who lived at headquarters year-round was unusual. "Dunnington's a good man," Volney said, "even if he do talk funny."

Crystal was toddling all around the house now, getting into mischief if she weren't watched closely. Since Dawn was not yet three, a close eye had to be kept on her, too. Dawn tended to follow Crystal everywhere, singing to the younger child. Crystal almost totally ignored Dawn, seeming hardly aware of her presence.

Gitty chuckled silently every time Dawn addressed her as "Madah." It was her imitation of Walks Softly's "Madame," which she used to address Gitty. It sounded so close to "Mother" that it made Gitty's whole being feel contented.

Gitty had a horror of one of the girls falling into a horse trough and drowning. Late one afternoon, Gitty noticed that Walks Softly was very tired from chasing the two active children around the house and grounds, so she hired Lena, a sixteen-year-old Deadwood girl as Walks Softly's helper.

"*Mon Dieu!*" Walks Softly laughed. "I move up in world. I have a maid!"

Gitty could see that the woman was pleased, and in a few days Walks Softly moved about again with a youthful bounce to her step.

By the end of summer, Gitty believed that she was pregnant again. This time there was no nausea. She felt wonderful. Though her body seemed fine, Gitty was still frightened and worried about the buffalo skinner. His foul-smelling shape seemed to lurk in every shadow. Would this dread hang over her the rest of her life? How she missed being able to ride Moonbeam out over the prairie! The threatening thought of the skinner made her captive of the ranch house.

Autumn was dry. There had been little rain. David worried constantly about the threat of prairie fire. Ranch hands were posted all over the Calico Butte spread. Three gunshots were the signal that a fire had been spotted, and everyone would ride toward the sound of the shots to assist in fire fighting.

No one could guess that the first fire spotted would be within sight of the ranch house.

Preparing to take Dawn and Crystal for a walk, Gitty had just stepped onto the porch. She smelled smoke before she saw the long line of flames, topped by gray smoke, just beyond the paddock.

"Fire! Prairie fire!" she screamed. She jerked the arms of the two little girls and pushed them back into the house. "Walks Softly!" she cried. "Get David's six-gun! Quick!"

Dark eyes wide, Walks Softly handed Gitty the long-barreled revolver. Gitty rushed out onto the porch, pointed the barrel skyward, and squeezed the trigger. Only a click. Gitty's heart sank. She pulled the trigger again. This time, a loud report rattled the windows. Twice more, she fired. When she lowered the smoking gun she remembered that David usually loaded only five cartridges. He let the hammer rest on an empty chamber.

With relief, Gitty saw men running from the stable toward the fire. With wet burlap feed bags, they pounded at the burning prairie grass. Gitty raced across the grounds to help. Two ranch hands mounted horses, circled wide around the fire, and rode off. For an awful moment, Gitty thought they were fleeing, but within a few minutes the same two cowboys returned, dragging between their two horses a freshly-killed steer which had been split in half. They straddled the fire, a horse on either side of the fire line, and dragged the bloody carcass across the crackling fire. The smell of singed hair and cooking beef mixed with the acrid stink of smoke.

Gitty swung a wet feed sack again and again at rivulets of fire which tried to sneak out from the main blaze. Dimly, she was aware of the arrival of other hands.

266

When at last the fire was quenched, Gitty stood panting, wiping perspiration from her forehead with the back of her hand. It was a chilly November day, but the heat from the fire had been intense.

David rushed to Gitty. "Are you all right, darling? You shouldn't fight fire! The baby!" Then he laughed. "You should see your face! Your whole nose is smudged black!"

Neither David nor Gitty noticed Uncle Volney stoop and scoop some of the cooler ashes from the fire. Carefully, as if they were something of great value, he placed them into his kerchief and rolled it up protectively.

Throughout the winter, storms followed periods of thawing. David said the cattle survived because during the thaws they could get down to bare grass. This coming summer, he said, he would put up a great deal more hay than usual. "If we have winter feed available," he maintained, "we wouldn't lose so many animals during storms. I'll store it in fenced enclosures at various sections of the ranch. Then, during a bad spell, if a cowhand can get through the snow to the fenced haystack, he can let down the fence and the cattle can eat."

During one of these thaws in early March, Gitty decided to walk around the grounds to get fresh air and stretch her legs. The baby was due in just three weeks, and Gitty found that if she walked regularly, she felt better and had less trouble with heartburn. She stopped at the stable to give Moonbeam an apple, a special treat, then sauntered on past the blacksmith shop, which was locked. As she cut between the blacksmith shop and the storehouse an arm grabbed her neck and shoulders. Gitty managed one high-pitched scream before a rough hand covered her mouth, bruising her lips. Using all the strength of her cheek muscles, Gitty fastened her teeth on loose flesh and bit down, hard. The salty taste of blood spread over her lips. The hand came off her mouth, and Gitty screamed again. It must be the buffalo skinner!

"You bitch! You bit my finger!" he growled. "I'm gonna kill you!"

Gitty gave a mighty kick backward. As he grunted, she heard the welcome sound of pounding boots on frozen ground. The strong arm whirled her. She faced the tangled, ugly beard of the buffalo skinner. As she looked into the small pig-eyes, she saw him draw back his right arm. When the blow came to the side of her head, she expected it. Even so, white light filled her eyes as her body thudded to the ground. Instinctively, she curled her arms around her belly to protect the child within. As a heavy boot drew back to kick her, she rolled over and took the blow to her back. Though her whole being was filled with pain, Gitty struggled to remain conscious so she could protect her unborn baby until help arrived.

Curled up on the hard ground, she braced for another blow, but it never came. Vaguely, she was aware of Uncle Volney and David kneeling beside her. Gitty looked up into David's white face.

"Where do you hurt, love?" he was asking. "I saw him kick you just before he ran off."

Ran off! Gitty groaned. He got away! She must continue living in fear!

"Did he hurt your stomach, love?" David persisted.

Gitty shook her head. She pointed to the left side of her head. "Here."

David carried her to the house. He and Walks Softly tucked her into bed. Though warm bricks were placed on both her sides, Gitty shivered. She didn't feel cold, just terrified.

Gitty heard the pounding hooves of many horses leaving headquarters. David must be taking men with him to search for the skinner. How she hoped they would find him!

An hour after the riders left Calico Butte in search of the skinner, Gitty went into labor. "Oh, it's too early!" she wailed to Walks Softly.

"May be small," the Indian woman replied, "but it can live. Only a few weeks early. Have warm bricks ready to keep tiny baby warm." Walks Softly sent one of the hands to town to fetch Ten-Fu.

This time, Ten-Fu wasn't cheated. When she arrived, Gitty was still in the early stages of labor. Though labor had been brought on unnaturally by fright and the beating, it progressed well. Just as the clock on the parlor mantel chimed ten, Gitty gave birth to a healthy, though small son. When Ten-Fu weighed him, the vegetable scale needle didn't quite swing to the five-pound mark.

Scarcely an hour after the birth there was a soft knock at the bedroom door. Walks Softly answered, murmured, the door closed. As the Indian woman moved to the basket containing the newborn babe, she carried a red kerchief. Carefully, Walks Softly laid the kerchief on top of the bureau and unfolded it. She took something out of it and moved toward the basket where she rubbed something on the baby.

"Walks Softly!" Gitty's voice was sharp. "What are you doing?" Walks Softly straightened, picked up the kerchief, and brought it to the bed. Gitty raised up on one elbow and peered at the unfolded kerchief. "Why, it's ashes," she murmured, puzzled. "Why?"

"Volney brought them. He saved ashes from prairie fire. Said I should rub on baby's head so he won't be marked." The Indian woman shrugged. "Not Indian custom, but can't hurt."

At midnight, Gitty heard the distant sound of horse's hooves pounding upon frozen ground. Within minutes, the horses trotted into headquarters. Shortly, David burst into the bedroom, his face flushed.

Gitty smiled a happy welcome. She didn't know that the left side of her face was swollen and purple. "He's here. Your son!" She motioned toward the wicker basket where Walks Softly sat protectively, one hand against the infant, making sure the bricks beneath the padding were neither too warm nor too cool.

After a quick look at his son, David rushed to the bed and sat gingerly on the edge. He picked up Gitty's hand. The smell of whiskey drifted from him.

"You won't ever be bothered by that scum again, love," he said.

Gitty's eyes lit up. "Are you sure? How do you know? Where is he?"

"He's dead."

Gitty's eyes narrowed. "How do you know? You're just saying that, so I won't worry!"

David winced. For a moment Gitty thought he was about to cry. "He's dead. I helped bury him. Volney is riding to Deadwood to notify the sheriff."

Though she sensed that David didn't want to talk about it, Gitty had to know. "How did he die?" she demanded.

David took a deep breath. "We were chasing him. He rode off a shelf." He shook his head. "Too bad about the horse."

Gitty's eyes searched her husband's. "David? Cross your heart and hope to die?"

"I promise you, love. He's dead."

Gitty closed her eyes, sighing. "What heaven to be able to ride Moonbeam around the ranch again! Oh, David, life will be so good!"

The dimples creased David's cheeks as he smiled. "It'll be good to see you carefree again. Now, my love, and mother of two, what are we to call our son?"

"What do you think of Peter Carleton Dunnington?"

"Suitably distinguished for a child who may become the 32nd President of the United States," David grinned. Then he sobered. "He seems a tiny chap. Do you think he's all right?"

Three months later, Gitty reminded David of his worry over whether Peter was healthy. They shared a good laugh. During the three months since his birth, Peter dominated activities at the ranch house. In his first week of life he'd slumbered quietly, apparently getting ready to face the world which he'd been thrust into ahead of schedule. At the end of that week, he howled his demands hourly. Gitty couldn't believe what a hungry baby Peter was. She nursed him until he fell sound asleep at her breast, her milk sliding out of his slack little lips. But then, almost to the hour, he howled for more. Consequently, Peter grew rapidly, quickly changing from the frail-looking infant, forced too-soon from the womb, to a chunky, strapping baby, folds creasing his wrists and ankles.

From the beginning Peter was the opposite of Crystal. While Crystal remained fine-boned and tiny, Peter grew large. Walks Softly predicted he'd be even taller than David. For several weeks, the baby remained bald, but then fuzz as black as ink began to sprout on his pink head. At first Peter's eyes were a smoky blue, but soon they changed to a honey color. The first time her son screwed up his face with gas pains, Gitty thought she detected dimples like David's. When he gave her his first real smile, she was sure. The dimples were David's. While his sister was quiet and sober, Peter was noisy and ebullient. He loved everything, smiled at everyone, and demanded that the household revolve around his desires.

"We're spoiling him," Gitty fretted to Walks Softly.

"Baby can't be spoiled. Give what he needs. Baby is a little bud, long way from a flower."

Before calf roundup, all the horses that had been turned out for winter were rounded up and brought to headquarters where, one-by-one, they were put into the paddock and re-broken. Some behaved well even after a winter of roaming wild and loose on the range. Others, bucking and rearing, had to be broken to the saddle again, misbehaving almost as if they'd never been ridden before.

It was entertaining to watch cowhands convert these nearly-wild horses into reliable, obedient mounts. Gitty leaned against the corral bars watching one of the younger hands — she suspected he wasn't yet sixteen — try to get a saddle on a horse. The boy vacillated from using sheer force, like biting the horse's ear, to being nice and trying to rub its muzzle.

The paint stallion was on the thin side, perhaps because of a winter fending for himself. Two cowhands lounged near the stable, unaware of Gitty's presence. She heard them talking.

"That paint's the skinner's horse," one of them said to the other. "You know, the stranger the boss kilt last spring."

A pounding began in Gitty's ears. The skinner's horse! David said the buffalo skinner had ridden his horse over a cliff! Gitty thought she even remembered David saying something about the poor dead horse.

Swinging on her heel, Gitty charged directly toward the two ranch hands. They paled as they saw who she was.

Gitty faced them. "Which one of you just recognized the paint?" she asked.

Both men swallowed, and she glared impatiently. She continued to stare at them until the shorter, fairer-complexioned one spoke. "You must be mistaken ma'am. I don't know that horse!"

"Which horse?" Gitty demanded.

"The paint."

"Listen," Gitty hissed. "My husband will never hear of this conversation. I don't ever want to discuss it with him as long as I live. But I want to hear from you what happened to the buffalo skinner. I swear to you on the lives of my beloved children, I shall never repeat to a living soul whatever you tell me. But," and she squinted hard at the shorter one, "if you don't tell me, I shall report to my husband that two of his hands were calling him a murderer!"

The shorter one pulled the crown of his dusty hat down farther on his head. His Adam's apple bobbed. Sweat beaded out on his forehead. "Tisn't fit story for a lady's ear, ma'am," he choked.

"Listen, fellow," Gitty rasped between clenched teeth. "On two different occasions this lady was beaten by the person in question. I would be able to sleep better if I knew for sure that he was dead."

"Oh, he be dead, ma'am," the cowhand nodded. "The baron smashed him again and again until there wasn't hardly a face..." He stopped, and his mouth gaped as he realized what he'd said.

"Tell me exactly what happened," Gitty snapped, "and I will give you twenty dollars."

It was hard for Gitty to believe that her gently bred husband was capable of the brutality described by the cowhand. Her eyes widened as she listened to the gory description. David must've been out of his mind with fury. She knew the cowhand wasn't making up the story. It had the

271

ring of truthfulness. No longer was there a doubt in her mind. The skinner was dead, killed by her husband's fists. Gitty shivered.

"I'll have your money for you tomorrow," she told the ranch hand. "Never speak of this to anyone."

The next day Gitty saddled Moonbeam and rode to Stardancer. She needed to borrow the twenty dollars from Cath. Though Gitty was the wife of a wealthy rancher, the granddaughter of a wealthy lumberman, she had no money of her own. Conway Carleton had invested for Gitty the money gained from the sale of her parents' estate. Hard cash was something Gitty never saw.

When she arrived at The Lucky Pearl, Gitty was surprised to learn that Cath had been about to send a messenger to Gitty, asking her to come visit. Cath said that Won-Tu needed Gitty's help.

"Why would Won-Tu need my help?" Gitty asked, puzzled. "Whatever could I do for him?"

"It's really about Henry. Won-Tu thinks you and David could get Henry into a good university back East."

Chapter 25
Saving the Buffalo

Had Won-Tu swallowed his pride and given up his hatred of all Englishmen including David Dunnington? During the three years since Gitty had moved out of The Lucky Pearl to marry David she had given little thought to Won-Tu's son, Henry Wadsworth Longfellow Hung. In fact, Gitty didn't think she'd laid eyes on the boy since the day of her wedding. Cath always insisted that Henry be kept away from The Lucky Pearl.

"Henry is old enough for college?" Gitty asked, surprised.

Cath chuckled. "He's been married for two years."

"Married? Oh, Aunt Cath!"

"Isn't it something? Of course, he's married only in word, not in deed, for the present." Cath fluttered her eyebrows. "The bride's a pretty little thing. She was only fourteen when they held the marriage ceremony."

"Did you go to the wedding?" Gitty asked.

"No. Won-Tu thought I'd feel uncomfortable with the strange customs. Henry got married in the Chinatown section of Deadwood at some place Won-Tu calls the "Joss House," over by Siever Street. It was an arranged marriage, of course, set up by both families. I'm not sure if Henry even had seen the little bride before the day of the ceremony.

"The wife's father is a Chinese undertaker," Cath went on. "I mean, he's Chinese and he's an undertaker for Chinese people." She giggled. "Oh, their customs are so strange. Won-Tu says that Henry's father-in-law is well-to-do, that he has a lucrative business. Apparently, Chinese people want their remains shipped home to China after they die. This undertaker arranges a regular below-the-ground burial for his customers. Then after six or seven years, when the bodies have decomposed, he goes to the cemetery, digs up the remains, separates out the bones and wraps them in newspaper and muslin. They put the wrapped bones into a zinc-lined box and ship it to San Francisco, where it's joined by as many as eighteen hundred other zinc-lined boxes all bound for China. Can you imagine?"

"Why did Won-Tu and Ten-Fu want Henry to get married so young?"

Cath shrugged. "Who knows? They say that Henry didn't just marry the girl — her name is 'Meng', by the way. He married her whole family, and she married Henry's family."

"When will Henry and his wife begin to live together?"

"I don't know," Cath said, "but I sure think that if Henry goes east to college that the little wife should go with him. He's at an age now where he has needs for a woman, and a wife might keep him out of mischief. Also, the girl is quite Chinese-Chinese, you know. She's always lived in Deadwood's Chinatown, and for a girl, that means very little contact with white people. If she's not to be a millstone around Henry's neck, she should be exposed to American ways."

Gitty nodded. "But would her family let her go?"

"They'd have no choice. Henry's her husband. A Chinese wife must obey her husband's wishes. If he wants her to go, she must."

✳   ✳   ✳   ✳

Early one morning in July Gitty and Walks Softly left Crystal and Peter in the care of the hired girl, Lena, and with Dawn happily seated in front of Walks Softly on the roan gelding, they headed out on the tawny prairie for a ride. By noon the sun would be too hot for a comfortable ride.

The short buffalo grass waved its gray-green blades in the ceaseless wind. As far as Gitty could see there was undulating buffalo grass, the grass that nourished David's thousands of cattle.

Walks Softly urged her horse into an easy canter. Dawn rocked easily with the gait. At only three and one-half years, the little girl already was a good horsewoman. Gitty touched Moonbeam with her boot heels, and Moonbeam began to canter, pulling alongside the roan.

They were perhaps an hour's ride from the ranch house when far ahead Gitty noticed what looked like boulders littering the prairie. As they rode close, she saw that the "stones" were buffalo carcasses, now only bleached bones, skulls, and huge oval rib cages. Gitty counted ten skulls.

"Indian-kill," Walks Softly said as she slid off her horse. She turned and lifted Dawn down to the ground. The child ran around examining each of the huge white skulls.

"Notice how eye sockets of skulls all watch the west, the great sun. That a service Indians do for their brother, the buffalo."

"Look at the size of this one!" Gitty said. "It must have been a monster."

Walks Softly said that there were few great herds of buffalo existing anymore. In huge numbers the hide hunters had swarmed over the plains, killing wantonly. Usually they skinned the animal, took the woolly robe, and left the meat to rot or to feed coyotes and wolves. The Indians were outraged over this terrible waste, since they were often hungry now that they'd been forced to remain huddled on their barren reservations. The military encouraged the buffalo hunters to continue their greedy killing because once the buffalo was annihilated, the Indians never would be able to feed and clothe themselves on the prairies. The fighting Sioux and Cheyenne, along with other plains Indians, had been dependent upon the buffalo to maintain their nomadic existence. The buffalos' hides made their tipis, their clothing, their meat fed them, the bones formed their utensils, the woolly robes kept the Indian warm in wintertime. With the buffalo gone, the plains Indians once and for all would be under the white man's thumb.

Cattlemen encouraged the slaughter of the great buffalo herds. The buffalo ate the grass the ranchers wanted for their cattle. The cattle business never could have gotten a start while sixty million buffalo roamed the prairies eating the grass.

Gitty was appalled as she learned about this systematic destruction, and she spoke of it to David. "It's outrageous!" she said. "It's wrong to kill off such a magnificent animal! Buffalo meat is better than the beef from our steers, isn't it?"

David agreed. "It has more flavor, and it's more tender."

"Can't we stop them?" she fumed.

"I'd just as soon try to stop a blizzard."

Gitty strode to the parlor window. "There must be something we can do." She stared out over the rolling acres of waving grasses. "I know!" she exclaimed. "We can capture all the buffalo that we can find, especially calves, and fence them in here on Calico Butte. That way they'll be safe. They can grow and multiply, and there will always be buffalo!"

"Whoa, now, love," David protested. "That's a man-sized job you're talking about, to say nothing about your asking me to give up some of my grass to feed buffalo instead of money-making cattle."

Gitty looked at David indignantly. "Surely, David, you're not so greedy that you can't give up a few acres for the good of the world?"

David knew that what his wife was talking about was more than "a few acres," but no man can argue money against "worldly good." He also sensed that he dared not be stingy about sharing some of his grass since Calico Butte Ranch was making huge profits. Gitty was aware of it since he'd bragged often to her about his 40 percent profits.

It was inevitable that David would give in. Still, he put the burden of preparing the project upon Gitty. "I'll help," he said, "but you're the boss of the buffalo section of Calico Butte. When you need something done, you can ask me or some of the ranch hands, but you're going to have to organize it."

At the very first step Gitty had to find out how to go about ordering barbed wire. She needed David's advice on how much wire she'd need to fence five sections. David whistled. "That's 3200 acres. You're leaping in big, love."

"This is a long-term project, David," she reminded him. "I intend these sections to be a preserve for buffalo for a long time, maybe forever."

David grinned indulgently. "Forever's a long time, my sweet."

When Gitty put the cow hands to work digging post holes for the fence posts they grumbled so much that she sent to Deadwood for four hired men willing to do farm work. Gitty had learned a lesson about cowboys. They were willing to do any kind of work that could be done from the back of a horse. They didn't take kindly to walking.

In August, the barbed wire arrived, coming all the way from Chicago, mostly by railroad boxcar, and then by bull train. Within a week Gitty's five sections of land, spoken of now as "the buffalo sections," were fenced and ready to become a protectory. David advised waiting until October to try to get buffalo calves away from their mothers. By then, he felt, they could get along without their mother's milk. Since November usually started the hide-hunting season, he said they should try to collect animals before the hunters fell upon the remaining herds.

Gitty didn't have to wait until October. One day in early September, she noticed a cloud of dust moving toward the ranch house.

She stepped out onto the porch. Animals were running and men on horseback were chasing them. It wasn't roundup time. Why were they bringing cattle in? As the round-up melee drew closer Gitty saw that the animals weren't cattle but buffalo! In the confusion, with all the billowing dust, it was impossible to count them, but there seemed to be half a dozen mature animals and perhaps that many calves.

The buffalo pounded through the wide opening in the barbed wire fence, and two cowboys jumped off their horses and quickly made fast the gate. The buffalo were enclosed!

David rode up to the porch wearing a satisfied grin. "Can you imagine that? Six cows, each with a calf. They were grazing alongside a coulee over by the southwest corner post. All we had to do was point them in the right direction." He looked back toward the buffalo sections, but the buffalo had galloped off, out of sight. "I'm still wondering if we can keep them in a fence. Nothing could hold those creatures if they had a mind to get out. We'll just have to wait and see. We'll leave them alone and see if they settle down."

It was two weeks before Gitty saw the buffalo again. Daily she'd ridden, sometimes with Dawn in front of her in the saddle, out along the fence line of the buffalo sections, hoping to catch sight of the brown woolly creatures. At last, on Dawn's fourth birthday, Gitty spotted six buffalo grazing on a rise. Six calves gamboled about, butting heads and kicking their hind legs in the air. The calves had lost almost all of their reddish color and were turning the same chocolate brown as their mothers. The animals seemed contented, and Gitty was thrilled. The buffalo had respected the fences! She'd hoped that if the animals had enough room, with plenty of grass and water, they'd be content to stay within their fenced acres.

Late that afternoon after the children had taken their naps, Walks Softly and Gitty put on a birthday party for Dawn. Cook baked a chocolate cake with chocolate frosting because Dawn had a passion for chocolate. Gitty made colorful paper cone-shaped hats. She and Walks Softly each wore one, as did Cook and Dawn. With a chocolate-sticky hand Peter pulled his hat off and tried to chew on it. Crystal solemnly refused to put on a birthday hat. "I don't want to," she answered coolly when Gitty attempted to put a blue and white flowered cone on her brown hair.

"But darling," Gitty protested, "it's a birthday party! We wear birthday hats to celebrate!"

"I don't have to!" Crystal replied. "It's silly."

Gitty was surprised that the word "silly" was even in the child's vocabulary. Crystal was always amazing people with words or actions beyond her years. Though she looked like a two and one-half year old toddler, she acted much older.

Walks Softly presented Dawn with a pair of feather-soft white doeskin moccasins with the name "Dawn" spelled in colorful beadwork across the instep. Gitty said they'd have to go out on the porch to see her present to Dawn. There, tied to the white hitching post, was a black Shetland pony. A hand-tooled California saddle was cinched to the pony's round belly.

Her dark eyes wide, Dawn looked up at Gitty. Though no sound came from them, her lips formed the words, "For me?"

Gitty nodded.

The child raced down the steps. In a flash she'd untied the reins and leaped into the saddle. She trotted the fat pony back and forth in the lane between the house and the store house, squealing, "See me! See me!"

David rode up from the direction of the bunkhouse. He grinned to see Walks Softly's little girl bobbing up and down the lane, her long black pigtails streaming behind. Gitty stood on the porch, beaming. She held Peter, and the baby smiled broadly at David and held out his arms for his father to take him. David jumped off his horse and picked up his son.

Walks Softly held Crystal, who had a smudge of chocolate on one cheek. David sauntered over to Walks Softly and Crystal. "And I suppose this sweet one will be wanting a pony before long, too," David said as he stroked Crystal's soft hair.

"No," Crystal said. "Don't like horses!" she lifted her small chin.

"Nonsense!" David chuckled, laughing at the stubborn little face. "All Dunningtons like horses."

Though David didn't notice, Gitty saw a contemptuous look flash across Crystal's baby cheeks. Gitty suspected that this daughter had an unyielding streak that might cause trouble in years to come.

Cath reported that Ten-Fu had received a long letter from Henry. He liked Harvard, and he wanted Gitty to be sure to convey his everlasting gratitude to The Honorable David Dunnington for the letters of introduction he'd given Henry. Meng, he wrote, had been homesick at first, but their landlady, a joyful Irish woman, had taken Meng under her protection, treating her like a daughter. She was teaching Meng English and instructing her how to cook potatoes and other American food. "And I'm glad, Mother," he wrote, "as I think I really prefer American food to Chinese."

"Hah!" Gitty laughed. "I bet Ten-Fu shot straight through the roof at that."

"Not really," Cath replied. "Ever since Won-Tu began planning our menus back in Stimsonville, he's been developing a taste for American foods. Like a good wife, Ten-Fu fixes them for him. In their household they eat both American and Chinese."

✳   ✳   ✳   ✳

Travelers reported the presence of a large buffalo herd northeast of the Black Hills between there and Bismarck. The first week in October David, Gitty and all available ranch hands rode out to see if they could capture some buffalo calves. Several miles from the ranch they spotted a large bunch, made up primarily of cows with calves and yearlings. There were no breed bulls in sight.

One of the cowhands threw a rope around the neck of a small red-coated calf. The moment the calf fell to his side, the angered mother grunted and charged horse and rider. While the cutting horse danced an evasive pattern from the attacking buffalo, the rider fumbled a moment and finally got the rope loosened from his saddle horn so he could drop the rope and get away from the roped calf and the maddened cow. This ruckus caused the main part of the herd to move off. Another rider got a rope around the neck of a second calf before it got out of range. This calf's mother didn't attack the horse, but she stayed protectively close to her fallen calf.

From the backs of their horses Gitty and David were watching the attempted captures.

"Oh, David!" Gitty cried, "the calf doesn't move!" They squinted, looking into the distance at the second roped calf, and they saw that it also lay perfectly still on the parched prairie sod. The mother of the first calf kept nudging it and licking its muzzle, but it didn't move.

"By George, I think they're dead!" David muttered. "How can that be?"

A cowhand, tanned face cross-hatched with lines, pulled his horse up beside David's. "Boss," he said, fingering his blue neckerchief nervously, "an Indian fellow was tellin' me once that he tried to rope a

279

buffler calf, and the rope killed it. He said buffler windpipes is close to the surface, that's why."

"Whatever the reason, it appears that your Indian friend was right. Well, we'll just have to get a rope on their hind legs, and then drive off the mother while those on the ground heave the calf into the wagon."

It was easy to say, but difficult and dangerous work. By late afternoon they'd collected only five calves. Gitty was dusty, exhausted, and thankful that no human had been hurt in the endeavor. Still, she was saddened when she thought of the two red calves killed.

David consoled her. "Remember, darling, in a few weeks this herd is going to be visited by hide hunters. Mothers of those calves will be killed. It's doubtful that the calves would survive the winter without their mothers. I'm sorry we killed them, but those calves were doomed. Civilization has no room for buffalo anymore. It strikes me that the fate of buffalo is rather like that of the Indian. Civilization doesn't want either buffalo or Indians roaming the plains. The Indian is probably doomed, too. Pity, you know. They're a fine people. I don't suppose you've ever known one?"

Gitty couldn't stop the pained look which spread over her face. David saw it and frowned. "Oh, you're thinking of Walks Softly. Well, she's half French, you know. She's a fine person, but not my idea of a true Indian."

The five calves were released in the buffalo sections. One calf limped a bit, and Gitty feared that his leg might be broken, but within a few days he was cavorting with the other calves, and there was no residual limp. In a few days the newcomers came upon the six cows and their calves and mingled with the original animals as one herd.

One thing David had warned Gitty about was that unless they were able to catch a yearling bull, there would be no calves born two years hence. "The six cows are probably pregnant now, so you'll have six calves born next spring. But the bull calves you have now, by next summer will be just yearling bulls, — too young to breed. The cows won't get bred next year."

When the hide-hunters descended upon the Dakota herd that autumn, some of the animals on the fringes of the great herd wandered into the foothills. One of David's outriders reported seeing two yearling bulls grazing not far from a bunch of Calico Butte cattle. David took six men with him and by whooping, waving their hats, and hollering, they drove two frightened yearlings back toward headquarters and into the buffalo compound. The two youngsters loped through the opened gate, tongues hanging out from the long run.

"Oh, David, thank you so much!" Gitty was ecstatic. Now her herd would increase. And she'd saved nineteen buffalo! That might not sound like many when one thought of the millions that had once grazed the prairies, but still it was a pocket of buffalo she planned to protect. She didn't really know how many buffalo her fenced 3200 acres could support. In a drought year it might not support large numbers. And Gitty had been a rancher's wife long enough to know that one never must overgraze prairie grasses.

David heard that the hide-hunters arrived earlier than usual, in October, not long after their capture of the calves. Sitting Bull and his hunters also shot animals in the great herd. Within weeks the big herd had been finished off. Only a few stragglers survived, like the two yearling bulls found near Calico Butte.

In the spring Gitty decided that Dawn was old enough to begin piano lessons. Dawn enjoyed the lessons and cuddled next to Gitty on the piano bench. Gitty suspected that Dawn liked the coziness more than the music. Dawn tried hard to follow Gitty's instructions. She practiced daily as instructed, but her blunt, short fingers hit as many wrong keys as correct ones. To make it worse, the child didn't realize when she hit a discordant note. It seemed as if Dawn had no ear for music.

One day after a long ride on Moonbeam, Gitty came into the house through the back door, wanting a drink of water. As she picked up the dipper, she heard the distinct melody of Stephen Foster's "Oh, Susannah" coming from the parlor.

Gitty moved quietly toward the parlor, almost tip-toeing, not knowing who she expected to see.

When she peeked around the ornate breakfront Gitty was dumbfounded. Crystal moved her delicate fingers easily across the ivory keys. A far-off look on her face, she picked out the lively melody. Not once was there a wrong note or even a hesitation.

Gitty moved into the parlor. "Darling! How nice it sounds." Gitty walked toward her daughter.

Abruptly, Crystal stopped playing.

"Sweetheart, don't stop," Gitty said. "It sounds so lovely! Please go on."

Crystal's lower lip pushed out obstinately. Her hands remained in her lap.

"Would you like me to give you piano lessons?" Gitty asked, as she picked up a strand of Crystal's baby fine hair, tucking it back out of the way.

"I *know* how," the child retorted.

"You're doing beautifully, darling, but I can teach you to play using both hands and all your fingers."

"I play the way I want to play," Crystal said as she slid off the bench. "I'm all done now."

As she watched the straightly-held back of her daughter leave the room, Gitty frowned. A three-year-old being able to pick out tunes on the piano by ear was extraordinary. Apparently Crystal had inherited musical ability. But her stubbornness was so difficult to deal with! However was she to help her youngest daughter develop the gifts she'd been born with? And how ironic. Dawn appeared to have no musical talent, yet she doggedly kept practicing her lessons. And here was Crystal with obvious talent who rejected any help or guidance. Gitty shrugged. They were both young yet.

But something in the back of Gitty's mind sounded a warning. Did people really change that much, or was character pretty much formed in those first years of life?

Gitty sighed and went off to find her son. Peter had just started walking. He was immensely proud of his new ability. When he caught sight of his mother he gurgled and held up his arms. Gitty swung him up into the air, and he laughed aloud. After giving him a big kiss on his warm cheek, Gitty laughed with him. Peter was a happy, uncomplicated child. Please God, he'll stay that way! she thought.

Though she was only twenty-two years old, and not a longtime mother, Gitty had a strong suspicion that Crystal was going to be a handful. And there would be complications with Dawn because of the Indian blood and because of her..., Gitty swallowed,... bastard status. Raising her daughters wasn't going to be easy. But, Peter — Peter was a happy one-year-old boy, a healthy, robust child who looked much like his handsome father. Gitty foresaw no problems raising Peter.

Chapter 26
Calico Butte in Shambles

Saddle leather creaked as Gitty swung herself onto Moonbeam's back behind Dawn. On this first warm June day, Gitty thought she'd make a leisurely morning ride, following Cottonwood Run upstream. Along its moist banks she was rewarded with the beauty of a glorious variety of colorful wildflowers.

She breathed deeply of the fresh summer air as she walked the horse slowly along the bank of the creek. The mare's hoofs scraped noisily against smooth rocks imbedded firmly in the soil. David said that long ago these round boulders had been carried downstream by this little creek when it was in full flood. The rocks, he said, were worn round by all their tumbling about in the torrent of rushing waters.

The gray-green prairie spread out in an endless sweep to the east. To her left, towering upward hundreds of feet, was Calico Butte. When Gitty was perhaps three miles from the ranch house a horse and rider appeared, coming out of a draw. It was almost as if the rider had been waiting there for her approach.

Moonbeam whickered, and Gitty pulled the mare to a stop. She squinted at the horseman moving toward her. The buffalo skinner is dead! she reminded herself. As he neared, she saw that the rider wore pale buckskins. He was an Indian. Gitty's hand flew to her neck. Blood rushed to her cheeks.

When the horse was within twenty feet of her, she was sure: It was Doe Eyes! Though she didn't realize it, tears streamed down her cheeks.

He guided his horse up to Moonbeam and stopped. "Little Flame," he said. His gentle voice was just as she'd remembered it these past years.

"The years have been good to you," he said.

Gitty couldn't speak. She could only stare at the beloved face. How long had she been deprived of seeing this dear one, of touching him, of being held in his arms? Six long, long years had passed since she walked away from Doe Eyes.

"Who's your companion?" He inclined his head toward Dawn.

Gitty leaned around Dawn to peer at the little girl's face. She saw that Dawn was examining Doe Eyes. He showed an equal interest in the child.

"This is Dawn, daughter of Walks Softly, my maid," Gitty said uneasily. Doe Eyes continued to study the girl. Gitty slid off Moonbeam and reached up to help Dawn dismount.

"Sweetie," she said to Dawn, "why don't you go down to the creek and play in the sand? Perhaps you can catch a frog if you're quick."

For a long moment Dawn continued to stare up at the Indian on the brown horse, then she obediently ran toward the creek.

"Who is she, really?" Doe Eyes whispered.

"I told you."

The hooded eyes flickered impatiently. "The child looks exactly like my sister Yellow Flower. When was the girl born?"

Flustered, Gitty said, "March 21, 1881," which was Crystal's birthday.

"She's older than that, my Little Flame," Doe Eyes said. His eyes rebuked her. "If this lovely child is from our love, how could you keep this from me? I told you I lost two sons. If I have a fine daughter, I sing of my joy to the clouds."

Tears flowed down Gitty's cheeks. She had thought to protect Doe Eyes from hurt by not letting him know about Dawn. She'd been wrong. "She's yours," Gitty admitted, rubbing the back of her hand across her wet cheeks.

Doe Eyes took a deep breath before he spoke. "After you left my tipi I try to learn if you are safe. No one know your aunt. I thought the earth had swallowed your footsteps. I grieved, feared you dead. But then a trader told of a beautiful woman with flaming hair married to an Englishman. To see if it was you, I came to the holy Paha Sapa for the first time. In Stardancer I saw you. You waited for the stagecoach. So lovely! You greeted an older man." Doe Eyes paused and straightened

284

his shoulders. "You are married now and have two other children," he said.

"How did you know that?"

"A trader from Stardancer comes to Pine Ridge Agency twice every moon. I tell him that years ago I save you from a pack of wolves, and that I'm happy to see you lead a normal life. He keeps me informed. What made you gather buffalo? My people wonder what you're doing."

"But how did you find me here this morning?"

"For three days I watched, waited to speak to you. Are you happy, Little Flame?"

Gitty swallowed and felt her lower lip quiver. "I'm not unhappy," she said honestly. "But a day never passes that I don't think of you."

Doe Eyes studied her, a sad look spreading over his face. "Often I wonder why you and I were born in different worlds. Or why Great Spirit allow us to meet and love. It seems a cruel trick. I pray about it to keep from growing bitter."

Abruptly, Doe Eyes tossed his head, and his black hair sailed across his shoulders. An almost teasing smile crossed his face. "I'm completely healed now. No more leakage from the cougar wound, and," he added, smiling wider, "no more bad smells."

She felt her face grow hot. Gitty knew it must be cherry red. "I, ...I," she stammered.

Doe Eyes leaned down from his horse, reaching across the space between them and placed his hand on Gitty's shoulder. "I know, Little Flame. I knew then. Don't mind feelings you cannot help."

Warmth grew in her shoulder where he touched her.

"I had a reason to tell you I was well," Doe Eyes said as he searched her face. "I hope you meet me alone without the child. My being aches to talk with you, to be with you."

Gitty sucked in her breath. She moved a step backwards to withdraw her shoulder from Doe Eyes's touch. Without her wanting it, a warm tingling feeling spread throughout her body. She closed her eyes. She almost could feel Doe Eyes's soft fingertips caressing her. She shook her head as if to throw off these disquieting thoughts. How could she even think of meeting alone with Doe Eyes? She was a respectable married woman and a mother. She took a deep breath. But how she wanted to be in his arms!

"On the northwest corner of your land," Doe Eyes said, "not far from trail to Deadwood is a linerider's cabin. It's used only during winter moons, for emergency shelter. There's a draw where our horses wouldn't be seen. My Little Flame, each day for the next three days when the sun reaches its high point I shall wait there for you."

He looked down at Gitty. There were tears in his eyes. "Please, my Little Flame," he whispered. He turned and looked at Dawn, splashing her hands happily in the rippling creek waters. A serene smile smoothed out the lines in the bronze skin beneath his eyes. When he returned his gaze to Gitty, his eyes once again grew pained. "Please," he said. With the touch of heels against its flank, the brown horse wheeled and galloped off.

That night Gitty lay awake beside her sleeping husband. The desire to be with Doe Eyes, if only for a few hours, overwhelmed her. Over and over, since her morning encounter with Doe Eyes, she'd cautioned herself that she must stay away from the Indian. You're a married woman, she told herself. Being with Doe Eyes would be adultery, breaking a Commandment. And if David ever found out! He'd — Gitty didn't know what he'd do.

Meeting Doe Eyes would be wrong. Even so, her thoughts kept drifting to Doe Eyes and how it would feel to lie naked in his warm arms.

By sunup she had made a pact with herself. She would try to ride out to meet Doe Eyes, but if something interfered, such as David or Walks Softly wanting to ride with her, that would be a sign that she should not meet Doe Eyes.

At breakfast David asked if she wanted to go to town with him. "I have to pick up some supplies that are coming in from the States," he said.

Gitty's heart jumped. David would be away from the ranch all day. She declined his invitation, saying that she had some sewing to attend to.

The moment that David guided the buckboard out on the track to Stardancer, Gitty ran into their bedroom to put on her riding breeches. She had no idea how far the linerider's cabin would be. Her heart thumped hard in her chest. Every time an unwelcome guilty thought pushed its way toward recognition, she shook it off. The door of permission had been opened. David had left for the day.

As Gitty guided Moonbeam through the waving buffalo grass she concentrated on Doe Eyes. If she thought of anything else, she would turn the mare's head and gallop back to the ranch house as if the devil himself were chasing her. It took Gitty more than an hour of riding before the cabin came into sight. This part of the vast ranch was unfamiliar territory. She'd taken a few wrong turns, once ending up in a box canyon. On top of a gentle rise Doe Eyes sat. As she approached, he stood.

When he walked toward her, his dark eyes shone. Taking Moonbeam's reins, he helped her dismount. "Over here is a good place to keep the horses. They can't be seen unless someone walks right up to the edge of the draw."

Doe Eyes grasped Gitty's gloved hand and led her toward the linerider's cabin. There was no lock on the door. The cabin was but one room, perhaps sixteen feet square. Three cots neatly made up with faded quilts filled one-half of its space. A stone fireplace was on one wall and the kitchen area occupied the rest.

Gitty began to pull off her riding gloves. Her heart waltzed beneath her breast.

Doe Eyes studied their surroundings. "I wish we were in my tipi instead of this ugly white man's cabin."

With a quick look, Gitty wondered if he regretted his invitation. "Yes," she said, "perhaps we'd better..."

Doe Eyes gripped her shoulders and pulled her to him. As his arms encircled her body, Gitty tipped her face up. His dark, heavy-lidded eyes fascinated her, drawing closer. Softly, his warm lips pressed upon hers, stroking her flesh gently at first, then more insistently. His hands clasped her waist and pulled her against his hard torso.

Gitty's body glowed, pulsing under his touch. Doe Eyes moved one hand to caress her cheek, his fingers traced her hairline, moved to her neck.

With a groan, the tall Indian pressed his lips to the soft skin of her neck just beneath the curve of her jaw. One hand lightly brushed her breast. Gitty caught her breath. Her hands caressed the firm, rounding muscles of his neck.

Waves of happiness swept through her. Once again she was a sixteen-year-old, melting into her lover's arms.

Lazily, they undressed each other, pausing for warm, moist kisses and soft, sensual caresses. When at last they fell together onto the cotton quilt of a cot, they became playful lovers, savoring the touch and smell of each other's bodies. Rather than hurry toward the unleashing of pent-up pressure, they slowly kindled their passions to new peaks of sensuousness. As Gitty's passion increased, she heard nothing, felt nothing but Doe Eyes's lithe body soaring with hers to peaks of desire.

After, as they lay damp and perspiring beside one another on the narrow cot, Gitty murmured, "I feel as if I've been away from home for a long, long time, and now I've returned."

"Oh, how I've missed you, little one," Doe Eyes breathed in her ear. "Each year without you was a lifetime of agony."

The next day, Gitty managed to slip away again. This time, she and Doe Eyes strolled to a thick stand of white birch and aspen. Doe Eyes spread a soft buckskin on the forest floor, and on it they made languid, sweet love.

Throughout the hot days of June and July, Gitty managed frequent clandestine meetings with Doe Eyes. Both preferred to meet in the woods near the cabin, but on calm, windless days, the black-flies drove them into the stuffy linerider's cabin.

On such a day in August, when not a breath of wind moved, Gitty tied Moonbeam next to Doe Eyes's horse in the out-of-sight draw. With pity, she saw that black-flies already pestered Doe Eyes's brown gelding.

As Gitty ran toward the cabin she didn't notice that she'd been followed. From a hundred yards away, Uncle Volney peered over a small ridge. His eyes burned with outrage as he stared at her back.

Two hours later when, hand in hand, Gitty and Doe Eyes came out of their trysting place and headed toward their horses, Uncle Volney lay flat, staring at them from a distance. The air wheezed in his throat with every intake of breath. The white knuckles of his fists threatened to burst through the skin. It took all of Volney's willpower to keep from jumping up and grabbing his rifle out of its holster on the saddle. He ached to shoot the miserable savage! But his Westerner's code of honor told him that the Englishman would want his own revenge. The cuckolded husband should have the right of punishment.

After the couple mounted their horses and rode away, Uncle Volney rose, pulled off his dusty hat and scratched his head. Clamping the hat back on his head, he swung up onto his horse. A deep scowl covered his face as he studied just how he should break this terrible news to his employer.

❋   ❋   ❋   ❋

The fall beef roundup kept all the ranch help busy. Clouds of dust hung over the cutting pens as Gitty rode in from her secret meeting with Doe Eyes. She went directly to Peter's crib, where she found him awake. He gurgled happily, trying to put a big toe into his mouth. After changing his diaper, Gitty carried him out onto the front porch where it was easier to view the branding operations beyond the paddock and chicken coop. The cloud of dust over the cutting pens obscured the cattle. The bawling complaints of the milling cattle filled the stifling air. If only a breeze would come up! It would cool things off and move the clouds of dust away from the ranch house.

Just then, David and Uncle Volney came out of the storehouse. Gitty could see that David's arm shook in a menacing gesture. Suddenly, he flung his arm straight out, pointing toward the cutting pens. "Round them up!" he shouted. "She stuff and all! They're *all* going! Every last damn four-legged creature!" He spotted Gitty on the front porch. A scarlet flush spread over his face. He spun on his heel and strode swiftly toward her. Something in his manner frightened Gitty. She whirled and went back into the parlor.

The slap of his boots on the porch planks echoed into the parlor. Gitty turned to face the door as David stormed in.

"Put the baby in his bed!" he ordered. Purple blotches spread over his flushed cheeks.

Swallowing, Gitty obeyed. Her mind worked furiously. Had he discovered her guilty secret? What else could make him so angry?

She trembled as David grabbed her elbow and jerked her into their bedroom. "What sort of woman are you?" he raged. "How can you look me or your children in the face? In fact, you won't *ever again* look your children in the face! I won't have them tainted by so much as a glance from you!"

"David, .." Gitty tried to speak.

David's right arm swung back. White lines ran alongside his nose. His arm dropped limp to his side. "No, by God, I'll not reduce myself to hitting a woman! Pack your belongings. You've got fifteen minutes. Whatever isn't packed, I'll have sent to you, back to your aunt. I'm sure she can give you a job that can use your inclinations. Only she doesn't take Indians for customers. Since that seems to be your taste, you may be disappointed." He glared, anger contorting his face. "I don't want to see you again — ever! Don't try to see the children! — ever."

Eyes wide with horror, Gitty protested, "David, I'm their mother!"

"You!" he spat the word. "You buck-fucker!" He whirled on his heel and left the room.

289

Though neither Gitty nor David had noticed, Crystal had been sitting quietly in the far corner of the bedroom, playing with a doll. Her yellow-brown eyes solemnly stared at her Mother's stricken face. The child showed no emotion.

Gitty's hands shook so badly that she could scarcely pack clothing into a carpetbag. There seemed to be nothing she could do but obey David's commands.

A fearful thought struck Gitty. Doe Eyes would know nothing of their discovery. Tomorrow he would show up at the linerider's cabin, expecting to meet her. What if David lay in wait for him? How could she get word to him? There was only one way. Gitty scribbled a hasty note. "They know. Don't come here anymore."

Fifteen minutes later Walks Softly tapped on the door jamb before entering the bedroom. *"Mon Dieu!* What has happened?" she cried."Tal is out front with the buckboard. He says he's to take you to The Lucky Pearl. What goes on?" She grasped Gitty's shoulders.

"I can't talk now, Walks Softly," Gitty replied. In a whisper, she said, "When you can get away, please, come to see me." Gitty pressed her note to Doe Eyes into Walks Softly's palm, gave the woman directions how to find the linerider's cabin and asked her to leave the note there.

Later, when Gitty walked into The Lucky Pearl carrying a carpetbag, Cath snorted. "So you and the Englishman had a tiff? I'm surprised you didn't bring the children. Thank God you didn't! Not that I don't love the darlings, but this is no place for them."

Before ushering Gitty into her quarters, Cath rang for tea. She arranged the voluminous folds of her blue skirt on the sofa and gave Gitty a worried look. Gitty wondered if her face mirrored the catastrophe that had befallen her.

"He sent me away, Aunt Cath," she said, her voice a whisper. "I may never see the children again."

Cath frowned. "This is no tiff. What happened? I thought David had a calm head."

Gitty lowered her head and stared at her folded hands. "Dawn's father returned. I was seeing him, secretly."

"Good lord!"

Gitty looked up. Cath's thoughts were racing across her face. Her aunt was puzzling how Gitty could possibly prefer an Indian to the handsome and charming David Dunnington. Cath looked as if she'd been punched in the stomach. "Oh, my dear," she whispered. "I just can't believe it! How could you?"

A stricken look passed over Cath's face. Her chin sagged. "He'll never forgive you. Never. Not with an Indian. Ladies don't have Indian lovers!" Tears flowed down Cath's rouged cheeks. "Even *I* find the thought disgusting. I don't see how..."

"Aunt Cath," Gitty interrupted firmly. "I don't need a sermon. I need you to keep a clear head to help me out of this mess. I want my children! He can't keep me from them, can he?" she wailed.

Gitty moved back into her old room near Cath's quarters. For ten agonizing days, she stewed, waiting, until Walks Softly finally arrived bearing news. "The Englishman is selling all the stock — cattle, horses, —everything. He's returning to England and" — she hesitated, taking a deep breath, "taking the children with him."

All color drained from Gitty's face.

"He asked if I wanted to go with them, said he knew Crystal and Peter were attached to me, but advised against my going. He said he thought Dawn and I would be happier with our own people. He felt we would be out of place in England. He is going to get an English nanny to raise the children. He will allow you to remain at Calico Butte as long as you wish. He is so angry! He said nasty things."

"Like what?" Gitty asked dully.

"Oh, that you would make a bawdy house out of Calico Butte ranch." The Indian woman's dark eyes looked sadly at Gitty.

Gitty closed her eyes, lowered herself to the sofa. Her head felt light. How could David be so cruel? To take Peter and Crystal far away, across an ocean, away from her? How could she bear it? Gitty saw only pity in the Indian woman's face. Surely, Walks Softly suspected the terrible thing Gitty had done to anger David so. If she had read the scribbled note Gitty asked her to take to the linerider's cabin, Walks Softly must suspect that the cabin was a rendezvous. Even so, the Indian woman's eyes bore no blame. For this, Gitty was grateful. She was heaping enough guilt on her own head. She needed no more from anyone.

The next day, Won-Tu drove Gitty to Calico Butte. As the buckboard rattled along the lane to the house, David stepped out of the stable. When he saw that it was Gitty, he strode into the lane, planted his feet. His arms akimbo, he blocked the way. Won-Tu halted the horse.

David walked around to Gitty's side of the buggy. Between clenched teeth, he hissed, "I told you I never wanted to see your face again."

"You can't take the children to England, David! You can't!" A sob burst from Gitty's throat.

"The hell I can't! I've consulted a solicitor. You have no rights. You've lost them. Now, get out, before I have one of my cowhands take a horsewhip to your Chink friend. He glared at Gitty, his blue eyes icy, the eyes of an angry stranger. "I said, 'get!'"

A week later, Walks Softly rode up to The Lucky Pearl on Moonbeam, Dawn following on her little Shetland. She reported that David had left the previous day. There was nothing at The Calico Butte. The stock were sold. Moonbeam and the pony were the only horses left. The buffalo were still there, but grazing off in an east section, out of sight. "It's lonely there for only me and Dawn," she said. "Won't you come home?"

Dazed, Gitty nodded.

The next day, Won-Tu delivered Gitty and her belongings to the ranch house. It seemed strangely silent. No bawling cattle milled in the pens, no clucking from the chicken coop. He'd even sold the chickens! Inside, the furnishings were unchanged. Darkened bare spots on the wallpaper were reminders of family paintings he'd taken. He had left all of the furniture. Gitty walked into the small bedroom adjoining theirs — Peter's nursery. Peter's empty crib held her eye.

One small thing to be grateful for. She was happy he hadn't sold Moonbeam.

The front door slammed. "Mada! Mada!" Dawn shrieked. "You're back!"

The little girl flew into the bedroom and threw herself into Gitty's arms. Gitty knelt to hug her. As she squeezed the sturdy body against her bosom, a sob racked her breathing, then another. Suddenly, she sobbed uncontrollably. Dawn soothed her with consoling pats on the back.

During this whole nightmare, ever since David had confronted her with his knowledge of her treachery, Gitty had not shed a tear. Shock and disbelief had numbed her. Now that she felt Dawn's warm body against hers, she understood the enormity of what had happened. Perhaps, until now, she had not been able to face the tragedy that had befallen her. One could bear only so much guilt without crumbling.

Over the next few days, she fought to keep her sanity. Gitty tried to remember how Doe Eyes said they came from different worlds. Even Doe Eyes had wondered why God had allowed the two of them to meet and love.

At night, Gitty looked up at the twinkling heavens and whispered, "Oh, God, if you planned this as a cruel joke, then you *are* a merciless God. Please help me: Either to forget Doe Eyes, or to make his world and mine one. I beg you."

Throughout the winter, once every week, Gitty wrote letters to Crystal and Peter, writing about Walks Softly and Dawn. She mentioned how Cottonwood Run had left pointed icicles on its stony shore, how Moonbeam loved trotting in the powdery snow — things she thought a child might remember. By the time she finished a letter, her tears had left small wrinkled brands on the stationery.

The following spring, in April, 1885, a large packet addressed to Gitty arrived from England. Eagerly, with trembling fingers, Gitty tore open the parcel. In it was every single letter Gitty had written to Crystal and Peter, unopened.

Chapter 27
The Winter of '86

Gitty gave away the crib and other reminders of Peter and Crystal. She kept the toys that Dawn liked. Dawn was upset by the upheaval of the household, the only family the little girl had ever known. She roamed through the empty house, bewilderment pinching her smooth cheeks. She missed Crystal especially, even though Crystal never had been a congenial playmate. Dawn's role in their relationship had been that of a shadow, but it had been *her* part in that child world. Now, Dawn had only Gitty and Walks Softly for companionship.

Toward autumn's end, Gitty hired three ranch hands. She didn't know if they would be worth their wages. When they first rode the fence lines, they reported seeing small bunches of cattle, apparently stragglers not gathered in David's hasty roundup. Gitty ordered the new hands to drive these cattle closer to headquarters, where they could keep an eye on them during the winter and get hay to them if needed.

Only once did Gitty hear from Doe Eyes. One day in December, when she was in Stardancer buying supplies, a one-eyed, buckskin-clad trader tipped his raccoon fur hat to her. "Got a message for you, Missus," he said. He pressed a damp, folded scrap of paper into her palm.

Gitty unfolded the paper. No greeting, no signature. The message said, "I am sorry. I brought great pain. I pray for forgiveness."

Tears stung Gitty's eyes as she tore the paper into small shreds and dropped them into the street where they mingled with horse manure. Typical! she snorted. Doe Eyes retreated into prayer, meditation. Even as she thought this, Gitty knew she was being unreasonable. Doe Eyes couldn't join her and Dawn at Calico Butte. The rumors about Gitty and an Indian had spread too far. People would suspect that Doe Eyes was "the one." One day some cowboy would get Doe Eyes into his gun sights so that he could brag that he'd avenged a white lady's virtue. Gitty couldn't trust Uncle Volney. She presumed that, if given the chance, Volney would kill Doe Eyes without a second thought. Walks Softly had heard that Volney had not gone to England with David, but no one knew where he was. Gitty had lived in the West long enough to know that if a white man kills an Indian, the issue seldom reached court. If it did, acquittal was a foregone verdict. West of "the river," an Indian's life was cheap. Sometimes Gitty thought Aunt Cath was right when she said this country was "west of God."

All winter, when weather permitted, Gitty's three ranch hands herded in more stragglers. David had put up a large supply of hay to feed his blooded breed bulls, so there was plenty of dry feed for the cattle.

Throughout that first lonely winter at Calico Butte, Gitty, Walks Softly and Dawn went about their lives in a near-dazed state. The once-busy headquarters was now a bleak, snow-swept settlement, an abandoned group of buildings clustered near the base of Calico Butte. The tall butte protected the house from the fiercest blasts of frigid wind from the northwest. Even so, evenings, the two women and Dawn huddled in the parlor with woolen shawls drawn tightly about their shoulders. When the wind outside rattled the windows as it whistled across the prairie, they pulled their chairs closer to the hearth where burning logs crackled out warmth.

In early spring, the cowhands reported the cows were fatter than they'd ever seen she-stuff after long winter snows. When the cows began dropping calves, the hands did a loose head count. They told Gitty there were close to five hundred cows and yearlings in the herd they'd gathered. Gitty was pleasantly surprised. This meant she'd need to buy only blooded bulls to get this seed herd growing.

The men also reported that whenever they caught sight of the buffalo, which wasn't often, these animals seemed to be faring well. During one long period of heavy snow, the ranch hands had made hay available to the buffalo, but they never touched it. "Them critters are tough geezers!" one of the men commented admiringly.

According to the weekly Black Hills Journal, the Wyoming Stockgrowers Association had been organized the year before. It covered all of Wyoming, western Nebraska and western Dakota. The association was divided into thirty-one round-up districts, two of which were in

Dakota. The paper said there were from five to twelve outfits to a district, depending upon the number of cattle run by each spread. Gitty wondered if David had joined this association.

The article went on to report that the range of southwestern Dakota Territory was pasturing seven to eight hundred thousand head of cattle, mentioning Dominion CC, Hash Knife and Western Ranches, Ltd.

Gitty named Floyd Humber, the oldest of the three hired men, as foreman. In the months he had worked for her, he'd proven himself reliable and blessed with good sense. The other two hands already turned to Floyd for orders, so his elevation presented no difficulty.

In May, right after calf round-up, where two hundred ninety new calves were branded, Floyd announced to Gitty that he was getting married to Carmel, one of the girls at The Lucky Pearl. When Floyd proposed that Gitty hire Carmel as ranch cook, Gitty immediately agreed. Walks Softly had been cooking for the six of them, and the Indian woman's menus were unimaginative, with little variety.

Carmel's cheery presence in the kitchen was like the sun coming out from behind a cloud. All the while she worked, she sang jolly songs. From sunup to dusk delicious odors swept through the house. Dawn began spending a lot of time in the kitchen, where the little girl listened to Carmel's stories about her girlhood in the old country, Austria. Dawn was fascinated to learn that Carmel's real name was "Hannah." At The Lucky Pearl she had been renamed "Carmel" because of her sweet disposition and because of the lack of glamour associated with the plain name "Hannah."

Regularly, Floyd and the two ranch hands dropped into the kitchen for coffee and for Carmel's freshly-baked rolls or sinkers. Once, Gitty walked into the kitchen and found Dawn perched happily on Floyd's lap, while she and the cowboys listened to another of Carmel's childhood stories. Gitty was glad to see Floyd treating the little girl like a member of the family. Without a father, Dawn needed attention from a man as a father-substitute.

Always, no matter where she was or what she was doing, a heavy lump lay in Gitty's chest. She grieved for her lost children as if they had died. Sometimes she had to remind herself that they weren't dead, only lost from her life. When she thought of Peter, she saw him always as a chunky one-year-old. Now he was past two. When she closed her eyes, she could see his dark, tousled hair, his honey-colored eyes fringed with black lashes. What a handsome man he would be! A sob caught in her chest. Would she ever see Peter again? And Crystal, who would be four now. Prim, quiet Crystal, like an old spinster aunt, soberly regarding the world and finding it not up to her standards.

Gitty forced her thoughts to return to Dawn, who was not far off in a foreign land but right here in her house. Always Gitty would be grateful to Aunt Cath for working that out. A small smile crept over her face as she remembered how her aunt had finagled David into bringing Walks Softly and Dawn into their household.

Gitty worried about Dawn's schooling. For a few years, she could teach Dawn herself. She intended to get started in the fall with McGuffey's reader and some simple sums and ciphering. Dawn would be six in September, old enough to attend school. Gitty supposed that eventually she'd have to send Dawn away for higher education, but she couldn't bear to think of that, now. Her wounds over losing Peter and Crystal were too raw.

That summer Gitty wrote her grandfather and instructed him to sell the investments he'd made with the money from her parents' estates. She used that money to buy blooded Hereford bulls for the herd of stragglers. Sometimes she wondered if David knew how many head of cattle he'd left behind. Gitty insisted that Floyd and the two hired men cut and stack a great deal of hay, though Floyd thought Gitty was unduly pessimistic about needing feed in the winter months. "Hardly any spreads put up hay, ma'am," he protested.

"I don't care what other ranchers do, Floyd," Gitty insisted. "I've spent nearly everything I have on these Herefords. I don't want them starving."

That autumn of 1885 was mild. The cattle grazed and grew fat. Indian summer haze seemed always on the horizon.

Gitty began Dawn's lessons. She was pleased with the quick intelligence of her daughter. Dawn reveled in learning. When she begged Gitty to give her longer and more difficult lessons, Gitty realized that life at the ranch house was dull for a girl with no playmates.

On the last day of the year, at mid-day, a drizzle began. Soon, the rain froze, turning to razor-sharp crystals which pelted the animals and landscape. By nightfall, Floyd reported all trails and landmarks were obliterated. For three more days the storm, accompanied by cyclone-like winds, kept on. On the fourth day, Floyd led the two ranch hands out to assess the damage. The winds were gusty, but the freezing rain had ceased.

When the men returned, Floyd entered the kitchen, stamping and blowing. Carmel fussed over him as she helped him remove his ice-encrusted greatcoat. Gitty came into the kitchen from the dining room and stopped, shocked, when she saw his reddened cheeks and tired eyes. Her heart sank. Was it disaster, then, for her cattle?

Carmel set a mug of steaming coffee on the table before pressing her husband into a chair. He looked up at Gitty. "You was right, ma'am," he said. "It's sure enough good we put up all that hay last July. The bulls broke down the wire around the haystacks, milled around the stack, kept warm, kept eatin'. We didn't lose a bull!"

Gitty dropped into a chair and covered her face with her hands. Though she tried hard to contain herself a sob escaped.

"But it's *good* news, ma'am," Floyd sputtered, bewildered.

"I know," Gitty gulped. "I'm just so relieved! If we'd lost the cattle, I couldn't stay on here. I have very little money, only the use of this spread." To herself, she added, and I need money if I'm to send Dawn to a proper school.

The rest of the winter was severe, but Calico Butte cattle survived because hay was there when the snow was too deep for them to graze. The first balmy day in March, Floyd took two skinners out to hunt down the dead cattle to get the hides before they were spoiled by warm weather. Buzzards showed them the way to the carcasses.

Floyd reported to Gitty that they'd found only twelve dead animals — one horse, seven yearlings and four cows. All the expensive Hereford bulls had survived because they'd been kept herded near headquarters and the largest haystacks.

Spring started auspiciously with a good calf crop. Because there had been a constant supply of nutrition, nearly every mature cow gave birth to a healthy calf. This year there were many more white-faced calves than the year before. Floyd hired three temporary hands to help with calf roundup in May. Gitty was in great spirits, watching her herd multiply and improve with the Hereford characteristics.

In June, things turned worse. The weather was scorching hot and dry. Water holes played out. The once lush buffalo grass shriveled. Floyd's ranch hands got only one-half as much hay to stack as they had the year before. With no rain, the prairie grasses remained stunted and sparse. Toward autumn, swarms of grasshoppers passed through, eating anything that had survived the burning heat of the sun.

In Stardancer, Gitty heard the tales of woe of other cattlemen. All the ranchers in the high plains were hurting from lack of moisture. Yet, from what Floyd said, Calico Butte was the only spread which even attempted to put up winter feed. The other large outfits relied on the toughness of their stock to survive long periods with no food.

In October a heavy snow fell, covering the ground. By December several blizzards had swept past. Cattle all over the western range drifted, piling up against fences and freezing. Floyd fought to keep the expensive Hereford bulls close for feed, but he couldn't contain all the wandering cattle. At times, the temperatures fell to sixty below zero. On those days Gitty wouldn't allow the men to go out. "I want those animals to live, Floyd," she said, "but not at the risk of human lives. There's hay out there. If they're too stupid to find it, maybe I don't want their blood in my cattle."

In January, a warm Chinook blew in, melting the snow to slush. That night, the slush froze, solid. Neither horses nor cattle could paw through the layer of ice. In some places, the cattle fell through the thick ice crust, and the jagged edges tore the flesh on their legs.

The winter of 1886-87 was the most severe in the history of the West. It would be more than sixty years before such a winter crippled the area again.

One April morning, a week after her 25th birthday, Gitty was delighted to see sun streaming through the window. *How good to see sunshine!* Her mother had often said, "Spring always comes when it's needed most." They certainly needed spring after this devastating winter. Floyd reported that some of the larger cattle outfits had been wiped out by winter-kill.

Gitty had lost over two hundred head of cattle. This was nothing compared to the outfits who had no winter feed for their stock. The Turkey Track, which had shipped in 27,000 head during the summer dry spell, rounded up 250. There were rumors that Alec Swan's huge outfit was in the process of going under. The Hash Knife lost three-quarters of their animals. Later, when head counts at the stockgrower's associations were assembled, cattlemen were appalled to learn that the average loss of most outfits was 85 to 90 percent of their animals.

That spring Gitty and her hands were impressed that they didn't find a single buffalo carcass. Every single buffalo had survived, even the calves. The hardiness of this woolly animal was impressive to men who had just spent two weeks skinning hides off dead cattle. Buffalo didn't drift with the blizzards, piling up to freeze at the fences as cattle did. Buffalo just hunkered down in their insulated coats and lasted out the frigid winds. "I wish my cattle had a little buffalo sense," Gitty said to Floyd.

"Yes, ma'am," he agreed. "Wish they had their warm coats, too."

At Calico Butte there was no time to grieve for lost cattle. Gitty hired a crew of workers to begin drilling deep wells at scattered locations so that the cattle wouldn't have to walk so far for water. This would open up more land for grazing. Men with teams of horses labored at building dams across draws, forming artificial ponds to catch and store rainfall and snow run-off in the spring. Though she knew they always would be whipped about by the whims of Nature, the more self-sufficient she could make Calico Butte, the more secure she'd feel.

In July, with Gitty's permission, two dozen Indians came from the Pine Ridge Agency to kill a buffalo to use in a religious ceremony. Wild buffalo roaming the plains were a thing of the past, and Gitty's small but growing buffalo herd awed nearby Indians. Only one of the men could speak English. Gitty wondered why Doe Eyes hadn't come with them. At least, he could have interpreted. She finally got it across to the men that they could shoot any of the two-year-old bulls, but absolutely not a cow or heifer. Gitty wanted all the females to survive so they could reproduce each year.

Through the main gate, Floyd let the Indians into the buffalo pasture. They mounted their ponies and galloped off, whooping and singing. Floyd, extremely uneasy having Indians on the place, mounted his big cutting horse and took off after them. He didn't trust Indians to take only one buffalo.

From a nearby rise, he watched them get their buffalo bull. The first arrow slowed the animal: the impact of the second brought it to its knees. Immediately, the Indians swarmed over the dying creature, carrying out what seemed to be a religious ceremony as they skinned the buffalo and carved its meat into carrying-size pieces.

When the Indians left, each one laden with parts of the bull, the one who could speak some English dismounted and shyly walked toward the porch. He carried something wrapped in pale doeskin. Gitty stepped out onto the porch.

"Thank you, Buffalo Lady," the man said slowly, as if he had memorized the sound of each syllable. He shoved the article into Gitty's hands and hurried back to his horse. In a cloud of dust, the Indians pounded off, heading east.

Inside the house, Gitty unfolded the doeskin wrapping. Inside was a dress made of the finest bleached doeskin for a small girl Dawn's size. The bodice was decorated with porcupine quills dyed many colors. A pair of matching child's moccasins lay beneath the dress. It must be a gift to Dawn from Doe Eyes. How else would the Indians have known her size? In vain, she probed the garment and moccasins for a note.

Oh, Doe Eyes, she sighed. Is there nowhere a world big enough for the two of us?

Chapter 28
Going Home

As the seasons slipped by, Gitty watched her herd of cattle increase. Now, all new calves bore the distinctive Hereford white face.

Intermittent moods of depression engulfed her unexpectedly. It took little to remind her of Peter and Crystal. The nasal "peent" of a nighthawk at dusk might bring memories of days when her home was filled with children's laughter. When she sat at the piano, Gitty wondered if Crystal was playing the piano in far-off England. The child would be nine years old. Darling Peter would be seven. Had he started school, or did they engage a tutor? Perhaps they'd sent him to one of those cruel English preparatory schools. Gitty's eyes filled with tears.

Cath tried to reassure Gitty that time would ease the terrible ache in her heart, but Gitty hadn't found it so. She hungered to throw her arms around Peter as much now as she had six years ago when David took him away. Sometimes she thought that her pain had grown worse. When the children were taken away, at first, shock and disbelief had deadened some of the ache.

All these years there had been no communication from any Dunnington. Her attempts to contact them had been rebuffed. Her letters were returned, unopened. The pain and depression she suffered now was from facing reality: the children were gone, perhaps forever.

Once, a few years back, Gitty had toyed with the idea of going to England to try to force David to see her; to convince him to let her see her children. The more she thought this over, the less she thought of the idea. She suspected that the children had been conditioned to think ill of her. Perhaps they wouldn't even want to see her! With a heavy ache in her chest, Gitty decided she'd have to wait for them to grow older. Then, perhaps, they would develop an independent interest in meeting their American mother. This one fragment of hope kept Gitty going. That, and the presence of Dawn, who grew taller and stronger with each season. Dawn was a feminine version of her father, though her skin was not so bronze. Dawn's large gentle eyes bordered by dark lashes were exactly like his. Each time Gitty looked into those eyes, she longed for Doe Eyes.

Stardancer expanded and The Lucky Pearl prospered. As the town grew more civilized, Cath had to be careful to accent the casino part of her operation, to be more subtle about the upstairs activities of her girls. Steadfastly, she insisted that they were dancers, entertainers. At election time Cath made generous contributions to campaign funds. That seemed to keep the law at bay. Since many gentlemen who also wore badges enjoyed spending an evening at The Lucky Pearl, Cath held few fears for her business's future.

One spring day in 1890 Floyd returned from Stardancer, the buckboard filled with supplies. He entered the house through the kitchen door, as was his habit. Gitty went into the kitchen.

"Could you get everything we need?" she asked him.

"Drill bits didn't come in. Got everything else. There's mail for you, ma'am." He laid an envelope on the kitchen table.

Gitty picked it up. The stamps on the envelope were English. The handwriting was youthful, not David's. She tore open the envelope. Gitty quickly turned to the second page. It was from Crystal.

The letter was dated February 20. Crisply, with almost spinsterish dryness, Crystal reported that her father had been killed two years earlier in a fall from a horse. Her Grandmother Dunnington had died at Christmas time. Peter and Crystal were living with their uncle and aunt, David's brother, Byron, and his wife.

It was signed "Your loyal servant, Crystal Dunnington."

Gitty blinked. David dead. Sybil dead. Her children living with strangers in a strange land! Was this letter from Crystal a plea for rescue? Of course! It must be! Why else would the child write?

Two days later Gitty was on a train heading for New York City.

The crossing of the North Atlantic was rough. The nauseating seasickness reminded her of her pregnancy with Crystal. Gitty acknowledged that her nervousness over what was to happen with her children was probably contributing to her illness as much as the rolling ocean swells.

When her ship sailed into Southampton harbor, Gitty squared her shoulders. From now on, everything she did or said must be carefully calculated. Much depended upon making each decision a correct one. Briefly, she wished she had accepted Walks Softly's offer to accompany her. It would be a relief to have someone to talk to, someone to look to for advice or reassurance. Gitty shook her head. No. Walks Softly would have been so in awe of all the strange experiences and sights and so lonely and worried about Dawn that she would have been a hindrance. This was something Gitty must do alone.

At the dock Gitty attempted to engage a hackney cab. The first driver she tried to hire turned her down when he found that he had to drive to Sussex and be gone perhaps a few days. "Me wife wouldn't like that," he shook his head dolefully. "Especially if she found out it was with a pretty lady." He leered. Gitty walked away.

An older, bearded man whose hackney coach looked in reasonably good shape was hired for the last leg of the trip. His name was Walt. Gitty told him her destination, the Dunnington's Green Manor, not far from Beachy Head in the South Downs.

Walt scratched his beard. "Two ways to go," he murmured. "One is rougher, but quicker."

Gitty left the decision to her driver, though she let him know that she was impatient to get to Green Manor. They took the rougher road.

That evening, not far from Eastbourne, Gitty got rooms for them at a pleasant country inn.

When she crawled between the crisp, clean sheets her whole body ached from fatigue, but sleep was a long time coming. Every muscle in her body was tense, waiting to react to some necessity.

The next morning the innkeeper gave them directions to Green Manor. Mid-morning, the hackney pulled into the circular driveway to the Dunnington's country manor house.

Gitty surveyed the vast expanse of grass, hoping to hear the laughter of playing children. She heard only the baying of a hunting hound.

A well-dressed man opened the door. Gitty figured it must be David's brother, Byron, but her instincts whispered, "Be very careful."

"I am Gitty Dunnington," she said. "I wish to have a word with either Lord or Lady Dunnington."

"Very good, madam," the man said. "Please follow me."

The erect figure led her into a spacious room, walls lined with bookshelves and books. A mounted globe filled one corner of the room.

The moment the man disappeared, breath exploded noisily from Gitty's lungs. That person was a butler! How embarrassing if she had addressed him as "Lord Dunnington!" She reminded herself that she must be very, very cautious. She was out of her territory — in a foreign land with foreign customs.

A tall gentleman stepped into the room. "I am Byron Dunnington," he said. "I've been told you wish to speak with me."

The older brother looked nothing like David. He was not handsome as David had been, but plain. His hair, eyes and skin were all a faded tan. There was nothing distinctive about him except for his clipped, upper class British speech and manner.

When Gitty explained who she was, the baron didn't flinch. Obviously, the butler had conveyed her name. Gitty told him that Crystal had written her, telling of her father's and grandmother's deaths, and that she had come to England to take her children to the United States for a visit. She was careful not to imply that she wanted to take them permanently.

Gitty ended her plea. "May I see my children?"

"They are away at school. As for your speaking with them, I think not. David never spoke of you, nor would he allow the children to speak of you. It would not be David's wish for them to have any conversation with you." He turned away. "Jarvis! Please escort Mrs. Dunnington out. She is leaving."

Gitty opened her mouth to speak.

"My decision is final," Dunnington said as he walked toward a wide curved staircase.

Back in the hackney, Gitty instructed Walt to drive to Eastbourne. There, she sought a barrister's office.

The name "George George" lettered in gold leaf on a second floor window attracted her attention. According to the sign, George George was a barrister. Intrigued with the double name, Gitty climbed the wooden stairs. Mr. George had time to see her.

Quickly, Gitty summarized why she had come to England. She told a true account of her background and why David took the children and left the states, omitting only that her lover had been an Indian.

For a long while after she'd finished, the barrister stared out his window. He chewed on his lip before speaking. "I fear I must dash your hopes. You would have absolutely no chance in an English court of gaining custody of your children. Even if you were English, it's doubtful. You see, in England, a man can get a divorce on grounds of adultery. Women cannot. For a woman to be granted a divorce, it must be adultery along with physical cruelty or desertion for two years."

"But I don't want a divorce!" Gitty wailed. "I want my children back."

The barrister shook his head.

"I must see my children," Gitty said. "How can I find out what school each of them is attending?"

"That shouldn't be too difficult," the barrister answered. "Our servant class functions as efficiently as the newly popular fictional character 'Sherlock Holmes.'" He scribbled a note. "I'll request my wife to speak to Cook and other servants. Most likely one of them will know someone in service at Green Manor."

Impatiently, Gitty awaited learning the whereabouts of her children.

Two days later when she strode into George George's office, the minute she saw the barrister's face, she knew he had been successful.

Mr. George handed her a slip of paper. It read, "Peter, St. Ode's at Seaford; Crystal, Holmby Hills Girls' School at East Dean." When Mr. George began to give directions for finding each of the boarding schools, Gitty summoned Walt so he could hear the instructions.

Early in the afternoon they found St. Ode's. Gitty presented herself to the headmaster as "Peter's American aunt, here to pay a brief visit to my orphaned nephew."

Primly, Gitty sat in the stark parlor, waiting. The minute Peter entered the room, she jumped up and held out her arms.

Though his lips formed "Mama," he made not a sound. Peter charged into her outstretched arms, nearly bowling her over. For long minutes they clung to each other, savoring the feel and smell of the other. Wrenched apart suddenly years before, they dared not let go. At last through tears, Gitty whispered, "Peter, my son."

"You're beautiful, Mama," he murmured. "Why did Father leave you in America?"

Gitty winced. Would she ever be able to explain?

Quickly, she told him why she had come to England — that she would like Peter and Crystal to come visit her awhile in their Dakota birthplace. Gitty described Dakota and Stardancer.

"Do you like ponies and puppies?" she coaxed. "You can have both a pony and a puppy of your own."

"School?" Peter looked up at her innocently.

"You're much too young to live away from home. I'll have a tutor come in to help you in your studies." The bribe was complete.

Peter clutched Gitty's arm, a wide grin creasing his face. "When do we leave?"

Gitty explained that she had yet to meet with Crystal this afternoon. "I'll be here at 3:00 o'clock sharp tomorrow afternoon. Then we'll pick up Crystal and be on our way."

Gitty knelt and took hold of her son's shoulders. Looking squarely in his eyes, she reminded him, "Remember, this is our secret. Your Uncle Byron wouldn't let you go, so you and Crystal and I must arrange this ourselves."

Peter squeezed Gitty and placed a damp kiss on her cheek. "See you at 3:00 tomorrow," he whispered, smiling broadly. His permanent front teeth were just coming in.

Gitty's reunion with Crystal was not warm, but that was nothing new in their relationship.

"Thank you for writing," Gitty said, looking into the yellow-brown eyes. Though taller, the girl remained slight and dainty. "It was kind of you to let me know about your father and grandmother, and your and Peter's circumstances."

"Kind!" Crystal enunciated loudly. "Since you didn't care what was happening to us I thought I should inform you. I know you don't care about your children, but..."

"Crystal!" Gitty snapped. "I'm here because I care! I want you and Peter to come home with me. To live with me. If you don't like it, I'll send you back to your aunt and uncle, but give me a chance! I love you!"

Crystal threw her mother a sullen look.

For over an hour Gitty talked to her daughter, coaxing, promising. Finally, Crystal agreed to meet her clandestinely in front of the school the next afternoon at 4:00 p.m. Peter, Gitty and Crystal would then be on their way to the United States.

"Don't forget that I'll be in a rented hackney," Gitty reminded Crystal. "I'll wear my emerald bonnet so you'll recognize me."

The following morning Gitty busied herself with the details of preparation. At the wharf she hired a sloop. The captain was to set sail immediately and anchor at Birling Gap, near Beachy Head in Sussex.

David had told her of this narrow depression in the chalk cliffs which pirates and smugglers once used.

She bought two valises and filled them with clothes, guessing sizes, for Peter and Crystal. She purchased three steamship tickets on *The Adventure,* which was scheduled to sail out of Plymouth later in the week. She dared not try to leave by way of Southampton. That was too close. They might be traced and stopped. She was careful not to let Walt know the name of the ship or what port she was sailing from, although she tried to give him the impression they were leaving from Southampton. Walt seemed trustworthy, but money could loosen tongues.

That evening at the inn in Eastbourne she and Walt shared a leg of lamb. "I think I've done all I can do," Gitty sighed.

Between bites, the hackney driver agreed. "You've been a busy lady."

"Walt," Gitty began hesitantly, "if anything should go wrong — and I don't expect it, but one never knows — is your hack good for speed?"

"It's a stout rig, ma'am," he answered. "And Curley's a strong horse."

Gitty reached into her reticule. "You've been efficient and loyal, Walt. Here's what we agreed upon. Tomorrow, if you get me and my children safely aboard that little sloop anchored in Birling Gap, there's another twenty pounds for you."

Walt's eyes met hers. "That's generous, ma'am. Do you expect the law?"

Gitty frowned. "I don't know what to expect. I don't know. I just want my children. I want to sail west with them to America. I want my children." Her voice cracked.

Walt bowed his head and nodded.

At noon the next day they loaded the valises into the hackney and headed west for Seaford. At the ivy-strangled wrought iron gate Peter waited. The moment he spotted the hackney he began jumping up and down. When Peter climbed in, Gitty's arms encircled him. Their coach clattered off.

An hour later as Walt guided the hackney down the narrow lane to Crystal's Holmby Hills school, the hairs on Gitty's neck began to prickle. Her stomach retched. Calm, calm, be calm. It's almost over.

When they stopped near the hitching post, Gitty searched wildly for Crystal. No one in sight.

Suddenly a black brougham pulled by a black mare pulled alongside. Inside were Byron Dunnington and Crystal. The girl pointed at Gitty. "There she is, and she's got Peter!"

For a wrenching moment Gitty stared into her daughter's hate-filled, blazing cat eyes.

Gitty swallowed. "Let's go, Walt!" she shouted. "Twenty pounds for you if we make the boat!"

The hackney lurched forward. Whip cracking, Walt urged Curley to a gallop. The bumpy country road bounced the carriage. Gitty and Peter were tossed about inside. Gitty managed to stick her head out the window. She peered behind to see if they were being pursued. Great billows of dust kicked up by the galloping horse and speeding hack obscured everything. She couldn't tell.

When their hack slowed to make a sharp turn, Gitty again looked out the window. There, perhaps one-quarter mile back, was the Dunnington brougham, speeding recklessly after them.

From his perch in front Walt roared, "Get going, Curley, or you be dog food!" The whip snapped. The hack leaped forward. When a wheel hit a large rock, the hackney leaned dangerously for a moment before it slammed back down onto all four wheels.

"Don't kill us for twenty pounds!" Gitty screamed.

"We're almost there, ma'am!" Walt shouted. "Have the boy grab his valise! You grab yours. I'll keep the bloke back with the buggy whip if I have to!"

As wheels crunched to a stop on rocks, Gitty dropped twenty pounds onto the seat. She opened the hackney door, pulling Peter out. There, as she'd instructed, was beached the small rowboat which would take them to the sailing sloop anchored out in deeper water. Gitty and Peter stumbled down the embankment toward the rowboat.

The Dunnington brougham skidded to a halt beside the hackney. "Bring my nephew back here, you wench!" Byron Dunnington roared. "I'll have the law on you. I'll have you in prison for kidnapping!"

A boatman picked Peter up and swung him into the rowboat. Gitty gathered her skirts and jumped into the boat. A second sailor pushed the boat away from shore.

Oars splashed. The rowboat headed for the waiting sloop.

Byron Dunnington stood at the water's edge, shaking his fist at the departing boat.

They boarded the sloop by climbing a rope ladder, which, with her long skirt, was difficult for Gitty. Once aboard, Gitty slumped heavily onto a coiled hawser, legs trembling.

A sail cracked as it filled with wind. The boat slid swiftly away from land, heading southwest into the English Channel. Gitty's teeth chattered.

When she glanced back at the white chalk cliffs she couldn't tell if anyone remained watching.

Peter stood beside her, concern twisting his young face. "Are you afraid, Mama? The ship seems seaworthy."

Gitty held out her arms, and Peter slid gently onto her lap. "I just need a cuddle from my Peter," she murmured, burying her face in his dark, tousled hair.

"I like hugging you, Mama," he said. "But Grandmother said it wasn't manly to want to be held on someone's lap."

"You've many years yet before you must be manly!" Gitty reassured him.

Her eyes looked to the west, out over the choppy green water. West. Heading home. And she had managed to wrest her son from his English relatives.

A frown hurried across her brow when she thought of Crystal, left behind. Perhaps someday Crystal will change her mind. At least Gitty had let Crystal know that she was wanted by her mother. Perhaps someday...

Peter snuggled happily, nudging his forehead into Gitty's neck. Gratefully, Gitty squeezed him.

"We're going home, Peter, home to Stardancer," she murmured.

"Yes," he nodded dreamily. "Home."

ORDER BLANK

Please send me the following books by Jean Cummings
(indicate how many)

_____Stardancer   @$12.50 each
_____Buffalo in Our Backyard   @$12.50 each
_____Shinglebolt   @$8.50 each
_____Alias the Buffalo Doctor   @$11.95 each
            plus $3.00 shipping per book
        Michigan residents please add sales tax

Mail to me at:

Name_____   _____

Address _____

        _____

If you would like your book or books autographed, please give
instructions:

Please visit our Web site at:
members.aol.com/buffalodoctor/BDHOME.HTM

e-mail: BuffaloDoctor@aol.com

Mail your order to:
Jean Cummings
2609 E. Fruitport Road
Spring Lake, MI 49456